"I have a new favorite historical author and she is Lucy Monroe."

—The Best Reviews

PRAISE FOR THE NOVELS OF LUCY MONROE

Tempt Me

"[A] wicked and wonderful temptation . . . *Tempt Me* is . . . for any reader hungry for passion and adventure. Give yourself a treat and read this book. Lucy Monroe will capture your heart."

—*New York Times* bestselling author Susan Wiggs

"If you enjoy Linda Howard, Diana Palmer and Elizabeth Lowell, then I think you'd really love Lucy's work."

—*New York Times* bestselling author Lori Foster

Touch Me

"Monroe brings a fresh voice to historical romance."

—*USA Today* bestselling author Stef Ann Holm

"Emotional, sexy and romantic. *Touch Me* is just plain wonderful!" —*New York Times* bestselling author Lori Foster

"A light read with many classic touches . . . Highly enjoyable." —*Romantic Times*

"Extremely romantic." —*Fresh Fiction*

continued . . .

PRAISE FOR
LUCY MONROE

"Lucy Monroe is an awesome talent." —*The Best Reviews*

"Monroe pens a sizzling romance with a well-developed plot." —*Romantic Times*

"A fresh new voice in romance . . . Lucy Monroe captures the very heart of the genre."
—*New York Times* bestselling author Debbie Macomber

"Fast-paced and sensual." —*Booklist*

"Romance as only Lucy Monroe does it . . . joy, passion and heartfelt emotions." —*The Road to Romance*

"A Perfect 10! First-rate characterization, clever dialogue, sustained sexual tension and a couple of jaw-dropping surprises." —*Romance Reviews Today*

"An intense, compelling read from page one to the very end. With her powerful voice and vision, Lucy packs emotions into every scene . . . [A] sizzling story with tangible sexual tension." —bestselling author Jane Porter

"Lucy has written a wonderful full-blooded hero and a beautiful, warm heroine." —Maggie Cox

"A charming tale . . . The delightful characters jump off the page!" —Theresa Scott

Berkley Sensation titles by Lucy Monroe

TOUCH ME
TEMPT ME
TAKE ME
MOON AWAKENING
MOON CRAVING

Moon Awakening

A CHILDREN OF THE MOON NOVEL

Lucy Monroe

BERKLEY SENSATION, NEW YORK

THE BERKLEY PUBLISHING GROUP
Published by the Penguin Group
Penguin Group (USA) Inc.
375 Hudson Street, New York, New York 10014, USA
Penguin Group (Canada), 90 Eglinton Avenue East, Suite 700, Toronto, Ontario M4P 2Y3, Canada (a division of Pearson Penguin Canada Inc.)
Penguin Books Ltd., 80 Strand, London WC2R 0RL, England
Penguin Group Ireland, 25 St. Stephen's Green, Dublin 2, Ireland (a division of Penguin Books Ltd.)
Penguin Group (Australia), 250 Camberwell Road, Camberwell, Victoria 3124, Australia (a division of Pearson Australia Group Pty. Ltd.)
Penguin Books India Pvt. Ltd., 11 Community Centre, Panchsheel Park, New Delhi—110 017, India
Penguin Group (NZ), Cnr. Airborne and Rosedale Roads, Albany, Auckland 1310, New Zealand (a division of Pearson New Zealand Ltd.)
Penguin Books (South Africa) (Pty.) Ltd., 24 Sturdee Avenue, Rosebank, Johannesburg 2196, South Africa

Penguin Books Ltd., Registered Offices: 80 Strand, London WC2R 0RL, England

MOON AWAKENING

A Berkley Sensation Book / published by arrangement with the author

PRINTING HISTORY
Berkley Sensation mass-market edition / February 2007

Cover illustration by Jim Griffin.
Hand lettering on cover by Ronn Zinn.
Cover design by George Long.
Interior text design by Kristin del Rosario.

For information, address: The Berkley Publishing Group,
a division of Penguin Group (USA) Inc.,
375 Hudson Street, New York, New York 10014.

ISBN: 978-0-425-21426-8

BERKLEY SENSATION®
Berkley Sensation Books are published by The Berkley Publishing Group,
a division of Penguin Group (USA) Inc.,
375 Hudson Street, New York, New York 10014.
BERKLEY SENSATION is a registered trademark of Penguin Group (USA) Inc.
The "B" design is a trademark belonging to Penguin Group (USA) Inc.

PRINTED IN THE UNITED STATES OF AMERICA

10 9 8 7 6 5 4 3 2 1

Moon Awakening

A CHILDREN OF THE MOON NOVEL

Lucy Monroe

BERKLEY SENSATION, NEW YORK

THE BERKLEY PUBLISHING GROUP
Published by the Penguin Group
Penguin Group (USA) Inc.
375 Hudson Street, New York, New York 10014, USA
Penguin Group (Canada), 90 Eglinton Avenue East, Suite 700, Toronto, Ontario M4P 2Y3, Canada (a division of Pearson Penguin Canada Inc.)
Penguin Books Ltd., 80 Strand, London WC2R 0RL, England
Penguin Group Ireland, 25 St. Stephen's Green, Dublin 2, Ireland (a division of Penguin Books Ltd.)
Penguin Group (Australia), 250 Camberwell Road, Camberwell, Victoria 3124, Australia (a division of Pearson Australia Group Pty. Ltd.)
Penguin Books India Pvt. Ltd., 11 Community Centre, Panchsheel Park, New Delhi—110 017, India
Penguin Group (NZ), Cnr. Airborne and Rosedale Roads, Albany, Auckland 1310, New Zealand (a division of Pearson New Zealand Ltd.)
Penguin Books (South Africa) (Pty.) Ltd., 24 Sturdee Avenue, Rosebank, Johannesburg 2196, South Africa

Penguin Books Ltd., Registered Offices: 80 Strand, London WC2R 0RL, England

MOON AWAKENING

A Berkley Sensation Book / published by arrangement with the author

PRINTING HISTORY
Berkley Sensation mass-market edition / February 2007

Cover illustration by Jim Griffin.
Hand lettering on cover by Ronn Zinn.
Cover design by George Long.
Interior text design by Kristin del Rosario.

ISBN: 978-0-425-21426-8

BERKLEY SENSATION®
Berkley Sensation Books are published by The Berkley Publishing Group,
a division of Penguin Group (USA) Inc.,
375 Hudson Street, New York, New York 10014.

PRINTED IN THE UNITED STATES OF AMERICA

10 9 8 7 6 5 4 3 2 1

For Christine Feehan and Sherrilyn Kenyon. Thank you for making me fall in love with the paranormal genre and for awakening new characters in my heart. Your books have given me many hours of pleasure. I hope my Children of the Moon touch my readers even half as much.

Sincerely,
Lucy Monroe

Prologue

Millennia ago God created a race of people so fierce even their women were feared in battle. These people were warlike in every way, refusing to submit to the rule of any but their own . . . no matter how large the forces sent to subdue them. Their enemies said they fought like animals. Their vanquished foes said nothing, for they were dead.

They were considered a primitive and barbaric people because they marred their skin with tattoos of blue ink. The designs were usually simple. A single beast was depicted in unadorned outline, though some clan members had more markings which rivaled the Celts for artistic intricacy. These were the leaders of the clan, and their enemies were never able to discover the meanings of any of the blue-tinted tattoos.

Some surmised they were symbols of their warlike nature and in that they would be partially right. For the beasts represented a part of themselves that these fierce and independent people kept secret at the pain of death. It was a secret they had kept for the centuries of their existence while most migrated across the European landscape to settle in the inhospitable north of Scotland.

Their Roman enemies called them Picts, a name accepted by the other peoples of their land and lands south . . . They called themselves the Chrechte.

Their animal-like affinity for fighting and conquest came from a part of their nature their fully human counterparts did not enjoy. For these fierce people were shape-changers and the bluish tattoos on their skin were markings given as a rite of passage. When their first change took place, they were marked with the kind of animal they could change into. Some had control of that change. Some did not. And while the majority were wolves, there were large hunting cats and birds of prey as well.

None of the shape-shifters reproduced as quickly or prolifically as their fully human brothers and sisters. Although they were a fearsome race and their cunning was enhanced by an understanding of nature most humans do not possess, they were not foolhardy and were not ruled by their animal natures.

One warrior could kill a hundred of his foe, but should she or he die before having offspring, the death would lead to an inevitable shrinking of the clan. Some Pictish clans and those recognized by other names in other parts of the world had already died out rather than submit to the inferior, but multitudinous humans around them.

Most of the shape-changers of the Scots Highlands were too smart to face the end of their race rather than blend. They saw the way of the future. In the ninth century AD, Keneth MacAlpin ascended to the Scottish throne. Of Chrechte descent through his mother, MacAlpin was the result of a "mixed" marriage, and his human nature had dominated. He was not capable of "the change," but that did not stop him from laying claim to the Pictish throne (as it was called then). In order to guarantee his kingship, he betrayed his Chrechte brethren at a dinner, killing all of the remaining royals of their people—and forever entrenched a distrust of humans by their Chrechte counterparts.

Despite this distrust, the Chrechte realized that they could die out fighting an ever-increasing and encroaching race of humanity, or they could join the Celtic clans.

They joined.

As far as the rest of the world knew, though much existed to attest to their former existence, what had been considered the Pictish people were no more.

Because it was not in their nature to be ruled by any but their own, within two generations, the Celtic clans that had assimilated the Chrechte were ruled by shape-changing clan chiefs. For the most part, the fully human among them did not know it; however, a few were trusted with the secrets of their kinsmen. Those who knew the secrets were aware that to betray the code of silence meant certain and immediate death.

That code of silence was rarely broken.

Chapter 1

"And so the werewolf carried the lass off and neither was ever heard from again." Joan's sepulcher tones faded as the dark shadows in the kitchen reached out to wrap around the two young women listening so avidly to her every word.

Emily Hamilton tried to imagine being carried off into the wild by a werewolf, or being carried off anywhere for that matter, but couldn't. She was nineteen, well past the age when most ladies were married, or even dowered into a convent. She would spend her life as her stepmother's drudge.

She sighed. Not even a werewolf would risk Sybil's wrath to carry Emily off.

"Are there truly werewolves in the Highlands?" her younger stepsister, Abigail, asked in careful Gaelic.

Joan shook her head, nary a wisp of her gray hair peeking from the housekeeper's wimple she wore. "Nay, lass. Though if ever there were a place such monsters might thrive, it would be that harsh and hilly land."

"I thought you said the Highlands were beautiful," Emily inserted, her own Gaelic more natural than Abigail's.

But that was hardly a surprise. Her younger sister speaking at all was the result of Abigail's tenacity. When the fever had almost taken her life three years before, it *had* taken her hearing. It had also destroyed what existed of family harmony in Emily's home.

Deafness was considered a sign of the damned by some and a curse by most.

Sybil made it clear that she would have preferred her daughter had died rather than be so afflicted. Overnight, Abigail had gone from being an asset her stepmother counted on to advance her own place in the world, to a problem best avoided. It was left to Emily to coax her younger stepsister back to health and into living amidst the household again.

Out of fear that Abigail would be rejected by the rest of the keep like she had been by her own mother, Emily had done her best to hide her sister's affliction. The younger girl had helped, working hard to learn to read lips and continue speaking as if she heard the voices around her.

So far, the deception had succeeded. Few people within the keep knew of the fifteen-year-old's inability to hear.

"It's a beautiful place, or so my mother always told me . . . but a harder land to live in. Och . . . the clans are so wild, even the women know how to fight."

Emily thought it sounded like a magical place.

An hour later, the rest of the family and the servants were in bed. Everyone that was, except her father and stepmother. They were in the great hall talking. Emily was usually the last of the family to go to bed and she burned with curiosity to know what was important enough to keep her parents from their slumber.

She stopped at the top of the stairs leading to the great hall and moved into the shadows. Eavesdropping might not be ladylike, but it was a good way to satisfy her curiosity and her need to stay informed of her father and stepmother's plans. Too many others depended on her to protect them from Sybil's machinations and her father's cold indifference to their welfare.

"Surely, Reuben, you cannot expect to send Jolenta!" her stepmother cried.

"The king's order is quite explicit, madam. We are to send a daughter of marriageable age to this laird in the Highlands."

Emily ducked behind a small table, making herself as diminutive as possible. It was not difficult. Much to her personal chagrin, she was not precisely tall. It was a fact tossed at her by Sybil often. She had no "regal bearing," as befitted the daughter of a landholding baron. She supposed there was nothing regal about hiding behind a table, no matter how tall she might have been. And that was that.

"Jolenta is far too young to be married," stormed Sybil.

"She has fourteen years. Emily's mother was a year younger when I married her."

Sybil, Emily knew, hated any mention of her husband's first wife, and she responded with acid. "And a baby can be betrothed in the cradle. Many girls are wed when they are a mere twelve years, but almost as many die in childbirth. You could not wish such a fate for our delicate flower surely?"

Her father made a noncommittal sound.

"You might as well suggest we send little Margery as send my dear Jolenta."

In her hiding place, Emily had to smile. Margery was a mere six years. Even the Church refused to recognize marriages contracted between parties under the age of twelve.

"If Jolenta is of an age to marry, then surely Abigail at fifteen is also. This will doubtless be her only opportunity," Sybil said callously.

Bile rose in Emily's throat. She'd always known the

other woman was cold, but such a suggestion was monstrous and her father had to know it.

"The girl is deaf."

Emily nodded in agreement and inched out of her hiding place so she could see her parents. They were sitting at the head table almost directly under where she stood and were too intent on one another to look up and see her.

Sybil said, "No one knows except the family and a few servants who would not dare to reveal our secret."

But Abigail could not hope to hide such an affliction from a husband, which was exactly what her father said.

"By the time he realizes she is so flawed, he will have consummated the marriage. Then he will have no recourse," Sybil said dismissively. "He's a Scotsman after all. Everyone knows they are barbarians, especially the Highland clans."

"And you are not concerned about what he will do to her when he realizes?" Sir Reuben asked.

Emily had to bite her lip to stop from screaming at the selfish woman when Sybil simply shrugged delicately.

"I have no desire to end up at war with one of the Highland clans over this."

"Don't be foolish. The laird is hardly going to travel this distance to take his anger out on you."

"So, I am foolish?" Sir Reuben asked in a dangerous tone.

"Only if you let old-womanish fears guide you in this decision," Sybil replied, showing how little her lord intimidated her.

"Aren't you the one who recommended I send the bare contingent of knights to assist my overlord in his last request for warriors?"

"We could hardly leave our own estates inadequately guarded."

"But his anger over my stinginess has led to this request."

"I was right though, wasn't I? He did not sanction you."

"You do not consider the loss of a daughter a sanction?"

"They must marry sometime and it is not as if we do not have a gaggle of them."

"But only one of whom you consider utterly dispensable."

"The others could still make advantageous matches."

"Even Emily?"

Her stepmother's scoffing laughter was all the answer her father got to that small taunt.

"I will send word to the king that he can expect my daughter to travel north to Laird Sinclair's holding within the month along with her dowry."

"Not Jolenta?" Sybil asked, her voice quavering.

Sir Reuben sighed with disgust. "Not Jolenta."

He meant to send Abigail. Horrified, Emily shouted, "No!"

Both Sir Reuben and Sybil started and turned their heads toward her like two buzzards caught picking over a carcass.

She flew down the stairs. "You mustn't send Abigail to such a cursed fate!"

Sybil's mouth pursed with distaste. "Were you eavesdropping again?"

"Yes. And I'm glad I was." She turned to her father, her heart in her throat. "You can't think to send Abigail so far away to a husband who might believe her affliction is a sign from God that she is unclean."

"Perhaps it is such a sign," Sybil inserted, but Emily ignored her.

"Please, Father. Do not do this."

"Your stepmother has pointed out that it may well be Abigail's only chance at marriage. Would you deny it to her?"

"Yes, if it means sending her to a barbaric Scotsman who will be furious when he realizes how you have tricked him." As her father's face hardened, Emily forced herself to reign in her temper. She did not wish to lose the battle before she'd begun because her demeanor offended her father.

She lowered her eyes, though it was hard to do. "Please, Father. Do not be offended, but I believe Sybil is wrong. I do not think a proud leader of a Scottish clan would take such deception in stride and be content to spend his fury on his hapless wife."

The fact that either of her parents thought that an acceptable alternative was more than she could bear.

"You believe the clan leader would declare war?"

"Yes."

"What does she know?" Sybil scoffed. "She knows nothing of the world."

"I have heard the tales of these fierce people, Father."

"Tales told to frighten foolish children," Sybil said.

"So my daughter is foolish as well?" Sir Reuben asked, proving he had not forgotten his wife's earlier insult.

Sybil's hands fisted at her sides as if she realized she'd made an error in speaking so plainly now that they both knew the conversation had been overheard. Her father's pride might accept such intransigence from his wife in private, but he would not tolerate others—even a lowly daughter—seeing him in a light that could make him appear weak.

Emily was determined to use that to her advantage. "Father, you are one of the wisest of the king's barons. Everyone knows that."

"Too wise to risk war with a barbaric people simply to placate an overmanaging wife?"

Emily knew better than to answer, so she remained silent while Sybil gasped in outrage.

"Who would you have me send in her place?"

"Jolenta?" she asked.

"No!" Sybil cried and then she grasped her husband's sleeve. "Consider, my dearest lord, the betrothed of Baron de Coucy's heir died of a fever not a month past. The baron will be looking for a new bride to contract very soon. His mother has already made it clear she finds Jolenta pleasing."

The younger girl had spent the last two years at Court, an honor Emily had never been extended.

"I thought you said she was too young to wed."

"A barbaric Scotsman, but not the son of a powerful baron."

"Then who would you have me send in accord with the king's order?"

"Abigail . . ."

"No, please, Father . . ."

"I do not fancy a war over the disposal of one of my daughters."

Emily winced at her father's comment. Silence had fallen between her parents and she feared its outcome if she said nothing. Yet terror at her own thoughts and what they would mean for the sister she would leave behind as well as for herself filled her.

She took a deep breath and then forced herself to say, "Send me."

"*You?* You think, my lord, that the Scotsman will not go to war over you sending such an undisciplined girl? She's sure to offend him her first week as his wife."

"You said it yourself, they are barbarians. He would hardly appreciate a true English lady."

Old pain seared Emily's heart. Her father had no higher opinion of her than her stepmother. She had known that particular truth since her own mother's death, when he had berated a small girl crying over her mother's grave with the knowledge that she was not the son he had craved. If she had been, her mother would not have died trying to give birth to another.

Emily knew the cruel words for the lie they were . . . now. But until she had seen Sybil grow large with child twice more after giving her father the heir he sought, she had believed them. And felt unworthy because of them.

But she no longer believed that to be born female made her unworthy. Six years of correspondence with a powerful abbess had healed her of that affliction. She reminded herself of that fact as she raised her gaze to meet her father's.

It was as if he had been waiting for her to do so. "Think you that you will fare better than Abigail in the wilds of Scotland?"

"Yes."

"I think perhaps you are right." He turned to his wife. "It is decided. I will send Emily in answer to my overlord's demand."

"And Abigail?" Emily asked.

"She will remain here, under my protection."

The large black wolf sniffed the air, his powerful body coiled to spring into instant motion if needed.

Away from his own territory, even in the presence of his companions, the situation was fraught with danger. He had not brought an attack force and the clan he had come to spy on had a full contingent of wolf warriors. Some of them were even as mighty as his own.

That meant treading carefully.

He made his way silently through the forest, knowing his two companions followed, though he could not hear them. The presence of all three went undetected by man or beast and that was as it should be.

His father had started teaching him to mask his scent from the night of his first change, and he had perfected the art. Other werewolves and even wild animals could come close enough to touch him in the dark and never know he was there. He had chosen two warriors just as skilled to accompany him.

Though he stopped often to sniff the wind, it was not his ultrasensitive nose that caught the first signal that his brother Ulf had been right. Rather, his ears picked up a sound no human could have heard at such a distance. From the clan's holding beyond the trees and across the expanse of heather-filled grass, he heard the unmistakable sound of the lass's laugh.

The femwolf, Susannah, was here.

Her soft human voice spoke, though even his superior hearing was not up to deciphering the words. She did not sound as if she were in distress, but that did not alter the facts or how he must respond to them.

Clan law . . . ancient clan law, known by most Celts and every Chrechte warrior who had joined them two centuries before . . . had been broken. A Balmoral woman had been taken to mate without the consent of the clan chief.

Lachlan, laird of the Balmoral and pack leader to the Chrechte contingent among them, would not tolerate the insult.

Ulf had been right about what had happened to the femwolf who had disappeared during the last full moon hunt. He had also been right when he said the Sinclairs must be made to pay. No Highland chief would tolerate such insolence leveled against his clan and himself as a person. It implied the Sinclairs thought he was too weak to enforce clan law, that his warriors did not protect their women.

England would be his ally before he would allow such a view of his clan to stand unchallenged. However, it was not a declaration of war that would give a message of the greatest impact to the other Highland clans, but well-planned revenge. As he had told Ulf when his brother had suggested mounting an immediate attack on the Sinclair holding.

Riding an exhausted horse and feeling less than wonderful herself, Emily surveyed her new home with both curiosity and trepidation.

The journey from her father's barony had been a long one and arduous upon reaching the Highlands. Shortly after reaching Sinclair land, an envoy of warriors had arrived to finish escorting her to their keep.

Emily had been both disappointed and relieved to discover that her husband-to-be had not accompanied them. Part of her wanted the first meeting over, but an even bigger part was content to put it off indefinitely.

The Sinclair warriors had refused to allow the English soldiers any farther onto Sinclair land. They had taken over her escort and Emily found them poor company indeed. They did not speak unless asked a question and then they answered in monosyllables if possible. Would her husband-to-be do the same?

Perhaps she would feel better if people would stop staring at her so. No one smiled, not even the children. Some adults openly glared at her. She turned to her nearest escort. "Some of the clan seem hostile. Why is that?"

"They know you are English."

Apparently that was supposed to explain it all because he stopped talking and even her curiosity was not up to questioning the soldier further.

So the clan knew she was English? That must mean they were expecting her.

For those in any doubt, her dress would have given her away, she supposed. She'd donned the dark blue tunic over her clean white shift with stylish wide sleeves three days ago. It was now as creased and bedraggled as the rest of her, but even if it had remained pristine, it was nothing like the garb of the Highlanders.

They all wore plaids, even the children. The colors were muted green, blue and black. It was a striking combination. She'd said something to that effect to one of her escorts upon first meeting—admittedly in an effort to pretend she wasn't noticing the fact that their lower legs were as naked as a baby being washed. He had growled that of course it was pleasing; they were the Sinclair colors.

She'd stopped trying to make small talk soon thereafter.

She turned her interest from the less-than-welcoming people to the Sinclair castle. The construction surprised her. She wasn't sure what she had expected, but something so much like her own father's home was not it. The ground had been raised to a hill with a moat around it. The keep, which looked like a single high tower, was built on top of the hill with a wall all around. The timber wall extended down the hill to surround the bailey as well.

She hadn't imagined anything so grand in the Highlands. Perhaps her husband-to-be was not such a barbarian after all. Perhaps he would even have a kind heart and allow her to send for Abigail to come live with them. That was her most fervent hope.

Her escort led her across the drawbridge toward the keep.

A group of soldiers on the steps of the keep caught her eye. They all stood with arms folded and scowling at her approach. One soldier, who stood in the middle and was taller than all of the rest, scowled most fiercely. She tried to avoid looking at him because the dislike, nay *hatred*, emanating off of him was frightening.

She hoped he was not one of her husband-to-be's close advisors. She scanned the crowd to find her future husband, their laird. Her escort had led her almost to the scowling soldiers before she realized that one of them must be him. Her only excuse for being so slow to realize it was her deep desire for it to be otherwise.

Please don't let it be the angry man in the center, she prayed fervently, crossing herself for good measure.

When the soldier in the middle stepped forward, she offered up a last desperate plea. But she knew it had been in vain when, without acknowledging her, he waved for her escort to follow him.

"Where do you want the English woman?" called the soldier nearest her.

Her future husband merely shrugged and continued inside. For the life of her, she couldn't think of any good excuse for his behavior. Even if he was a barbarian as Sybil claimed.

She could only be glad that Abigail had not been sent in her place. God alone knew what kind of horrible things he might have done to her gentle sister. Or perhaps it was the devil himself who knew.

She banished the wicked thought, but could not dismiss as easily the sense of doom settling over her.

Chapter 2

Emily's escorts swung off their horses and two young boys rushed forward to lead the animals away. She made haste to climb down from her own weary horse and nearly landed on her bottom in the process. Her legs had fallen asleep on the long ride since daybreak and they ached like blue blazes.

Weak tears pricked her eyes, but she blinked them away. Suddenly a hand stretched out to steady her. Startled, she looked up. It was one of the clanswomen.

She was lovely with curling dark hair and slightly tilted, velvety brown eyes. She was also pregnant. Emily couldn't miss the protruding bulge under the woman's plaid, but if she was not mistaken, the other woman was only about five months into her confinement.

She curtsied. "My name is Caitriona, but I am called Cait. I am to be your sister." The woman spoke slowly and with a thick brogue that reminded Emily how far north into Scotland she had traveled.

"You speak English?" Emily asked in shock, returning the other woman's curtsy, her own a little awkward because her muscles still did not want to cooperate.

"Yes."

"I'm most pleased to meet you, Cait. My name is Emily Hamilton, daughter of Sir Reuben," she said in Gaelic.

"I had drawn that conclusion," Cait said with a teasing glint in her eye. "You speak our tongue."

"My father's holding is on the border."

"Ah. I knew only that you were English."

"I don't suppose you know where I am supposed to go now?"

The soldiers had all disappeared.

"You will stay with me until the marriage. I am sorry you cannot have your own room, but there are no empty sleeping chambers in the keep at present." Cait smiled apologetically, her face shining with even more beauty when she did so.

No wonder Emily's intended was upset he had been ordered to marry her if Highland women were all as lovely as this one. She had no illusions about her own looks. Sybil had made sure of that. Her lack of height was not the only thing the older woman found lacking in Emily's appearance.

According to Sybil, Emily's hair was too curly and too bland. Unlike the lustrous dark locks of the woman standing in front of her, Emily's hair was a cross between blond and light brown. Sybil had often commented that it could not make up its mind what it wanted to be.

She also lamented the fact that Emily's eyes were the color of lavender. Who ever heard of purple eyes? Sybil had said more than once in Emily's hearing that she thought it might be a sign from above and not a good one. But by far, Emily's worst shortcoming, according to her stepmother, was her well-rounded body, too curved to fit the aesthetic ideal of tall, regal and *understated* femininity.

"Won't your husband mind me staying with you?" she

asked as her stiff fingers worked to untangle the ties that held the satchel attached to her saddle.

Cait took over the task. "My mate died in battle these four months past."

Emily didn't ask what battle. According to the English and even the lowland Scots, the Highlanders spent all their time at war, or preparing for one. "I'm very sorry." She reached out and impulsively squeezed the other woman's hand. "Are you sure you won't mind sharing your home?"

A grieving woman might very well want her privacy.

"No, I will like the company. It is very lonely at the keep sometimes, being the only woman in residence."

So, Cait lived in the keep? Emily wasn't sure if that was good or bad news since so did the scowling warrior she was supposed to marry. "There are no female servants?" Emily asked, aghast as the full import of the other woman's words sank in.

"Some, but they live in the bailey."

"None live in the keep?" Emily asked, eyeing the large towerlike building. Close up it looked even bigger than it had upon first sight, definitely large enough to house a family and their servants comfortably. "Who fills the sleeping chambers?"

"Warriors."

"Isn't that unusual?"

Cait sighed. "Not here."

"Is the laird planning war? I could not help but notice he did not greet me or show any reaction to my arrival." Well, nothing but dislike and she wasn't going to come right out and say so. She was hoping he was simply in a bad mood . . . not that he truly hated her as much as his sulfuric look had implied.

"Do not mind Talorc. He is not reconciled to this marriage, but he will come around," replied Cait encouragingly as she led the way inside.

She said something else, but Emily had stopped listening. The keep's great hall was cavernous and poorly lit. It was also filled with soldiers wearing the Sinclair plaid. The men ignored Cait and Emily, and for that she was very grateful.

She'd thought her escorts intimidating enough, but en masse the warriors of her new family were downright terrifying.

She scooted closer to Cait and followed the other woman to the back of the hall and down a set of stairs. An open doorway off to the right revealed a storage room, but Cait led her into a room on the left. It was a small bedroom. Unlike most rooms on the lower level of the keep, it had a series of tiny boxlike windows near the ceiling that let in light.

It was clean and much more cheerful than the unadorned great hall. Emily set her satchel on the bed beside several bundles she recognized as the ones her escort had carried on their horses after sending her father's soldiers away.

The bed was covered in the Sinclair plaid. Another plaid was draped over the single chair in the room and there were two small trunks along one wall.

Cait lifted the lid of one. "You can put your things in here."

"Thank you." Emily wanted nothing more than to curl up on the bed and sleep until the next century, but she began putting her belongings away. "You said your brother was not reconciled to this marriage?"

Cait helped the obviously exhausted Englishwoman by handing her bundles from the bed. "Yes."

"Why? Did he want to marry someone else? Does he hate the fact that I'm English?"

"It is very unusual for a Highlander to marry outside of the clans," Cait said diplomatically.

But the truth was, she was still shocked her brother had acceded to the king's demand that he marry an Englishwoman. Talorc had more reason than most to distrust both the English and humans. Since Emily was both, Cait couldn't help worrying that the match was doomed from the start.

She tried to look at the positive and believe her brother would get past his prejudices. He simply refused to see that not all humans were untrustworthy because some were capable of betrayal. Some of the Chrechte were capable of betrayal as well; it wasn't simply a human weakness. But it made no difference to Talorc. He chose to view all humans as weak and unprincipled.

Similarly, one couldn't lump all the English together; they couldn't all be heathen usurpers, could they? Certainly the sweet woman beside her did not have the scent of betrayal or greed clinging to her person as their stepmother had.

"You mean to say that they are as appalled by the fact that I'm English as my parents were to discover one of their daughters had to be sent to marry a Scot?" Emily asked.

Cait sighed. "Appalled is a mild word for Talorc's reaction when he received word from Scotland's king."

"I see."

"Do not take it personally," Cait said earnestly.

"How can I? The man has not spoken a single word to me."

Cait relaxed, relief flaring through her. "I'm glad you are so sensible." She sighed again. "I cannot say the same for my brother."

"Has he upset your king to be punished this way?"

"No," Cait gasped. Where did the English get their ideas? "King David respects my brother a great deal, but he has been influenced by the Normans of England and adopted many of their ways. It is for that reason he wanted

Talorc to take an English bride. He is hoping you will tame him."

It was Emily's turn to gasp. She looked like she'd just swallowed a fish whole. "Your brother told you this?" she demanded. "I would not have thought such a fierce warrior would confide so personal a thing to his younger sister."

Cait had to laugh at that. "Oh, no. I listened to the soldiers talking."

Emily grinned and then laughed as Cait blushed at what she'd admitted to.

"It's a shameful habit, I know, but . . ."

"How would you learn anything otherwise?" Emily finished for her.

Feeling like she'd met a true sister of the heart, Cait asked, "You don't think I'm terrible?"

"I've overheard many an important conversation in my father's keep." Emily shrugged. "Men keep women in the dark when they shouldn't . . . and parents are not always as forthright with their children as one might wish."

"Amen to that. My brother has been like a father to me for many years. He didn't even tell me he had arranged my marriage until I was called to the great hall to speak my vows."

"Were you happy in your marriage?"

Cait wished she could say yes, because it was so obvious her new friend was looking for some kind of solace, but she couldn't make herself lie to the other woman. Even for Emily's peace of mind. "It was a good match to cement my brother's power in the clan, but Fergus and I had little in common."

"Still, it must be difficult he is gone now that you are pregnant with his child." Then Emily's hand flew to cover her mouth. "I'm so sorry. I know I shouldn't speak of it."

"Is that an English custom, to pretend ignorance when a woman is increasing?" Cait asked, trying not to laugh at the idea. She did not wish to offend the other woman.

"Yes, actually."

Cait shook her head. "I am due in four months and I cannot wait. To be a mother is a great blessing among my people."

"The abbess says that according to the Church, to give birth is to rectify the sins of Eve." Emily's brow furrowed. "It is considered evidence of Heaven's blessing on a marital union."

"An *abbess* said that?" It sounded more like something an English priest would say to Cait.

Emily's mouth tipped in a small grin and she winked conspiratorially at Cait. "Well, she didn't say she agreed."

"I have heard that an abbess can be a woman of great political power in England."

"Yes."

"You're lucky then to be related to one."

"Oh, I'm not."

"Then were you sent to an abbey for schooling?"

"No, but a very learned abbess came to stay in my father's holding while traveling from her abbey to the home of one of her former students. She was wonderful. She was never too impatient to answer my questions and even tried to talk Papa into allowing me to attend schooling at the abbey. My stepmother refused and later I had cause to be glad, but I was allowed to correspond with the abbess frequently. I think more because my stepmother did not wish to make an enemy of her, but whatever the reason, her missives will be one of the things I shall miss most living here." She smiled valiantly, though her violet eyes were rimmed with fatigue. "I'm sure I'll find other things to make up for it."

Cait admired Emily's spirit and only hoped the other woman's faith would be rewarded.

Emily found many odd things about her new home over the next few days. Not least of which was the fact that her intended husband had yet to speak a single word to her. For the most part, he ignored her. However, when he did deign to notice her, his scowl was every bit as furious as it had been the first time she saw him.

She made no effort to introduce herself, determined to save meeting him for later, when he was in a better mood. She thought that just might happen about the day she went to meet her Maker.

She helped Cait with the chore of running the keep, much as she had with Sybil, but enjoyed the task more. She and Cait had a great deal in common and grew to be good friends very quickly.

The two women were crossing the great hall one evening after her arrival when Talorc turned to them. "Cait, bring the woman here."

Cait grimaced at her brother's surly tone, but turned to obey.

The woman? Emily couldn't believe the laird's effrontery. If he didn't start showing some manners soon, she was going to give him a lecture that would make Sybil's seem like friendly gossip. Her temper, which had been pricked on her arrival, climbed toward a boil.

As Cait walked past she whispered to Emily, "Don't let him frighten you. His bark is worse than his bite."

She almost laughed because it was obvious Cait was at least a little frightened herself. However, she soon became angered at the thought. A pregnant woman should not be upset in any way. Hadn't her father often said so when Sybil was carrying? Emily turned and glared at Talorc, but did not move to obey.

"Is she stupid then? Why isn't she following you?" Talorc demanded loudly of his sister. "You told me she spoke our language."

Cait turned a worried look to Emily and her eyes widened to round saucers when she saw Emily's defiant stance. Then she smiled.

Emily didn't give her a chance to answer her brother. "Why don't you ask *that woman* yourself?" she challenged Talorc. "That is if you can bring yourself to speak to her."

If he thought she was saying her vows to a man who would not even address her, then he was sadly mistaken.

"Or perhaps I'll just tell you. I am not stupid, nor am I deaf. You do not need to shout your requests like an old man who no longer hears properly."

"You dare to insult me?" Talorc roared.

"Of course she does not insult you," Cait interrupted with speed.

Emily started walking toward the clan leader. "Nay, I do not insult you."

Talorc nodded his head at her statement, apparently mollified. However her next words had him red with anger.

"When I wish to insult you, I can think of things much more offensive to call you than an *old man*. It is more of an insult to old men to compare their deaf shouts to your rude bellows," she replied, nodding for emphasis.

This had Talorc bellowing again about the barbarous tongues of English women. She laughed out loud to be called a barbarian by someone so uncouth as the man yelling at her. She noticed Cait smiling, too. Looking at her, Emily was sure her newfound friend understood her amusement.

Talorc felt like exploding. He grabbed the woman when she reached him, but stopped himself from shaking her. His strength was too deadly to allow it free reign against an innocent, even a rebellious Englishwoman. She was pretty with her purple eyes and womanly curves, but he felt no physical reaction to touching her.

He pulled her close until their thighs brushed and . . . nothing. No lust stirred in his loins, no desire to mate with the female. Just as he had feared when the order had come from his king. Talorc was a werewolf and even mated to a femwolf, the possibility for offspring was low, but with a human it was almost nonexistent.

Only in a true mating could a wolf and human joining result in children. He did not know how to tell if a woman was his true mate. According to the elders of his pack, there was no way . . . not until after the physical mating took place. But once that event took place, there could be no going back. His pack's laws stipulated that a physical mating dictated a lifetime bond.

However, he was certain of one thing. He would at least physically desire the woman if they were destined to be true mates. He did not want this woman. Though he admired her spirit, he did not even like her. How could he? She was English.

His own father had learned the folly of wedding the treacherous English. They could not be trusted . . . ever. And he would not have his mate chosen by a *human* king all too enamored of their southern foe.

He pushed Emily away, his repudiation reflected back at him in the lavender eyes spitting fury.

His clanswomen were not so undisciplined, but he had no desire to tame this English wildcat. "Listen well, woman, I'll not marry my enemy even to please my king."

"Splendid," she replied. "I believe I would rather be married to a goat than you!"

Cait took advantage of her brother's spluttering to whisk Emily up the stairs to her room. She hurried her inside and shut the door.

She looked at Emily with a mixture of disbelief and amazement. "Are you daft?"

"No, is he?"

Cait smiled. Her smile turned into a laugh and soon they were both laughing so hard that Cait collapsed on the bed and Emily leaned against the wall for support.

"I can't believe I'm laughing when my brother is surely going to kill us both," gasped Cait.

"I suppose I have gotten you in trouble with my hasty tongue, haven't I? Although, how Talorc could hold you responsible for me after such short acquaintance I don't know."

Cait shook her head. "He won't be truly angry with me, but I think he meant what he said about not marrying you."

"That's a blessing as far as I can see," Emily said with some asperity.

Cait pushed away from the wall, tucked in her stray pleats and shook her head. "If he doesn't marry you, what will happen?"

Emily's sense of victory faded. "I do not know." He sure as certain wasn't going to send for her sister Abigail to come live with them in his current state of mind.

"Did you really tell my brother you would rather be married to a goat?" Cait asked, as she smoothed her now tidy pleats over her swollen abdomen.

Emily felt herself blush at the remembrance and chagrin filled her. She'd left England determined to make herself indispensable in her husband-to-be's household so that he would let her bring Abigail to the Highlands. Now, he was likely to send her home in disgrace.

And she had no doubt Abigail would be sent in her place, even if he didn't request a new bride. Emily's stomach contracted at the thought.

She sighed in vexation with herself. The man's rudeness was no excuse for *her* losing her head like that. "Aye, I did. I don't know what came over me. Sybil is always telling me I need to be more ladylike. I suppose your brother thinks I'm not and there's no hope of changing his mind."

Cait laughed again and shook her head. "That is an understatement. My brother is not used to men challenging him. A challenge from a woman is bound to keep him in a foul mood a good long while." Cait sobered a little at the thought.

"Do you think he meant what he said about not marrying me, even against the orders of his overlord?"

"You needn't sound so happy about it. Talorc isn't that bad," replied Cait reprovingly.

"Yes, of course, you should say that. You are his devoted sister after all. And I'm not hopeful . . . not exactly." Not when her duty to her sister dictated she marry the cranky warrior. "But do you think he meant it?"

"I don't know. Talorc rarely says something he does not mean. In fact, I am not sure I remember a time he has done so," admitted Cait.

"Do you think he will send me back to England?"

Cait's eyes filled with worry. "I do not know, but I do not want you to go. I have come to rely on your company."

It was a question that had still not been answered the next afternoon. Emily desperately wanted to go home, but knew that no matter what Talorc had decided for her future, she had to talk him out of sending her back to England. Sure as certain, she was going to have to apologize.

And the thought of apologizing to the laird was as unpleasant as the prospect of marrying him.

But Abigail would never survive life amidst the Sinclair clan. They were a prejudiced people, and Abigail's affliction on top of her being English was bound to make her life a misery.

Cait was the only person in the clan that made Emily feel welcome in any way. Everyone else either ignored her or was blatantly hostile. Especially the soldiers. It was as if they were personally offended she had been chosen to marry their laird. She felt like a leper and without Cait's friendship, she would have despaired.

As it was, when the two women went to the stream the other clanswomen used for washing, they were greeted by glares and not a single welcoming smile. Emily did her best to ignore the waves of rejection rolling over her and began washing her gowns marred by dirt on the journey north from England. But one by one, each of the clanswomen left, making it clear they did not want to be soiled by her presence. Stupid, weak tears filled her eyes.

"Are they like this with all outsiders?" Emily asked Cait as she blinked back the wetness in her eyes and tried to pretend it did not bother her.

"No. One of our warriors has just mated with a woman from the Balmoral clan and the other women accepted her warmly." Cait sighed. "I fear news of your confrontation with my brother has reached the rest of the clan. They're very loyal to their laird."

"And I called him a goat."

"Not quite," Cait said with a smile.

"You're loyal to your brother, but you don't hate me, do you?" she asked, realizing Cait's kind heart might be moved to pity, but she could very well dislike Emily as much as the rest of the clan.

"Of course not. And the other women won't once they get to know you either."

"Don't they care that he called me his enemy?"

Cait shrugged. "You *are* English."

"And therefore the enemy?"

The other woman sighed sadly. "Yes, but it is more than that. I suppose I should have told you. Only I had hoped Talorc would learn to be reasonable about it."

"About what?"

"Our father married an Englishwoman."

"Your mother was English?"

"No. She died when I was very small. Our father remarried when Talorc was fourteen. I was five at the time. The woman was very beautiful, but not trustworthy. They had only been married three years when she betrayed our father to an English baron, greedy for more holdings. It cost our father his life and that of many clan members. Talorc has never forgiven or forgotten the offense."

"He wouldn't, but does he truly believe I would betray him too . . . just because I am English?"

Cait looked away. "Yes."

* * *

The next morning, Emily approached Talorc. She knew she had to apologize to him and now was as good a time as any. Besides, she wanted his permission to walk to a small lake Cait had told her about.

She wanted a bath and did not want a repeat of the day before. Naturally, she would not tell Talorc that bit of her plan.

"What do you want?" he demanded.

"I wish to apologize . . . for saying I would rather wed a goat than you."

"Why?"

"I was angry with you."

"I know why you insulted me. Why are you apologizing?"

"A marriage begun with insults has little hope of harmony."

"There will be no marriage."

"But your king—"

"Will forget such an insignificant order in due course."

"You believe an order to wed insignificant?"

"Yes."

"I see. What do you plan to do with me then?"

He shrugged as if her future was of no consequence. And undoubtedly, to him it would be. But she could not be so sanguine. "I do not want you to send me home."

"You lie, just like all the English."

"I do not lie."

"You do not want to live here."

"That is true."

"Then you lie."

"I don't."

She saw nothing for it and explained about Abigail.

"So, you came in hopes of saving your sister from having to come here and marry me?"

"Yes."

"That is commendable." He said it grudgingly, but he was no longer scowling at her.

"She is gentle. She would not understand the coldness of your clan toward an English bride for their laird."

"And you do?"

Emily didn't, but she wasn't about to destroy the little rapport they had managed to achieve by saying so. "I do not want my sister hurt."

"I will not hurt her."

"So, you will not send me back?"

"I have not decided."

He stood up as if to go and she understood their discussion was at an end. She hurriedly made her request about the lake. He did not acknowledge it directly, but assigned a single young soldier to escort her, thereby giving his tacit approval and underscoring just how unimportant she was in his estimation if he would not waste a seasoned warrior on her escort.

But he had seemed to understand about Abigail at least. That was something. When Cait heard where Emily planned to go, the other woman insisted on accompanying her.

They reached the lake after a half an hour of brisk walking. Cait ordered the young soldier to wait for them with his back turned on the other side of some bushes. After realizing the two women intended to bathe, the boy turned bright red and hurried to obey his laird's sister.

As always, Emily was careful to stay in the shallowest water, refusing Cait's invitation to swim with hidden revulsion. The thought of going into deeper water made her sick to her stomach as it always did and she had to hide that as well. She was proud of her ability to do so.

Emily and Cait were finished bathing and redonning their clothes when Cait went utterly still. She turned toward where the Sinclair soldier had gone as if trying to see through the thick plant growth.

"What's the matter?" Emily asked. "He's not peeking, is he?"

Cait shook her head and put her finger against her lips in a sign to be quiet. Emily couldn't imagine what had her so agitated, but she did as Cait said and finished dressing as silently as possible. Cait did the same, her expression stark with worry.

She went rigid with tension, grabbing the small knife she used at mealtimes from her belt. Her eyes were fixed on the foliage several feet from the water's edge. Emily's gaze followed Cait's, though she had no idea what they were both watching for. A wild animal perhaps? But she hadn't heard anything and she had very good hearing.

The answer came a second later as five gigantic warriors, their faces painted with macabre blue designs and wearing a plaid of dark blue, green and pale yellow came out of the forest. They were riding the biggest horses she'd ever seen . . . bareback.

Chapter 3

Emily thought she had been prepared for anything in this Highland country, but she hadn't been ready for this. If someone had told her the day before that there were warriors more intimidating than the Sinclairs, she would have laughed in the person's face. She wasn't laughing now.

Nay. She was too busy praying.

The giant men rode toward her and Cait, their fierce scowls made even more menacing by the blue war paint. It was not so much that they were bigger than the Sinclair warriors as that they carried themselves as if they owned the world and all that was in it. Considering they were on another clan's territory, that said something. She'd never seen such arrogance and she'd been raised by one of England's most ruthless barons and was now betrothed to the formidable Sinclair laird.

The sound of Cait's frightened intake of breath reminded Emily she was not alone in facing the menace. Relief turned to chagrin in the space of a second. Emily didn't want her friend hurt . . . or frightened. She turned to Cait, whose face had drained of color. She was looking with terror at the warriors on horseback.

Emily tried to smile reassuringly. "Don't be frightened, Cait. It's only some friends of your brother, I'm thinking."

They looked mean enough to be friends to the Sinclair laird.

Cait shook her head slowly, her eyes never leaving the approaching warriors. "Friends? Nay, Emily. These are Balmoral soldiers and they have already killed Everett," she said, speaking of the boy sent to guard Emily, "or they would not be here."

Emily turned eyes filled with fury to the warrior closest to her. "Surely, not. You did not kill that boy. For it would be a sin for a grown man to kill a child . . . even here in the Highlands."

The warrior she addressed, a redheaded demon with eyes the color of grass, raised his brows but did not answer. He watched her silently, causing her to nervously twist and untwist the folds of her dress. She felt goaded into speaking again.

"Do you not know it is impolite to ignore a lady when she is speaking to you?" She'd been using Gaelic the whole time, so she knew the heathen monsters had to understand her.

A warrior from her left spoke. He could have been the first one's twin but for his brown eyes. "We did not kill the boy."

Emily turned back to her friend. "There now. Do you see? These are merciful men. I'm sure we have nothing to fear."

She prayed God would forgive her for the lie, but she hated the look of dread in Cait's eyes.

Cait's snort of disbelief turned into a scream as the green-eyed warrior swiftly rode forward and swung her onto his horse. He disarmed her in a move too quick for Emily to see, but she saw the small knife fall to the ground. Forgetting anything resembling ladylike decorum, she dove for it.

Grasping it in her hand, she scrambled to her feet and went for the warrior's unprotected calf.

The horse backed up and the knife swished uselessly through air. She lurched forward to try again, but was caught from behind by an arm as big as a pine tree. At least that was how it felt ramming into her stomach and knocking out her breath as she was lifted off her feet and dropped into a totally indecent position in front of one of the Balmorals.

She couldn't even scream, but she could bite and that's what she did, turning and sinking her teeth into the shoulder not covered by the warrior's plaid.

He grunted.

She bit down harder and tried to stab him in the thigh with the knife. Suddenly, instead of the arm being around her waist, it was wrapped around both her arms, holding them tight to her sides. The thumb from his free hand pressed against her wrist and her hand released the knife of its own volition.

The horse beneath them started moving and the warrior growled in her ear. "Stop trying to eat me, woman. I dinna think even the English infidels practiced cannibalism."

Emily tasted blood and yanked her mouth away from the huge warrior's shoulder. She spit to get the taste from her mouth and then turned to glare at her captor, but her attention was caught by Cait's wildly flailing body.

The other woman fought desperately, trying to free herself. The warrior holding her wasn't working too hard to subdue her, but was concentrating on protecting her from the tree branches as they rode swiftly through the forest.

Unconcerned about her own plight for the moment, Emily yelled, "Stop fighting, Cait. You'll hurt the baby."

"We can't let them take us!" Cait cried back. "If we do, it will mean war between the Sinclairs and the Balmorals."

Emily didn't see why that should be so upsetting to Cait. From what she had heard, the Highland clans were always at war with each other.

"If your brother did not want war, he should not have allowed his warrior to keep one of my clanswomen," the warrior holding Emily said.

Cait turned and glared at him, still struggling to be released, but not thrashing as wildly. "She was outside your holding . . . hunting on our land. Her loss is your own responsibility."

The man holding Cait said something to her. Emily could not understand the words, but his harsh tone was unmistakable. Cait said a word that Emily didn't know and the warrior's profile hardened with anger. Emily's own captor stiffened with affront, indicating he knew just what the word meant and it wasn't good.

Apparently there were worse things than being likened to a goat.

Suddenly the horses picked up their pace. There was no chance to speak for the next several minutes as the men rode hard. Emily worriedly watched Cait and was glad to note her friend no longer struggled for release. She must have realized a fall from a galloping horse could make her lose the babe.

They came to a clearing and stopped as suddenly as they had begun.

Her captor swung down from his horse, taking her with him, and then turned her to face him. Standing, he was huge and she had to tilt her head back to see his face.

Dark brown eyes encircled by gold stared down at her, no softness in evidence. They were wolf 's eyes, but instead of making her shiver, they made her burn in places she could give no name. She could not believe she was noticing something so shameful, especially in her current predicament, but the man was altogether too much for her senses to remain unaffected.

"Leave her alone," Cait yelled.

Emily's gaze skittered to her friend. Her redheaded captor had a more effective hold on her now and Cait's arms were pinned to her sides much the same as Emily's had been.

Her own captor's hands squeezed her shoulders in a demand for her whole attention. "Tell the laird we are keeping his sister and the babe in her. 'Tis fitting retribution for Susannah."

She stared at him in horror. "You can't mean that. Please, you mustn't take her away."

He didn't bother to reply and she hadn't expected him to. After all, why should he care for her pleas? The man's mind was obviously made up to do this heinous deed.

Still, her mouth opened to argue further, but he squeezed her shoulders again, this time his thumbs brushing along her collarbone. She gasped, no words making it past her suddenly tied tongue. She couldn't think. Not with him touching her in that inappropriate manner. She wanted to tell him to stop, but something about him mesmerized her.

He had not hurt her.

It was a puzzle, but even more so was the question of why he stood staring down at her, saying nothing.

He was frowning, but he didn't look particularly angry.

Didn't the men in the Highlands ever smile? What a foolish thought. Was he waiting for her to agree to be his messenger? If so, he would be waiting a long time.

"You cannot mean to take Cait on an arduous journey on horseback. Surely you have noticed she is with child."

He said nothing, giving her a glare meant to intimidate and it worked.

He was the most daunting man she'd come across in her life. He was also the most appealing one. The blue paint on his face could not disguise the masculine beauty of his features. Hair like shining obsidian hung past his massive shoulders and even the intricate tattoo around his bicep added to his appeal. It looked like a blue armband and none of the other soldiers had one.

Not that she would have seen any such thing on the Sinclair warriors. They had the decency to cover their upper torsos with saffron shirts under their plaids. Not so with these barbarians. His chest and one shoulder were bare. She could see a purplish bruise forming where she'd bit him as well as a smear of blood.

She winced, pained that she'd done that to another person.

His face held an impassive stare, yet she felt as if he were reading her every thought. She did not know how she was going to stop him from taking her friend, but stop him she must.

She pulled a handkerchief from where she had it tucked in her kirtle and wiped gently at the blood on his chest, not completely aware of what she was doing because her mind was spinning so furiously. She had to protect Cait.

"The journey could hurt the babe," she pointed out.

"Balmorals do not hurt women. Drustan is keeping her, but she and the bairn will not be harmed."

Emily pressed the cloth over the small wound she had inflicted. "Would not taking the laird's wife give you more revenge?" she asked, a desperate plan forming in her mind.

The warrior's eyes narrowed. "He is not married."

"Well, that was true a few days ago, but it isn't anymore."

At her friend's quick intake of breath at her lie, Emily silenced her with a look.

"Where is this wife then?" asked the warrior, in spite of himself.

He did not know why he hesitated and was actually listening to the Englishwoman. She was lovely, but he had never been swayed by a beautiful woman before. Perhaps it was her courage, or the way she tended the wound she had inflicted. The contradictory behavior intrigued him.

As did she. Her obvious concern for Talorc's sister confused him. He would have expected no less from another member of the Sinclair clan, but this woman was not a Sinclair. She was English. Unmistakably so from the way she was dressed and spoke their tongue with the accent of their southern foe.

English or not, he liked watching her. She tried so hard to hide her fear from him, but her trembling gave her away. Despite her nervousness, purple eyes shot fire at him and this amused him. She looked ready to go to battle. Against him.

And she was not even a femwolf.

Amazing.

Where had the Sinclairs found a jewel such as this?

"I am his wife."

The words hung in the air, slicing through his pleasure in her company. This jewel belonged to the Sinclair? He would not believe it.

He shook his head.

She nodded emphatically.

He turned to the Sinclair woman. "Your brother chose an English mate?"

"No."

Lachlan tilted the woman's chin up so she had to meet his gaze. "I do not like being lied to."

"I-I'm not lying."

"You say your friend is a liar?" he asked in a voice that had sent grown warriors running.

"No, of course not. Talorc did not choose me. Your king did it for him."

"You won't convince me that he married an Englander." The other man's hatred of the English was too strong. He'd lost a father and a brother to a greedy English baron and his cohort, the English woman who betrayed the Sinclair clan.

"Talorc hates the English more than he hates the MacDonalds," Drustan said, echoing Lachlan's thoughts.

"I know Talorc hates the English and it has not been a happy relationship." There was too much truth in her tone for Lachlan to continue to dismiss her claim. "But I am his wife. Your king and my king ordered it and my dowry was substantial."

He did not think Talorc would be moved by any amount of money, but he could not guess at the workings of the other clan chief 's mind.

"Why aren't you wearing his plaid?" he asked, while his mind latched on to the ease with which his revenge could be enhanced in this fortuitous circumstance.

"His willingness to marry did not extend to having an Englishwoman wearing his plaid. He is not entirely reconciled to this marriage."

Lachlan had no trouble believing that. Looking at the all-too-innocent expression in the woman's eyes, he could not help wondering if that lack of reconciliation meant the marriage had not yet been consummated.

"If you are his wife, he would only thank the Balmorals for ridding himself of you," Ulf said from behind them.

Hurt flared briefly in her eyes and then she shielded them with her lashes, shrugging. "His pride would not like it, even if his emotions found only relief."

Curiously, her hurt feelings moved Lachlan and he turned, glaring his brother into silence.

Ulf's eyes widened, but he said nothing, merely frowned.

Lachlan did not understand the fury coursing through him or the profound disappointment on finding that this unique and lovely woman was the wife of his enemy. However, he did understand that it would be cruel indeed to leave her to face Talorc's wrath when he learned of his sister's capture.

He focused on the woman. She had regained her composure and was speaking again.

"Even if I am English," Emily added under her breath, inexplicably hurt by the Balmoral soldier's cruel words.

She should not care what any of these barbarians thought.

Her captor heard her and smiled. Her heart almost stopped. An enemy's smile should not look so heavenly, particularly in a face painted for war.

Without another word, he grabbed her and swung up on his horse again, dropping her in the same embarrassing perch she'd been before. Her legs straddled the horse and her backside sat against his hard thighs. She gave a gasp of surprise, but otherwise tried to hide her fear now that her plan had worked.

She turned to her friend and said, "You must not concern yourself for me, Cait. I shall be fine. You can see that these warriors are kind and honorable."

Cait simply shook her head, apparently struck dumb.

Emily tried to smile, but didn't quite make it. "Goodbye, Cait."

At that moment the horses started moving, but the warrior her captor had called Drustan did not release Cait.

"You must let Cait go now that you have me."

Her captor said nothing.

She pinched at his thigh, but it was like trying to pinch a stone. "I said, you've got to let my friend go."

"Nay."

"Yes."

"*Silence*."

"I will not be silenced. Let her go, or I'll start screaming so loudly, they're bound to hear me all the way back at the keep."

"One sound like that and I will gag you."

She gasped.

His hold on her tightened . . . a warning squeeze she wasn't about to ignore. She had no desire to be gagged.

Her situation was dire enough. Her plan hadn't worked. Instead of releasing her friend, the warrior had kidnapped them both. What kind of man was this Highland laird that the prospect of stealing another laird's wife was not enough vengeance to take?

She had to make one last attempt to change his mind, as futile as it might be. "But if you don't leave one of us behind, who will tell Talorc that it was the Balmorals that did this thing?" she asked, desperately.

"The boy who was guarding you had opportunity to see our plaid before we knocked him asleep," the warrior said in a tone that discouraged further questions.

She didn't see what she had to lose. "You left that poor boy senseless? What if wild animals get him? Then who will tell? What if wild animals had gotten me on my way back to the holding if I *had* been your messenger? I suppose that wouldn't have mattered to you, me being English and all."

Her captor did not bother to answer. The horses gradually picked up speed until the war party was galloping away from Sinclair land at a speed that made Emily's head spin. She prayed for the safety of the unborn baby in her friend's womb and then prayed the man holding her would not drop her.

Several hours later, after riding rigidly in her captor's arms, she was praying for the strength to withstand just one more minute of this torture before disgracing herself and crying like a baby. When she thought she could not take another moment of the pain in her back from trying to sit away from the man carrying her, he raised his hand in a silent command to halt.

He swung down from his horse, bringing her with him. But he let her go immediately as if he could not stand to touch her. Foolishly offended by his rejection, she groaned in pain as she straightened her back, sure the moisture burning her eyes was from that pain alone. Truthfully, it was all she could do not to sink to her knees in weak relief. She walked gingerly, making her way to her friend's side to check on Cait's condition.

"Are you all right?" she asked with concern.

Cait smiled wearily. Emily was obviously in pain and trying to hide it. She was only human after all and the ride had been a punishing one . . . even for Cait. And she was a femwolf. "Yes. Drustan held me very gently and took care that I was not jostled by his horse."

The warrior's consideration made her feel strange. She knew their plan was to keep her in retaliation for Susannah, but he was not being cruel to her. In fact, he'd been more careful with her than her husband had ever been.

But if he could be so careful of her, why had the clan been so careless of Susannah? A femwolf left to hunt alone, especially when she was in heat, was fair game for an unmated werewolf and well they should know it.

"You on the other hand look as if you were forced to ride balancing on a mace," Cait added.

Emily grimaced, her heart-shaped face pinched and pale with exhaustion. "You are not far from the truth. The effort to sit forward and maintain my balance has left my back feeling like it will never straighten completely again."

"Why did you not relax against Lachlan? Surely he could withstand your weight if Drustan could withstand mine."

Emily looked askance at her. "*Relax against him?*" she asked incredulously.

Cait shook her head. Was it Emily's Englishness or the fact that she was a human that made her so prim? Cait would never have spent such a grueling ride trying to maintain propriety, but then she was a wolf and they were taught from the cradle to be more practical about their bodies than the human members of her clan tended to be.

"How did you know my captor's name?" Emily asked. "Have you seen him before?"

"No, but he's obviously the leader and he spoke possessively about Susannah, so I'm guessing he is the laird of the Balmoral clan . . . Lachlan. He could be her brother, but if I'm to be kept by Drustan, I can't help thinking he's Susannah's brother. He has not said." In fact, he hadn't said a single word since she'd called him that nasty name.

"Oh."

"Do you want me to ask if I am right?"

"No. I'm sure you are. It was a clever guess, but I was too busy trying to think of ways to escape to work it through. I should have figured out he was the laird anyway. It's obvious now that you say it."

Cait had to smile at her friend's chagrin. "Do not be too hard on yourself."

"I'm so smart I got both of us kidnapped. If I hadn't, I could have raised the alarm and gotten your brother's warriors in pursuit all the faster."

Cait felt badly that Emily had been kidnapped, too, but considering the way she and Talorc got along, Cait didn't think the other woman being left behind would have been an improvement. Especially if she didn't succeed at escape. And, in her condition, she had very little hope of doing so.

"By the time you had walked back to the keep, we would have been too far ahead to do me any good. Remember, we had ridden a fair way before the laird was prepared to release you. As it is, Everett has raised the alarm, I'm sure."

"I hope you're right and that no wild animals got him."

"He is no unprotected human." Cait grimaced at her slip, but Emily didn't seem to notice.

She was too busy looking around her. "Why did we stop here, do you think?"

"To get in the boat."

"Boat?" Emily asked, going pale. "What boat?"

"The Balmoral clan live in a fortress on an island. Once we are in the boat, it will be much harder for my brother to rescue us."

"There will be no rescue, lass," Drustan called in a hard voice from a distance away.

Emily gasped in shock even as her whole body shook with fear at the prospect of being dragged onto a boat. "How did he know we were talking about that?"

"He could hear us."

But Emily shook her head. "We're too far away and we've been speaking in undertones. He must have made a clever guess."

Cait looked as though she were going to argue. "Emily . . ."

"What?"

Then Cait shook her head. "Never mind. Do you speak Latin?" she asked in that language in a bare whisper.

"Yes."

"I'm hoping they don't."

Emily understood immediately. In case one of them did have particularly good hearing, it wouldn't hurt if she and Cait spoke in a foreign tongue. She would ask another time how her friend had learned Latin. It wasn't an uncommon accomplishment for women of her status in England, but she'd always heard the Highlanders lived near barbarianism.

Though, so far, that belief had been shown up as a gross exaggeration.

"What are we going to do?"

"Keep pretending that you are debilitated by the ride."

"That should be easy," Emily said with a grimace, her sore muscles making it not much of a pretense.

"We have to steal some horses."

"But they will only follow us."

"Our one hope is to stay ahead of them long enough to meet up with my brother."

"If he is following."

"He is. Trust me. Do you notice how they are letting the horses drink without a guard?"

Emily looked to the water's edge where all five horses drank. The men were busy readying the boat Cait had mentioned and some kind of contraption that she thought might be for the horses. It looked like a floating raft, but with openings for the horses to be harnessed to it, so they could swim behind the boat, but be kept afloat? At least that is what it seemed to her.

"We need to get closer to the horses and when they have two of them harnessed for crossing the sea and are busy with the third one, we will grab the last two and run. We must be swift."

Emily nodded and then had an inspiration. "Laird?" she called.

He looked at her, his expression thoughtful.

"Cait and I need a moment of privacy."

His dark brow rose, the only indication he gave that he heard her.

She felt a blush climb her cheeks. "To, you know . . ."

Lachlan had to bite back a smile, which was a very different reaction for him. He wondered if he should tell the women he spoke Latin as well? Not yet.

Since he knew their plan was to try to steal horses, he wasn't concerned about allowing her the moment of privacy she asked for, but he did wonder what she thought it would gain her.

"Be quick," he barked.

She jumped, nodded and turned to hurry into the bushes. Cait was right behind her.

He listened to them as they left.

"He's awfully surly, isn't he?" the Englishwoman asked.

"He's laird," Cait replied.

"And that's his excuse for rudeness? I don't know why I'm surprised. It's your brother's as well."

Mention of her husband, the Sinclair laird, irritated him and Lachlan scowled.

"They're spirited lasses, aren't they?" Drustan asked from beside him.

"That is one way to put it," Lachlan growled.

"Cait called me a horse's backside."

"I heard."

Drustan laughed. "I'll have her apology tonight, along with other things."

Lachlan nodded. "Be gentle with her. She's carrying."

"The Balmorals don't hurt women."

"I know that."

"They don't bed other men's wives either."

A warning growl rumbled low in Lachlan's throat. "I know that as well. But if her husband has bedded her, I'll bury my claymore. She's too damn innocent."

"And that bothers you?"

"Yes," he bit out.

"Would it be easier to keep your hands off her if she weren't, do you think?"

Lachlan had no answer. He had never anticipated wanting an Englishwoman and would sooner tear out his own throat than bed another man's wife. But he wanted this purple-eyed spitfire . . . enough to make his body rigid with desire and his sex ache.

"I should have left her in the forest."

"You could still leave her. The Sinclair is probably only a couple of hours behind us."

"If that."

"So, leave her."

"I can't."

"Hell."

"My thoughts exactly."

"If you kill him, she would be a widow," Drustan said helpfully.

"I'm still not convinced she is a wife."

Chapter 4

"What's the matter?" Emily demanded of Cait.

All of a sudden, her friend looked ready to cry.

"I don't want him to kill my brother."

"Who?"

"Lachlan . . . the laird of the Balmorals."

"Why would he kill him?"

"To have you."

"Don't be ridiculous."

But Cait wasn't listening. She was like she had been earlier . . . intent on something Emily could get no glimmer of.

"What is it, Cait?"

But Cait just shook her head.

"Don't you think it is odd they did not send a guard with us?"

"We could never outdistance them and they know it."

"But if we hid . . . perhaps we could delay their departure until your brother caught up with us."

Cait's face leached of color. "I do not want that to happen."

"What? Why?"

"The Balmoral laird could kill Talorc. I'm not even sure that Drustan couldn't. It wouldn't be a given, but it is possible. I don't want to lose my brother."

"But won't there be a battle when we meet up with them with the horses?"

"I am hoping they won't follow once we get away. They will know their attempt at taking us has failed."

"I don't see Lachlan avoiding a fight."

Cait's eyes filled with tears. "I don't either."

Emily put her arm around her. "What do you want to do?"

"If we don't escape, my brother will come for us on the island. And there is an even greater chance he would be killed then."

Although the cranky laird's death would solve her own problems, Emily wasn't tempted in the least to wish for it. First, because it would be a terrible sin, but second because it would hurt her dear friend. "Then we must escape."

"Yes."

"But you do not wish to run and hide now?"

"Hiding would never work." Cait bit her lip. "They could find us no matter how good our concealment."

"You speak as if they are gods. They are merely men, Cait."

"No. They are not. They are more . . ." She made a sound of distress. "I wonder if they heard our plans, perhaps they can hear us even now . . ." Cait shook her head. "No, I think we are far enough away to be out of earshot. I don't hear them anymore. We did walk a good long distance."

"If we don't return soon, they are bound to come looking for us."

A pained expression came over Cait's features. "They already have. We must return now."

Emily nodded, unwilling to argue with her distraught friend. If she said the men were coming, she must have heard something. She'd certainly heard them before Emily had at the lake.

However, her pretense had not been all deception. "I still need a few moments of privacy."

Cait looked startled and then laughed jerkily. "Me, too. I've found pregnancy makes this aspect of life quite challenging at times."

Emily smiled, remembering other women having made the same complaint in her father's keep. Cait had returned to the clearing when Emily finished dealing with the pressing need of her bladder. Drustan was there with her.

He wasn't saying anything and Cait's eyes were filled with hopeless desperation.

Emily glared at the warrior.

He jerked slightly as if surprised by her hostility, which made her want to scream like a fishwife. Were all men in the Highlands so dense?

"What you are doing is wrong."

"Nay, lass. Retaliation is law among the clans. Right is on our side."

Cait spoke then, her eyes burning with anger. "Was it right to allow your clanswoman to hunt during a full moon away from Balmoral territory? She was not protected. She was in he—" Cait snapped her mouth shut and looked at Emily, then back at Drustan. "You know what I mean. You neglected to protect her and now you would punish me for your own weakness."

Drustan swelled with affront. "I did not neglect my sister's protection. Whatever lie your clansman told to justify his actions, she was not hunting off the island. Your clansman came to our territory and took her, just as I am taking you now. And it is not you who pays the price, but your brother in losing you and the babe in you from his pack."

Emily had never heard a clan referred to as a pack before,

but now was not the time to ask about it. "Susannah is happily wed to a Sinclair. Surely that is all that matters," she said.

"The Sinclair should have asked permission on behalf of his clansman. He did not, which is a breach of clan law that my laird and I, as Susannah's brother, cannot tolerate."

Cait crossed her arms over her chest and glared at the Balmoral warrior. "Deny it all you like, but she was a lone wol—woman! She was fair game when Magnus came across her and she *is* happily wed. She loves Magnus and our clan has accepted her with open arms."

Emily tried not to wince at the reminder that she had not received such acceptance.

"Clan law must be satisfied," Drustan stubbornly maintained.

"Even if it means going to war?" Emily asked.

"Of course." The daft man looked like he couldn't understand her need to ask the question.

They headed back, Cait taking pains to keep distance between herself and the Balmoral soldier. Emily felt for her friend. Her own situation was precarious, but the truth was . . . she was no worse off than she'd been before. Living amongst the Balmorals couldn't be any worse than living with the Sinclairs. And as long as she was captive to the other clan, she didn't have to worry about Talorc sending her back to England and Abigail being sent in her place to fulfill the king's edict.

But Cait was obviously and justifiably upset by their predicament. She didn't want war with the Balmoral clan and she didn't want to live with them either, from what Emily could see.

They reached the water and both she and Cait stopped a few feet from where the soldiers readied the horses. The contraption they were using looked odd, but she remembered seeing something like it in a painting of a Viking raid once. It looked like a floating raft that the horses would be attached to in harness as they swam. The raft would make the crossing easier on them. It would keep their heads above water, with slots in it for each horse's body to fit into, so that they would be together and afloat and share the burden of the crossing, conserving their equine strength. The horses didn't seem to mind it.

Regardless, Emily was glad she and Cait planned to escape before getting on the boat. The sea was not exactly calm. Waves crashed against rocks a good distance from the shore and she had no desire to be in a boat amidst such awesome movement of the deep, dark water. She had no desire to be in a boat at all.

She had grown adept at hiding her terror of the water, but it was there inside her, a dark force that would consume her as surely as the murky depths.

"Eat this." Drustan held an oat cake and apple toward Cait.

She shook her head.

"The babe needs nourishment."

As much as she hated to, Emily agreed with the warrior. "Eat, Cait. He's right."

Cait took the food and bit into the apple.

Drustan handed a similar offering to Emily in silence. She accepted it without a word. If they were going to run, they had to keep their strength up.

She took one bite of the oat cake and realized why Cait had chosen to eat her apple first. The bread tasted like wood, but she choked it down. She immediately took a bite from her apple to clear the awful taste from her mouth.

She looked at Cait and grimaced. The other woman laughed.

"What is so amusing?" Drustan asked.

Cait lost her smile. "Emily doesn't seem to like the oatcake."

"It is merely that the flavor took me by surprise," Emily hedged, not wanting to be rude even amidst her enemies and then got angry with herself for caring whether or not she offended them.

They bloody well deserved to be offended.

"I don't like them either," Cait assured her. "Only warriors lack taste enough to find them palatable."

"That doesn't surprise me," Emily said with asperity.

They finished the repast quickly despite its unappetizing nature.

"Come here, English." It was Lachlan. He was twenty feet away, standing by the boat that looked much too small to transport five giant warriors and two women anywhere across the water. He was so close to the edge, he was practically standing in the water.

She had no desire to get that close to the sea. "My name is Emily, not English."

The big warrior just shrugged. And waited.

She crossed her arms and gave him a look that told him he could wait until her father came calling from England. She wasn't getting that near to the water. She measured the distance to the horses out of the corner of her eye. If Drustan wasn't so close, they would have better luck escaping, but they had to try.

She turned to signal Cait, but she was too late. Without so much as a muscle twitch of warning, Drustan swung Cait up in his arms and headed toward the boat. She yelled and shoved against his chest, but he kept hold of her.

"Ulf," the laird said.

A second later, Emily found herself swung high in another warrior's arms and then thrown over his shoulder. It was the man who had said Talorc would thank Lachlan for stealing her because she was English. She immediately tried bucking out of his hold, but his grip tightened painfully across her thighs and she yelped.

His shoulder rammed her stomach with every step he took and she found it difficult to breathe. She was not happy about hanging upside down either. His backside was right there and she averted her face so she was at least looking at the ground. He felt different from Lachlan and she didn't want him holding her. Even briefly.

His glare had been filled with a malevolence she had not seen in Lachlan's eyes either.

"Put me down," she demanded when she could get enough breath, only to lose it again as she realized the warrior had walked right into the water.

He put her down all right . . . straight into the boat on a tiny seat beside Cait. The craft rocked dangerously and she gasped in fright. Drustan was in front of them and Ulf climbed into the boat behind them. He sat down right behind her, his hostile presence too close for comfort. She felt trapped and her body twitched with the need to get away from him.

The water was shallow here. She noticed his legs were only wet up to his knees. No matter how dark it looked, it was not deep. She must remember that. Emily pinched Cait lightly. It was now or never. Her friend dove out one side of the boat while Emily forced nausea-producing fear down so she could dive out the other. Ulf caught her by the skirt of her overtunic and held her hanging above the water.

The sound of splashing and Drustan's bellow told her Cait had been more successful.

"Save yourself, Cait," Emily screamed as she scrabbled to get back in the boat and do what she could to hamper efforts at catching her friend.

She was just in time to grab Drustan's ankle. She clung for all she was worth with both hands, but he gave a mighty yank, straining her shoulder joints. He dove after Cait, but it was the other redheaded soldier who caught her as she tried to mount the single horse remaining on dry land.

Cait fought like a wildcat, biting and clawing, screaming for the man to let her go.

But it was Drustan's lethally quiet command that accomplished that. The other soldier released her and Drustan grabbed her in the same motion. He subdued her almost instantly and tied her hands behind her back with a leather strap, his face set in a black scowl. He then did the same to her feet.

Cait was sobbing by the time he was done. "Don't do this," she begged through her tears. "Please, don't do this. I'll talk to Talorc . . . there will be an apology. Please . . ."

But Drustan just picked her up, cradled her to his chest like a small child and carried her back to the boat.

She looked up at him. "I h-hate you. I'll never be yours. N-never!"

He looked down at her and his anger was terrifying. "You'll be mine, lass. Hate me if you will, but I am keeping you just as Magnus kept my Susannah."

"I'll kill you first, or die trying," Cait said, her tears giving way to fury.

After that, she said nothing, sitting ramrod straight on the small bench beside Emily. With a sideways look, Emily noted that Cait was glaring a hole in Drustan's back. And the horrible man deserved it.

Emily did not know how to help her friend, but her mind was reeling in horror from what the angry warrior's words had implied. Less than five minutes later, they cast off. The warriors rowed with practiced movements that showed they'd made this crossing together many times before.

She was trying not to imagine how deep the water was or how flimsy the boat felt. She valiantly ignored the spray from waves that crashed against its bow. Her eyes were fixed firmly on the back of Drustan's wet plaid, but the image of the furious soldier was no more comforting than the terrifying water.

She turned to Cait. "Are you all right?" she asked in Latin.

Cait met her gaze with troubled brown eyes. "The babe and I are not physically harmed," her friend replied in the same language. "But I am not all right."

Emily nodded, understanding better than another woman might what it meant to feel her life had been taken out of her control and the best she could do for those she loved still left them vulnerable. "I am sorry."

"Thank you, but you know it is not your fault."

"I insisted on bathing outside the walls . . . because I was weak."

"We were on Sinclair land. We should have been safe."

"You should not have been with me. If your brother had known you were going, he would have sent more soldiers to guard you . . . probably older ones, too."

"The boy he sent with you is known to be fierce. Unless he had sent a contingent of his personal guard, like he did to fetch you from the border, we could not have been better protected. Even then, it would have been an uncertain outcome with the Balmoral soldiers."

"They are that fearsome?" Emily asked.

"These ones are."

"It is still my fault we were outside the walls."

"Emily, I would have taken you to see the loch sometime. They would have been waiting then."

"You think they were watching for their opportunity?"

"I am sure of it."

The wind gusted and despite the summer sun, Emily shivered. Cait was wet and she wasn't. She patted her friend's shoulder in commiseration. "You must be awfully cold."

Cait looked surprised by the comment. "Nay."

Her friend certainly wasn't shivering like Emily was and she did not understand it. She'd noticed at the Sinclair keep that they often didn't light a fire in the hall until evening although it was certainly chilly enough for one much earlier in her estimation. There was no doubt about it, the Highlanders were a hardy people.

But even a strong woman like Cait could be broken by the kind of plans Emily suspected Drustan had for her friend.

"Cait . . ."

"Yes, Emily?"

"What does it mean to *keep* someone in clan law?"

Cait grimaced. "You mean like Drustan has threatened to keep me?"

It had sounded more like a promise to Emily's ears, but she nodded.

"Between a man and a woman, it means he intends to take her for his mate."

"Drustan is going to marry you?" It was as she feared, but something still did not make sense to her. "But is not Church law the same in Scotland as it is in England? Your king accepted Rome's authority, did he not?"

"The clans are not much bothered by the dictates of Scotland's king."

Talorc certainly had not been. "So you do not have to agree to the marriage for it to be valid?"

"Well, yes, but when a man keeps a woman, he will settle for a clandestine marriage."

"You mean he will take you to his bed without the benefit of the Church's blessing?" Emily demanded, appalled. It was even worse than she had thought.

"Yes."

"That is barbaric."

Cait shrugged, but her eyes belied the relaxed pose.

"Lachlan told me that the Balmorals did not harm women or children." And she had believed him. "But he lied."

"Yes, he lied."

"I did not lie," Lachlan said in Latin, his voice hard.

He'd understood the entire exchange.

Cait flinched and then her shoulders sagged. "I should have guessed. My brother told me the Balmoral laird was more learned than other Highlanders. He considered it a weakness."

"You have learned differently, have you not?"

Cait refused to answer Lachlan's taunt and Emily was too furious to say anything at all.

The man was a monster!

Drustan asked for a translation of the conversation and Lachlan gave it to him. Word for word. Despite her anger, Emily blushed to be caught discussing such private things in mixed company. The embarrassment did not last long as fury that Cait could be treated so horribly overtook every consideration, even her fear of the water.

It was not right.

She surged to her feet and spun to face Lachlan. He stood at the front of the boat, his stance arrogant and commanding, while the other soldiers manned the oars. His rugged masculine appeal mocked her, for it masked a black heart she would never have guessed at.

The pain of having believed him to be something he wasn't mixed with her fear for her friend and exploded in a deluge of angry words. "*You are nothing but a lying savage*. Do you hear me?"

"I believe they hear you in England, lass," one of the soldiers said. He was the only blond one among them and up to now he hadn't spoken.

She glared at him before turning her frown on Lachlan once again. He looked unaffected by her outburst. She didn't care if her words impacted him, or not. She was going to have her say and that was that.

"And Drustan is a thief. No . . . he is worse than a thief," she said with relish. "For he intends not only to steal that which does not belong to him, but to hurt an innocent woman in the process. And most likely her unborn child. You're all a bunch of cowards, too, taking your revenge on a woman rather than facing your opponents in honest combat."

Several grunts of annoyance met that statement, but she ignored them. She had one last thing to say to the man watching her so impassively.

"You may be more learned than the other Highland lairds, Lachlan, but to my way of thinking, you are the most ignorant, not to mention heartless man I have ever met here or in England."

Then she sat back down with a flounce that rocked the boat, reminding her just where she was and making her stomach churn.

Cait was staring at her like she'd lost her mind. "Are you wanting them to throw you out of the boat then?"

Still too angry to heed her words, she said, "I wouldn't be a bit surprised if they did, considering the wicked plans they have for you."

Ulf grabbed her shoulders as if prepared to do just that and she bit back a scream. She would not let them see her fear, but inside her heart raced with terror at what he would do.

"Let her go!" The whiplash of Lachlan's voice had immediate impact.

Ulf released her instantly, but snarled, "It is no more than she deserves for casting such slurs on the Balmoral clan."

"Not the whole clan, just the warriors here." Unlike some of the Highlanders she had met, she did not judge an entire group of people by the actions of a few degenerates.

She didn't guess they liked that opinion either when fury-filled silence greeted the airing of it. A large wave crashed against the bow, sending sea spray over all of them. Now, on top of her anger, she had to deal with the fear that the ocean was going to swallow their boat.

Her nails dug into her palms and she prayed drowning wasn't as horrible a death as she had always feared.

The strangest expression crossed Cait's face. "I've enjoyed knowing you, Emily."

Coming on the heels of her anxious thoughts, the words were not in the least welcome. Emily sucked in a breath and tried to calm herself. It didn't work. The boat road a high swell and the bow came out of the water before hitting it again with a jar. She gasped and then bit her lower lip to keep from making another noise.

Movement behind her rocked the boat from side to side and she wondered who could be so daft that they were moving about at a time like this, but she refused to turn to see. She would rather be surprised by her fate if Lachlan had changed his mind and decided to have her tossed overboard.

A big hand landed on her shoulder. Lachlan had come for her himself.

"I don't know how to swim," she blurted out and then practically bit her tongue through, chagrined to have shown such weakness.

"That would hardly matter if I were the man you believed me to be, would it?"

He was right and she knew deep inside he would never throw her overboard, or was she only deceiving herself? She refused to face him. "You have aided in the abduction of a woman with the intent to harm her."

"I have exercised my right as laird to exact justice between the clans."

"I don't care how you justify it to yourself. What you are doing determines what kind of man you are."

His sigh was loud and long. "Your opinion of me and my clan does not matter, English."

"I never thought it would." But his words had hurt her and it was all she could do to keep that out of her voice. Her opinion should matter. His would matter to her.

Horror filled her at the recognition of that appalling truth. She should not care.

"Yet you expressed it."

She shrugged, or tried to with his heavy hand still on her shoulder. "It matters to me."

"I see."

"I doubt it."

"If you are about to insult me again, I warn you . . . dinna do it." His quiet tone was more lethal than if he had shouted the warning.

Her mouth snapped shut.

He growled. "I do not like talking to your back. Turn around."

"No."

But he was already picking her up to do it himself.

She cried out as she was lifted off her seat completely. "Do not drop me. You shouldn't be moving so much. Don't you notice how rough the sea is? We could capsize." She nodded, wishing she could appeal to a sense of reason she feared he did not have.

The man thought he was indestructible.

"The water is near smooth as glass."

"You jest. I know you do, but this is no laughing matter."

"I am not jesting." He held her close against his chest, his eyes filled with a dark intensity she could not interpret. "No harm will come to you at my hand, English."

She wanted to scoff, but she couldn't. Because Heaven help her, she did believe him. What did that say for his plans for Cait then?

She did not realize she'd asked the question aloud until he answered it.

"It is Drustan's responsibility to convince Cait she wants to be kept."

"And if he can't?" Emily asked, trying to read the level of Lachlan's sincerity in his gaze.

A small smile played at one corner of his mouth. "He can. He is a Balmoral."

"That doesn't make him a magician," she whispered, once again falling under the spell this man seemed to cast every time he turned his whole attention on her.

He set her down on the bench beside Cait, but this time so Emily faced where he had taken Ulf 's seat at the oars. The other soldier now stood in the bow of the boat, turned away from them all, his body stiff with rage.

Lachlan took up the oars and began to row in perfect unison with the others. "He is man enough to make his mate want him . . . to bed her without hurting her or the bairn she carries."

Emily couldn't believe Lachlan had said such a thing to her and Cait's loud gasp said she didn't appreciate his candidness either. "If he's thinking I'll submit, he's wrong," she said, her tone as mean as any of the warriors had been.

Drustan gave a low chuckle that sounded diabolical to Emily's ears. "Aye, you'll submit, lass, and like it."

Cait made a strangled sound and lurched forward. Emily turned her head just in time to see Cait's mouth closing on the back shoulder of the man taunting her. Drustan didn't react any more than Lachlan had when Emily had bit him.

"I see you've taught your heathen English ways to the Sinclair lass," Lachlan drawled, inexplicable amusement in his voice.

"I am not a heathen," Emily spluttered.

Drustan made quick work of breaking Cait's hold on his skin. Then he pulled her into his lap, whispered something about teaching her better things to do with her mouth and kissed her.

It wasn't a brutal kiss even though Cait tried to bite him again. He simply laughed and kissed the corner of her mouth, her eyes and her temple before returning to her lips. Emily looked away, unwilling to witness such a scene, but couldn't help peeking again and saw that her friend's struggles had ceased.

She was afraid Drustan had hurt her after all, but Cait was kissing him back, her body turned toward his, not writhing to get away. Emily could not look away. She had never seen anything like it. Surely it was the sort of intimacy that should be saved for the bedchamber, but none of the other soldiers seemed in the least embarrassed by it.

Cait wasn't embarrassed either. She was too busy to notice anyone else, Emily was thinking.

What would it be like to be kissed in such a manner?

Would she like it? Surely that sort of thing happened in the marriage bed, but it was not Talorc's face that came to her mind when she tried to imagine it. No, the face in her disturbing fantasy was of another Highland laird, a man who went looking for revenge with his face painted blue and riding a horse that could be mistaken for a dragon.

Chapter 5

After long minutes, the warrior finally lifted his mouth from Cait's. She was panting and had the most astonished expression on her face . . . but she did not look angry any longer. Or even a little bit frightened.

"You will want me when I take you," Drustan promised in a voice that made Emily feel funny and crave such words for herself. Only not from him.

It was wicked . . . some kind of Highland sorcery she did not understand. She was not the heathen around here . . . it was the Balmoral wizards who could turn a woman's thoughts to mush.

Using the corner of his plaid, Drustan gently wiped away the blue paint that had been smeared on Cait's face from the kiss. "I will not harm you. Never doubt me again."

Cait turned her face away, but Drustan gently pressed it into his chest, cradling her close as if she were a precious treasure.

For some reason, the action brought tears to Emily's eyes.

"You will apologize now," Lachlan said, drawing her attention back to him.

"For what?" she asked, making a valiant effort to meet his wolflike gaze.

Those eyes were so uncanny, she knew she would see them in her dreams.

As usual, when the stubborn warrior did not want to answer, he didn't. He merely stared at her. Well, she could be stubborn, too. She pressed her lips together, determined not to speak. She had nothing to apologize for. Just because Cait appeared to enjoy Drustan's kisses didn't mean Lachlan had been right in the form of revenge he had chosen.

The silence between them stretched on and on, broken only by the sound of the oars slashing through the water and the waves breaking around them.

"I will win," Lachlan promised quietly, then dismissed her as surely as if he'd turned away.

Inexplicably hurt by his rejection, she focused on the view out the side of the boat. It was no more comforting than it had been the first time she'd looked. The island they were obviously headed toward didn't seem to be getting any closer and the water stretched in an expanse of dark swells around them.

Drustan untied Cait and helped her back to her seat beside Emily before taking up his oars again.

Without the anger to bolster her courage, it deserted her and horrible images of the boat tipping to one side or huge crashing waves washing over it and taking her and Cait overboard tormented Emily's brain.

"Are you going to tolerate the insult of the English wench?" Ulf demanded in a furious tone, interrupting her waking nightmare.

"She will apologize," Lachlan drawled with utter certainty.

"No, I won't." She muttered the defiance without thought and was surprised she could force the words out of her tight throat afterward.

Lachlan growled low in his chest, the sound so far from human, it made her shiver and added to the sense of doom taking over her senses. Her gaze flew to his and she wished it hadn't. His eyes were even less human than usual with the gold almost overtaking the brown of his irises. She just knew that meant he was well and truly annoyed with her.

If she wasn't past the age of believing in monsters like dragons and werewolves, she'd think he was one. An atavistic chill skittered down her spine and it was all she could do not to whimper in fright.

"Are you admitting she is right then? That you are weak and a coward to take your revenge on women instead of men?"

Lachlan stood and faced the angry soldier, his own body vibrating with deadly tension. "You dare to challenge me?"

"I am not the one challenging you. *She* did and you do nothing to punish the insolence."

The boat swayed and a scream locked in Emily's throat, making her jaw ache with the effort it took to hold it back. She shut her eyes tight, trying to block out the reality of her surroundings, but the sounds of wind on the water would not let her.

"Perhaps he thinks forcing her to endure your company is punishment enough," Cait taunted.

There was a scuffle above Emily and the boat swayed in alarming dips first to one side and then to the other. She sank further and further into the fear swirling through her. Her eyes flew open, her despairing gaze searching out the strongest person on the boat . . . Lachlan.

He stood above her, holding Ulf, as if stopping him from going for Emily's throat.

Her hand flew to protect it in a totally futile gesture.

Ulf's eyes spit angry recriminations at his leader. "I won't tolerate such insults, even if you will."

"You will tolerate whatever I tell you to tolerate." The tone of Lachlan's voice was the meanest she'd heard it yet.

"You would choose your enemy over your brother?"

Ulf was Lachlan's brother? Emily supposed there was a slight family resemblance, but they seemed so different.

"Balmoral warriors do not prey on women."

"She insulted us all!" he yelled, jerking his head toward Emily.

"She is English, and therefore ignorant of our ways. She will learn."

A tiny part of her mind was offended by the pronouncement, but she was too preoccupied with the prospect of dying at sea to work up any real anger.

The summer sun had not quite set when they reached the Balmorals' island.

Emily was breathing shallowly, her fingers curled like talons around the edge of the wooden slab she and Cait sat on. Her usually resilient nature had been eclipsed by the ongoing torture of crossing the roughened waters and doing it sitting across from Ulf, who glared at her like he hated her.

Lachlan had traded places with his brother moments after their brief scuffle and she'd spent the rest of the trip being glowered at by the angry soldier. She'd wanted to turn around, to face Drustan's back, but her fear of the water had complete hold again. Moving even an inch had been beyond her . . . and continued to be.

The sight of land so close was so welcome, tears sprang into her eyes, but she could not utter a word.

The brown-eyed soldier with the red hair, whom Emily had heard Lachlan refer to as Angus, jumped out to pull the boat to the shore while Ulf and the blond soldier went to tend to the horses. It took less than fifteen minutes to bring both the boat and horses ashore. Drustan lifted Cait to dry land and turned to do the same for Emily.

"Come." He put his hand out.

She stared at it. He expected her to stand, she knew he did, but for the last hour or more, her only grip on safety had been her tight hold on the bench beneath her. She willed her fingers to let go, but they did not move.

"What is the matter?" Lachlan asked Drustan.

"The English lass is being stubborn about getting out of the boat."

Lachlan turned to her, his frown fierce. "Do not try my patience."

"You don't have any," she muttered.

"If that were true, I would not be waiting for my apology."

She didn't respond to that bit of arrogance. She couldn't. She was too busy trying to make her fingers obey her.

"Come here," he barked, his gaze searing her.

Her body jerked and her fingers finally unbent from the seat. She shot to her feet, grateful for his brusqueness, but with no intention of telling him so.

Drustan's hand was still outstretched, but she ignored it, swaying toward Lachlan. He reached into the boat and grabbed her by the waist with both hands, then lifted her as if she weighed nothing. He set her on the ground, frustrated anger emanating off of him in waves that buffeted her overwrought emotions as powerfully as the water had crashed against the boat's bow.

She turned away and her attention was caught by the horses. They appeared no worse for their journey across the channel. She wished she could say the same. In order to return to the Sinclair holding, she would have to go back the same way. Sick at the thought, she barely stopped herself from praying she would remain captive until the end of her days.

"How far to your holding?" she asked Lachlan without looking at him.

She got no answer and sighed. "I am sorry for being difficult about getting out of the boat."

When she received no reply to that either, she looked back to see if Lachlan was still behind her.

He was, a strange expression in his gold-rimmed eyes. "You're wasted on Talorc, English."

She shook her head, not knowing what he meant.

"Aye, you are."

Cait made a sound of distress, but when Emily's gaze found her, she could see no reason for her friend's upset.

"My home is there," Lachlan said, drawing her attention back to him.

He was pointing and Emily followed the direction of his finger with her eyes, then gasped at what she saw. A sheer cliff rose fifty feet in the air and on top of the cliff was a huge stone castle that looked worthy of a king.

"It's massive," Cait whispered, her voice filled with awe as she came to stand beside Emily. "My brother's forces will never make it inside."

Emily had to agree. She didn't think the king of England would have much luck in a siege against the Balmorals.

"What we have we hold," Drustan said arrogantly, laying a proprietary hand on Cait's shoulder.

"Except Susannah," Cait pointed out.

"Rest assured, whatever mistake led to her mating with Magnus will not be repeated with you."

"I should hope not. I have no desire to mate with my brother's blacksmith," Cait said teasingly.

Drustan did not smile at the joke. If she hadn't thought it improbable, Emily would have said he looked severely offended by the remark. But even a too-serious Highlander had to realize Cait's words could have been nothing but a jest.

For no reason she could discern, he turned his glare from Cait to encompass Emily as well.

"How many live within the castle walls?" Emily asked, trying to turn the topic, her mind still boggling at the size of the castle atop the cliff.

"Think you we would give secrets like that away to our enemy?" Ulf asked, his contempt flaying her.

Emily's emotions teetered on the edge of an abyss as deep as her fear of the water. "I am not your clan's enemy."

She'd spoken in a whisper that was barely audible, but Ulf laughed deridingly. "You say that after the insults you leveled against our clan? You are our enemy right enough. Not only are you the wife of the Sinclair laird, but you are English. That makes you our enemy twice over."

The words poured over her like acid, burning and destroying what was left of her emotional well-being.

She'd been met with almost nothing *but* hatred since coming to the Highlands. Ulf's words told her that she would be despised even more amidst his clan than she had been among the Sinclairs'. She could not bear to face such a prospect.

Back in her father's keep, she was well-liked by the servants, if not valued by her family. Some, like her old nurse, even loved her. Her sister Abigail certainly did.

But here, she was surrounded by people who believed she was beneath their contempt. Even Lachlan had shown he found her more annoying than anything else and that hurt more than all the rest, though she could not have said why. She'd only just met the man and he wasn't exactly pleasant company.

On top of it all, Cait thought it was Emily's fault the laird might try to kill her brother. Emily didn't understand her friend's reasoning, but in that moment, she understood very little. Only that she could not bear one more scowl leveled her way simply for being born.

She turned and started walking. She didn't know where she was going, but it didn't matter. She could not go to that castle, an impregnable fortress where she would meet nothing but more rejection and malice. She shivered as she remembered the look of the stone wall and the towers rising up above it.

There would be no Cait there, ready to stand sister. She would be taken from Emily . . . by Drustan. It had been decreed.

For a moment, her thoughts left her own dire straits and her worry centered on Cait. Would the women of the clan shun her as the Sinclairs had shunned Emily, or would they accept her as the Sinclairs had accepted Susannah? She hoped for her friend's sake it was the latter, but *she* wasn't going to the Balmoral holding.

She had been shunned enough.

In fact, she wasn't going anywhere other people told her she had to go. Never again. If she disappeared in the forest, Talorc could not send her home. Then Abigail would be safe. Yes, that was the way of it. As hard as life within her father's keep was, it would be easier for Abigail than braving the sickening prejudice she would face in the Highlands, and that was before the Highlanders discovered her deafness.

Emily stumbled on something, but managed to stay upright. She could not see what it was through the moisture glazing her eyes. She was not crying. She would not cry; it was merely that she was cold and her eyes stung because of it.

There were voices behind her. Cait and the soldiers. She had to get away from them. She started walking faster.

A hand landed on her shoulder. "Stop, Lady Sinclair."

It was the voice of the blond soldier. She didn't know his name and she didn't want to know it. She didn't want to know another thing about this land that was so inhospitable. Its beauty hid a terrible flaw.

She tried to keep going, but the soldier's hold tightened, pulling her to a halt. "You must come with me."

"No." She jerked out of his hold and started running.

He chased her and she ran faster, swiping at her eyes so

she could see. Her tunic caught on a branch and she tore it yanking free, then held her skirt as high as she could, running as fast as her legs would go. She had to get away.

She had no warning before the soldier grabbed her again.

She didn't think about what she did next, but acted on the instinct to protect herself. She bent and grabbed a piece of driftwood from the ground, then swung it in an upward arc with all her might, hitting the soldier where her father had taught all his daughters it would do the most damage.

The soldier yowled like a scalded cat and grabbed between his legs, falling to his knees, his face contorted in agony.

Emily was too distraught to feel remorse and she started running again, this time intent on making it to the forest before another soldier tried to stop her. If Ulf came after her, he would probably hurt her, no matter what Lachlan had said about Balmoral soldiers not harming women.

Ulf hated her . . . just as all the Highlanders hated her. Except Cait. She hoped Cait would find happiness with Drustan.

"Emily, stop!"

That was Lachlan's voice, but she couldn't obey. If she did, he would take her to his castle made of stone and her heart would be ground to powder by more hatred from his clan.

"Emily!"

She pushed herself to run faster, but she was still several feet from the edge of the forest when a heavy body landed against her, knocking her to the ground. She fought, but she could not dislodge his weight. She kept trying, but no matter how hard she tried to get her legs under her, she failed. Finally, spent from her efforts, she lay still.

Lachlan rolled off of her and turned her onto her back before standing up.

"Why did you run away?" he demanded, his voice tight

with fury, his expression set in stone harder than his castle walls.

Did he hate her, too? "Please let me go."

"Where, you daft woman? You have nowhere *to* go. Surely you must see that."

The smell of the sea surrounded them, reminding her that she could not go back. "The forest. I want to go to the forest."

"Have you really gone daft then? There is nothing for you there but wild animals."

"At least they won't hate me. Please, Lachlan. I can't go to the castle . . . I don't want to meet your people."

"You have no choice."

She scrambled to her knees and scooted away from him.

"If you run again, I will lock you in the tower. Your door will only be opened to serve your meals."

Emily jumped to her feet and ran. He caught her before she'd taken four steps. She hadn't expected any less.

He turned her to face him, his expression good and mean. "I meant what I said, lass."

"Yes." Tears were streaming down her face now and she could not stem their flow. "Lock me in the tower and I won't have to see anyone. I will not have to face their hatred."

It was a much better plan than her confused notion of hiding in the forest.

"Hatred? Whose hatred?"

"Your clan's. The women will be just like the Sinclair women . . . or worse. They'll believe I soil the air they breathe just because I'm English and the soldiers will all glare at me all the time. If I do something wrong . . . they'll hurt me. I was just waiting for it before and now I know it will happen. Ulf already wants to hurt me," she reminded Lachlan of that irrefutable fact before bursting into more sobs.

He pulled her roughly against him, his hand patting awkwardly on her back. "I won't let him."

"You will. You hate me, too. You have to. I'm your enemy." Even as she said the words, she pressed into the solid safety of his body.

Somehow, this all had to be a nightmare and therefore she was not acting forward. Nothing had to be proper or make sense in dreams.

Lachlan could not stand Emily's bereft tone and having her soft curves so close to him was driving him as daft as she sounded. But he did not believe she was crazy. Just hurt, very, very hurt. It was true that the Highlander's dislike of the English was deeply ingrained, but the Sinclairs had obviously taken it to levels far beyond anything he had seen before.

"The Sinclair soldiers hurt you?"

"Not yet, but it was bound to happen. Don't you see?"

"And Talorc?"

"He hates me most of all. He called me his enemy and no one cared, but they all think I'm wicked because I said I would rather be married to a goat than to him."

"Was this before or after the marriage?" he asked, feeling his first twinge of sympathy for the Sinclair laird.

To have his bride chosen for him would have been insult enough, but to have her say in front of witnesses that she would rather be married to a goat would have been galling indeed.

"Before." She hiccupped on a small sob and burrowed closer to his rapidly growing arousal, but she did not know it.

She was too innocent to realize it. He was sure. And the knowledge tormented him.

"I do not like your tears."

"I'm sorry."

"Stop crying."

"I'm t-trying . . ."

He could tell she was. She sucked in one small, shuddering breath after another.

He could hear his brother making disparaging comments and Cait was upset that he was holding Emily so close. He frowned. His life as a laird made for very little privacy, but right now he wanted the prying eyes and ears of his fellow werewolves off of the vulnerable woman in his arms.

He swung her up against his chest and something strange twinged inside him when she wrapped her arms around his neck and buried her face in the curve of his throat. Lust. 'Twas all it was. He wanted her and he could not have her. It was nothing more than that. If he could bed her a few times to rid himself of the affliction, it would leave him.

He carried her into the forest, far away from the watchful eyes and superior hearing of his soldiers. It was not a smart thing to do. He was taking time they should be spending returning home and getting the women to certain safety.

Yet he could not make himself turn around and return to his soldiers until he had calmed Emily's fears.

He stopped only when he could no longer hear the others. He forced himself to let the woman go, lowering her to her feet carefully.

She looked up at him, her eyes still drowning. "Have you decided to leave me in the forest then?"

"Tell me why you ran away," he said instead of answering her ridiculous question.

"I told you. I can't stand any more hatred." She sighed, making an obvious bid to get control of her emotions. "I looked up at your castle and suddenly all I could think of were all the people who lived there . . . every one of them prepared to dislike me because I am English. On top of that, I am the Sinclair laird's wife and they will hate me for that too because he is your enemy."

"You believe this because . . . ?"

"It's true. I wish it weren't, but I've come to accept it. The Highlanders hate the English."

"You said that you told the Sinclair laird you would rather marry a goat. Do you not think that has as much to do with his clan's hostility to you as your being English?"

"Cait said that, but no one smiled at me upon my arrival either." She took a deep breath and let it out.

"We do not smile at strangers. Is that an English custom?"

She thought about it for several seconds while she blinked the last tears from her eyes. "Perhaps not, but I was supposed to marry their laird."

"By the king's edict."

"Well, yes."

"That would sting the pride of the clan. Their laird is their chief, they are loyal to him over their king."

"But you are supposed to be loyal to your king above all."

"In England this is true and mayhap in the Lowlands, but not here, lass."

"But that is wrong. It is a sin to put a clan chief above the king of your country."

"By whose edict?"

"The Church . . . I am sure the Church has taken such a stand."

"Are you?"

"Doesn't that matter to you?"

"No."

She stared at him as if she could not imagine such a thing. "Are you not worried about being sanctioned by the Church?"

"Nay."

It was almost worth saying it just to watch her reaction. She looked thoroughly scandalized. "But that is terrible."

"Do you think so?"

"So, Cait was right . . . Drustan will not be marrying her with the blessing of the Church."

"I did not say that."

"But no priest would come to your holding if you have such disrespectful views."

"Our priest does not find our views distressing."

"He doesn't?"

"No."

"*Your* priest? Does he live amidst your clan then?"

"Yes."

"Do you hate me, too?" she asked in a small voice.

"Why would you ask such a thing?"

"You acted like you hated me."

"When?"

"When you lifted me from the boat."

"You inconvenienced me. I was angry."

"I am sorry."

"You were obviously feeling overly emotional."

"Yes." She took another deep breath and waited.

He waited for what she planned to say next.

Finally, she let the breath out in a disgruntled sigh. "Well . . . *do* you hate me?"

"No."

"I don't hate you either."

Chapter 6

He didn't understand why, but he liked hearing those words. Nevertheless, he said, "It does not matter."

"No, I don't suppose it does. Just as it does not matter to you that I think you are wrong to have kidnapped Cait and me."

"You are better off with my clan than the Sinclairs."

She bit her bottom lip, her eyes questioning him. "I don't see how."

"No one here will hate you, Emily."

"Ulf already does."

"Ulf is offended by your plain-speaking and your insults."

"He's surly."

Lachlan laughed. "'Tis good of you to notice."

"I wasn't complimenting him."

"He would take it as such."

"You Highlanders are a strange lot."

"You have no idea."

She looked at him with such an air of innocence, he

could barely refrain from touching her. "Your husband has not bedded you yet, has he?"

She gasped, her pale skin going rose red. "You should not ask such a question!"

"But I am right."

Her blush deepened and she looked away.

"Tell me the truth, English."

"It should not matter to you."

"Tell me."

She hugged herself, as if grabbing for courage. "No, he hasn't." She glared at him. "Are you happy now?"

He had guessed she was untouched, but to hear her say so affected his libido with cruel intensity. "He has never even kissed you, has he?" he asked, embarrassing her further and tormenting himself, but he had to know.

"Lachlan, please . . . don't ask such personal questions."

"I want to know."

"I don't want to tell you."

"I could kiss you and find out."

"It would be wrong to kiss another man's wife."

He didn't answer, waiting to see if she would give in and tell him the truth. She watched him as if waiting for him to withdraw the question. It was not going to happen.

He moved toward her.

She took three hasty steps backward. "No. He's never kissed me. Are you satisfied? He hates me. I told you, but the truth is . . . I don't want his touch."

That final whispered admission almost sent him to his knees because she did not mind *his* touch. His body still throbbed in reaction to her burrowing into him for comfort, even though she had seen him as the enemy.

Her violet eyes searched his during several seconds of silence he was content not to break. "If your people hate me, will you let me go?"

"They will not hate you." He would make sure of it. He

knew the Sinclairs had more reason than most to despise the English, but to take their anger out on a tenderhearted woman like Emily was wrong.

"Will the women be kind to Cait as the Sinclair women are to Susannah, or will they shun her for being their enemy?"

"Drustan would challenge any man whose wife or daughter shunned his mate."

She nodded, apparently satisfied by that. "That is good to know. He's a strong warrior. Few would challenge him."

"You've got the right of it."

"Lachlan?"

"I am standing right here, lass."

"Are you married?"

He shook his head, wondering why she asked the question.

"Oh. Why not?"

"I do not want to marry yet."

"Oh." She went silent, apparently deep in thought.

What she had to think about, he could not guess. "Why do you ask?"

"Not for any particular reason." She licked her lips, blushing a bright pink and looking like she'd lost her train of thought.

"But you were curious?"

"It was merely a general curiosity. I don't care *personally* if you are married," she emphasized. "I am a very curious sort of person. Sybil always says my curiosity will get me into trouble, but I cannot seem to help myself."

Women were odd. Particularly human females, but this one was stranger than most. And even harder to understand was the fact that he liked it. He liked her.

"If I weren't married, would you let one of your soldiers keep me like Drustan is keeping Cait?" she asked, her expression going from worried to embarrassed.

"Nay. I would let no other man keep you."

"Cait believes you mean to kill her brother because of me."

"It is a move worth considering."

Emily paled, all traces of her blush fading along with her natural color. "But I don't want you to kill him!"

She should, or was she too tenderhearted to realize that? "You do not want to be married to him."

"That is no reason to kill him."

"But you do not wish to be his wife." He wanted to hear her say it, though why he should he could not understand. Her desires in the matter made little difference. Still he prompted, "Do you?"

"No, may God forgive me."

"Then his death would be to your benefit."

"Are you truly that cold?" she asked in a shaken voice.

"I am practical."

"Killing a man is not practical. It is wrong."

He did not understand her view. "Your father is a warrior."

"Yes."

"He has killed."

"Yes, but only his enemies."

"Talorc is my enemy."

"Were you at war before your clanswoman married his clansman without permission?"

"No."

"Then he is not your enemy." She seemed relieved by her conclusion. "You have no reason to hate him . . . or to kill him for that matter. I'm sure everything can be worked out if the two of you met . . . to talk I mean."

He didn't bother to scoff at her belief, but it was laughable. He and Talorc would not talk if they met face-to-face. They would fight.

"Stop looking like that."

"Like what?"

"Like you plan to kill him."

"Perhaps I do."

"You can't. Talorc is Cait's brother. It would upset her. Don't you see that? According to you, she is soon to be one of your clanswomen whether she wants to or not. Doesn't that mean that her happiness is your responsibility? You are the clan's laird after all."

The woman's ideas were downright daft on occasion and why that should make her even more appealing, he could not begin to fathom. "Cait is already upset."

"It would upset her more."

He shrugged. "She would get over it."

"She would hate you . . . and Drustan. She would hate him even more. You can't go killing her brother."

The discussion was getting to him, but not in the way he was sure she wanted it to. The thought of killing Talorc and claiming Emily as his lover was too damn tempting for Lachlan's peace of mind.

"He is also your husband. He hurt you. He should die." It made perfect sense to him, but Emily looked appalled.

"You can't kill the man on my behalf!" she shouted. "He didn't hurt me, not more than my feelings anyway. And I've come to believe that feelings are not overly important to you Highlanders. Leastways, not to warriors."

He shrugged again. Feelings *weren't* important, but if he chose to be offended on behalf of hers, that was his right. He was laird and pack leader. He could do anything he wanted.

"You shouldn't want to. I mean nothing to you, but then I don't suppose it takes one of you Highlanders much in the way of incentive to start killing each other." She paced away from him, muttering things that even his hearing could make no sense of. Finally, she stopped and faced him from several feet away. "I am not Lady Sinclair."

He heard the words, but could not take them in. She

was not Lady Sinclair? That would mean she was not married to Talorc. "You are saying you lied to me?" he demanded.

"Only that one time. I wanted to save Cait and I thought you would believe that as his wife I was enough of a sacrifice to the clan."

"But you are *not* married to the Sinclair?"

"No." She was wringing her hands now. "We are supposed to marry, but he hates me. I don't know what I will do if he sends me back to England. I have to save my sister."

The words made no sense, but perhaps nothing would have at that moment. All he could think about was that it was not a smirch on his honor to kiss her. Right now.

He could not keep her, not a human . . . but he could kiss her and perhaps more. He smiled. "Emily . . . come here."

Her violet eyes flared warily. "I don't think that is a good idea."

The words were barely out of Emily's mouth before Lachlan crossed the distance between them and grabbed her by both arms. She gasped in shock, both at his touch and the fact that he'd traversed the distance so quickly. How had he done it?

Her eyes must be playing tricks on her. She had thought she was farther from him than she had been. That was all, but she hadn't seen him move either. Only a blur and that too was odd. She was sure she'd been watching. Only she must have looked away.

He looked at her like he planned to devour her.

Was he furious about her lie? Had he decided to kill her instead of Talorc? She thought about mentioning that that was sure to upset Cait as well, but that argument hadn't swayed Lachlan in regard to the other woman's brother.

"You do not belong to him, then?" Lachlan asked, his voice rumbling like a predator's growl.

She shook her head. "I am his betrothed."

"But not his wife?"

"No, not his wife."

Lachlan pulled her closer until not even a breath separated their bodies. He was so big and hot, his heat seared her right through her gown and shift. She'd never been held like this. It was indecent, but she could not force sound from her dry throat for a protest. She could barely breathe.

Her breasts pressed against his chest and every time she pulled in a shallow puff of air, they moved in a most disturbing way that made them tingle and ache mysteriously.

Lachlan's eyes were narrowed and fixed on her. He did not look beset by strange feelings from their closeness. "And you told me the truth before, that he has not touched you?"

"Yes." She could barely get the word out.

He said nothing more, but his head descended slowly toward hers, his gaze trapping hers the whole time.

He stopped his mouth hovering just above hers, so close she could feel his warm breath on her lips. A strange kind of fearful excitement shivered through her. Was he going to kiss her then?

She should not want him to. It was wicked, but she did.

Lachlan's lips closed over hers not a second after the thought formed. They were warm and firm, unlike anything she had ever known and she strained upward, needing to feel more.

He made a sound low in his throat, his mouth molding hers. It drew a response from her that was wholly instinctive and she moved her lips in unison with his. It was the most amazing experience she had ever known. Her insides popped and sizzled like a sap-covered log in the fire. She never wanted him to stop kissing her.

In this moment in time, nothing existed that could harm her. No parents who would dismiss their own children as expendable, no angry Sinclair warrior who would send her home only to force her parents to send Abigail in her stead, no Balmoral warriors waiting to carry her to their castle where she would be prisoner.

She was no captive in this moment, but a woman. She had never felt so free and did not think she would ever feel such sensations again. Right or wrong, she wanted to feel them for as long as she could.

His body was so hard against hers, so different from her own . . . big and powerful, emanating a scent that filled her senses. It was spicy and uniquely male. And it called to something deep inside she could not name, making her feel hollow and empty. Not in a bad way though, not like true hunger for food. No, this felt all too good, as if she had a peculiar hunger only this man could fill. Warmth and an ache connected in some mysterious way to that emptiness pulsed between her legs.

Her hips moved of their own volition, brushing his hard thighs and increasing the maelstrom of feelings storming through her. She didn't understand what was happening to her. It frightened her, but it entranced her as well. She needed to get closer to him. She didn't know how though. Their bodies were as close as two beings could get.

It was not enough.

Her lips parted, softening against his and she could taste him. His flavor was sweeter than honey, which was strange because the man was so far from sweet, but she had never known anything as delicious as Lachlan's kiss.

Craving more of that flavor, she touched his lips with the tip of her tongue. He growled like a hungry wolf, his entire body vibrating with the sound. It shivered through her, too, making her shake and her knees grow weak, but she did not want to stop the kiss.

Far from willing it to end, she wished to do wanton things . . . to touch him and to be touched by him. She wanted his hands on her face again, cupping her cheeks while he kissed her.

She wanted to feel his skin, imprint his scent and the feel of him on her mind to carry with her into eternity. Her fingers itched to trace the pattern of the tattoo that circled his bicep and then the one of the animal on his back. She wanted to run her fingers through his hair and the dark curls scattered over the sharply defined muscles of his chest and torso.

She allowed herself to press one hand, open palmed, against the front of his chest on the side not covered with his plaid.

Everywhere her skin touched skin, it tingled. It was the oddest sensation she had ever known and it fed the desire burning her insides. It felt as if she were meant to do this, as if she had been born to connect to this man alone.

That could not be true. He was not her intended. She could never be his bride. Tears leaked from behind her eyelids from inexplicable pain at the thought.

She should pull back. She had to stop this before she lost her heart and her honor. Propriety and sanity demanded it, but her heart cried that this was her one chance to taste true desire. Once she was married to Talorc, she could never experience anything like this again. She couldn't. Not with him. Talorc did not smell right . . . he would not taste right.

Most likely, he would not even kiss her.

He hated her.

How could she belong to a man who hated her?

But her brain insisted that this kiss was still wrong.

Finally, she forced herself to listen and tried to break away from Lachlan, but he responded by moving his grip to her waist and lifting her into more intimate contact with his big body. The apex of her thighs met a hard ridge and with a groan, he pressed her against it. Pleasure suffused her on a wave of such overwhelming delight, she cried out against his lips.

"What the hell are you doing?"

The raucous voice infiltrated Emily's thoughts just as Lachlan went stiff, his hold on her biting into her waist.

He lifted his mouth from hers. "Go away, Ulf."

"Balmoral warriors do not bed married women," Ulf said, spitting the words out with enough disgust to make Emily's face flame with shame.

She buried it against Lachlan's neck.

"She is not married."

"She said she was."

"She lied."

"And you have only her word for this?" Ulf demanded.

"Yes," Lachlan ground out as he lowered Emily until she was standing on her own two feet again.

He turned to face his brother, stepping away from her at the same time. Chilled by the loss of his touch, she rubbed her arms. He stood between her and Ulf, but she did not feel as if he stood with her—only in front of her. He was a barrier, but not an ally.

Shame that she wanted him to be suffused her. She was not married, but she was promised. *To a man who has flat-out refused to marry you*, her brain reminded her. Did that negate the betrothal? It couldn't when Abigail's future was at stake.

"Why should we believe you now, English? One way or another, you are a liar." Ulf sneered at her.

"I'm not lying."

He abruptly turned his attention to his brother. "What the hell were you doing kissing her, regardless? She is our enemy."

"She is not our enemy and you will not call her such again." Lachlan's tone was so harsh, she could barely make herself believe he had been the man kissing her so tenderly only moments before.

Ulf did not appear impressed by his brother's ire, however. "I bloody well will. Just because you're controlled by that beast inside you does not mean I will abandon reason for such base urges as lust. It's obvious to the other soldiers as well. They're back at the beach betting on whether or not you have tupped her yet."

Emily gasped at the crude terminology and the implication of Ulf's words. The others knew that Lachlan wanted her? They thought he was having her . . . right now? By the saints, didn't they realize she was a chaste and honorable maid?

She hadn't been acting like either a moment before though. She'd touched a man's bare chest . . . and wanted to do more.

Perhaps she was depraved.

"I am not governed by my beast, I am benefited by him," Lachlan said in a hard voice.

"So you say."

What was all this talk of beasts? Was Ulf trying to say that lust was a beast? She'd heard it described thus by the priest that served her father's barony, but Ulf did not seem a religious man who would eschew the pleasures of the flesh. Did he mean to imply that he did not have the same beast raging in himself, or simply that he felt no such thing for her?

She suspected the latter and did not feel in the least offended by it. Relieved more like.

Ulf's sneer was now directed entirely at his brother. "Then prove your superiority instead of making a mockery of it."

Lachlan sighed. "She is innocent."

Emily was confused. Of what had she been accused?

"You kissed her to determine if she had been touched or not?" Ulf asked, sounding marginally approving. "To test whether or not she told the truth?"

"Yes."

Emily stared at both men for several seconds before fully comprehending the import of their conversation. When she did, she wished the earth would open up and swallow her. She had responded with lascivious abandon to a test the odious laird had been making on the veracity of her words. While she had been lost to something beautiful and she had believed meaningful, he had merely been trying to discern if she told the truth or not.

It was humiliating . . . and it hurt.

Nevertheless, she was shocked he'd drawn that conclusion, considering how wantonly she had incited his ardor.

"He might refuse to touch an English wife," Ulf mused.

"Not even for the sake of his pride would a Chrechte warrior refuse to mate his wife. Honor demands he touch no other." Lachlan shook his head. "Nay. She is not his wife and we have only her word she is his betrothed, though I am inclined to believe that part of her story."

"You are certain of her innocence?"

"He has never even kissed her."

Ulf looked at Emily, his expression mocking. "She is that unskilled?"

"She is completely untouched."

"She *was*," Ulf said with a smirk, now obviously thinking his brother's actions bordered on the heroic.

Why shouldn't he? She had been thoroughly humiliated by her response to the kiss. And that had to be obvious by the blush burning her face and neck. No doubt Ulf was most pleased by such a circumstance, but she wanted to strangle Lachlan.

He had promised not to hurt her, but once again he had lied . . . for he had hurt her more than she wanted to admit, and not merely her pride. She felt wounded, but she would not give him or his horrible brother the satisfaction of knowing that.

And she was never going to believe another word Lachlan said. A man who could kiss like he meant it—but didn't—could not be trusted.

* * *

When they got back to the others, Emily forced herself to apologize to the warrior she had hit with the driftwood. Her words were met with a shrug and then the man turned his back on her.

Fine. She wasn't going to be hurt by his rejection. She was through being so tenderhearted around these barbarians. She took their feelings toward her entirely too seriously. Hadn't she lived almost her whole life with her father and stepmother thinking less of her than if she were a servant in their household?

The only person in the world who truly loved her like family was supposed to was her sister Abigail. And Emily was in the Highlands to spare her sister the same fate. She could face anything and anyone for such a cause.

She wasn't going to run again . . . unless she was sure of her destination and her chances of true escape were high. She was going to endure and do it with a smile on her face just to confuse them. She would show them she was no weakling, no matter how foolishly she had behaved thus far.

Cait rushed to her side and took both Emily's hands in hers. "Are you all right?"

Emily squeezed Cait's fingers. "I am fine. I do not know why I ran. It was foolish."

"Your emotions overcame you. I could see it happening, but could do nothing to help you. It was not surprising after the time in the boat. You were terrified; I could smell your fear. You masked it well, but I was right beside you," Cait said with obvious admiration. "I did not know huma . . . I mean the English had that skill."

Emily shook her head. "Sometimes you say the strangest things. Do you know that? Just because I am English does not mean I am a weakling."

Cait laughed. "I'd say, after the way you handled that soldier who came after you. It is obvious to everyone here you are no weakling."

"I did not handle Lachlan as efficiently."

"Naturally not. He is laird. He would not be so if he was not stronger than all the others," Cait replied consolingly.

Was that why his kisses had turned her inside out? If it were true, then perhaps Talorc's would be just as powerful, but somehow she could not believe that would be the case.

Chapter 7

She was not surprised when Lachlan ordered one of the other soldiers to take her up on his horse for the ride to the castle. After all, now that he had answers to his odious questions, he had no need to touch her. She refused to be bothered by that.

The warrior named Angus put his hand out to her and she smiled at him as she took it for a lift up. He looked confused by her smiling all right and stopped in the act of pulling her onto his horse with a stupefied expression on his face.

She simply waited, wondering how simpleminded were these soldiers that her poor plan was having such success so quickly.

"Angus!"

Lachlan's command snapped the soldier from his reverie and he swung Emily into his lap.

She sat primly forward, but turned to smile up at him once more. "Thank you kindly for allowing me to ride with you."

"He allows nothing. I have ordered it," Lachlan growled.

Emily ignored him, deciding then and there that her campaign to confuse the soldiers with her cheerful countenance would not stretch to their leader. She never wanted to speak to him again.

She faced forward without another word. The trip up the cliff was not as harrowing as the water crossing, but she did give thanks to God more than once that she had no fear of heights. The trail zigzagging up the side of the cliff was barely wide enough for the large war horses, its right side a rock face and the left a sheer drop back down.

Unless there was another path to reach the cliff-top castle, she could not imagine a force of any strength could ever surprise the Balmorals with their arrival, or even make it as far as the castle unless the Balmorals wanted them to.

Cait had been right. There was no way her brother would be able to rescue them once they were inside the castle walls.

When they reached the top of the cliff, they could see the drawbridge was down and so they rode right into the lower bailey before they stopped and dismounted. Men and women wearing the Balmoral plaid looked with open curiosity upon Emily and Cait. They didn't scowl like the Sinclairs had even though Emily knew her dress had to give away her Englishness.

One older woman with a kind face and eyes very like Angus's even came forward. "Who is that you have with you, son?"

"The Balmoral's captive. She's promised to the Sinclair."

"So, we've taken two in retaliation for Susannah, then?" The woman's face creased in a satisfied smile.

"Aye, we have."

Drustan laid a possessive hand on Cait's protruding belly. "Nay, we have taken *three*."

Cait's eyes filled with tears and Emily wanted to smack him.

But keeping with her intent to confuse them, she smiled instead. "I still say it is a poor man who takes his revenge through women and a child."

She'd said the words sweetly, so Drustan's scowl didn't come for two heartbeats after she'd spoken. When it did, it was fierce enough to fell the monster werewolves Emily's faraway housekeeper had told her and Abigail so many stories about.

Cait, however, no longer looked ready to cry and that was all Emily wanted. She was shaking her head, her eyes questioning Emily's sanity.

Angus laughed though.

"You find the insult to your brother amusing?" the older woman censured.

"Our laird has said she is English and will therefore have to learn our ways to understand them. I'm inclined to agree."

His mother shook her head. "An insult is an insult, Angus . . . even to an Englishwoman."

"Enough of this foolish talk." Lachlan's harsh voice came from directly behind Emily. "The priest waits for us up at the keep."

And that was when she learned there was to be a wedding between Cait and Drustan. Immediately.

"But the marriage sacrament is to be spoken in the morning," Emily said, scandalized as she followed the soldiers to the keep. She was still intent on ignoring Lachlan, so she was haranguing Drustan instead. "And Cait cannot go to her wedding without the opportunity to prepare her person. This is too barbaric even for you Balmorals."

"You would prefer I took your friend to my bed tonight without making her my wife?" he asked in a lazy drawl that made her want to scream.

"I would prefer you waited until she has had sufficient time to prepare."

"And how long would that be, English?"

"It takes time to organize a wedding . . . days, weeks even."

"On the contrary, the wedding is already set." Lachlan's voice came from her left, but she refused to look at him.

"Drustan . . . please, you must reconsider."

"My laird has ordered the wedding take place now. It shall be done."

They had reached the keep and the small group swept into the great hall where a priest did indeed wait near the fireplace. He wore the proper vestments and his expression was kind, but the image of him sent Emily's heart pounding.

Cait did not look similarly affected. Her expression was stoic, but that was a far cry from serene and Emily wished there was something she could do to save her friend.

She was even willing to renege on her promise to herself never to speak to Lachlan again, if it would help. Spinning to face him, she grabbed his arm in urgent appeal. "Please, don't do this. Not tonight. Give her time to . . . to . . ."

"To what, English? Waiting will not change her fate."

"But she never even met Drustan before today."

"How many times had you met Talorc before your father sent you here?"

"That is not the same thing. This is not by order of the king. And Talorc did not force the marriage upon my arrival."

"He would if he had wanted to bed you."

Emily reeled back from the brutal crudity of the words, but she could not allow herself to become overset. She had to keep fighting for Cait's welfare. "Nevertheless—"

"Enough," he said, cutting her off. "If you do not cease this tirade, I will have you taken to the tower before the wedding takes place."

Emily's mouth snapped closed on another argument. She was Cait's only friend present. She had to stay. With that thought in mind, she went to stand by Cait's side.

Cait did not look at her, but she squeezed Emily's hand

as if to tell her she was glad she was there. Then she clasped her own hands in front of her, her mouth set in a firm line. Drustan took his place on the other side of Cait and Lachlan moved to stand beside him. Angus and the older woman who had spoken outside stood nearby. Everyone in the hall grew silent.

The priest began the marriage sacrament with the right words, but Emily could not help feeling it was sacrilegious to speak them in the evening rather than the morning. Was the marriage valid if the procedure dictated by Rome was not followed to the letter?

She prayed for the sake of her friend's soul that it was.

Drustan spoke his vows in a firm voice, but when it came time to speak her vows, Cait remained mute. The priest repeated his question, but Cait acted as if she had not heard.

Emily did not blame her. In fact, it was a clever plan. According to the laws of the Church, a marriage could be annulled if both parties did not enter into it willingly.

Frowning, Drustan took Cait by the shoulders and turned her to face him. "You will be mine regardless of what you do here."

Face averted, Cait shrugged, but Emily could see the tension in her friend's body.

The priest looked to Lachlan for instruction.

Lachlan looked at Drustan. Drustan crossed his arms, his intent clear. He would not budge on his stand.

Emily was proud of Cait's strength of purpose, but it worried her. Better to be wedded before being bedded, or so Sybil had always said. Emily didn't make it a habit to agree with her stepmother, but in this case . . . she did. And after the kiss she'd witnessed on the boat between Cait and Drustan, she had no doubt just where Cait was going to end up sleeping this night.

Lachlan crossed his arms over his broad chest, his expression bored. "The priest will speak the blessing over you on my say so."

The holy man winced, but nodded.

Cait did nothing . . . said nothing.

"I prefer her to speak her vows. I am content to keep her without the benefit of marriage until she does so."

"No," Emily gasped, but no one paid her any heed.

Lachlan considered Cait for several long minutes of silence. "Very well, until you speak your vows to my soldier and bind yourself to him willingly and forever, the English woman will warm my bed."

Blackness washed over Emily and it was all she could do to remain standing. "You lied again," she whispered.

But he heard her. So did everyone else from the reaction she received, but she didn't care. The soldiers could glare all they liked and the priest might as well stop looking like she'd spoken a blasphemy. Lachlan of the Balmoral was no god to be blasphemed, no matter what the arrogant man might think.

"My patience with your insults grows thin."

"And I have no patience at all with your lies," she said, her voice stronger now, though her knees still felt wobbly.

"Tell me when I lied."

"You said you would not allow anyone to keep me."

He had the audacity to shake his head at her.

She scowled and nodded right back. "Yes, you did."

"I said I would not let any of my soldiers keep you."

"But—"

"I made no promise not to keep you myself."

"You can't," Cait said, her voice laced with shock. "If you do, Talorc will consider her mated to you and he will refuse to marry her."

"He has already refused."

"But he will come around."

Lachlan didn't even bother to shrug, but the dismissal of that paltry consideration was written into his very stance. He did not care about her future . . . only about getting his own way. He wanted his vengeance and he would not be denied.

"Emily, I . . ." Cait looked like she was ready to cry again.

Emily soothed her as best she could. "Do not worry about me. I will be all right," she lied with what was left of her courage.

But Cait shook her head. "No. You will be ruined . . . you'll be mated to him. They don't see it that way here . . . Susannah told us, but the Sinclairs will. I'm sure your English father will."

"You mean if Drustan takes you to his bed, he will not see himself committed to you?" Emily asked.

"Of course he is committed to her. What do you think the priest is for?" Lachlan asked with obvious exasperation.

Emily turned on him with fury. "He said he would take her to his bed regardless."

"He wants her promise."

"And you . . . all you want is your own way."

His dark brow rose.

Emily opened her mouth, but did not know what to say. She did not want to be the lever used to force Cait into marriage, but she was also worried for her friend's virtue. Regardless, she would not lend her voice to the others in putting pressure on her friend.

She snapped her mouth shut and turned away.

"I will speak my vows."

"Not on my account," Emily said fiercely, grabbing her friend's arm.

Cait shook her head. "It is an empty gesture to refuse." She sighed, her shoulders slumped. "As I said, my clan sees the physical act of joining as a lifelong commitment. My brother will consider me mated regardless of what words I speak here."

"But you do not want to promise your loyalty to Drustan, do you?"

She finally understood why Cait wanted to avoid saying her vows regardless of Drustan's threat.

"No, but even if I do not say the words . . . I will belong to the Balmoral clan come sunrise. According to the laws of my people, I will belong to Drustan."

It wasn't right, but it was the way of the world. It only shocked Emily that Cait claimed the Balmoral clan did not see it as such. Well, without the wedding . . . an Englishman could walk away from a woman he had compromised as well. Was Cait saying that a Sinclair could not?

It was all very confusing, but one thing was clear. Cait was not happy about speaking her vows.

Drustan did not look too happy either. In fact, he looked downright mean. He grasped Cait's shoulders and turned her to face him again. "Becoming my wife is not a punishment."

"I know," Cait whispered, shocking Emily and making Lachlan grunt with approval.

Drustan's green gaze softened. "I will care for you and watch over you and your bairn."

At mention of the babe, Cait shook her head.

Drustan sighed and pulled her closer. "Yes. You will learn to trust me, lass."

Then, before Cait could argue again, he kissed her. This time Emily did not watch. She turned her head away, but could not help noticing the tiny sounds of pleasure her friend made.

After what seemed like a very long time, Drustan spoke, "Repeat the vows for my mate, Father."

The priest repeated them and Cait spoke her responses in a dreamy voice that gave Emily her first true smile in a long while. Cait did not like having her decision made for her, but she was not averse to marrying Drustan. Not really. And truly, it was no worse than when Talorc had informed Cait on the day of her first wedding that she was to be given to one of his soldiers. That had been no great love match from what Emily could tell.

A woman's lot was not an easy one, but Cait could do

worse than to marry a strong man who had not resorted to violence to get his way.

They celebrated the wedding with a toast before Lachlan instructed his brother to escort Emily to the east tower.

"Can she not stay with us?" Cait begged Drustan, then turned to Lachlan. "You cannot truly mean to lock her in a tower?"

"Do not question your laird," Drustan said before Lachlan got a chance to answer.

"He's not my laird."

"As of fifteen minutes ago, he is."

"But—"

"There is only one bed in our quarters."

"Emily can sleep in it with me."

"I will be in it with you and we will not be sleeping," Drustan said in a voice that made Emily embarrassed to hear it.

Cait looked at Emily with an apology in her eyes.

"It is all right. Truly. I am happy to go to the tower. You must not worry about me."

The older woman who had approached them in the bailey came forward and put her hand on Cait's arm, nodding to her son. "I am Moira, mother to Drustan, Angus and Susannah. Welcome to our family, child." Moira looked at Emily then. "You are English."

"Yes."

"You are betrothed to the Sinclair."

"Yes."

"How can this be?"

"By order of both our kings."

"Ah." Moira nodded again. "That explains the mystery. Why is our laird bent on locking you in a tower? Have you been difficult?"

"Perhaps, a bit."

Ulf grunted and grabbed her arm. "Come."

Emily turned to her friend and hugged her tight with her free arm. "All will be well, Cait. Truly it will."

"Yes." Then, seeming to know what had Emily most worried, she said, "He will not hurt me. He promised."

Emily swallowed down her emotion and nodded as she stepped back. Then she looked at Drustan. "Be kind to her. If she is to be your wife, you must realize you are duty-bound to protect her from harm."

Instead of getting angry, Drustan nodded solemnly. "I would ever do my duty."

Emily turned to Ulf. "Please release my arm. You are hurting me. I will follow you without argument."

He ignored her and started dragging her toward the main entry to the great hall. Suddenly, he stopped and his grip fell away from her arm.

Lachlan was there, his face inches from Ulf 's. "I gave you an order, it did not include touching her. Do not do so again."

Ulf said something vicious, but he did not take her arm again. He led her across the great hall to the entrance to a stairway in the eastern corner. They started up a set of spiral stairs in total silence. She kept several paces behind him, afraid of what his temper might make him do. The steps felt like they went on and on.

She and Ulf passed three landings on their way upward, but did not stop on any of them. When he finally did stop, it was on a small landing that had only one door. He pushed it open and she stepped inside, careful not to touch him as she squeezed into the room.

The door shut behind her with a bang and the unmistakable sound of the bar sliding in place let her know she'd been locked in good and tight.

Shivering, she hugged herself and looked around her new accommodations. The circular area was small and sparse. It had a bed covered with the Balmoral plaid, but no rugs over the window to keep out light or wind, no tapestries on the cold stone walls to relieve their monotony, no fireplace for additional warmth, and not even a chair to sit on. There was a small table with a wooden pitcher, a bowl, a cup and a cloth. She looked around for a chamber pot, but saw a garderobe with no door on it instead.

The tower room looked exactly like what it was, a place designed to keep prisoners.

But it was clean and it could have been worse.

She could have been warming Lachlan's bed.

Cait stood in the middle of her new home, her insides shaking. She was married. Again. She did not want to be.

No, that was a lie.

Part of her very much wanted to be a lifelong mate to the werewolf leaning against the door, his big body pulsing with energy denied by his negligent stance. Already, she could not imagine her life without him. And that terrified her more than the fact that she had been kidnapped and forced into a marriage born of the Balmoral laird's need to redress an insult.

She should not feel so much. Indeed, she should not feel *anything* after such a short acquaintance.

She had not felt this way about Sean, not before or after marriage. She had wed him because her brother had commanded it, but she had never fallen in love with him. She very much feared she was halfway there already with Drustan. He'd been so careful with her, even when she'd tried to escape. And when he kissed her, she experienced cravings she had never known existed, even when she had gone into heat and mated with Sean during a full moon.

"You look worried." His voice sent shivers over her flesh though the air was not cold.

She took a deep breath and almost choked letting it out when he stepped away from the door . . . toward her. She quickly moved in the opposite direction. "I'm simply making myself acquainted with my new home."

Drustan's quarters were directly above the soldiers' quarters on the opposite side of the keep from where Emily had been taken. No matter how hard she tried, Cait could hear nothing of her friend. In fact, with the heavy door shut, she could hear nothing at all through it or the thick stone walls. It afforded a level of privacy unknown among the Sinclair pack members. She liked it.

The room they were in was not a bedroom, having a table and chairs in one corner near a fireplace, which was an extravagance she never would have expected in a room besides the main hall. Two benches lined the opposite wall near a large chest. There was an open door close to one of the benches which she surmised led to a bedroom because she distinctly remembered him saying he had a bed.

She scooted around the table as her new husband stalked her. "Your mother seems very nice. She welcomed me into the family."

"As she should." Drustan's eyes glowed with unmistakable hunger. Only he looked as if food were the last thing on his mind.

Her heart pounded so loudly, she was sure he could hear it. He took a step closer, coming around the table.

She backed up, toward the wall. "Where do you sleep?" she asked in a bid to distract him.

"*We* sleep in there." He nodded toward the doorway she had noticed earlier, confirming her guess it was the bedroom.

"I was thinking we could wait."

"To sleep?" His teeth flashed white. "Yes, that will come later."

Oh, heavens above, how could he put such strong sensual promise into a few short words?

"I meant before we mate . . . I would like to know you better."

He came closer, his scent growing stronger, letting her know that he was aroused. Her body reacted to it even as her mind scrabbled for logical reasons why he should not claim her.

Reaching out, he brushed his fingertips down the side of her face, making her shiver. "You have very soft skin."

"Thank you," she said primly.

He smiled as if her words amused him. "How well did you know your first husband before you mated?"

"He was a member of my clan. I had known him since childhood."

"Did you? Or did you know his face, his name . . . rumors of what kind of soldier he was?"

"I don't understand." But she did. He was implying she had not known her first husband the day they had wed any better than she knew Drustan. And he was right.

"Don't you?"

Silence was her best defense and she made use of it.

He touched her again, this time brushing his thumb across her lips. "Did your first husband court you?"

She almost laughed at that, but Drustan's touch drowned her humor in rapidly growing desire. Sean had never even run with her during a hunt before her brother decreed the two of them should wed.

Scurrying backward, she bumped her shoulder on the wall, changed course and increased the distance between them. "No. He did not court me."

"Did he wait to claim you as his until after the wedding?" Drustan sounded only mildly curious as he stalked closer, making her feel like prey for the first time in her life.

As a femwolf, she had hunted, but had never been the prize to be caught. Even when she'd gone into heat the first time, she'd already been mated and there had been no "hunting" involved.

She shook her head at Drustan, unable to talk because, try as she might, she couldn't seem to get the table between them again. She was panting in a combination of atavistic fear and excitement.

He got closer with each passing second, maneuvering her with the skill of a master predator until she was up against the wall beside the open doorway to the bedroom. Another step and she would be in the room. He did not stop until his body brushed against hers. Then, he caged her in with one hand against the wall on either side of her.

His head lowered until their lips almost touched. "I make you this promise, Cait. You will know me very well come morning."

Then his mouth covered hers in a kiss that burned her remaining resistance to cinders. She was clinging to his shoulders with both hands when he lifted his mouth from hers.

Drustan's wolf looked at her through his eyes, turning them dark green like emeralds. "You belong to me, Caitriona. You are my mate."

"Not yet," she said, shocking herself as her own wolf came out to defy him in a mating rite as old as her people.

Nevertheless, she had experienced no desire to indulge in this sort of behavior with Sean. They had mated like humans. It had been pleasant, but she had never craved physical joining with him as she did now with Drustan. She wanted to have his body connected intimately with hers, but she could not simply submit and let it happen. She needed him to prove himself a strong and worthy mate in the most primitive way. That need frightened her, but it excited her even more.

The scent of her arousal mingled with his now, letting him know what she felt without a word being spoken or even a slight movement on her part.

He growled, the sound blatant affirmation of her body's response to his. "I want you," he said gutturally. "I will have you."

"Do you?" She licked her lips, sliding her hands away from his shoulders. "Will you?"

His eyes narrowed. "You want me, too."

Her head cocked to one side. "Perhaps." But first he had to prove he was powerful enough to mate her wolf.

He rubbed against her, marking her with his scent, but with their clothes on, it was not a full claiming. She smiled, dropping down and ducking under his arm before moving quickly out of his reach again.

She stopped by the door, ready to flee, to force him to chase her as a wolf chases its mate. "But then perhaps not."

Chapter 8

Drustan had spun to face her and his expression was grim. "I cannot let you run, Cait."

Her entire body tensed with the need to do just that. "You must."

"No," he gritted, as if the single word was hard to get out. He wanted the chase, too. She could see it in his face. He took a visible rein on his desires. "I promised not to hurt you or the babe. I cannot let you do so either."

She didn't want to hurt her baby, but she had to run.

With two deft movements, he removed his plaid. Suddenly the air crackled like it did during a lightning storm and before she could take a breath, he had taken wolf form. He bounded to the door, leaping past her and landing against it. He circled to face her and growled, baring his teeth.

She'd been around werewolves and femwolves her whole life, but she'd never known fear in the presence of one. She knew it now . . . a primal fear that had nothing to do with concern he would harm her. It was a sexual fear of being dominated and yet it was mixed with the need for just that.

She could not change during pregnancy, but she felt no disadvantage facing him as a woman rather than a femwolf.

She took a step toward the door. "You won't hurt me."

But he didn't have to. He blocked the door as effectively as a stone wall. He was huge as a wolf, almost as tall on all fours as she was standing up.

"How long will you keep your wolf form?" She smiled provokingly. "You cannot claim me that way." And then she would win. The taunt hung, unspoken, in the air between them.

He began to stalk her again, a fierce growl rumbling in his chest, his ears pinned back, his tail straight up, his huge animal body shouting intimidation in every sinuous movement. And in spite of herself she backed up and kept backing away from the threat that her brain told her was not a threat. Her instincts demanded she avoid contact with the wolf that looked at her with eyes shining with a man's intelligence . . . and determination.

He wouldn't attempt to claim her as a wolf, not when she couldn't make the change. Her mind told her that, but his feral behavior mocked her certainty. So, she kept moving, no longer caring whether or not she reached the door, only that she kept distance between them. She didn't realize where he had herded her until she stepped backward into a dark room.

The bedroom.

The air shimmered again and then he was there, a warrior towering over her, his body no less intimidating than it had been in wolf form . . . perhaps more so because she knew that as a man, he really would claim her in the ancient mating rite. His fully aroused nudity was silhouetted in the doorway to the other room, which was still lit by candlelight.

Her gaze skimmed his body—she could not help herself. And she sucked in air when she saw the size of his male organ. He was bigger than Sean. Much bigger. Dark, angry veins pulsed on Drustan's erect flesh, reminding her that he came to her as a werewolf, not merely a man.

A responding rush of wetness between her legs told her what her femwolf thought of his readiness to mate with her.

He grinned, his eyes lit with arrogant certainty. He knew her wolf wanted him. "Undress yourself, Cait. Claim me as I plan to claim you."

She stared at him, inexplicable emotion curling inside her heart. The claiming was supposed to be mutual, but often it was not. Werewolves and men alike often saw their wives as possessions rather than true mates. Drustan's words said he thought differently, that he recognized her worth and strength. Of their own volition, her hands began to peel her clothing away until she stood before him as naked and proud as he was.

Her stomach protruded, but she was not embarrassed by it. Femwolves did not become pregnant easily and to be with child was evidence of the deepest level of her femininity, not something to be ashamed of. The changes in her body made her more beautiful. Any wolf would say so.

Drustan's gaze, so intent on her, reflected agreement with those thoughts. "I have never touched a woman with child," he said hoarsely.

She reached for his hand and laid his palm against her belly. The heat of this simple touch seared her and a shudder went through his big body, showing he was as affected as she was. Tears she did not understand welled in her eyes. Everything was different with him. Everything.

He swung her up in his arms and carried her to the bed, then laid her out on it, his touch possessive. "I cannot let you run from me, but I will prove my strength to be your mate."

She stared up at him, her whole body shaking with the

need to feel his in intimate contact. "How?" she asked in a bare whisper.

"You will beg me to take you and in this way I will prove the rightness of our mating."

He thought to make her plead? A femwolf never begged. Not ever. "You cannot do it."

She wasn't taunting him, but was truly concerned. He'd set himself an impossible task and she didn't want their mating to be impossible.

"You doubt my strength?"

"I am a femwolf," she reminded him, knowing better than to make a direct challenge.

"And I will make you beg. Believe it." He inhaled deeply and smiled like a Viking conqueror. "The scent of your arousal is like an aphrodisiac to my blood. You will beg, you will plead . . . you will ache for my possession before I claim you."

Sean had never made her ache.

She realized she'd said the words aloud when Drustan chuckled. "He was not a Balmoral."

"He was wolf enough to make me pregnant," she snapped back, unwilling to accept the implied slight on the clan of her birth.

Drustan did not look even mildly offended, but smiled again . . . a predator's smile that made her shiver. "I will make you wish the baby were mine."

Then he touched her, his fingertips gliding along her skin, the caress so soft, it made her fine hairs stand on end and goose bumps form on her skin. He used his mouth, his hands and his body to mark every bit of her exposed flesh with his scent and in the process, he brought her excitement to a fever pitch.

She arched off the bed, her body in an agony of pleasure. "Drustan!"

He laughed low, the sound another impossible caress. "Do you want me, little one?"

"Yes!"

"Enough to beg?" he demanded.

Her mouth clamped shut on the words she wanted to utter and then opened again immediately in a gasp of delight as his fingers trespassed her most private flesh.

"You are wet and luscious."

She made a garbled sound, unable to talk.

He pressed his fingers deep inside her, but was careful not to touch the small nub of her utmost pleasure. He played with her, sliding his big fingers in and out and all around her swollen folds.

Then he put his fingers to his mouth and sucked. "Delicious."

She moaned.

He pushed her thighs wide and then lifted her hips with his werewolf strength before lowering his mouth to the exposed heart of her desire. He kissed her with closed lips all over her sensitized flesh. Then he kissed her with his tongue in shocking intimacy. Sean had never done this and she could not believe it was permissible, but it felt too wonderful to question.

Besides, if she opened her mouth to speak, she feared broken words of pleading would be all that came out.

He tasted her for long minutes, drawing away when her body trembled on the brink of spending. He did it over and over again until she was writhing below him, trying to get that final touch that would send her over. But he held her where he wanted her and continued to pleasure her until she was mindless with need. He pulled his mouth away and sat up between her spread thighs. She cried out in protest, only to moan again when his fingers delved deep within her once more.

He pulled them out and her wolf 's vision could see her glistening wetness on them, even in the shadowed darkness.

His expression was somber as he marked first his penis and then his chest right over his heart with her intimate scent. She broke, unable to hold back her words of need any longer, and cried out with guttural pleas for him to take her.

He did with one hard thrust, joining their bodies in complete oneness. He was big and she was swollen with excitement. She felt stretched to the point of pain-edged pleasure. He pressed against her from head to feet, careful to curve himself over her protruding middle, affecting the final marking of their scents on one another's bodies.

"You are mine," he said in age-old tradition.

"I am yours," she replied, her voice filled with emotion she did not want to name.

He withdrew until only the tip of his large member rested within in her and then waited in silence, his body rigid with the tension of controlling the urge to drive for both their fulfillment.

"You are mine," she said in an ancient dialect the Celts of their clan would not understand.

"I am yours," he responded in kind and then thrust to the hilt.

She cried out, her body bowing with the intense pleasure of the mutual claiming. He set a rhythm that brought gut-wrenching pleasure with every stroke until her entire being clenched in need, on the edge of a precipice higher than any she had ever known. He ground his hips into her, rubbing her sweetest spot once, twice and then she exploded, stars bursting behind her closed eyelids and inside of her until all she knew was blackness.

When she came to, he had her cradled against his body and no candlelight glowed from the other room.

She touched his chest, right where he had marked himself with her sexual scent. "We are one now."

"Yes." The word sounded more like a growl, but she understood him.

And he had been right earlier . . . in that moment, she wished more than anything that the babe inside her were his. Because the fact that it was not was the one thing that might have the power to tear them apart.

There was no warning knock before Emily heard the bar sliding against the outside of her door as it was lifted from its place. Ulf was probably the soldier accompanying the housekeeper this morning. He was rude enough not to bother with such a common courtesy.

The night before, Angus had been with the housekeeper and not only had he knocked, but he had waited patiently while she and the housekeeper visited. The servant hadn't been in the least surly toward Emily, which had lifted her spirits considerably. She'd been so busy talking, in fact, that she'd eaten very little and was subsequently starving now.

She'd been up since sunrise after getting very little sleep the night before worrying about Cait. She'd done everything she could do to occupy herself, including making her bed and using the water in the pitcher and the small towel to clean her room. She'd even given her hair one hundred strokes with the brush the housekeeper Marta had provided.

So, even if it was Ulf on the other side of that door, she welcomed the intrusion.

But when the heavy wooden door swung open, it wasn't Ulf's scowling countenance she saw, but Lachlan's. He wasn't scowling though . . . not precisely, but he wasn't smiling either.

She wasn't about to smile at him either, not after his threats the evening before. She ignored him completely, greeting the housekeeper. "Thank you kindly for the food, Marta. I wondered . . ."

She paused and gave Lachlan a sidelong glance, unsure whether her request would better be saved for a time when he wasn't with the servant. After all, if the intent of locking her in the tower was to punish, then giving her something to keep the boredom and worry at bay would be the last thing he would allow.

"Yes, milady?" Marta prompted when Emily didn't speak again.

What if Marta left and did not return again until the midday meal? Emily could not bear the thought of hours more spent doing nothing but thinking about what terrible fate might have befallen her friend. She bit her bottom lip and then smiled tentatively. "I had hoped you might have some chore for me to do to help me pass the time."

Marta looked uneasily at Lachlan and he gave a slight shake to his head.

"I am sorry, milady, but I do not." Her eyes expressed pity for Emily's plight though.

Filled with disappointment, Emily acknowledged the woman's words with a nod. "Thank you all the same."

Lachlan dismissed the servant with a flick of his hand and she left. Emily stifled a sigh. She would have liked to chat with the other woman again, but his presence made that difficult anyway. She straightened the already-made bed and wondered how long he planned to stand there watching her.

"Your porridge will grow cold if you don't eat it."

Right now cold porridge was the least of her problems. She shrugged, busying herself by giving her already shining hair a few unnecessary strokes with the brush.

"Emily." The warning was there in his voice, but she chose to ignore it, instead rearranging the things on the small table.

"I do not like being ignored, English." He said it as if he truly believed she might not realize that truth already.

He was probably too arrogant to latch onto the fact that she was baiting him on purpose. Not that her behavior was more than a paltry defiance at best. He did not care for her opinion, so the fact that she chose to ignore him was barely worth his notice. But he had noticed, she reminded herself. Her lips twitched in satisfaction.

She did not like being kidnapped, but that had not stopped him from taking her and she did not think she owed her captor polite consideration.

She didn't hear him move, but suddenly his big hand landed on her shoulder. He turned her to face him, but she refused to look at him and kept her eyes averted.

He sighed.

She considered what she wanted most—to annoy him further or to ask about her friend. Her concern for Cait won. "Have you seen Cait this morning?"

"Look at me when you speak to me."

She thought about it and then stiffened her spine. "No."

"If you want me to answer your question, you will."

Deciding news of her friend's well-being was more important than her pride, she did. And wished she hadn't. He was so handsome and it made her angry that such a beautiful man could have such a black heart.

"No."

She stared, thinking she must have misheard. "You haven't seen her?"

"No."

"You made me look at you only to tell me no?" she demanded, incensed.

"Do not raise your voice to me."

"You tricked me."

He shrugged. "You should not have denied me."

"Why, pray tell?"

"I am your laird."

"I am not a member of this clan. I am your captive and I owe you no allegiance."

"You owe me respect."

"I owe you nothing."

Instead of getting angrier, he shook his head with a

strange smile, making him look even more appealing than normal. "My fiercest warriors would not talk to me so and yet you, a mere slip of a woman, defy me without pause."

"I'm not afraid of you."

"No, you are not." He sounded bemused by that fact. "I do not expect to see Cait or Drustan for a day or more," he offered without further prompting.

"You are not serious?"

"I am."

"But that is . . ." She stopped, unsure what to call it. She supposed that a newly wedded couple might want time to themselves. She could hardly fault that, but Cait and Drustan had married under anything but usual circumstances.

"It is normal," Lachlan said in a hard voice.

"Is it?" she asked, finding it difficult to keep track of their conversation with him standing so close.

"Yes."

"I have no experience in these matters." Not yet anyway. "But I am worried about her. I hardly slept last night for thinking about what might be happening to her."

Lachlan stared at her and she blushed, realizing how her words sounded.

"I wasn't thinking about that."

"What?" he asked, a devilish glint in his dark eyes.

"*That* . . . you know. The bedding."

"What else did you think might happen to her on her wedding night?"

"She might have refused him."

"She didn't. You saw how she responded to his kiss on the boat. The lass wanted him."

Emily's hand flew up to cover his mouth. "Don't say such things. It isn't seemly."

He kissed her palm and she jerked her hand away as if burned. Worse, she felt marked . . . as if his kiss had seared her palm with the imprint of his lips.

He smiled. "You watched them. You know I speak the truth."

"I didn't watch," she lied.

"You did and it excited you."

"It didn't!"

"It did and that made me hot."

"Hot?" She shook her head, unable to believe they were having this conversation.

He nodded. "Oh, yes. Your lips parted as if you were ready to be kissed yourself."

"I did no such thing."

"You did. And I liked it."

"You shouldn't have noticed. It was rude."

"You think I'm a barbarian."

"A barbarian who speaks Latin," she said wryly.

"I am interested in many things."

"Well, I am interested in my friend's welfare. Will you allow me to visit her?"

"There is no need. You will trust me when I tell you she is content to be with my warrior and you will stop worrying. Drustan gave his word he would not hurt her."

"As you gave your word you would not hurt me?"

"Yes."

Then she had plenty to worry about.

Her opinion must have shown on her face because he said, "You will cease believing my choice of reparation for insult is some horrible fate that has befallen your friend. Cait is unharmed."

Emily laughed. She couldn't help it. The man was daft. "It is a horrible fate."

"No more so than any other woman given in marriage."

"She had no choice!"

"Most women have little choice in who they wed."

"This is different, you must see that."

"How?"

"You chose for her."

"And was she allowed to select her first husband?" he asked in a tone that implied such a thing highly unlikely. "Were you allowed a choice in whether or not you were sent to marry Talorc?"

There had been no choice . . . not if she wanted to spare her sister. "No." Sighing, Emily also remembered what Cait had told her about her first marriage. "Cait's brother decided on her first husband."

"Ah," Lachlan said with satisfaction. "Her first marriage was arranged by her brother who was also her laird and now her new laird has chosen her second husband. It is no different."

"It's different all right." How could he be too stubborn to see that? "She didn't choose to be a member of this clan."

"Did she choose to be a Sinclair?"

"She was born a Sinclair."

"And now she has been made a Balmoral."

Implying neither had been her friend's choice. Looked at in that light, she could see his reasoning, but it was flawed. Only she did not know how to explain that fact. "You are trying to confuse me."

"No. I'm only trying to make you see the truth."

"What truth?"

"That I have done nothing reprehensible in commanding this marriage take place."

"You said my opinion did not matter."

"I have changed my mind. I want you to stop thinking I am some kind of monster."

"Why?"

He glared at her. "You did not eat your dinner last night, and this morning you have not touched your porridge."

"What does that have to do with anything?"

"You will eat. I command it."

"And if I don't . . . what threat will you use against me to make me obey? Will you take me like a whore to your bed?" She couldn't believe she had asked that, but he certainly didn't hesitate to discuss issues best left unmentioned.

"To warm my bed would not make you a whore," he growled.

"Wouldn't it? What do Highlanders call women who share their bodies with men who are not their husbands?"

"Accommodating."

Emily gasped, unable to believe her ears. "You did not just say that."

"I did. I am no Englishman to say one thing and mean another."

"How dare you?"

"I dare anything I like. I am laird here." And according to him, that made him tantamount to being a king.

Well, he wasn't her king and that was that. With a huff, she spun away.

"If you want to see Cait, you must eat."

"So that is to be the threat?" Not that he needed to threaten her to eat. She'd only been waiting for him to leave before she ate her porridge, but he was right. It was going to be stone cold if she didn't eat it soon.

"If that is what it takes to make you act reasonably, then yes."

"I did not realize that prisoners were expected to be reasonable." Because she wanted to anyway, she sat on her bed and began to eat.

He moved to stand near her, propping one foot on the bed frame. "You are not a prisoner."

She tried not to look at the muscular leg so close to her, but could not keep her gaze from straying to it. Englishmen covered their legs, but she did not think it would matter if he wore hose and a long tunic. Lachlan was so very masculine that he called to everything feminine in her even when she was angry enough to throw her porridge right at his head.

"So the door is not barred on the other side when the servants leave?" she asked with faint mockery. "I must have imagined hearing it slide into place then."

"I warned you that you would be locked in a tower if you ran from me again yesterday. You ran."

"And you followed through on your threat, but you didn't tell me you were going to torture me with boredom."

Chapter 9

Lachlan watched Emily eat, lascivious thoughts that would send her running if she could read them going through his mind. He wanted that mouth on him, not the spoon. When he had threatened to keep her in his bed the night before, he had known it would convince Cait to speak her vows. That did not mean he had not wished for the opposite outcome.

He did not pine for women, but he'd spent a good part of last night sleepless and aching. And it was all this Englishwoman's fault.

"I am not torturing you."

She was the one torturing him with his need to touch and taste when he knew he should do neither.

She finished her breakfast before saying, "I saw you shake your head at Marta. You wanted her to tell me she could not give me any chores to do when we both know there must be dozens in a keep this size."

He could not believe she was acting offended because of that. "You are not a servant in my household."

"I would rather be a servant than sit around all day doing nothing."

"Is that why your hands are chapped from work? Because you did not like doing nothing in your father's household?" He had noticed that yesterday and wondered at it.

She winced, tucking her hands into the folds of her skirt. "My hands are not unsightly."

"I did not say they were."

"You did."

He sighed. "Will you argue over everything I say?"

"I don't mean to."

"Then stop."

"You make me angry."

"I had noticed."

She cast him a disgruntled look. "Then why don't *you* stop?"

"I am laird."

"Is that your answer for everything?" She sounded so incensed, he had to bite back a smile.

"It is my answer when it is the right answer."

"Which seems to be all the time, in your opinion," she grumbled.

He stepped away from the bed. He had accomplished his purpose. She had eaten. Now, he had other more important duties to attend to.

She jumped up and grabbed his arm. "Please . . . do not leave me here again with nothing to occupy my time."

"What would you have me do?" he asked out of curiosity.

"At the Sinclair holding, I helped Cait oversee the running of the keep. I did the same with my stepmother in my father's home as well as seeing to many chores myself. I am used to being busy."

"I have a housekeeper and women to help her."

Emily's face fell and her small hand dropped from his

arm. "Very well. I will not keep you from your duties any longer with my unimportant problems."

"They are not unimportant," he denied, even though he had told himself that very thing only a second before. "I simply do not know what you would have me do to fix them. I will not have you treated as a servant and you must wait to see your friend until she and Drustan emerge from his quarters."

Which did not mean Lachlan could not think of *anything* to occupy Emily's time. He could, all too easily, but it had nothing to do with work and everything to do with getting her naked. He did not think she would appreciate his solution.

"At least let me stay in a room that is not a prison."

"You said you preferred to be kept from my people." She'd been adamant on that point.

"I was overwrought yesterday. I wasn't thinking clearly when I ran from you."

"Why?"

She looked at him as if she could not believe he had needed to ask. "I was kidnapped, then I discovered the only friend I have in the Highlands was to be forced into marriage to exact revenge on her brother, then you made me sit in that tiny boat to cross water so deep there is probably no bottom while your brother glared at me as if I were his worst enemy. When we landed on dry land, my emotions got the better of me."

"The water frightened you?" he asked, wondering if she would tell him the truth.

Knowing an opponent's fears made them vulnerable to you and she did not realize he knew hers already. He'd been shocked when he heard her and Cait talking about it. He had not smelled Emily's fear on the boat and he should have. Humans were not trained to mask their scent.

"Yes."

"Why?"

"I don't want to die by drowning."

"A sound plan, but that does not explain your concern when you were in a seaworthy boat."

"The boat could have tipped. A wave could have crashed over the bow and knocked me into the water."

"I would have pulled you out."

She stared at him, an odd expression on her face. Then she sighed. "I don't expect you to understand, but I don't like the water and the sea terrifies me."

"Why?"

She looked away, her face schooled into an impassive mask that impressed him all the more for the fact that her features were usually so expressive. "It does not matter."

"I will be the judge of that. Tell me."

"You are even more demanding than my father."

"Did your father instill the fear of water in you because he was afraid you would drown?" It was not such an uncommon practice, but it was a foolish one. Better to teach a child to swim than to teach them fear.

She did not answer and she did not move. There was a quality to her stillness that bothered him. It was too absolute. She was barely breathing.

"Emily?"

She looked at him then and her violet eyes were filled with an agony he could not stand.

Without considering his next actions, he sat beside her on the bed and then pulled her into his lap. It was a measure of her inner turmoil that she did not fight his hold, but burrowed against him as if hiding from her own thoughts.

It shamed him that while she was so obviously upset, his body reacted to her nearness with primitive intensity. He wanted her and his sex was soon rigid with the need to take her.

Forcing his thoughts to other paths, he repeated, "Tell me."

She shook her head.

"Why not?"

"It is long past."

"But haunts you like a specter of the night."

She shuddered. "Yes."

"Tell me and I will vanquish your ghost."

Emily marveled at his confidence. Did he really think it was that simple? "You are a man, not a magician."

"I am a laird."

"There you go again, thinking that's the answer to everything," she said teasingly, but her voice was not as light as she wanted it to be.

"It is." No doubts. No questions. Just absolute certainty in his own power.

Was he right? Could telling him cauterize the wound that had bled inside her for so long? She had never told anyone, not even Abigail, why she was so wretchedly afraid of the water.

"My mother died giving birth to a boy child who also died." Memories crowded her mind and she curled instinctively further into Lachlan's strength and heat. "Until then, my father loved me and called me his precious daughter. He was kind to me and smiled often. He loved my mother very much. His grief at her death was terrible. And his affection for me turned to hatred. He blamed me for being born a girl and for Mama's death in the attempt to give him a son and heir. He drank wine by the pitcherful the first months after her passing."

She could still remember the stench of it on his breath, his clothes. She'd been a small child, hurting and frightened by her mother's death and her father's withdrawal.

"One night, I went to him . . . I wanted to comfort him. I wanted him to hold me and call me precious as he had before she died. But he did not want my comfort and he abhorred my touch. He started shouting at me, telling me how useless I was. He said that when animals give birth to useless offspring, the babies are drowned. That I should have been drowned at birth, I was so useless."

Her throat convulsed and she had to take several breaths before going on.

"He stumbled to his feet and grabbed me. He carried me like a sack of wheat, his big arm pushing into my stomach. It hurt. I was crying and begging him to let me go, but he acted like he didn't hear me. He kept muttering about drowning a useless pup. He carried me outside. It was dark and there was no one around. He took me to the small pond behind the keep. The water was dark and black. Terrifying. I started screaming, but no one came. He gave an anguished roar and threw me in."

Talking about it brought back the feeling of the cold water closing over her head, the terror as she realized she could not breathe. She'd flailed in the water, but could not swim and her head broke the surface only once. She'd been sure she was going to die, but then her father's hand had been there, grabbing her, pulling her into the cold night air.

She'd coughed and sputtered, throwing up water, sobbing so hard she could not breathe. He'd held her then, rubbing her back, telling her over and over again how sorry he was. He'd carried her back to the keep as if she were a baby, cuddling her close to his chest, trying to comfort her. But all she had wanted was to get away from him.

When they reached the keep, the housekeeper was there. With terror-based strength, Emily had torn herself from her father's arms and thrown herself at the housekeeper. She'd wrapped her arms around the woman's legs and sobbed and sobbed.

"Father told her to give me a hot bath and drink. Then he left. The next day, he found me in my room and I screamed when I saw him. He went away after that. When he came home, he had my stepmother Sybil with him and my two stepsisters."

Emily had needed her father's love, but had not been

able to bear being close enough for him to touch her for years after that. Sybil had finished the separation his drunken rage had started, and by the time Emily was old enough to begin to understand her father's pain and drunken cruelty, she was too estranged from him for it to make a difference.

"He has never had a drop of wine since then that I know of, even when Sybil insisted he toast the birth of their first son. He drank water."

She looked up at Lachlan, wondering what he thought of her awful tale. His eyes were filled with banked rage and a compassion that touched her in places she could not afford to be touched. She scrambled off his lap and stood. He made no move to grab her back, but she felt the need for more space between them nevertheless and moved to the other side of the room.

She crossed her arms protectively over her heart. "Now you know."

"He was crazed with grief."

"Yes."

"But there is no excuse for what he did. I would kill a soldier who acted likewise."

She shivered, knowing he meant it. "I didn't want him killed. He was my father."

"He never touched you again?"

"No."

"But you are marked by his brutality."

"You could put it that way. My fear of the water is not usually a problem. I can hide it mostly. Other than kidnappings, I've never been forced into a boat."

He did not smile at her small jest. "You still cannot swim?"

Revulsion at the thought swept over her and she made no attempt to mask it. "*No.*"

"I can."

"Oh." She did not know what else to say.

"To live on an island and not be able to swim would be foolish."

"I suppose so."

"I will teach you to swim as well."

Horrified, she shook her head vehemently and then said, "No," for good measure.

"It is necessary, both for your safety and to vanquish your ghost."

"It's a memory, not a ghost."

"Call it what you like, but I have promised to defeat it and I will."

"By teaching me to swim?" she asked incredulously.

"Yes."

"You're daft. I want to stay away from the water, not get into it."

He was right in front of her without her knowing how he'd gotten there again. Maybe the man was a magician. "Most lairds would not take kindly to being called daft," he told her in a mild voice.

She bit her lip. He was probably right.

He reached out and gently pulled her lip from her teeth with his thumb. "Do not do that, you will draw blood."

She jerked backward, his touch more provocative than her memories. "I'm sorry."

"For biting your lip?"

"For implying you are daft."

"Then you agree to learn to swim?"

She swallowed, her mind whirling. "You truly believe doing so will drive the memories away?"

"If I teach you, it will."

Of course he thought he was the only one who could do anything important. He was the laird after all. She had to clamp down on a hysterical giggle. There was nothing funny about this situation. But what if he was right? She hated her fear of the water, but even more she hated her fear of her father. She would most likely never see him again, but if she did . . . she would like to be able to touch him without cringing.

There was also the fact that if she did not conquer her fear of the water, if she ever did find a way to escape, she would not have the ability to take it. She'd made the boat crossing to the island because she had no choice. She'd been physically forced to get in the boat. She did not think she had the fortitude to force herself to make the return journey.

"The lessons will keep you from getting bored," he said with sly persuasiveness.

"It will get me drowned."

He shook his head. "You have very little faith in me."

She should have no faith in him at all, and why she did was a mystery she could not fathom.

"I cannot trust you," she reminded herself as much as him.

She wondered if the words sounded as false to his ears as they did to hers. Because against her own best judgment, she could not deny that deep down inside, she did trust him. And knowing that made her furious with herself.

"You damn well can."

"You broke your promise to me." She should have remembered that truth before spilling her most secret memories all over him.

What was it about this man that sent her most logical thoughts scattering to the four winds? How could being with him make her feel safe when he had proven she was anything but secure in his company?

He looked mortally offended. "I have not."

"You have."

"How?"

"You promised not to hurt me, but you did . . . very much," she added for good measure.

"What the hell are you talking about? I have not harmed you in any way." His voice came out more like a growl.

The man was very animal-like sometimes. It must be a

Highlander trait because she had not seen anything like it amongst her father's soldiers. No matter how fierce, they never conjured images of predatory beasts.

"How can you say you have not harmed me? You kidnapped me! Before I told you I was married to Talorc, you were going to leave me in the forest to be eaten by a wild animal. You forced me to cross the sea in a boat. You kissed me just to see if I was lying. Then you told your brother I was so inept at it, I was most certainly innocent." Her anger grew as she enumerated his sins.

"The kidnapping saved you from having to marry Talorc. That is a gift and well you know it."

"That is entirely beside the point, since your intent was to harm me, and the fact that your actions indirectly benefited me in some small measure does not negate your many other sins."

"I am surprised your father did not settle you in a nunnery. You speak like an abbess."

"How would you know that?" she asked deridingly.

"Knowledge of the world is necessary to keep my clan safe, so I acquire it."

"Humph."

His eyebrows rose at that and then that tempting gleam was back in his wolflike eyes. "I would not have allowed you to be eaten by wild animals."

"And how would you have stopped it? You intended for me to return to the keep on my own."

"My soldiers would have watched over you."

"A likely story. When you dropped me off your horse with the intent of sending me back to Talorc as message bearer, your soldiers were going with you."

"I left behind two warriors you never saw."

"What? Why?"

"They are watching the Sinclairs."

"You left spies behind?"

"Yes."

"And you expected them to watch over me when I traveled back to the Sinclair holding?"

"Yes."

"Oh." So, she hadn't been an expendable pawn. She wasn't sure why, but that knowledge made her feel much better.

"You still forced me to cross the water in your small boat."

"It's a very sturdy craft and I did not know of your fear of the water when I decided to take you."

"Would it have mattered?"

He shrugged. "I might have knocked you out so you would not be unduly distressed."

"You think knocking me asleep would have been an improvement?" she demanded in outrage.

"Over you spending more than an hour locked in terror, yes."

She shook her head, unable to think of a single thing to say to that audacious comment.

"I have kept my promise to you and I will have you admit as much. Now, English," he added when she said nothing.

"You did hurt me . . . with your kiss." Far more than kidnapping her from a clan she did not wish to belong to.

"I did not. I was gentle." His voice suggested he'd made a major concession.

She didn't remember much gentleness . . . only heat and pleasure and then terrible shame. "You humiliated me . . . and in front of your brother, too."

"I did not humiliate you."

"Must you disagree with everything I say?"

"If you are wrong, yes."

"But you did humiliate me. You made me enjoy it. You made me kiss you back, but all you were doing was testing me." Could he truly not fathom how horrible that would be for a woman, to believe she was wanted and discover belatedly, after exposing her own inappropriate desire, that it was all a stratagem? "I acted like a wanton and it was nothing but a horrible, rotten test on your part," she whispered, her head down because she could not stand to look in his face when she said it.

"You are upset you responded to me?"

Were all men so ignorant of the way a woman thought, or just this one? "Yes."

"Then it is not my fault you were embarrassed, but your own."

She looked up at that, unable to believe he had said something so cruel.

"My fault? I did not invite your kiss."

"You had lied to me. I had no choice but to test the veracity of your claims. And by your own admission, it was not my kiss that caused you to be hurt, but your response to it." He sounded like he was terribly proud of that logic.

She was stunned because he was right of course. Oh, he had hurt her all right, but she could see where his male reasoning had led him to believe it was the only course of action. Had she not responded to his kiss, Emily would only have been angered by his boorish behavior, not humiliated. It was her own weak behavior that had hurt her the most.

A lump formed in her throat. Why did life have to be so painful? She could look back over her years and see a pattern that shredded the very depths of her soul. It was her reaction to her father's visit the day after he tried to drown her that had sent him off to find Sybil. It was her inability to warm to her stepmother and be the lady Sybil wanted her to be that had kept a mother's love far out of Emily's grasp.

She had ruined her own chances with Talorc by responding with temper instead of understanding to his impatience and rude behavior. She had ruined her chances of effecting a rescue for Cait by getting herself kidnapped as well with her lies, and she had sown the seeds of her own humiliation when she had responded to Lachlan's kiss.

A small voice in her head said she was painting too dark

a picture, but at that moment she could not see beyond her misery. She seemed to invite rejection like an old friend wherever she went and whatever she did.

A sob escaped before she pushed her fist into her mouth to prevent another sound coming out.

"Emily?" Lachlan sounded worried.

He probably thought she was going to succumb to another bout of ill humor again, but she was not that weak. Unutterably foolish sometimes, but not hopelessly weak.

She swiped at her tears. "I am s-sure y-you are right." She hated the way her voice broke, but she could not help it.

However, her tears did not mean she was going to lose control again.

"Do not cry. I forbid it."

"I'm not . . ." She sucked in air so she could talk without stuttering. "I'm not crying."

He said a word she did not recognize. It didn't sound Gaelic, but it might have been. She was not totally fluent, especially when it came to curses and the like.

"Responding to my kiss should not embarrass you," he informed her.

She almost laughed at that, but she was too busy trying to control the tears she had denied. "I should not have blamed you for my lack. I'm no better than a strumpet," she admitted.

"Strumpets have a lot more experience."

"Is that supposed to comfort me?" she demanded, glaring at him. Bad enough to behave like a woman of ill repute, but to have him tell her she wasn't very good at it was hardly flattering.

"Do you want me to comfort you?" he asked, looking slightly green at the prospect.

"Why not? There is no one else here to do it." Though she'd spent most of her life without someone there to comfort her. Abigail tried, but Emily had always been careful not to visit her worries on her younger sister.

The girl had enough of her own with her hearing affliction.

"I am a laird, not a nursemaid."

"I would not have known that if you hadn't told me so." She'd meant the words to come out mocking, but they ended on a sob and she turned from him, desperately wanting to get her feelings under control.

He pulled her back around and into an embrace that should have been awkward, but was not. It felt so natural she had to remind herself that he was the enemy. She fit against him as if their bodies had been made to be pressed together in just such a fashion and his arms felt secure around her.

It was comfort when she needed it most and she could not turn away, though her logical mind told her she should.

Wasn't she proving her weakness to him yet again?

His hand smoothed down her back. "Tell me why you are so upset. I do not understand."

"You kissed me and I liked it." She sighed. "I thought you liked it, too, but then I realized you didn't . . . that it was simply a test. You weren't affected by our embrace, but I was. That must mean I'm a true wanton. Even when you pulled away, I did not want you to stop."

He smiled down at her, his eyes warm with something she did not understand. "You are no wanton."

"I am. I know it, though I appreciate you trying to comfort me." She sighed. "Perhaps marriage to Talorc will not be so bad after all."

Lachlan went absolutely rigid and the hand rubbing her back now grabbed her shoulder with bruising bite. "What the hell are you talking about?"

She had no idea why he was so upset. Surely she was the one who should feel out of sorts for being forced to see a side of her nature she would rather have remained in ignorance of. "If I am wanton, I will find some solace in the marriage bed."

"You are not a wanton. Your response was for me, not the other laird." He looked ready to do violence.

But she did not feel any fear in the circle of his arms. Still, she had allowed the liberty of his holding her long enough. She needed to start acting like a lady if she wanted to believe herself to be one. She would never live up to Sybil's exacting standards, but Emily had her own code of honor and would not compromise it further.

She pushed out of his arms and indicated the door with the sweep of her hand. "You have other, more important matters to attend to, I am sure."

"You do not dismiss your laird. You wait for him to dismiss you," he growled, as if instructing a child in basic manners.

She rolled her eyes. "I cannot go anywhere, therefore I cannot be dismissed."

"Which means you wait for me to leave."

She bit back another frustrated sigh. No doubt he was right, but she wanted him to leave now. "I wish for a moment of privacy."

"You dare to order me?"

"I am not trying to offend you. I did not order you, if you will remember . . . but merely spoke my opinion. That is allowed, surely?"

"I did not ask for it."

"I must always wait until you do?"

His jaw looked hewn from granite and she wondered at his apparent anger.

"Lachlan?" she prompted in a soft voice.

"You do not have to wait for me to ask for your opinion to give it . . . in private," he said as if making a major concession.

"Thank you," she replied, though she personally thought she should not need his permission to do so. She was smart enough to refrain from saying so, however. No doubt Sybil would have agreed with him. She had certainly never encouraged Emily to speak her mind. "Well . . ."

"What?"

"Are you going to leave now?" she asked, trying not to sound overeager and offend him again.

"Not yet."

"Why not?"

"There is something I must do first."

Chapter 10

"What?" Emily asked.

Her eyes were wide with shock when Lachlan's lips closed over hers. Which would have been amusing if he wasn't aching so much from having her tell him how much she had enjoyed his kisses. Had the lass really not expected him to claim her lips again after that?

But to say in almost the same breath she thought she would respond to Talorc the same way had brought Lachlan's beast raging to the surface with more than desire fueling his blood. He'd wanted to rip the other laird's throat out for nothing more than the image of Emily sharing her body and her passion with the other man.

Her mouth was open on a gasp and Lachlan took immediate advantage, delving inside with his tongue to sip at the nectar waiting for him there. How could she believe he did not enjoy her like this? He had needed to test her yesterday, to see if she was as innocent as she claimed, but he'd never said he did not enjoy it.

She didn't fight him, but hung suspended in his grasp as he tasted her mouth and imprinted his wolf senses with both her flavor and feminine scent.

He lifted his mouth only a breath from hers. "There is no shame in this, Emily. I want your response. I crave it."

"Is it another test?" she asked, vulnerability shimmering in her violet eyes.

"No."

"Then why?"

"Because I want to. Because I want you."

"Oh. But I don't want to be a wanton."

"I won't let you become one," he promised.

He connected their mouths again, exultation roaring through him when she made a small sound and melted into him.

He was a fool for kissing her again, for tempting his beast as well as his manly desire.

But there was something so perfect about this woman. She was destined for his rival, but she smelled right, she felt right, and she tasted like ambrosia. His beast howled with the need to come out and claim her. His bones ached with the desire to make the change, to show her his power. It was insane and he could not give in to it, but his body shook with the craving and a growl her human ear could never hear rumbled low in his chest.

If he did not do something quickly, he was going to lay her on her bed, strip her clothes from her body and make love to her until neither of them could walk. Not only was she too fragile for such handling, but she was human and she was English. She would believe that if he took her completely, that it would mean they had to marry. Hell . . . even the Sinclair Chrechte saw mating that way.

He shoved her away from him and then grabbed her again before she fell on her backside. "We will have our first swimming lesson now."

He only hoped that the cold water of the loch would restore some of his self-control.

Emily swayed in his grasp and blinked at him, her purple gaze hazy with passion. "I really am a strumpet."

He glared at her. "Liking my kisses does not make you a whore."

"It does when I am promised to another."

"No, it does not."

"There are those in the Church who teach woman is evil, a temptress. I feel like a temptress now." She blinked up at him, her lips parted, her breasts rising and falling with each rapid breath she took, their turgid peaks pressing against her bodice. "I want you to kiss me again. Surely that means I am depraved."

"It means I have roused your passion. 'Tis good to know." He placed his fingertip over the quickly beating pulse in her neck. Her blood was rushing for him and for no other. That did not make her a wanton; it made her more alluring than any other woman he had known. "I am tempted by your sweet innocence, but that does not make you a temptress. I kissed you, English, not the other way around."

"That is true. Does that mean you are the seducer?"

"You have not yet been seduced."

"I haven't?"

"Am I buried between your thighs?"

She gasped. "No!"

"Then you have not been seduced."

"Oh . . ." She chewed on her bottom lip.

"You would not respond so easily to another man."

"Are you certain of that?"

"Yes."

"You are very arrogant," she said speculatively. "Perhaps it is only that arrogance speaking now."

She had no idea what the thought of her being attracted to another man did to him, how angry it made him. But he could tell from the way she spoke that she was not trying to make him jealous. She was genuinely worried about her morals.

It would have been bloody amusing if she didn't look so upset.

"Did you ever want to touch one of your father's soldiers?" he asked, convinced the answer had to be a negative for her to be as wholly innocent as she was.

"No." She clasped her hands, as if pleased by that reminder. "And they were not all surly men. Some were quite pleasing to look at, but I did not feel the things I do when I am near you." Then her expression took on a worried cast again. "Of course I did not spend much time with them. It would not have been proper."

"You rode on Angus's horse with him. Did his nearness affect you the way mine does? You smiled at him," he reminded her. It rankled, that smile. For she'd given his soldiers many such looks while ignoring him completely the evening before.

"That was to confuse him, but no . . . I did not want to get nearer to him as I did when I rode with you."

Everything she did confused Lachlan, but he wasn't about to admit that sorry truth. The woman was a puzzle, but an appealing one. "Are you sure you had no desire to have Ulf kiss you, or one of my other soldiers?" he teased, knowing the answer to that question with certainty.

She grimaced, distaste at the idea written all over her expressive features. "Of course not."

"Then how can you believe yourself to be a woman of misplaced morals?"

"It is not my morals I'm concerned with, but my urges. *It is you*," she stated with conviction. "I must stay away from you. You bring out the worst in me."

He did not agree. "I bring out the woman in you."

"I am supposed to be a lady, but you give me impure thoughts. It is wrong."

He pulled her close into his body so she could feel the evidence of his desire, the result of his own thoughts where she was concerned. "It is hot."

"Hot?" she asked, her voice squeaking with alarm.

"Very hot." He rubbed himself against her and groaned. "And now, unless you want me to act on those impure thoughts, we need to cool down."

"How can you act on my thoughts? You don't know what they are."

"Don't I?"

"Do you mean to say you have the same ones?"

That made him smile. "You are too innocent to have my thoughts."

"But you said—"

"That it is time for your swimming lesson."

"I am not taking my tunic off. It would not be decent." She couldn't believe he had suggested such a thing.

"You cannot learn to swim wearing it."

"My shift will be as good as gone if it gets wet."

"Then do not wear it in the water." He made that impudent suggestion without so much as blinking an eye.

"I can't do that!"

"Why not?"

"You are not serious."

"Explain this aversion you have to disrobing."

"I don't mind disrobing." But even saying the word made her blush. "In the privacy of my chamber, *by myself*," she stressed, "but I'm not about to do so in front of you."

"I admit doing so is not likely to have the calming effect on my sex I had wanted, but naked works best for swimming."

She knew the Highlanders looked at things differently, but this was totally outrageous. "You can't mean men and women swim naked together."

He shrugged. "Balmorals learn to swim when they are still babes. It is the way of things here."

"I am not a child."

"No. You are not."

"You said it works best to swim without your clothes." She paused, finding it difficult to utter the question that comment elicited. "Do you mean to say that you intend to take your plaid off as well?"

He gave her the devil's own grin and she knew he was enjoying her discomfort far too much. "Aye."

"You're daft! If your kisses are not bad enough, you cannot possibly expect me to do as you suggest."

"I told you *daft* is not a polite thing to call a laird."

"It is much ruder for you to demand I take my clothes off."

"I did not demand it. I suggested it."

"So I can keep them on?"

"Not if you want to avoid sinking to the bottom of the loch."

She went cold at the thought and felt her face draining of color. "This swimming thing is a bad idea. We will have to accept that I do not know how and leave it at that."

He shook his head. "You are becoming too excited over this. I am not suggesting you take your clothes off in front of my soldiers."

"Just you."

"You are going to be naked for me one way or another, Emily. You do not find my kisses bad at all . . . they make you hot, and merely being near enough to touch you makes me hotter than Hell in the summertime. I will try to preserve your maidenhead, but I am going to see you naked and caress you and learn your body's secrets."

Her entire body suffused with heat at his words and it wasn't embarrassment. He did make her *hot* like he said, but that didn't change anything. She could not give into him. "No."

"Yes."

"I am promised to Talorc."

"That is not something you should remind me of often. It makes the beast in me want to claim you as mine."

Did he really consider his lust a separate beast within him? Perhaps it was. She certainly felt urges that did not come from any place inside herself that she recognized. It was as if there was another Emily when she was in his company . . . a woman who craved things ladies were not even supposed to think about.

"Because he is your enemy?"

"Because you do not belong with him."

"You are so sure?"

"If you reacted to him the way you do to me, you would not have seen the kidnapping as a reprieve."

"I must marry him. I have no choice."

"You could stay with the Balmorals."

"You would give me sanctuary?"

"Yes."

But he said nothing about wanting to keep her for himself. In fact, as much as he wanted her, he had been careful to make no promises for the future. He was not looking for a wife, but for a woman who would slake the lust that raged like a beast inside him. She should be offended, mortified and a lot of other things her stepmother would have screeched at her, but all Emily felt was longing.

Nevertheless, she sighed and said, "I cannot stay."

"Tell me why."

So she told him about Abigail and her fear that her sister would be sent in her place.

He said nothing, but his expression turned thoughtful. "You wanted to bring your sister to live here in the Highlands."

"Yes."

"Talorc will not welcome her."

"I had hoped to change his mind."

"By calling him a goat?"

She blushed at the reminder. "I apologized."

"Did you?"

"Yes."

"What about my apology?"

"You want to apologize to me?" she asked facetiously.

His glare said he did not appreciate her humor. "You will tell me you are sorry for your insults to myself and my clan. I have waited long enough, English."

"And if I do, will you give up this idea of teaching me to swim?"

"No."

"Then I don't see why I should apologize."

"Because you were wrong."

"Perhaps . . ." She paused and then said, "Then again, perhaps not."

He shook his head. "Do you hope to make me angry enough to forget your lesson?"

He was far too clever for her liking. It was a ploy that had worked for her with her stepmother and father more than once. "Maybe," she admitted, "but truly . . . Lachlan you cannot expect me to disrobe in front of you. Not to mention the possibility of someone else coming along."

"I would hear their approach before anyone could get close enough to see you."

He really did have an exaggerated view of his strengths. "I don't think so."

"Come here, English."

"Why?" Did he plan to undress her himself? She truly must be depraved because the prospect was as thrilling as it was shocking.

"I want to kiss you."

"Oh." She had enjoyed their kisses to this point. Very much. More than she should, if she wanted to admit the truth. "But I don't think you should keep kissing me. I am promised to Talorc."

The muscle in Lachlan's jaw tensed. "This is the last

time we will discuss this. I do not wish to hear of him again from your lips. Understand?"

"But, laird—"

Lachlan rudely interrupted, "The Sinclair has said before witnesses that he would not marry you."

"So?"

"Until he recants that statement, you are not betrothed to him."

"But our kings—"

"I told you, lass, we Highland lairds make our own laws. We cooperate with Scotland's king when it suits us. And only then."

"You mean you are *all* that way?"

"Aye. Even the lairds that are mere humans are still Celts. They will never submit to absolute rule by another."

"You think you are more than a mere human?" she asked, amused by his arrogance and secretly relieved at his interpretation of events.

If she did not belong to Talorc, then her honor was not compromised by the feelings Lachlan stirred in both her body and her heart.

"Come here and let me kiss you and then you may tell me your opinion of the matter."

She shivered to the depths of her being at the promise in his voice. "I think you plan to do more than kiss me."

He wanted to see her naked. He wanted to touch her. By the saints, she craved that touch more than she had hungered after acceptance in her own family.

"Perhaps . . . then again, perhaps not," he said, mocking her with her own words.

"And perhaps I will let you," she said with more boldness than sense.

She found true joy in his arms and a pleasure that was unimaginable. Once she left the Balmorals, she would never know either again. She decided in that moment to fully experience everything Lachlan would give her.

He had promised not to take her virginity and she would trust him to keep that promise. She was not so naïve that she believed women did not engage in the sort of touching he spoke of outside the bond of matrimony. Jolenta had told Emily and Abigail stories of the goings-on at Court. Those tales had shocked and sometimes sickened her, but she did not feel in the least sick at the prospect of doing any and all of the things Jolenta had spoken of and alluded to with Lachlan.

If that made her wanton, then so be it, she would be wanton. Because deep in her heart she knew she would only ever be that way with this one man . . . a man who thought he was more than a mere human. And looking at him with his wolf's eyes and power radiating from him like a palpable presence, she thought she just might agree.

Having made the decision, she did not want to wait for him to act, but needed to make the first move herself. She stepped up against him, cupped his face with both her hands and reached up on her tiptoes to kiss him.

Making a feral sound, he dipped his head and took possession of her mouth with mind-numbing intensity. He kissed her like he meant to devour her, eating at her lips, his tongue tangling with hers and pervading her mouth with his spicy flavor.

Her knees went weak. She wobbled and fell against him, confident that he would hold her up and keep her safe. His big hands clamped to her waist and lifted her right off the ground.

She wrapped her arms around his neck and kissed him back with every ounce of the passion she'd tried so hard to suppress until now. His hold changed, one arm wrapped around her back, his fingers brushing the side of her breast through the fabric of her shift and tunic. His other hand cupped her bottom, kneading her with erotic gentleness that sent a wash of humidity to the juncture of her thighs.

This was how men touched women they wished to mate

with. It was incredibly intimate and yet not enough. She wanted more, but had no experience with which to determine what more might be. The things he made her feel were so very unique to her that she grew light-headed from the myriad sensations. And it was a good thing he was holding her so tight, for she was beyond remaining upright, even leaning on him.

Their surroundings ceased to exist for her and she knew only the taste and feel of his lips . . . the possessive hold of his hands. Nothing else mattered. Not her future, not her past and not even the present, except this man in this moment.

She did not know how it happened, but with only a couple of brief separations of their mouths, she found herself as nude as he'd promised her she would be. And she was not embarrassed. She felt no shame in allowing him to see her, to touch her . . . to know her like no one else ever had.

She belonged to him for this moment in time and she refused to consider anything else.

The summer sun warmed her skin, but not nearly as much as the heat of his gaze. Gold-rimmed brown eyes seared her with elemental fire while her own gaze became locked on the part of him that declared him fully male. He'd taken off his plaid and he stood proud and glorious in his own nudity. His masculine sex was swollen and rigid as a staff, pointing at a sharp angle toward the sky.

Oh, my. "I never thought it would be so big," she whispered.

"It?" he asked with strangled laughter in his tone.

She pointed to his male member. "That."

"That?"

"Your penis," she said defiantly.

But he just smiled. She liked his smile. It made her feel warm in a way that even his touch did not.

"You spent much time thinking on the matter?" he asked.

"Only in recent days."

His eyes glowed with masculine satisfaction. "Since you met me?"

"Maybe," she hedged.

"A man is large . . . a woman small. The fit perfect."

But, according to him, that "fit" was one delight she would not know in his company. She said nothing, simply staring at him and trying to control the urge to reach out and touch. She would never have anticipated wanting to, but she could barely stop herself.

"You want to feel it?" he asked, as if reading her mind.

"Yes."

"Then do so."

Her gaze flew to his, but there was no mockery evident. He meant it. He had put himself at her disposal and her passion and curiosity demanded she accept his invitation.

She stepped closer and then reached down to brush one fingertip along his shaft. It moved and she jerked her hand away.

He laughed. "It is all right."

"But . . ."

"I like your hand on me."

She looked into his eyes and saw a hunger that matched her own burning in their depths. A sense of exultation made her want to laugh, but not with humor . . . with sheer joy. She had no experience of men, was not the favored daughter in her father's household, but she could affect the powerful laird of the Balmoral so much that his body trembled with his need for her.

Amazing.

Lachlan watched the sense of feminine sensual power dawn in Emily's violet gaze and had to fight the urge to tumble her onto her back and bury himself in the silken wetness he knew waited for him between her legs. There was no calculation in her expression, only pure happiness.

She *liked* affecting him so strongly. It was an honest reaction, one worthy of a femwolf, though she was no more than human.

He must remember that truth, no matter how she delighted him. He would not claim her body completely, he would not spurt his seed into her womb. He had promised her that he would not breach her maidenhead and he would keep that promise. Equally as important, to take a virgin was to imply the willingness to mate for life, and he had no such intention.

No matter how much he might want this human woman, he would not travel the path his father had taken. It was too fraught with danger to his kind.

Emily curled her fingers around his sex as if she had done it a thousand times and rubbed up and down. "You are so soft."

"Soft?" he asked on a choking laugh. "I think not."

"Your skin," she replied with a great deal of seriousness. "Have you ever felt silk?"

"Nay."

"We have silk tapestries in our great hall . . . or rather my father had. Sybil insisted. They feel like air against your skin, so thin and smooth."

"You are saying I am not more substantial than air?"

"Oh, no. You are quite substantial, laird. But so smooth here over the hardness." She caressed him along his length again, this time taking twice as long to make the journey from base to tip.

If he did not do something, he was going to spill and his pride would not let him do so without giving her pleasure first. Only he could not trust himself to pleasure her right now without swiving her. He had never been so lacking in control, but even his pride could not pretend his mind governed his body at that moment.

He swung her up in his arms and kissed her to stifle any

protest she might make. She instantly began kissing him back with a passion that threatened his very sanity.

Using the last bit of self-discipline he had remaining, he forced himself to walk toward the water and not stop until he was in the chilly depths up to his waist. The shock of the cold did little to impact his arousal and he shook with the need to lower her hips and position her to take him inside. He moved toward deeper water. He was up to his chest and her whole body was practically submerged before he broke the kiss.

"Are you ready for your first swimming lesson?" The words came out strong, but his body was weak with desire.

She stared up at him as if she did not understand what he was saying and then her eyes widened and she gave a small shriek. "I'm in the water. And it's cold!" She drew out the last word in a complaining wail.

He shook his head. "Not cold enough." Not nearly cold enough.

Chapter 11

"It's not?" Emily looked like she was considering calling Lachlan daft again.

"No."

"But I'm freezing."

He looked down at her and saw that she did indeed have goose bumps all over her body. He wanted nothing more than to smooth them away with one hot caress after another. "We will start with floating."

"F-floating?" She was cold, but he thought the stutter a result of the nervous fear in her eyes.

"I will not let you sink, Emily."

Her eyes filled with resolve. "I do not want to be afraid."

"You will conquer your fear."

"I want to, but I don't know if I can." She did not sound happy with that fact, but resigned to it.

"You can." He was impressed that she did not insist he take her out of the water.

The longer they stood there, the more rigid she became

as terror that was so great it even masked the scent of her excitement overcame her. Something shifted inside him as he saw it happen. He hated to see her afraid and was determined to help her. Even his sexual desire took a secondary role to that determination.

"If you drop me, I'm afraid I'll sink into a dark abyss, that the water will hold me down until all my air is gone, until I die . . . I . . . I feel like the lake is bottomless, that I will be lost forever. Promise me, you will not drop me."

He was impressed with her for having the courage to voice her fears. "I have already made this promise."

"Say it again."

"I promise I will not let you sink."

She smiled gratefully, though it was a poor attempt. Her mouth trembled and she had turned the color of parchment. "Thank you."

"The loch is not bottomless either, lass."

"I know, but . . ."

"I am standing on the bottom now and it does not go over my head for a dozen or more feet out."

"I would like to learn to swim here then."

He kissed her softly on her partially parted lips. "All right, sweeting."

A hot blush stole over her cheeks at the endearment and it was all he could do not to kiss her again. She was so damn precious. And she made him smile. He'd been laird for a decade, ever since his father's death in battle, taking on the responsibilities shortly after his voice changed. He'd learned restraint early. He'd also learned duty was more important than pleasure and he had spent the last ten years proving that.

This slip of a woman made him crave the pleasure. She was dangerous, but she was also irresistible.

She gasped and grabbed onto his shoulders the first time he tried to let her go. He found himself almost forgetting their shared nudity in his quest to help her overcome her terror of the water. It took an hour to get her floating with his hand only lightly touching her back, but he was so proud of her for getting that far that he was grinning when he heard an approaching soldier.

He looked down at her lovely body exposed to his gaze and the summer sun and for the first time in an hour saw her as the soldier approaching might see her. Her breasts, belly and thighs floated above the water, while the rest of her was revealed through its crystal clear depths. He had swum naked with femwolves before, and even had sex with them afterward, but never before had he felt the sense of possessiveness he did toward Emily right now.

She was not his woman, but he did not want anyone else to see her this way. Her berry-ripe nipples were beaded from the cold water, and the golden brown curls on her feminine mound glistened with droplets of moisture. Her thighs were apart just far enough for his hand to slide between them and touch her delicate folds if he wanted to.

His hand itched to do just that, but his senses told him the soldier would be there soon.

He sighed soundlessly and then spoke. "Someone is coming."

She'd been floating with her eyes closed upon his instruction, but now they flew open and she tried to sit up. Because she was in the water, she started to sink instead, of course, and he had to grab her to keep her face from going under.

She spluttered and latched onto his shoulders with urgent fingers. "Where? Who?" She frantically looked around the clearing. "I don't see anyone."

"He will be here in a few seconds."

"I suppose you can hear him," she said sarcastically.

"Yes."

She frowned and shook her head. "It makes no sense and I don't know why, but I believe you."

"I do not lie."

"I need my clothes." When he didn't move fast enough to suit her, she tried to shake him. "Now, before he gets here."

He was in complete agreement, but it still took him a moment to force his muscles to obey the command to leave the water. Now that he wasn't focused on teaching her to swim, his need for her was taking precedence over his common sense. His wolf wanted to touch and taste her delectable naked curves.

"Lachlan!"

The wolf would have to wait along with his wholly human need. Using the speed of his inner beast, he carried her to the shore, and then threw his plaid around her like a blanket. The soldier was approaching at a run and would break through the concealing trees in a few seconds. She grabbed the edges of the plaid, making sure it covered her. It was not a woman's plaid and though he was much bigger than she was, a good portion of her legs was still exposed.

He shoved her shift and tunic at her. "Go over there and dress." He pointed to a dense clump of bushes that would hide her from even a werewolf 's gaze, though the man approaching was only human.

Lachlan didn't need to be in wolf form to pick up Ulf's scent at this distance. His senses were superior even in his human body, but not quite as good as when he changed.

Emily had grabbed her clothes and disappeared behind the bushes. "You are going to meet your soldier naked?" she called.

"It is my brother."

His plaid landed on the ground a foot or so from the bushes. "Get dressed."

"A captive does not give a laird orders," he instructed her.

"This one does."

He almost laughed at her impudence. He knew no other woman like her . . . femwolf or human. He had just picked up the plaid when Ulf came into the clearing.

He was scowling. There was nothing new in that. His brother smiled less frequently than he did, but the look of accusation in his eyes irritated Lachlan. Ulf believed his family position gave him the right to question his laird, and Lachlan often humored him. It was not his brother's fault he had not been born werewolf.

He had pitied his older brother since the year came for Ulf's first change and it did not happen. Their father had been disappointed; their mother had been relieved and Ulf had learned that unlike what he had believed since childhood, he would not one day rule the Balmorals. There had been signs that his brother was fully human all along, but their father had ignored them, insisting his sons were both wolves.

He had been wrong. Only one had carried the ability to change and it had been Lachlan. From the week after his first full moon as a werewolf, he had been trained to take over the clan one day. Ulf had never protested. It would have done no good. A human could not survive a challenge by a werewolf and Lachlan would have challenged Ulf's leadership if he had tried to assert it. For the good of the clan.

His entire life had been lived toward that greater good and he was not about to forget his responsibilities now.

"Where is she?" Ulf demanded by way of greeting.

Lachlan could hear Emily pause in her struggle to tug her clothing on. She'd also stopped breathing, as if waiting to hear how Lachlan answered.

He nodded toward the bushes with his head while he secured his plaid.

Ulf's scowl grew more pronounced. "What is she doing over there? You're wet. You were naked when I arrived. Have you taken to tumbling your enemy's castoffs in the water? I thought you only indulged in that sort of thing with femwolves."

Lachlan knocked his brother to the ground with a hard shove. "Guard your tongue."

Ulf had the grace to look chagrined when he realized what he had said. Emily was no more aware than most of the humans in the Highlands of the wolf nature inhabiting some of their clanspeople. Ulf knew the penalty of betraying the Chrechte's secrets to those who should not know.

Death. And being the laird's brother would not save him.

Lachlan did not know what Emily would do if she knew the pack's secret, but she was human and that meant they did not take the chance.

Then, to cover both Ulf's blunder and his own correction, he said, "She is no one's castoff, as I have told you."

Emily muttered something about arrogant men poking their noses into business that was not theirs and he had no doubts she could hear every word he and his brother spoke.

Ulf showed no evidence of hearing her low-voiced grumbling as he climbed to his feet. "Yet she does belong to your enemy."

"He refused her." Lachlan was bloody weary of discussing the Sinclair laird.

"And you plan to keep her in his place?" Ulf asked with derisive bite.

"No." Lachlan did not understand his brother's derision.

Emily was human, but so was Ulf. She was not the other laird's castoff and if Lachlan chose to keep her, he could not see what objection Ulf might raise. Unless he, too, was concerned about Lachlan's children being born wolf.

Ulf, better than anyone, knew the price paid when a child

born to a Chrechte and a human took human form instead of a wolf's. Their race did not reproduce easily, but to do so and not pass on the gifts of the Chrechte was a tragedy.

"You are giving a great imitation of a man governed by his lust rather than his head." Ulf 's criticism stung because it was so close to the truth.

Lachlan was too proud to admit such a thing though. "I grow weary of your harping, brother. You sound like a fretful old woman."

"Better than a man at the mercy of his beast."

Lachlan usually let comments like that slide, but enough was enough. His brother needed reining in. "Be careful I do not unleash my beast on you," he said with chilling bite.

Ulf winced, but quickly controlled his features. His strength in the face of even a Chrechte's threat impressed Lachlan. He had always admired his human brother and while he had pitied Ulf 's inability to make the change, he'd never made the mistake of thinking the older man was weak for what he was.

Not wanting to risk Emily hearing anything more that might betray his secrets, he led his brother far from the bushes she was now simply hiding behind. She'd finished dressing but had not come out, and he didn't know if it was because she was embarrassed or because she didn't like his brother, or both.

He stopped a good thirty feet away. "Say what you came here to say."

Ulf's hands fisted at his sides. "First tell me honestly if you have plans to marry the woman."

"You should know better than that. I will not marry a human."

"Not even a clanswoman?" Ulf asked.

"Nay."

"You're worried the Chrechte's secrets will be revealed."

"That is part of it." Intermating always carried such

a risk. There had been a time when it had been expressly forbidden, but that was before the Chrechte joined the Celtic clans. Many maintained the ancient ways though.

His father had not.

"You're afraid all of your offspring would be like me, instead of just one, aren't you?" Ulf asked, sounding bitter.

"It is the responsibility of all Chrechte, but especially the leaders, to make sure our race does not die out."

"I am no less a Chrechte warrior than you because I have no beast to overcome my human logic."

Lachlan did not agree, but he could not explain to his brother, who had no wolf, what it meant to know the beast lived inside him giving him strength and superior abilities. Far from diminishing his ability to think logically, his beast added an animal cunning to his thoughts that no human could emulate.

"There is no need for this argument. I have told you I do not intend to keep the Englishwoman. Why is not important."

"To you maybe."

"To you either. My decisions are not subject to your approval, nor are my thoughts."

"You're so damn arrogant."

"Emily thinks that's a Highland trait."

Ulf did not smile at the jest. "She has a low opinion of us all."

"That you have done nothing to rectify."

"Why should I? I care not what my enemy thinks of me."

"She is not your enemy."

"I do not dismiss the truth in favor of my cock's urgings. She is English and she is promised to the Sinclair laird. That makes her my enemy."

"She is a Balmoral captive, which puts her under my protection. Consider that the next time you are tempted to treat her like your enemy," Lachlan said in clear warning.

"I came to tell you that Duncan is here to give his

report." The lack of urgency in Ulf 's manner indicated the spy's report was not to tell them that the Sinclair had gathered his troops and was even now crossing the sea to lay siege to the castle.

"I will return to the keep shortly."

Ulf nodded, his mouth set in a tight, grim line, and left.

Lachlan could have ordered the soldier to escort Emily back to the keep and therefore left sooner himself, but he worried Ulf would hurt her tender feelings. When he had started worrying about such inconsequential matters, he did not know, but he refused to leave her to the not-so-tender mercies of his brother.

Emily paced the tower room, her emotions and thoughts in turmoil. She had done and felt so many shocking things she could not decide which one was the most astounding.

She'd exposed her deepest fear and told Lachlan her darkest secret. He had not mocked her fears or implied there was something lacking in her that her father could do such a thing. She had always worried that if she had been more lovable her father could never have rejected her so completely, but if Lachlan saw things that way, he had not said so.

She still struggled with accepting the fact that she had trusted him so utterly.

But then he elicited a unique response in her in more ways than one. She did not find his mouth or touch intrusive, but diabolically tempting. She'd returned his kisses with an ardency she had never dreamed a lady could be capable of. Then she'd let him undress her and when he had removed his own clothes, far from running, as any other unmarried lady would have done, she had touched him. Intimately.

She went hot all over remembering the feel of his hardness in her hand. He had liked her caresses and instead of embarrassing her, that made her feel proud. But he had not taken advantage of her wantonness to tumble her as Ulf had insinuated. Lachlan had used her distraction to get her into the water.

She could barely accept the memory of her being in the lake was real and not a dream. She had floated. Okay . . . with his support, but for a woman who refused to bathe in water that went above her knees, that was an amazing feat.

And he had not laughed at her nervousness even though it was obvious he was very comfortable with the water himself. He also had not exposed her to his brother's ridicule, but had sent the soldier back to the keep before calling her from behind the bush so he could escort her back. His consideration left her as breathless as when his lips were on hers.

Lachlan had walked her all the way to the tower room and left her here. But he had not barred the door. She'd been listening closely for the sound of the bar sliding into place, but it had not come. Did that mean she had the freedom to leave the room if she wished?

Despite her emotional outburst the day before, she had no desire to hide from his clan. She was not so weak-minded. If she could face Sybil every day of her life from the time she was eight until she'd left for the Highlands, she could face a few possibly hostile Scottish women.

She could have asked Lachlan what her position was if he had stayed even a few moments, but he had not. He had seen her into her room, told her they would repeat the swimming lesson the next day and left without a backward glance. It had taken all her self-control not to reach out and touch him as he left. She had wanted him to stay and now missed him as if she were used to seeing him every moment of every day of her life—an odd thing to feel for a man she had met only the day before.

She picked up the brush from the table, meaning to tend to her hair, but she went still at that last thought.

She had known him for two days and she had shared more of herself with him than she had anyone in her whole life. She remembered reading a poem about love at first sight, but had thought it rather silly at the time. She could not imagine such a thing. She could imagine it now.

She sat down with a thump on her bed and began to brush the wet tangles from her hair. How could she be so stupid? If she loved anyone, it should be Talorc. She would have to marry him. She had no choice. How could her heart have betrayed her this way? Or were her feelings nothing more than an instinctive trust in a strong man and a strong lust she had no experience controlling?

She could only hope it was the latter, because if she did love the laird, she was destined to have her heart broken.

Love or desire, she had not acted like a lady with Lachlan, but she could not regret it. No matter how shocking the events of the morning, Emily would not undo any of them. And she would be ready for her swimming lesson tomorrow morning with Lachlan, too. If he kissed her, she would kiss him back. If he touched her, she would learn pleasure at his hand and not regret it.

She had enjoyed every moment in his company . . . except when she overheard him tell Ulf that he would not keep her. That had hurt, but it should not have. It was not as if his stance had come as a big surprise. He'd told her the same thing, only using different words. He did not want a future with her, but that shouldn't matter because a future was out of the question anyway.

She would not love him. Only a fool loved where heartache was sure to follow and she was no fool. She would enjoy this time as a captive as a respite from the life she was committed to living, but when the moment came to return to that life, she would return.

Highland warriors were not the only ones who knew their duty.

Cait was snuggled into Drustan's body, her own a boneless mass of satiated pleasure. She had never known lovemaking could be like it was between them. It certainly had not been in her first marriage, but she did not tell Drustan that. The werewolf was arrogant enough as it was.

And he had made her beg.

She wasn't ashamed of that fact. She was impressed with his strength.

It had been a mating night filled with unbelievable pleasure and when they had woken that morning, he had renewed their intimacy. She'd remained hidden in bed when a servant brought them breakfast and had only protested weakly when he'd taken that as an invitation to explore the desire between them further. She wasn't sure now why she had protested at all.

His hand brushed up and down her side. "You are a passionate femwolf, Cait. It will be a pleasure to have you in my bed for the years to come."

She didn't know where he got the energy to talk. It was all she could do to kiss his chest where her face rested against him in acknowledgment of his words.

A rumble of pleasure rolled through him.

She was contemplating whether she should actually attempt to get out of the bed when a knock sounded on the door. It was too early for the noon meal, but late enough that she would be embarrassed to be caught lazing in bed. She was usually up with the sun and it had risen hours ago.

"Do you have duties today?" she asked, trying to work up a little guilt for keeping him from them and not succeeding.

It had been his idea to make love yet again, after all. Not hers.

"Nay. It is probably my mother come by to find out what we discovered of Susannah's plight. She showed great restraint not asking a dozen questions last night."

That woke Cait up as a bucket of frigid water would not have and she sat straight up in bed. *"Your mother?"*

"Yes."

She jumped off the bed and started scrabbling for clothes. "Susannah is not in a plight, she's in a marriage and she's happy. I can't believe your mother is here to visit and we're naked in bed." She sniffed herself. "I smell like you . . . I smell like sex. She's going to know what we've been doing."

"Even those members of my clan who do not come visiting this morning are going to know what we did. We are married and last night was the claiming, although the humans would call it the wedding night."

She glared at him. "That general knowledge is not the same as being caught *in bed* by your mother."

Drustan got out of the bed and tugged her plaid from her hands. "You are to wear Balmoral colors from this point forward," he said with gentle censure, indicating a plaid folded neatly on top of the small chest beside the bed. He leaned down and kissed her. "Take time to wash and compose yourself. I will let Mum in and talk to her while you do."

Cait threw him a grateful glance before he walked out of the bedroom carrying his plaid, which she sincerely hoped he planned to don before letting his mother inside. He shut the door behind him, but it wasn't as thick as the door to their quarters and she could hear him letting his mother inside a few moments later.

Cait did wash, not because she thought she could rid herself of his scent—she didn't want to—but because she was sticky with dried sweat and wetness between her legs.

It felt good to be clean, but she would have preferred a swim. Her muscles and the tender flesh between her legs ached. She felt marked by Drustan inside and out.

It was a new sensation, but not unpleasurable.

She hurried through her ablution, listening with only half an ear to Moira and Drustan's conversation. His mother asked about Susannah and if Drustan had seen her. He told her he hadn't, but that he'd heard her and she sounded happy. It gave Cait chills to think the Balmoral soldiers had gotten that close without being detected by the Sinclair werewolves.

She supposed there were wolves in her pack that adept at hiding their scent, but she'd never had occasion to know about it. She certainly wasn't. Her brother might be. Did that mean he would be able to breach the security of the Balmoral fortress? If he did, would he take her away?

Unfamiliar fear washed over her.

As a femwolf prevented from the change by her pregnancy, she had few options to protect herself. The babe had to be kept safe at any cost. She'd almost forgotten that yesterday when she had fought like a madwoman for her freedom, but she would not forget again. The responsibility to reproduce was a sacred one the Chrechte continued to honor.

No matter how difficult the task.

She could only hope Drustan was as good at protecting her as he had been at taking her . . . and that he did not kill her brother in the process. As surly as Talorc might get, she loved him. He would not come for her, but for her baby. He lived by the old ways and that meant he would respect her bond to Drustan; however, he would not tolerate the loss of a future Chrechte warrior to his clan, nor would he tolerate the insult of her kidnapping without redress.

He and Lachlan were very much alike in that way.

In all likelihood, he would demand the babe's return to the Sinclair holding. If she chose to come with it and live as a widow, he would allow that, but she had little hope he would allow the Balmoral clan to keep her child. Especially if she gave birth to a son. There was also the very real possibility he would declare war over the insult of her kidnapping well before the babe's birth.

Her heart heavy and her mind spinning with possible outcomes to her situation, she finished dressing. She brushed her hair with several quick strokes before going into the outer room.

"Susannah is happy with Magnus," she said by way of a greeting, wishing that truth could make a difference but afraid it would not. "She has found many friends among the Sinclairs."

Both Drustan and her new mother by marriage looked toward her. Moira sat on one bench and he sat on the other. He beckoned her to come and sit beside him. She did, but it felt odd. Sean had never been this possessive.

"You have seen her?" Moira asked, hope alight in green eyes so like her son's.

"Yes." Cait reached out and squeezed the older woman's hand. "Magnus lives in a cottage in the bailey. He is the blacksmith for our clan and very good at it, too. My brother relies on him. You would like him, I'm sure of it."

"Why did he take my daughter?"

Cait knew her answers were going to anger Drustan, but she could not lie. "Magnus did not take her. Not exactly. He mated with her in the fur and then, according to the custom of our pack, insisted she return to our clan as his wife. It happened on Sinclair land."

That was the part she knew Drustan would not like. She herself didn't understand why Susannah had been on their land, but she knew her brother's blacksmith had not lied. "Susannah told him that she had her laird's permission to hunt off the island during the full moon. She said she was not yet ready to take a permanent mate."

Moira's gaze clouded. "She wasn't. She'd gone into heat

and she knew that if she ran with the pack during the full moon she would end up mating in the fur."

Cait could imagine the girl's thoughts. Every werewolf and femwolf knew that if an unmated female ran with the males of the pack when she was in heat, their wolf natures would take over. The unmated males would fight for the privilege of mating her, even if they didn't like each other as humans. The winner would then woo the femwolf and they would end up mating. It was inevitable. What the femwolf 's mind told her in her human form would not hold sway in her animal form, and most were smart enough to realize it and take action accordingly.

Susannah had thought she was protecting her independence by hunting alone. Though in ancient days, she would not have been allowed to do so, no matter what her personal desires. Not all femwolves went into heat, but most did. And when they did, they were expected to mate and have children to increase the numbers in the packs.

Most packs still adhered to that tradition, much as human fathers insisted their daughters marry when they came of age. She'd already been mated the first time she went into heat, but she knew her brother would have insisted she take a mate at the time if she hadn't been.

"I thought the wolves among the Balmoral do not consider physical mating a life commitment." That attitude had caused Susannah and Magnus some conflict in the beginning and Cait had wondered why the girl had chosen to hunt alone if it were the case.

Wouldn't she have been safer running with her own pack?

Moira sighed. "Mating in the fur when a femwolf is in heat usually results in pregnancy. Susannah knew this. In our pack, making a cub together means a lifelong bond that cannot be broken under any circumstances."

That made sense. The Balmoral wasn't the only clan who had a pack that practiced physical mating outside of life bonding. Since the act of physical intercourse was the trigger for so many werewolves gaining control of their change after their coming of age, some packs believed it should be practiced without lifelong consequences. To Cait's way of thinking, that was giving in too fully to their wolf natures.

But she wasn't about to get into a morality argument with her new husband and mother-in-law right now. But woe betide any werewolf who mated a daughter of hers without promising a lifetime commitment. She would rip his throat out and Drustan would have to learn to live with it.

She wasn't going to allow any barbaric custom like that to hurt a child of hers.

"Why was Susannah encouraged to hunt on Sinclair land?" Cait asked, still confused on that point.

It made no sense in light of what Susannah had been trying to do . . . remain unmarried. Whether the wolf was Sinclair or Balmoral, the femwolf was going to end up mated once her scent in heat was caught. Which was exactly what had happened.

"She wasn't," Drustan said harshly.

She turned to her new husband, unsure how to take this change in his demeanor, but not about to back down. "Your sister told Magnus she was instructed where to hunt during the full moon. She did not know it was Sinclair hunting ground, but you cannot tell me the males of your pack were as ignorant. It is a thing the lairds take care to learn about each other."

It was supposed to be a secret, but the packs spied on each other and knew much more than they admitted about one another. There had been a time when all Chrechte were one pack under a common king, but that was not the way they lived now. Not since MacAlpin's betrayal. Even so, they did not war as much with each other as they did with the wholly human clans or with those to the south. There were unspoken laws they all lived by, and those governing mating with a femwolf from another pack were some of the most sacred. But they had not been breached for the reasons Drustan thought.

Cait's brother respected ancient tradition, very much. He would never have allowed Magnus to keep Susannah without a formal request of the Balmoral laird. If the request was denied, he would not have ordered his blacksmith to return her to her former clan. That was governed by the even more ancient law of true-bond matings, but none of that mattered.

Talorc had not made the formal request because he considered Susannah's presence on Sinclair hunting lands the result of shameful neglect for the femwolf 's safety by her laird and family. Soldiers as adept at hiding their scent as the Balmoral werewolves would know more than most. They would have known the land they sent Susannah to was hunting ground for the pack within the Sinclair clan. It was inconceivable that they would not.

"Of course we know where the Sinclair pack hunts," Drustan growled, confirming her thoughts. "Neither Lachlan nor I would have instructed her to hunt there alone, or otherwise."

"But she said you did."

"Susannah did not say I gave her these instructions," Drustan said in a voice that dared her to disagree . . . at her peril.

"I don't know who she claimed instructed her in this matter. I never asked. I just assumed it was your laird."

"Your assumption would have been right . . . *if* she had spoken to anyone. She *would* have sought permission for such a thing from me or from Lachlan." Anger sizzled in the air around Drustan, and Cait would never have known they had spent so many hours locked together in passion from the way he looked at her now if she did not have her own memories to go by. "She came to neither of us and if she had, we damn well would not have instructed her to hunt where she was likely to end up mated against her will."

Cait laid her hand on his forearm in entreaty. "She did not mate against her will. It doesn't work that way and you know it."

He shook off her touch, wounding her. "But she did not want to mate yet," he gritted out.

"But she is happy to be married to Magnus now. Truly. She is. You say you heard her . . . you know she is content to be his wife. They are good together. He's very tender with her," she said wistfully, thinking how gentle-spoken Magnus was with Susannah, while Drustan was practically yelling at her. "They love each other now."

"Is she pregnant?" Moira asked.

"Yes. And they are both very happy about the coming baby." She rubbed her own protruding tummy as her babe kicked. "It is a blessed event."

Moira's eyes filled with tears. "I will never see my grandchild."

"Talorc will give you permission to visit. I'm certain he will. But if you are worried, I could ask him for you."

"You will not be seeing your brother."

She tried to dismiss the biting tone of her husband's voice, but it was hard. He was obviously not as content as Magnus in their marriage born of the disaster of Susannah hunting alone during the last full moon.

"You must see that there is a misunderstanding that needs to be addressed. My brother did not dismiss ancient law on a whim. He and Magnus believed your clan had failed in its duty to protect Susannah. That is why the formal request for her hand was never made to you or Lachlan. I'm sure if I talk to him and explain, the situation can be resolved."

"You are going nowhere near Sinclair land."

Cait had known he would take that stand, but it still hurt. He didn't even act like he believed she'd told the truth about Susannah, and she didn't know how to convince him. Presumably, Susannah was not known as a liar and thus, he thought *Cait* was lying about what his sister had said.

After the night and morning they had spent together, she needed him to trust her. She had given him more of herself than she had ever done with Sean, but apparently that was not enough to merit belief in her integrity. What had been cataclysmically emotional for her had been nothing but physical lust for Drustan . . . and perhaps the fulfillment of his duty to his clan.

She was his wife by edict of his laird. He had not chosen her and she had best remember that before giving her heart away to be trampled. She was nothing more than the captive he had married, not a wife he valued or trusted.

She stood up. "Would you like some refreshment?" she asked Moira. "A cup of water, some wine?" Her eyes took inventory of what was on the shelves by the table as she spoke.

"No, thank you, child."

Cait nodded. "Drustan?"

"Water."

She poured him a cup and one for herself. She handed him his before sitting at the table and taking a long drink of her own. Her throat was suddenly very dry and tight. "I would like to see Emily."

He frowned. "She is in confinement in the tower. I do not know if Lachlan will permit her to have visitors."

"I do not think our laird considers her a prisoner," Moira offered, a worried expression on her kind features as she looked at Cait, but she spoke to her son.

"Why?" Drustan asked.

"He took her swimming in the loch and personally escorted her back to her room not thirty minutes past."

"He took her swimming?" Cait demanded, fear for her friend clawing at her insides. Emily was terrified of water. Had the laird been torturing her?

She had not thought Lachlan that cruel, but Emily would never have willingly gone swimming. After the boat crossing the day before, Cait was absolutely certain of that. Then another thought hit her with the force of an anvil. Emily could not have gone into the water in her gown.

She jumped up from the table as the implication of that truth seared her mind. "I am going to see Emily right now."

She rushed out the door and was halfway down the stairs to the great hall, using one of the few wolf strengths left to her in her pregnancy (her speed), when Drustan's big hand clamped onto her elbow.

He dragged her to a halt. "What do you think you are doing?"

"I told you. I am going to see my friend." She yanked her arm, but there was no give in his hold.

"You did not ask my permission, nor did you even have the courtesy to say good-bye to my mother or thank her for her visit. On top of that, you are running at speeds guaranteed to harm you or the babe if you were to fall. Have you no sense at all?"

"I was in no risk of falling." Moira was right behind them and Cait turned her body toward her, wishing she could dismiss her husband's presence as easily as she did the sight of him. But his hold on her elbow made such a thing impossible. "I am sorry. Thank you for visiting. I would love to talk more some other time."

Moira nodded, her expression showing concern, not annoyance. "I'm sure we will find the time."

To Cait's sensitive ears, the words were more threat than courtesy, though she was sure her mother-in-law had not meant them that way. They reminded Cait that she was stuck with the Balmorals. She had thought she had accepted her fate the night before when she spoke her vows, but that was before she realized her husband meant to keep her from her brother entirely.

She knew some clans were that way. Indeed, Talorc had become increasingly wary of outside contact since the betrayal of their clan by their English stepmother. However, she had not expected the Balmorals to be so isolated from others. A rather shortsighted conclusion she realized now. After all, they lived on an island and had a castle that would keep out all intruders. She'd never seen anything like it.

Despite standing on a stairway and the crush of her thoughts, Cait managed a credible curtsy toward Moira. "I look forward to many more visits."

It was not a lie. She did look forward to getting to know the older woman better and she knew Moira would want more details about Susannah's life. Especially if her laird refused to allow her to visit her daughter. But that would have to wait. Right now, Cait needed to assure herself that Emily was all right. She did not know what she would do if she found out the contrary, but she would help the sweet Englishwoman somehow.

Moira nodded her head and then reached up to kiss Drustan's cheek. "I will be leaving now. Bring Cait for the nooning meal tomorrow."

Cait saw Drustan nod out of the corner of her eye. Moira left, skirting nimbly around them.

Cait turned to her husband, removing all warmth from her expression. She did not feel even remotely charitable toward him at the moment. "Will you release me now? I wish to go to Emily."

"You have yet to ask my permission to do so."

"May I please go to visit Emily now?" she gritted out.

"I will ask Lachlan. If he agrees, then you may go."

Cait wanted to scream, but instead, she asked, "Will you ask him *now*?"

"I would prefer to return to our quarters."

"I would prefer you find your laird and ask permission for me to see Emily," she said stubbornly.

"You defy me at your peril."

"Do I? What more can you do to me, Drustan of the Balmorals? You have taken me from my clan, forced me to marriage and decreed I must remain estranged from my family for the rest of my life. I do not see how you can hurt me further, unless you wish to beat me . . . but we both know you will not do that while I am pregnant with a Chrechte child."

Chapter 12

Drustan's glare was hot enough to singe stone, but he said nothing. He simply swung her up into his arms and carried her back up the stairs, his body rigid with fury. Though his hold was tight, it was not bruising.

He kicked the door closed behind them and set her on her feet.

Neither of them spoke for several long seconds, then he sighed. "You are concerned for the Englishwoman and because of that I will make allowances."

"Will you?"

"I would not beat you, pregnant or not. Ever."

She shrugged. She had known that already. A Chrechte warrior would be ashamed to beat a female. She was not about to apologize for the insult though. She was too angry with him.

Surprisingly, Drustan smiled. "You are very stubborn, wife." When she said nothing in reply, he added. "We will see Lachlan at the nooning meal and I will ask him about you visiting Emily then."

Did he expect her gratitude for the concession? He wasn't getting it. Cait's concern for Emily was so great, it made her stomach roll with nausea. Making her wait another two hours to discover if she would even be allowed to visit the other woman was cruel, but she wasn't the only stubborn wolf in the room. She realized well that no amount of arguing on her part would change his mind. So she did not bother to try.

She turned away and saw her half-full cup of water on the table. She finished it before speaking. "I would like to explore the keep and the castle. Do I have your permission to do so?"

"I can think of a better way to pass the time between now and the nooning meal," he said in a voice filled with masculine promise.

Her pulse leapt in instant response, but she shook her head without deigning to glance his way. "Thank you, but I am in no mood to rut with you again. If it is all the same to you, I would rather see the rest of my new home."

"It is not all the same to me," he said gutturally and then turned her with implacable hands to face him. She had meant to irritate him, but she had not anticipated the fury that exploded from his green eyes and made his body go rigid with battle-ready hardness. "We did not rut last night."

"What would you call it? There is no love between us so it cannot be called lovemaking. It was no communion of souls. You claimed my body with yours. You marked me with your scent and your seed. We rutted," she said again, not understanding why she felt this need to push him so hard.

His hands dropped away from her shoulders as if he could not stand to touch her any longer. "Are you saying you knew something better with your first husband? Did you love the man your brother chose for you? Did he make you scream with ecstasy and cry for more?"

There was something more than anger in Drustan's eyes and she knew instinctively that she could hurt him with her answer. She should want to hurt him as he had hurt her with his lack of trust and lack of concern for her feelings, but she didn't. The simple knowledge that she *could* hurt him soothed some of the ragged edges inside of her.

But that did not make her anger at his cavalier treatment go away. "No. I was not in love with Sean, nor he with me, but he did not treat me like a dog to bring to heel either."

"I did not do that."

"You did. You implied I have to have your permission to see my friends. You criticized me in front of your mother. Sean never pretended to love me, but he would never have done that. He treated my concerns with respect and sought to alleviate my worries when he could." Those she had shared with him. They had not been close, but that was beside the point. "And he did not demand I ask his permission before taking a step I called my own either."

"You offended my mother."

"I offended *you*. *She* understood my worries even if her son is too cruel to do so. Do not lay your sins at your mother's door."

"I am not cruel."

"You would make me suffer your touch while my mind and heart are consumed with worry over my friend, rather than do something to alleviate that worry. But then what do my feelings matter? I am nothing more than a means to an end to you."

Drustan's expression turned colder than the winter moon. "I would not want you to *suffer* my touch. I will find Lachlan now and seek his permission on your behalf. That is apparently all you want from me."

He stormed out of their quarters before she had time to reply. Not that she knew what she would have said. She did want to check on Emily. Desperately.

But after he left and she felt herself breathing easier, she had to admit that she also wanted a chance to come to terms with her overwhelming response to Drustan. His lack of faith had hurt her, but the fact that she had secretly wanted to return to their bed almost as much as she had wanted to see to her friend's welfare, terrified her.

She did not want to love a man who had married her only as an act of vengeance and who cared nothing for her feelings.

Emily was contemplating testing the boundaries of her captivity by leaving her room when a knock sounded on the door. She rushed forward and pulled it open to find Cait on the other side. Wearing a Balmoral plaid and an expression of deep anxiety, she stood there alone.

Emily drew Cait into the room with a hand on her arm. "Are you all right? You look upset. Are you?"

"No."

"Good." Emily dragged Cait over to sit on the bed. "Lachlan said I would not see you today. I am so glad he was wrong. He was sure that as newlyweds you and Drustan would not venture forth from his quarters for a couple of days at least. Lachlan thinks he knows everything, have you noticed that? I suppose Drustan is similarly inclined. He is a Highlander, after all."

Cait nodded, her anxious expression having turned to one of bemusement.

"But even he can be incorrect in his assumptions, can't he? I mean to say Lachlan can be," Emily said with satisfaction as she took a seat beside Cait, very, very glad to see her friend and not just because she did not relish the absolute solitude of the tower room.

Some of the anxiety returned to Cait's velvety brown eyes. She looked very closely at Emily. "I was worried about you."

"I was worried about you, too." Emily studied Cait for evidence she had been through an ordeal, but could see no signs of it. "Tell me truly. How are you? Was it awful?"

"It?" Cait asked with a faint smile.

"The wedding night," Emily clarified with a roll of her eyes. As if her friend did not know what she had been referring to.

Cait glanced around her as if seeking answers to the question in the smooth stone walls of the round room. Her gaze seemed to be caught by the open door and she jumped up to close it before returning to sit beside Emily.

"Well?" Emily prompted when she still said nothing.

"Last night was the most amazing night of my life." There were sad undertones in Cait's voice totally at variance with such a statement.

"You do not sound happy about that." But Emily was feeling a great deal of relief on her friend's behalf.

"I'm not. It wasn't the same for him. I'm sure of it."

"He told you so?" Emily asked, scandalized that even an arrogant warrior would be insensitive enough to utter something so callous.

"No. Not in so many words, but he doesn't believe me that Susannah said she had permission to hunt on Sinclair land."

"Why would a woman go hunting alone? That is the chore of the soldiers certainly?" Everything was so different here and she really wasn't sure what this had to do with Drustan being as moved as Cait was by their intimacy.

Cait bit her lip, her expression pained. "It isn't usual, but she did have permission and she did do it. And because of that she ma—met Magnus and they ended up married. Only Drustan is still convinced Magnus came to the island and took Susannah."

"That's ridiculous. How is a lone soldier supposed to cross the sea and kidnap a woman without being detected? If Susannah was within the castle walls, she could not have been taken at all. Were they thinking she was taking a stroll on the beach and got kidnapped?"

"No. Oh, this is so hard."

"What?"

"Trying to explain."

"I'm sorry. I should not interrupt."

"No, it isn't that. It's just . . . you don't know everything."

"And you cannot tell me?" Emily asked, hurt that her friend did not feel she could trust her with the clan secrets.

"I wish I could."

"Do not concern yourself. Please, just tell me what you can."

"Well, you know I was taken in retaliation for what happened to Susannah. According to clan law, Magnus or my brother should have requested permission from either Lachlan or Drustan to keep Susannah in the Sinclair clan."

"And neither of them did."

"No. They felt the Balmoral clan had failed in their responsibility to protect her and therefore were not deserving of the courtesy."

"I see. Highlanders are very proud people are they not?"

"And the Chrechte even more so."

"Chrechte? I heard Lachlan call himself that. What does it mean? It is not a word I am familiar with."

Cait stared at her. "Lachlan said that . . . in front of you?"

"Yes. Didn't I just say so?"

"I'm surprised, but I suppose it wouldn't hurt for you to know some of our past. Until about one hundred years ago, there were a people in the Highlands that called themselves the Chrechte; the Romans called us the Picts."

"Us?"

"I am Chrechte as well."

"Oh. I remember hearing of the Picts. They had tattoos . . . like the ones on Lachlan's arm and back," she said as realization dawned. "Does Talorc have them, too?"

"Yes, but the band on his arm is different from the Balmoral's."

"Didn't the Picts have their own king until MacAlpin joined the clans from the Highlands and the Lowlands under one Scottish king?"

"Yes. When he declared himself king and used deception to murder the remaining royal Chrechte, our people were devastated. After much argument and discord, it was finally decided in a council that we would join the Celtic clans. Though it was over a century ago, the Chrechte have never forgotten MacAlpin's treachery."

"I see. So, even though the king that now rules Scotland did not perpetrate the original betrayal, the Chrechte do not submit to him fully."

"No Highlander would submit fully to any rule but that of the clan chief. The current king is more English than Scottish anyway. He'll turn Scotland into a Norman outpost if the people let him."

Emily wasn't bothered by Cait's feelings. She understood them. Scotland was not England and therefore should not have a king who tried so hard to emulate the English way of life. There were many in England who were similarly incensed over the way the English royal court so closely followed traditions established in France.

"I think I understand your brother's behavior better. I can imagine he was well and truly offended to have a king he only grudgingly serves dictate his choice of wife."

"Offended is a mild word for the way the whole clan felt."

"Except you."

Cait gave a tiny laugh. "Oh, I was offended too . . . until I met you. I liked you on sight, Emily."

Tears pricked her eyes and Emily blinked them away. She was being maudlin and it was silly. "I am glad. I liked you, too."

Cait squeezed her hand. "Even if you do not marry my brother, I will always consider you my sister."

One of the tears spilled over and Emily hastily wiped it

away after returning the affectionate gesture. "Thank you. I feel the same."

"Emily . . ."

"Yes?"

"I was worried about you for a reason."

"Because Lachlan had locked me in a tower? I appreciate your concern, but you should not worry. I am fine, as you can see, and the door is no longer even locked."

"Truthfully, that was only part of it." Cait paused and looked like she was trying to find words. "Moira said that Lachlan took you swimming this morning."

Emily smiled, remembering her triumph of almost floating alone. "Yes. It was wonderful. He is teaching me to swim so I will not fear the water any longer."

"He is?" Cait asked as if such a thing were too astounding to be believed. "So you won't be afraid?"

"Oh, yes. And he's a very patient teacher. You wouldn't think so by the way he acts the rest of the time, but he did not yell at me once."

"I see . . . I think." Cait frowned and sighed. "Actually, I don't understand anything."

"What do you mean?"

"His patience and the kindness in teaching you to swim . . . it doesn't fit with what I was thinking about him."

"What were you thinking?" Emily asked, not surprised Cait was confused by this side of Lachlan.

She was as well. The man could order the kidnapping of two innocent women to assuage his pride and then go out of his way to help her conquer a lifelong fear. She'd read of a creature who changed color with its surroundings and wondered if Lachlan wasn't a bit like that.

"Well, I do not believe Susannah lied. She is really too sweet to have done so," Cait said as if trying to convince Emily. "Besides, why would she lie? Unless she was afraid Magnus would think less of her otherwise. Yes, that is possible, maybe even probable. Only I had about convinced myself that Lachlan was the one who was lying, you see."

"What? Why would Lachlan lie?"

"Because he wants war with our clan and doesn't want his clan to blame him for starting it, so he sent Susannah off by herself and pretended outrage when the inevitable mating took place."

"I don't see how he could think a woman going off hunting was going to end up married."

"Trust me, in this case, he would have been certain."

"Hmm . . . Even if that is the case, you are attributing terribly devious thoughts to Lachlan and I don't think he's like that."

"You don't think he's capable of deception?"

"Not that exactly, but I think he's too arrogant to believe it's necessary. If he wanted to go to war with your clan, he'd declare war and be done with it. It would never occur to a man of his temperament that he needed to deceive his own people like that. My father's much like him, too arrogant by half."

"Really?" Cait asked, looking diverted.

"Oh, yes. I'm in this mess because of his arrogance. He likes to blame my stepmother because she made the suggestion, but he only does what he wants."

"What did he do?"

"The king issued a call for soldiers and my father sent the bare minimum under his lord and vassal agreement. His stinginess angered our king and in revenge, he decreed that Father had to send one of his daughters north to marry your brother."

"He believed that marriage to my brother was punishment?" Cait asked, outraged.

"Losing his daughter to a marriage that could not benefit him in any way was the punishment," Emily soothed. "A Highland laird is hardly likely to become a baron's ally, even if he is married to the baron's daughter."

"Oh, I see." Cait looked somewhat mollified. "You said one of his daughters. You have sisters?"

"Three. Two are my stepsisters and Margery, the baby, is my half sister. I also have two half brothers."

Cait frowned. "You have a stepmother?"

"Yes and she's annoying, but she would not betray my father like your and Talorc's stepmother betrayed your clan. Sybil loves my father, but it is a very jealous love."

"That must have been hard for you . . . living with her."

Emily nodded. "But I loved my sisters and brothers. Especially Abigail. She's the reason I cannot return to my father's house." And she explained her fear for her sister and why she had to stay to marry Talorc, no matter what she wanted.

"And do you want something else?" Cait asked when Emily was finished.

She felt herself blushing even though Cait had said nothing embarrassing.

The other woman smiled. "You are attracted to Lachlan."

"How did you know? Is it that obvious? I shouldn't be. He's rude and grumpy and impatient except when he's teaching me to swim. I wouldn't think my feelings for him were so easy to see." After all, more often than not she felt like strangling the man, but here Cait was saying she thought Emily was attracted to him.

Which she was, but still . . . it should not have been evident.

"You cannot learn to swim in a gown," Cait said dryly.

"Oh. Um, no, you can't."

"If he convinced you to take it off, he must have been very persuasive indeed."

"He was."

Cait was back to looking worried. "Talorc will not marry you if Lachlan has mated you."

"Lachlan said he would not breach my maidenhead."

"Oh, my." Cait fanned herself.

Emily straightened her shoulders. "I have determined to allow him to teach me to swim and . . . and other things if he is so inclined."

"The English and Highlanders are different. Talorc would have ripped my throat out for doing similar."

Emily shivered at the gruesome image. "My father would no doubt beat me, but he is not here and I am and when I am with Lachlan like that . . . I am happy. I want to taste happiness before I must submit to duty."

Cait eyes filled with understanding. "Do you love Lachlan?"

"I hope not."

Cait smiled ruefully. "I understand. It would hurt too much, would it not?"

"Yes," Emily whispered.

But then she thought Cait understood only too well. If her wedding night had been so special for her and she was convinced it had not been for Drustan, the pain of caring was already in her heart. Emily could only hope the Balmoral soldier would realize quickly what a treasure he had in Cait.

A peremptory knock sounded on the door and then it opened. Drustan stood in the opening, his expression void of emotion. "It is time to go down for the nooning meal."

"Is Emily to come, too?" Cait asked.

"Yes."

Relief brought a smile to Emily's face. So, she was free to leave her room. That was very good news. She would also see Lachlan. Her heart sped at the thought.

Lachlan was sitting in the center chair at a long table at the far end of the hall when Emily, Drustan and Cait walked in. All of the other places were taken at his table except for two to his right. No doubt who those were for: Drustan and Cait.

Emily looked around for a place to sit herself and saw an empty spot at the table where Angus sat. Ulf was also at that table, but that could not be helped. She would know at least one person.

She told Cait where she was going and why and started her way toward Angus's table. The soldier saw her when she'd drawn near and nodded in greeting. She nodded back and he bumped the man beside him, forcing him to move on the bench so the empty spot at the table was beside Angus.

Emily smiled her gratitude, but before she could sit down a strange look came over Angus's features and the blood drained from his face. Two of the other soldiers at the table looked up as well, their features expressing shock. All three of the soldiers looked toward Lachlan. He was scowling, which was nothing new really, but he hadn't been doing so when she first entered the great hall.

Angus jumped up from the bench. "I believe the laird wants you to sit at his table, Miss Emily."

"I'm sure you are wrong. There is no place for me at that table."

"I believe he has just instructed one of the soldiers to move to a different table."

She shook her head. "I'm sure you are mistaken."

"No. I am not. I just heard him."

"You couldn't possibly hear your laird over this din." There were at least seventy-five soldiers eating in the hall and the noise was enough to mask even a loudly spoken conversation.

Emily grabbed Angus's arm, so she could step over the bench to take her seat without falling.

The soldier went absolutely still. "Please, Miss Emily, do not touch me. I like my throat just the way it is."

Emily didn't understand Angus's comment about his throat, but she yanked her hand back from touching him. Had her action been considered forward? None of her father's soldiers would have thought so, but this was not her father's keep and these men bore little resemblance to English soldiers.

"I am sorry. I didn't mean—"

"The laird would like you to join him," Angus said urgently.

She couldn't understand what was wrong with the soldier, but she turned obligingly so she could see Lachlan again. Sure enough, the spot to his left *was* empty now and he crooked his finger at her. She stared, unsure what to do. His summons and the attention she was receiving from the others in the hall embarrassed her. Out of the corner of her eye, she noticed her friend looked worried again, but her gaze was not on Emily. It was on Lachlan. What had the laird done to upset Cait?

"Miss Emily?" Angus asked, sounding harried.

"Yes?"

"Would you like me to escort you to the laird's table?"

"That would be nice, thank you, Angus."

The soldier nodded and led the way, his movements jerky, like he was nervous. When they reached the head table, he left her standing beside Lachlan with a quick farewell.

Lachlan wasn't looking at her. He was talking to Drustan, so she scooted around both men to lean over and whisper in Cait's ear, "Are you all right? You're looking worried again."

"We'll talk about it later . . . in the tower room. But I think you had better sit down, Emily."

Emily did as her friend suggested and then was surprised to find Lachlan serving her. It was really very odd. Her father would never have served anyone but Sybil, even the most important guest and especially not a female one.

Emily could not figure out why Lachlan had made a point of having her sit beside him because he ignored her for most of the meal. She was too shy to speak to anyone at first, but the priest was seated across the table and he was quite friendly. She also found the soldier to her left very amiable and by the time she had eaten and drunk a single cup of wine, she was feeling much more comfortable and sharing in the conversation.

She leaned across the table, not wanting her voice overheard and said, "Father?"

"Yes?"

"I was wondering something about the marriage sacrament last evening."

"What was that, child?"

"Doesn't the Church stipulate that the Sacrament must be spoken in the morning?"

"That is Rome's tradition, yes."

"But you spoke it last *night*," she emphasized.

"That was my laird's will."

"But is it valid then?"

The priest looked at her as if she'd lost her mind. "You're wanting to know if the marriage ceremony I spoke last night was valid?" he asked, making no attempt to keep his voice down.

Conversation stilled around them and suddenly, Emily was the cynosure of all eyes. She felt heat climb into her face and fervently wished she'd kept her question for another time. But since she hadn't, she might as well brazen it out now.

"I am concerned for my friend's standing with God and the Church. Surely you can understand why. If her marriage Sacrament was not valid, neither is her marriage." She wished Lachlan had thought of that before commanding the holy man to do his duty in such an extraordinary way.

"I assure you the marriage is valid."

"Recognized by the Church?" Emily pressed.

"Yes."

"Oh." She still wasn't convinced.

"The marriage is valid," Lachlan said, speaking to her for the first time since she had sat down.

She frowned at him for his arrogance. "Are you implying that not only are you above the king when you feel like it, but the Pope as well?"

"Do you think to try to give my wife an excuse to run from me?" Drustan asked in a hard voice before his laird could answer her impudence.

Emily shook her head vehemently. "Oh, no. That would not be in her best interests after well . . . *after*. If you know what I mean. It is the *next day*, after all. I am merely concerned for her standing with the Church, but if the priest is not worried, then I realize I should not be either."

"The marriage Sacrament is no less holy spoken at night than in the morning," the priest hastily intervened. "There are dispensations for unusual circumstances to almost all of Rome's traditions."

"There are?"

"Especially here in the Highlands," Lachlan said in a mocking voice.

"Why especially here?"

"Because it was the king who chose to follow Rome's dictates, not the lairds."

"But the lairds must follow the dictates of their king." Even if they grudged him his place of power.

"Must we?"

"You speak treason."

"Nay, simple truth."

The others around them nodded their agreement. Even Cait. And Emily stifled the urge to argue further. The Highlanders saw the world differently and that was that.

One thing was certain. They all believed Cait to be well and truly married.

Thank goodness.

Chapter 13

After the nooning meal, Emily was unsure if she was expected to return to her tower, or not. Lachlan left before she had a chance to ask, which might have been for the best. Since he had not expressly ordered her to do so, she could tell him later—if the matter came up—that she had assumed his silence meant it was all right for her to stay in the great hall. She didn't plan to wreak any mayhem anyway, just find something to keep her occupied.

And really, *couldn't* she assume he meant to allow her the freedom since he had not expressly denied it to her? He was, after all, a man who did not mince his words.

"Emily, Drustan has said it would be all right for you and me to explore the castle grounds." Cait spoke from behind her and Emily spun to face her friend.

"Oh, that would be lovely. I've seen some of it, walking to the loch and all, but honestly my mind was too busy with other things to take it in."

And her courage had not quite extended to making such

an exploration on her own without express permission. She didn't want to end up locked in the tower again.

They started by touring the upper and lower bailey. There was a tanner's cottage, a blacksmith and an area where the women of the keep laundered, including a grove of lilac and heather bushes on which to dry the clothes so they would smell sweet. The stable was large, with over a dozen horses all as big as the ones they had ridden the day before.

The priest's cottage was behind the chapel and the two women stopped to chat briefly with him when they saw him sitting outside his door enjoying a little sun.

"Are you worried about the validity of your marriage, lass?" Father Paul asked Cait.

Cait smiled and shook her head.

"I am glad." He patted Emily's shoulder. "It is good to show such genuine caring for your friend's spiritual welfare. It gladdens my heart to see it."

Emily blushed under the praise. "It is no more than she would do for me, Father."

They declined his offer of refreshment and continued on their walk. When they had fully explored the upper and lower bailey, Cait asked Emily to show her the way to the loch. It wasn't within the castle walls, but when Cait explained they had Drustan's permission, the women were let through the gate onto the drawbridge.

The loch was only about a ten-minute walk from the castle and more cottages dotted the landscape along the path. They met several Balmoral clanswomen who seemed pleased to make the acquaintance of the new wife to the laird's first-in-command and her English friend. Some had also seen Emily pass by that morning with Lachlan and were curious about a woman he chose to spend time alone with.

"This clan is certainly friendlier than the Sinclairs," Emily remarked and then wished she'd kept her mouth shut. Her dear friend might be a Balmoral now, but she'd been born a Sinclair.

Cait sighed, her eyes sad. "My brother's clan would have welcomed you more readily under different circumstances. You must believe me on this, Emily."

"I do," Emily hastened to assure her. "I understand better since our chat this morning. I didn't mean to offend you with my remark."

"You didn't."

"Are you certain?"

Cait laughed. "Yes. The women did go out of their way to make you feel like an outsider and I am not so easily insulted, trust me."

"Your brother is. Imagine getting so testy over being likened to a goat," Emily teased.

"Well, it is better than a horse's backside."

They were both laughing when they came into the clearing beside the water.

"Oh, it is gorgeous here," Cait exclaimed.

Emily looked at the lake shimmering in the sun and could not believe she had gone out far enough for the water to reach Lachlan's chest and be over her head. The gift he had given her that morning was greater than any she had ever known. Lachlan could be harsh and he was certainly bossy, but he was also gentle and passionate with her. And he cared enough to help her. That made him a hero in her eyes, even if he was an arrogant one.

Thinking out loud, she said, "I have another swimming lesson tomorrow morning."

"With Lachlan?" Cait asked in a strange voice.

"Yes, who else?"

"But I'm sure you won't be alone. There will be other soldiers nearby."

"If there were this morning, I didn't notice them. He has really superior hearing and he heard his brother approaching before he ever broke the cover of trees."

"Still, I'm sure Lachlan had guards with you." There was a strange urgency in Cait's voice and Emily didn't understand it.

"No, really. I don't think so. He's so sure of himself, he probably doesn't think he needs guards. Especially on Balmoral land."

Cait made a sound of distress, her gazed focused on something across the lake.

Emily turned to look and saw a huge gray wolf. He was too far away to leap at them of course, being on the other side of the water, but the aura of menace around him was enough to make her shiver. He didn't have the boney look of a desperate, hungry animal though, and she doubted the wolf would try to harm them. They were shy creatures as long as they weren't hungry . . . or establishing territory.

"I'm married now," Cait was saying. "The wedding was last night . . . and the claiming."

"Yes, I know," Emily replied, thinking it an odd topic when they were facing down a wild animal.

"There has been a misunderstanding. Susannah did not have the laird's permission to hunt alone. Her brother insists she was taken from the Balmoral's island."

"So you've said." Cait touched her friend's arm. "Are you all right?"

"The Balmoral laird is looking for an apology."

The wolf shook his head at them and snarled, showing his sharp teeth. Emily jumped back even though a whole wide lake separated them.

"Please, I don't want war between our clans," Cait pleaded.

"Well, I don't either, but I don't know what you expect me to do about it."

The wolf turned and disappeared into the forest on the other side of the lake.

Emily turned to Cait. "That was a close call."

"Closer than you know." And tears were trailing down Cait's cheeks. "Emily, you must not come tomorrow morning for your swimming lesson."

"But I want to learn to swim now."

"It isn't safe."

"I would have agreed with you this morning, but Cait, Lachlan is helping me to conquer my fear."

"Please, Emily. *You must not come*."

Something very disturbing was happening with her friend. "Tell me why."

"I can't. Not here. Just accept that it isn't safe. I think Lachlan plans to seduce you."

"I already know what Lachlan wants to do with me, and I want it. I'm sorry if you don't understand, Cait. I don't mean to disappoint you. Your opinion matters to me very much. You are my only friend here and as dear to me as Abigail, but I want this little bit of happiness in my life. I need it. For all the lonely years ahead."

"Talorc will reject you if he believes Lachlan has mated you. Even if it isn't true."

"Talorc has already rejected me."

"He'll send you back to England in disgrace."

"He can't possibly know about my swimming lessons with Lachlan."

Cait did not reply, but started dragging Emily back toward the way they had come. She refused to answer any questions or slow down until they were inside Emily's tower room with the door firmly shut.

"You certainly move quickly for a pregnant woman," Emily said, panting herself from the exertion of climbing the stairs at a near run.

"Femwolves are like that."

"Fem . . . what?"

"There is something I have to tell you, Emily. So you will understand." Cait rounded on her, her expression desperate.

"So you can help me avoid a war and the death of my brother or Lachlan."

"What?"

"Do you remember when I told you about the Chrechte people?" Cait asked.

"Yes, of course. It was only this morning. I'm English, not forgetful."

Her jest fell flat as Cait's agitation only seemed to grow. "You are also human and I am not. Not fully."

Concern for her friend had Emily standing and pushing her to sit on the bed. "You are distraught. It has been an eventful time for you and you are pregnant. Let me get you a cup of water to help clear your mind."

"My mind is already clear. Believe me, Emily. *You've got to believe me,*" Cait said with a wild look in her eye. "Sit down and listen. *Please.*"

Emily could not ignore her friend's plea and she sat.

"The Chrechte are shape-changers."

"Shape-changers?" Emily asked faintly.

"They have more than one form, both animal and human."

Oh, no. Last night had been an ordeal and it had broken her friend, only Emily had been too blind to see it. She stared at Cait, unsure what to say to help. If anything.

"Have you ever heard stories of werewolves?" Cait demanded.

"Yes," Emily whispered, her heart breaking.

She could not stand to see her friend like this and in that moment, if either Lachlan or Drustan had been there, she would have attacked them with her eating knife. They had done this to Cait. Damn their vengeance-loving natures.

"That's what the Chrechte are, a race of werewolves and femwolves. That gray wolf we saw beside the water was my brother Talorc." Oblivious to Emily's tormented thoughts, Cait continued in an urgent tone that pleaded for belief. And even though she knew it was all fantasy, Emily almost did believe, Cait was so earnest. "Some wolves cannot control the change like that until they are mated, but he has been able to since his first full moon in wolf form. I have, too. Our mother was a white wolf and she passed the ability on to us."

"White wolves can control their change?" she asked for lack of anything better to say while her mind tumbled with thoughts of how to react to Cait's words.

"Yes."

"I see."

Cait clenched her hands into fists, her face contorted with despair. "You don't believe me, do you?"

Emily's eyes filled with tears as she shook her head. "How can I? You are talking about children's fairy tales, not reality. Please, Cait, stop and think. What you are saying is impossible."

Cait shook her head. "It isn't. Please, don't cry, Emily. I have proof."

"Proof?"

"Yes. I can't make the change right now because I'm pregnant, but I want you to think about some things."

"All right."

"Remember in the forest yesterday, when I heard things you couldn't and how Lachlan heard the approaching soldier earlier today when you couldn't?"

"Yes."

"That is a werewolf trait."

"Superior hearing?" No, it couldn't be, but in both cases they *had* heard things she hadn't and she knew her hearing was good.

Only, was she trying to believe the unfathomable because the alternative, that her friend had gone daft, was too untenable to accept?

"That isn't all," Cait said sincerely. "We are stronger and faster than humans, too."

Without warning, Cait surged from the bed. Emily

blinked, saw a blur of movement, and then the other woman was on the far side of the room.

"Do you see?" Cait demanded.

Emily shook her head. It couldn't be true, but hadn't Lachlan played this trick, too? And according to both Lachlan and Cait, he was Chrechte. It was too much to take in. Perhaps she was the one going daft.

Cait did it again and she was in front of the entrance to the garderobe without Emily seeing how she got there excerpt for a blur of color shifting across the room. She rubbed her eyes.

Cait laughed, the sound lacking any real amusement. "You are not seeing things. We move that quickly. I'm not supposed to be running like this right now. It upsets Drustan. He thinks I could hurt the babe if I fell."

"Could you?" Emily asked stupidly, her mind refusing to take in the evidence of what her eyes had seen.

"Yes, I suppose. If I fell, but I don't plan to fall." Cait came back over to Emily and sat down again, taking Emily's arm in a near bruising grip. "*You've got to believe me*. That wolf we saw *was* Talorc. Didn't you see him shake his head when I told him Lachlan wanted an apology? He didn't like hearing that. But he heard everything else we said, too. He heard about Lachlan's plan to take you swimming in the morning. Alone. You can't go, Emily. Talorc will challenge Lachlan and then one of them will end up dead."

"How can Talorc be on the island without Lachlan knowing?"

"He swam over in his wolf form and he's good at masking his scent. Far better than I ever suspected and much better than I am at it."

"This is impossible," she said again, but part of her was starting to believe. No matter how unlikely it all seemed, she had seen or heard so many inexplicable things since coming to the Highlands and these strange claims Cait made would explain most of them.

"I know it seems that way, but it's not. Chrechte have been around as long as every other race of humanity, but we have always kept ourselves hidden."

"Why? And how could MacAlpin have betrayed the Picts . . . Chrechte I mean, if they are stronger than normal humans?"

"Strength isn't everything. MacAlpin was of the Chrechte, but not a shape-changer. It happens sometimes when a human mates with a shape-changer. His mother was a femwolf, but his father was a Scott. He had the animal cunning, but not all the other traits of the Chrechte. He also had werewolves on his side, those that were willing to betray their people for the power he represented. For hundreds of years, war was the only life we knew, but it took its toll on our numbers. MacAlpin's betrayal decimated what was left of the Chrechte. When we became part of the Celtic clans, we were protecting the future of our people. It was our only hope."

"But you're saying not all the clans have werewolves among them?"

"No. Not even close. Our numbers have risen, but less than one in ten clansmen are Chrechte. When a pack *does* exist within a clan, you can be assured the laird is Chrechte. We do not tolerate being led by any other."

"This is all so fantastic." But the sheer scope of Cait's story made it more credible somehow.

"You've got to believe me." Cait dropped to her knees in front of Emily, that Chrechte pride she'd spoken of earlier humbled and that was as convincing to Emily as anything Cait had said so far. "I'm begging you. You have to keep the Balmoral away from the lake tomorrow."

"I can't," Emily whispered, feeling like the worst friend in the world. "I tried today and he wouldn't take no for an answer. He's incredibly arrogant and very good at getting his own way."

"But you must." Cait pounded the thresh-covered floor

with her fist. "I know you can do it, Emily. He wants you. He staked his claim on you. That has to mean something. He'll listen to you. He has to," she said frantically.

"Come, sit back on the bed. This upset cannot be good for the baby," Emily said, tugging Cait off of her knees. "You must regain your composure."

"I know you are right, but I'm so frightened, Emily. I love my brother. I do not want war between my new clan and my birth clan."

"Neither do I." Emily bit her lip, trying to think, but it was hard with so many new ideas vying for attention in her mind. "You said Lachlan staked his claim. What did you mean?"

"He did it at the nooning meal. He growled. You couldn't hear it. The pitch was set for the werewolves of the pack. For Angus because you were touching him. And then Lachlan insisted you sit beside him at the table. You cannot think that is normal for a captive and a laird."

"I thought it was a Highland idiosyncrasy," Emily admitted. She'd dismissed many things as unique to Highlanders when in fact they might well be related to the fantastical tale Cait had told her.

Cait shook her head.

"I don't understand this claiming. He ignored me all the way through the meal."

"I do not think he is happy about wanting you, but he has made it clear no other wolf is to have you."

"Because I'm promised to Talorc?"

"That wouldn't matter if he meant to keep you."

"But he doesn't."

"No. I don't think he does."

Emily knew he didn't. "He promised that no other soldier could keep me. Maybe this growling business was his way of making sure the others knew that."

Cait shook her head. "All he would have to do is to

decree it and none of his soldiers would dare defy him. A clan chief stays chief by being stronger than all the other warriors and they know it."

"I don't understand."

"I don't either entirely," Cait said, sounding calm for the first time since they'd seen the wolf across the lake. "The Balmoral pack does things differently than what I am used to. For example, a physical mating does not bring with it a lifetime commitment unless pregnancy results."

"Can I get pregnant by him?"

"If you are true-mated, yes."

"What does that mean?"

"When a shape-changer and a human mate, if they are true or sacred mates, they can sometimes hear each others' voices in their heads and the union will result in children."

They could hear voices in their heads? She had heard of magicians claiming such a thing, but Sybil had always dismissed them as charlatans. Though Emily supposed the ability to hear someone's voice in her head was no more incredible than the idea that humans really could turn into wolves. "What about werewolves?"

"If a werewolf and a femwolf mate when she is in heat, there is almost always a pregnancy. In fact, I've never heard of a time that did not happen. The problem is that femwolves do not go into heat very often and we are independent by nature. Before joining the clans, Chrechte females would sometimes go their whole lives without mating."

That was interesting. No wonder the Chrechte had found it so hard to survive. "But werewolves do not have to be true-mated to make babies?"

"No, but they can be and if they are, they can mind-speak, too. They also suffer the other consequence of a true-mating."

"What is that?"

"When the Chrechte find their true mate, they are incapable of mating with anyone else until the death of that mate."

"Incapable?"

"Yes, you know . . ." Cait bit her lip and then continued in almost a whisper, "The males cannot achieve erection with anyone but their true mate and a femwolf 's body will not accept penetration from anyone else either."

"What about the human in a true-mating?"

"They are human. They can mindspeak, but as for the other, I don't think they are so limited, but I cannot be entirely sure. I never asked my mother when she explained about the bond between true mates."

"I don't believe this." But even as she said the words, she realized they weren't entirely true. Cait's claims were becoming more and more plausible by the minute.

"Mindspeak is strange," Cait said as if that were the only element of this conversation that was even slightly odd. "I've never experienced it myself. My parents were not true-mated either. I have heard of family members that could hear each other, too, but I cannot hear Talorc and he cannot hear me. I couldn't even smell his scent until he unmasked it briefly at the loch. He was giving me a message."

"That he is here to save you?"

"Not me. He respects the laws of mating too much to dismiss Drustan's claim on me, but he could be scouting for war, though his actions do not suggest that at least. I think he wants my bairn. Another Chrechte warrior for his clan."

"But that is barbaric. He cannot take your baby away from you."

"Not until it is born, no."

"Even then."

"I do not know what will happen then. I cannot bear to give up the babe. I love it already, but he may well go to war over the child even if he does not over our kidnapping."

"What if it is a girl, will he be less insistent on her return to the Sinclairs?"

"No, women are prized for their ability to have more Chrechte warriors and men for their ability to fight."

"It's the same with humans." Goodness, was she really ready to accept this fantastic tale?

Cait seemed so serious, so very certain of her facts. If she wasn't telling the truth, she was doing an admirable job of acting sane and honest.

"To an extent, yes," Cait agreed sadly.

"What are we going to do?"

"I don't know, but I don't want either laird killed."

"Do you think Talorc was there earlier this morning?" The thought that the Sinclair laird had seen her naked with Lachlan sent waves of revulsion and mortification rolling over Emily.

"He may have been. He would have waited to challenge Lachlan until he knew where I was and what had happened to me."

"Now he knows."

"Yes."

"Are you sure he will come to the lake tomorrow morning?"

"No, but it's highly likely. If he can kill the Balmoral, the clan would think twice about keeping my babe for its own."

"That is brutal."

"It is the way of life here."

Emily shivered. "Why does it have to be so hard?"

Cait sighed, but didn't answer.

Emily bit her lip and thought furiously. "Maybe I could keep Lachlan from the water by offering myself to him."

Cait shook her head. "Oh, no. You cannot do that. I know I said to use his desire for you, but it is not fair to you. It was very wrong of me to suggest it."

"You don't understand. I want his desire. I've spent my whole life living in the shadows of my father's new family.

When I'm with Lachlan I feel like I'm in the sun. It won't last. I know it. It can't, for so many reasons, but I want to experience as much of this newfound passion as I can. Do you think I am terrible for feeling that way?"

"No. I think you are brave, but Lachlan could marry you, if he wanted to."

"According to what you said, there would be the risk of my not having children. No man would embrace such a future willingly, but most especially not a laird."

Cait nodded sadly. "I think you are right. Many Chrechte discourage human matings because of that very thing and the possibility of having human offspring instead of shape-changers."

"You mean that can happen?"

"Yes. Lachlan's mother must have been human because Ulf is."

"Ulf isn't Chrechte?"

"He has no wolf. I'm certain of it."

"Oh, but how can you be sure it was their mother that was human?"

"Because their father was laird and he would not have been if he had been human."

"So no clans with Chrechte have human lairds at all?"

"None that I know of. It's possible I suppose, but I cannot imagine it."

Emily didn't know what to think. "Will you go to the lake and try to talk to Talorc tomorrow?"

"No. I can't be sure why he is here. Maybe he's only checking on me, but I'm afraid he would take me back until he receives a formal request for my hand or the babe is born and then the Balmoral would declare war. Maybe Talorc wants to declare war. Maybe he won't respect the mating bond in this instance. I just don't know." Cait sounded increasingly distressed with each possibility she listed off. "I should not withhold news of his presence from Drustan, but I cannot betray my brother—especially when I am not sure of his motives."

Emily understood Cait's dilemma and sympathized. "If I can keep Lachlan from the lake tomorrow then you have nothing to worry about. Your small deception will hurt no one."

"Do you think that is true?"

"Yes."

"Does this mean you believe me now?"

"I'm not sure," Emily admitted honestly, "but it's impossible to dismiss all that you have said and I believe you believe it. Which is halfway to believing it myself, really." She sighed. "I know you are frightened and I want to do whatever I can to hold that fear at bay."

Cait's eyes filled with tears. "Thank you."

"I will do everything I can to keep Lachlan away from the lake tomorrow."

Cait nodded. "There is one thing."

"What is that?"

"Please do not let anyone know you are aware of the Chrechte's true natures."

"Why?"

"Few humans within the clans know and those that do, guard the secret with their lives. If they betray it, the punishment is death."

Emily felt her face leach of color. "I see," she said faintly.

"As your betrothed, Talorc had the right to tell you, but I did not."

"You mean you could be killed for telling me?"

Cait grasped her hand and squeezed it. "I do not think it would come to that since you are betrothed to Talorc."

"But you are not certain. You risked your life to tell me this."

"I did not know what else to do."

"I will not betray you, Cait."

Her friend gave her a tremulous smile. "I know."

Cait left a short time later after a servant had come to tell her that her husband wished her return to their quarters.

Chapter 14

Emily's thoughts buzzed inside her head like a hive of bees upset by someone trying to harvest the honey.

There were so many of them that she could not make sense of even one. Images and words tumbled together in an incomprehensible mass more daunting than her first Latin primer. She wished she had the abbess here to help her decipher her current situation as she had helped Emily understand the language of the Church.

The stone walls of her room felt like they were closing in on her and she jumped to her feet. She needed to get out of the keep, to breathe some fresh air. Her thoughts began to settle as she was forced to focus on her step so she did not trip climbing down the circular stairs.

Of all things, the first real image she could hold on to was that of the monster werewolves her father's housekeeper had told her about so many nights beside the kitchen fire. The Scotswoman had used words to draw the monsters in vivid detail for her audience until some nights, Emily had dreamed about them. And when she was small, she could remember wishing she could be as powerful as the fabled creatures so she would not be so afraid anymore.

Not of water. Not of her papa. Not of Sybil's disapproval. Not of the monster Death, which had claimed her beloved mama. Not of anything.

But she had never in her wildest fantasies dreamed she would ever meet someone who claimed to be one. Only Cait claimed to be a *femwolf*. She said that Lachlan was a *werewolf*. The small hairs on the back of Emily's neck rose and goose bumps chased themselves up and down her arms at the thought.

She found exquisite pleasure in his kisses and craved more of his touch, but if Cait's claims were true . . . Emily wanted the caresses of an animal. Did that make her depraved? But he wasn't an animal . . . not wholly. He was a man who could take animal form. That was not the same, *was it?* Cait did not act like an animal; she acted like a woman and Emily was sure her friend was not depraved, but she obviously was content in her marriage bed. Of course, she was part animal, too.

On another burst of confusion, Emily reached the bottom of the stairs. She was happy to discover the door leading to the outside was not closed. It was heavy and when she had tried to open it earlier today, Cait had gently pushed her aside to do it herself. Emily had surmised at the time that there was a trick to it that she did not know. Now she had to wonder if the door had been easier for her friend because of Cait's femwolf strength.

With that disturbing thought, Emily nodded at a group of soldiers coming up the steps. She peered intently at them, trying to guess which were werewolves and which were human. She couldn't see any discernible differences. Was there a way to tell? How had Cait determined that Ulf was human? The soldiers gave her some odd looks as they passed and she had to fight a blush as she realized it looked as if she were ogling them.

Sybil would have pitched a fit if Emily had done anything of the sort to her father's soldiers.

She averted her eyes, but was soon studying everyone around her with more than her usual interest again. Cait had said that only a small portion of the clan were shapechangers, but Emily didn't see any way of telling who was and who wasn't. Did that mean they were all human? Even if that was the most logical conclusion, Emily was far from convinced it was the case.

Lachlan had said so many things that implied he saw himself as more than human and if he was a werewolf, that made sense. He was naturally arrogant, but even so . . . his attitude and actions did seem to imply it was more than the mere conceit of the powerful leader a clan. Hadn't he referred to his beast within more than once? Plus, his sense of hearing was astounding. To say nothing of his sense of smell.

She stopped and chatted with some children playing near the kitchens. Try as she might, she could see no differences between the children. They were all curious about England though, and were delighted she spoke Gaelic.

"So, are there monsters in England who eat bad children?" a tiny girl asked.

Emily laughed. "I believe some parents tell their children this, but I've never seen one."

"Were you bad as a child?" a little boy asked.

"Not usually."

"Then, you wouldn't have seen them, would you?" he asked with irrefutable child's logic.

"Our cook's son was certainly bad. He liked to jump out of dark corners and scare people, especially children smaller than he was. He never got eaten by a monster."

"Maybe the cook made something else for the monster to eat."

Emily laughed. "Are there monsters here in the Highlands?"

The little girl wrinkled her nose. "I think there are giant serpents in the lochs, but Mum says there aren't. She says I shouldn't be afraid to bathe because I might get eaten."

Emily dropped to her haunches and cupped the wee girl's cheek. "I think your mother is right."

"We've got lots of wild animals and they're scary as monsters," one boy boasted.

"Aye. Our wolves are bigger than any you'll find elsewhere and the wild boars can kill even a warrior with their big tusks."

Emily gave an exaggerated shiver. "I shall avoid them at all possible costs then."

The children laughed and one of the boys said, "You don't need to worry, English lady, our warriors protect the clan and no one can beat a Balmoral warrior."

"You'll be one someday, won't you?" she asked with a smile.

The boy nodded self-importantly. "I won't never let no serpent eat my little sister."

The small girl who had first voiced that fear looked on with awe and adoration and Emily could not hide her own smile in response. "I'm sure you won't."

"I still say there are monsters in England. They don't have any Chrechte to slay them."

"Chrechte?" Emily asked, her breath stilling in her chest.

"Our fiercest warriors."

"My dad's a fine warrior and he's not Chrechte," another boy said.

It looked like a fight would break out and Emily intervened. "I'm sure both your fathers are fierce."

The Chrechte boy nodded, but there was an expression in his eyes that said he knew something the others didn't. Maybe it was all her imagination, but it seemed to Emily that he carried himself with an arrogance a lot like Lachlan's.

Her mind whirled as the children went back to their play. Their certainty that a creature did not have to be seen to exist reminded her that many things in life had to be taken on faith. She'd never seen the king in person, but she knew he was a real man. Because her father and others had seen him and told her. She'd never seen God, but she didn't doubt his existence. She crossed herself quickly.

No, she knew her Maker was real. She knew her king was real and she knew her mother waited in Heaven to be reunited with her one day. Cait had told Emily that werewolves were real and she could accept that on faith, or continue to doubt until she had irrefutable proof. She had some evidence already, if she chose to interpret the odd behavior of the Highlanders in a certain way.

Was her trust in her dear friend enough to convince her of an impossible truth?

Not certain of her answer, she went into the kitchens and asked if she could help with anything, only to be shooed out again, but not until Emily had made the acquaintance of the other women who helped with the cooking. They were not overly friendly, but they were not unkind either and they seemed pleased she'd made the effort to learn their names and compliment them on the nooning meal.

She saw the priest from a distance when she came out, but he did not notice her. She wanted to ask him if there were werewolves in the clan. She was sure he knew, but she could not risk exposing Cait to censure. The possibility that sharing the clan's secrets had put the Scotswoman at risk made Emily's stomach cramp with worry.

She could not stand the prospect of something bad happening to her friend. Which must be how Cait felt about her brother. The truth was that while he was surly, he was probably no more annoyingly arrogant than Lachlan. Only she had not felt the strange erotic feelings toward Talorc that she did with the Balmoral laird. Cait loved Talorc, though, and must be beside herself with worry over his fate.

Whatever her doubts regarding the werewolves of the clan, Emily must keep her promise to do all she could to prevent Lachlan from going to the lake the following day.

With that thought firmly in mind, she helped some children get water from the well in the lower bailey before going back to the keep with the intention of tidying herself before the evening meal.

Cait sat on one of the benches, brushing her hair and waiting for Drustan's return to their chambers.

She had thought when he had requested her presence earlier that he might have intended to make love again. Now that she knew Emily was relatively safe and unharmed, she had not been averse to the idea. She had craved the closeness they shared the night before, especially in the face of her knowledge that Talorc was nearby and possibly intent on wreaking havoc.

Only she had arrived to find a coldly implacable husband and the housekeeper waiting for her. He had informed Cait that her new duties were to include overseeing the running of the household in the keep since the laird had no wife. He then introduced her to the housekeeper and left.

Marta had given Cait a tour of the keep from tower to cellar. It was more than twice the size of her brother's keep, which she found disconcerting. Not only did over two dozen soldiers have their quarters in the barracks below her and Drustan's rooms, but the housekeeper and her husband and their two children lived in quarters off the great hall. The laird's quarters were above the great hall along with a solar that the voluble Marta informed Cait was never used. Not since the laird's mother's day.

An image had risen in Cait's mind of Emily and her in the solar, surrounded by children. It had seemed so real, she'd had to blink her eyes to dispel it before attending to what Marta had been saying. But the image had come back to haunt her again and again and she could not stop herself from wondering if God had brought Emily to the Highlands, not for her brother . . . but for the Balmoral laird.

It was probably just wishful thinking, but she'd dreamed of it when she laid down for a rest after the housekeeper left Cait once again in her own quarters. She'd gotten very little sleep the night before and her pregnancy dictated she required more rest than usual anyway. She'd woken a while ago, both disturbed and intrigued by her dreams.

Drustan had still not returned.

Emily had remarked that Lachlan had said that he did not expect to see Drustan for a couple of days, which meant her husband had been released from his duties for that much time at least in celebration of their marriage. Apparently, he had decided after the lack of enthusiasm she had shown for remaining in his company that such a dismissal of his duties was unnecessary. Why that truth should make her teary-eyed she could not imagine, but she did her best to think of something else.

Goodness knew she had enough worries to occupy her mind. Not least of which was the fact that she had told a human the clan's secrets without asking her laird's permission. Should she tell Lachlan what she had done? If it were Talorc, she would, no matter how much she knew he might bellow. But she trusted her brother. She had yet to feel the same confidence in her new laird.

But should she tell Drustan anyway? If she did, he would no doubt tell his laird. Should she inform her husband about her brother at least? Her heart twisted at the prospect. Loyalty to her new clan dictated she do that very thing, but she couldn't. If she exposed Talorc's presence on the island, the pack warriors would go looking for him. If they found him on Balmoral land, they would kill him.

And if she did tell Drustan about her revelations to Emily, Cait would have to lie about why she had done it.

Was lying worse than withholding information? She didn't want to do either with her new husband and yet she felt she had no choice.

She was so intent on her chaotic thoughts that the first inkling she had of Drustan's presence was when her eyes focused enough to take in the fact that he was standing right in front of her.

She jumped with shock and her gaze flew to his. "Oh. You have returned."

He put his hands on her shoulders, his thumbs brushing her collarbones, his darkish red brows drawn together in concern. Green eyes probed her like fingers dipping into her soul. "Are you all right?"

"I'm fine," she rushed out, terrified he could somehow read her thoughts. "Why would you think otherwise?"

"You did not hear me enter."

"How do you know?"

His mouth twisted mockingly, but he did not answer. Of course it was obvious she had not heard him enter. She'd acted like a scalded cat when she realized he was in front of her. Little surprise he asked if anything was the matter. He had not read her mind, not that he could. Even if they were true mates, mindspeak did not include being able to see into the other person's thoughts, only an ability to hear them when they directed those thoughts at you.

And she and Drustan were not true-mated regardless. She was his vengeance wife. No more.

"I . . ." Her voice trailed off to nothing when she noticed a bloody gash on his chest, a bruise on his arm and dirt smudges on the rest of him. She jumped to her feet, knocking his hands from her shoulders. "What happened? Was there a fight?"

Had they found Talorc? Her throat closed tight as terror clenched at her insides.

Puzzlement creased his features, as if he could not

understand her reaction to such minor wounds. "I was practicing with the soldiers."

"Oh." Relief flooded her, quickly followed by concern. "I will get a damp cloth and cleanse your wounds."

"Wound. There is only one cut, but you can wash the rest of me if you feel the need." The sexy intonation in his voice sent her nerves rioting.

His teasing and concern were a huge improvement over his coldness earlier.

She scooted around him to cross the room to the fresh pitcher of water. She was clumsy getting the cloth wet, sloshing water onto the table as she poured it into the large basin. "I would be happy to wash you . . . if you like."

"Would you? Is it perhaps less onerous to suffer touching me than to suffer my touch?"

She gasped and swung around to face him. No expression showed on his face, but his eyes were alive with something that made her melt deep down inside.

Her gaze locked with his. "I did not mean to imply this morning that I did not enjoy your touch."

"You did not imply anything. You said it outright." Crossing his arms over the bulging muscles of his chest, he leaned back against the wall, his stance relaxed.

"But I did not mean it that way."

One brow rose in lazy query. "What other way could you mean it?"

She crossed the room to stand in front of him and wiped at a smear of dirt on one of his cheeks. Her body reacted instantly to his nearness, but she continued what she was doing. "I was worried about my friend and hurt that you did not care how worried I was, that you were more interested in finding pleasure in my body than helping me to allay my fears."

"You consider it my responsibility to allay your fears?"

"When you can . . . yes." She bit her lip as she dabbed

at the cut on his chest. It was not deep and the blood had already dried.

"Was Sean so considerate of your feelings?"

"I rarely shared my fears with him. The situation did not arise."

"Do you mean to tell me that this paragon of husbandly virtue and you were not as close as you implied this morning?"

"No."

"So you were not true-mated?"

She finished cleaning his chest and began wiping at the dirt on his arms. "No."

"Odd. I got the impression this morning that he was an impossible ideal to live up to."

"You are a Balmoral wolf. You do not believe that of any man."

"Don't I?"

She laughed, the sound husky and constrained from the feelings rioting through her as she touched his body with what should have been pure innocence. "No, you don't. You are even more arrogant than my brother."

He uncrossed his arms and settled his hands on her waist. "Is that a complaint?"

She licked her lips, her hand stilling in its task. "No."

"I did not intend to embarrass you in front of my mother."

"I know our marriage came about because of unusual circumstances, but it is still a marriage and it is important to me that she likes me."

"She already thinks you are wonderful."

Cait was not sure that was true, but it was kind of him to say. "Thank you."

"You were hurt when I said I wanted to go back to bed this morning?"

"Yes."

"I did not dismiss your worries. I told you that Lachlan would not harm the Englishwoman."

And he had expected her to believe him without a further word on the subject. She sighed. "I needed more. I needed to see her, to assure myself that was the case."

"And when you saw her, was Emily well?"

"Yes. Very well. Lachlan is truly teaching her to swim."

"Your fears were groundless. You should have trusted me."

"How could I know that?"

"I am your husband."

"What does that signify? I do not mean anything to you . . . not personally. I am just a means to an end. Your laird wanted vengeance for a perceived insult and keeping me was the way he chose to get it." She tried to tug away from Drustan's hold, but he would not let her go.

"I am the one keeping you and I have as much right to vengeance on the Sinclairs as Lachlan does."

"Which makes you my captor, not my husband, and I am nothing more than *your* instrument of revenge as well as the laird's."

"I am your husband," Drustan grated down at her.

She sighed, knowing he spoke the truth. For better or for worse, he was the man she would be mated to for a lifetime. "Yes, you are my husband. By the laws of the Church," she couldn't resist adding on.

"By your own vow and admission last night."

She refused to acknowledge that thrust. "But I am not someone you care for, am I?"

"Do you want me to care for you?"

"What woman wouldn't? I am your wife, after all. We have many years ahead to be together."

"You did not confide in Sean, but did he care for you?"

She really did not know. If he had, he had never said so. "He was considerate of me."

"And I am not?"

"You dismissed my concerns for Emily as if they did not matter."

"I told you they were groundless. Even knowing that, I agreed to speak with Lachlan at the nooning meal when I had at first planned not to leave our quarters until tomorrow at the earliest. That is not dismissing your concerns."

"But—"

"You have no patience."

"I was afraid for Emily, can't you understand that?"

"If you trusted me, you would have no fear."

"How can I trust you?"

"I am your husband," he repeated, as if that single fact alone should set all her fears at rest.

"Because of vengeance."

"Does it matter why we married? You are now my wife. Not some woman who warms my bed when the occasion suits me. You will bear my children and be my companion into our old age."

"I want to trust you," she admitted. It would be so much easier if she could be certain her feelings and desires mattered to him, that he would act in her best interests.

"Then do."

"It is not that easy."

"It is if you let it be."

"You may end up killing my brother."

"Only if he declares war or tries to take you from me."

Which was no comfort at all. Both circumstances were all too likely. "What about my baby?"

One of Drustan's hands slid around to her stomach and settled possessively over the babe. "What about it?"

"Talorc will want it for the Sinclairs."

Drustan's face twisted with disgust. "It is wrong to separate a mother from her child."

"He won't care." She loved her brother, but Talorc could be single-minded to the point of pain at times. "Sean was Chrechte, the baby will be Chrechte."

"I will not let Talorc take the bairn."

She was equally comforted and frightened by the promise. "I don't want war."

"It is the way of our people."

"And we almost died out because of it. It is not the right way, Drustan."

"Would you have me dismiss an insult? Would you prefer I gave the babe over to your brother? Will you only be content when the Balmorals are crushed under the Sinclairs' heels?"

"No!"

Then what do you bloody want, damn it?

Cait heard the words in a shout loud enough to fell a pine tree, but Drustan's lips had not moved.

Did you just speak in my mind? she asked with her thoughts directed at him.

His green eyes widened and then narrowed. *Not intentionally. What did you hear?*

"I heard you yell, *Then what do you bloody want, damn it?*" she said out loud. "Only it was inside my head."

His hand lifted to touch her face almost reverently. "We are true-mated."

Cait shook her head, unable to believe it. They could not be true mates. Not after only one night . . . not when their marriage had been the result of his desire for revenge against her former clan. Cold gripped her and she shivered, feeling woozy. The room grew very dark and Drustan's face swam before her eyes.

She woke lying on their bed with Drustan leaning over her.

He smiled, but his gaze was narrowed with concern. "I do not believe I have heard of a femwolf fainting from the news her husband was her sacred mate before."

Her heart squeezed at the ancient term. "But . . . isn't it impossible?" It had to be impossible.

"Why? Because you are a Sinclair and I am a Balmoral? We are both Chrechte."

She'd always thought that being a true mate would include loving her mate. Did it? Her feelings where he was concerned confused her. And what about him . . . did Drustan feel more than lust for her? He said he wanted her trust. Was that mere male posturing, or an expression of a deeper need he had not yet put into words? Or was true-mating as basic as going into heat? A very physical thing that she had always believed was more than physical.

"I don't know," she said finally.

"You were not true-mated with Sean." He sounded very pleased by that fact.

"No, of course not. I already told you, but how could I be and be true-mated to you anyway?"

He brushed her hair back from her face. "I have heard of Chrechte being blessed with more than one true mate in their lifetime."

"Is it a blessing . . . for you?"

"Yes. No matter why we mated, I want our marriage to be strong. I want you to be happy, Cait."

"You do?" Had Sean wanted her to be happy? She'd always had the impression that her brother's gratification was more important than her own to her first husband.

"Yes."

"Oh. That's nice."

Drustan smiled. "You are still a little befuddled by your faint, aren't you? It must be a pregnancy thing."

"I suppose."

"What about me?"

"What about you?"

"Do you want me to be happy, too?"

His happiness should not matter to her. She had not wed him by choice or by duty, but because of coercion. That was why she found it so peculiar that he wanted her to be content in their marriage. Her feelings did matter to him, if only just a little, but she did not understand why.

Unless it was his duty as a husband prompting him to be solicitous.

Regardless of why he felt as he did, she, too, cared if he was satisfied with her as his mate. Very much. "Yes, I want you to be happy."

"Then we will be."

"I will not be happy if you kill my brother," she warned.

His glare was ferocious enough to make her flinch. "Do not try to use our bond to manipulate me. I will do what I must do as a warrior."

"So, you lied?" she asked, trying to get away from the circle of his arms without success. "You only want me to be happy if it means you doing what you want?"

"A warrior does not always have the luxury of doing what he wants . . . he does what he must."

"But if you would just talk to Talorc, instead of fighting him . . . you would find out that there is no reason for war between our clans."

"I do not think he would agree."

"The babe is not born yet. God willing, we will have arrived at an agreement that will not tear my heart out before that, but that is not the immediate issue."

Drustan sighed and rolled onto his back. "Lachlan would never have given Susannah leave to hunt alone and my sister would not lie. Ever."

Perversely, she missed his surrounding warmth, but the implication of his words was even more chilling. "So, you are saying I am lying?" *I'm not,* she cried into his mind.

He rolled back toward her and pulled her close. "I do not wish to discuss this now."

She avoided his lips while her own ached for the contact. But this was too important to dismiss with physical need. "Because you don't want to admit that you are wrong, but just stop and think. What if Susannah went across the water believing it was her best hope for making it through the full moon unmated? Then she ends up mated to Magnus and she doesn't want him to think she is disloyal or disobedient, so she . . ."

"Lied? My sister is not such a weak woman."

"Please, Drustan, just consider the possibility."

He shook his head and kissed her, but she refused to respond. It was hard. Harder than anything she'd ever done, but she could not give herself to a man who thought she was a liar.

"What is the matter?" he demanded, lifting his head.

"You think I'm a liar."

He took a deep breath, his chest filling up and hard muscles pressing against her side. "I do not think you are a liar."

"But you do. Either Susannah is lying, or I am." Or Lachlan, but she thought Emily's point of view on that was sound. The man was too arrogant to think he needed to lie.

"I have known Susannah her whole life. She does not lie."

"And you have only known me two days and one night, but I don't lie either." Her heart was cracking in her chest and she didn't know why. She should be offended by his lack of trust, not hurt. What was the matter with her?

"Perhaps Magnus convinced my sister to tell the story."

"For what purpose? He is not so shy he would have balked at asking for her hand and since chances were she was pregnant, that request would have been granted . . . no matter how she came to be in his keeping."

"But if he took her, Lachlan might still have declared war."

"And convincing her to tell that lie to our people wouldn't have prevented that. No, he had no reason to request such a thing of her."

"So, you want me to denounce my sister as a liar?"

"No. I want you to talk to her . . . talk to Talorc. Please."

"How do you propose I do this?"

"You could go to the Sinclair holding in open parley."

"And I suppose you would expect me to take you along?"

"He might listen to me more readily than he would you, but no . . . not if you don't think it is best." She'd been dealing with prickly soldiers all her life. She knew when to push and when to retreat.

"And if I refuse, do you plan to deny me access to your body?"

"No."

"Prove it."

She did, letting go of all of her worries and embracing the pleasure she found in his arms. Emily thought she did not understand her decision to allow Lachlan to touch her, but Cait did. Too well. She needed the intimacy of two bodies coming together with her husband. She needed to feel connected to him, even if it was an illusion.

But how much of an illusion . . . when they were sacred mates?

Chapter 15

Once again, Lachlan insisted on Emily sitting by his side for the evening meal. Cait and Drustan were absent, so Ulf sat on the other side of the laird and monopolized Lachlan's attention. Emily could not be sure the soldier cut her out of the conversation on purpose, but she suspected that was the case. Ulf really did not like her.

He might be Lachlan's brother, but she wasn't overly fond of him either.

She picked at her food, her attention on the warriors in the hall. Angus was Chrechte. So was Lachlan, but she didn't know about any others. It was easier to watch Angus and look for differences in his demeanor than to watch the laird by her side, but Emily tried to do it covertly.

"Why do you keep looking at my soldier, English?"

So much for subtlety. "Was I?"

"Maybe she prefers his company," Ulf said from the other side of Lachlan.

Emily frowned at him. The man was a troublemaker and that was that.

Lachlan looked down at her. "Is it true? Would you rather sit at his table?" He didn't sound particularly worried by the possibility, but he did look puzzled.

"Would it matter if I did?" He certainly hadn't hesitated to insist she leave Angus's table to join him at the nooning meal.

"No."

Just as she'd thought. "So, why bother to ask?"

"I want to know."

Ulf made a disparaging sound.

Emily leaned around Lachlan to give his brother a good glare. "Must you always be so rude?"

He surged to his feet and the look he gave her and then his brother made Emily's glare feel like a smile. "I suppose you expect me to tolerate this insult as well?"

"If you find truth such an insult, perhaps you should change your behavior so you cannot be called to account for it," she said before Lachlan could open his mouth.

"Are all English women so sharp-tongued?" Lachlan asked while his brother spluttered more displeasure.

Emily's face heated, embarrassed by the accusation inherent in his words. "No. My stepmother would be appalled at my plain-speaking." But what bothered her most was knowing Lachlan had the same opinion. How long before he started to see her as an unpleasant nuisance just as Sybil had done? Or did he already? She sighed and met Ulf 's glowering gaze. "I am sorry that my words caused offense."

He did not acknowledge her apology, but he did return to his seat and proceeded to eat with gusto.

Upset by the confrontation, Emily gave up trying to eat altogether. She let her gaze flit around the great hall, lighting on first one soldier then another. The only place she did not allow it to go was to the man beside her. She did not want to see the same look of disgust on his face that so often marked Sybil's countenance when she talked to

Emily. Just as painful would be to see that he was ignoring her altogether.

By not glancing at him, she could avoid both possibilities.

"If I did not know better, I would think you were spying on my men with the intent to report to the Sinclair." Amusement laced Lachlan's voice.

Emily could not dredge up a corresponding smile as she forced herself to meet his gaze. "I am a captive, not a spy."

"Certainly you would find reporting your discoveries to Talorc a great challenge."

Thinking it would be all too easy to go back to the lake and talk to the wolf as Cait had done, Emily choked on the wine she'd been trying to drink.

Lachlan's eyes narrowed as the man to Emily's left started pounding her back. She coughed and then wheezed in a great breath of air before turning to thank the soldier.

She turned back to Lachlan to find him staring at her speculatively. "You are innocent. You are not mated to him, I am sure of it. You cannot be his spy."

"Do we have to have this discussion here?"

"You are skittish for a woman with a tongue as plain-spoken as yours."

"I may not be as much of a lady as my stepmother would have liked, but I am not totally lacking in decorum. And I do not wish to discuss my most personal business in front of your soldiers."

"What is your preoccupation with my soldiers?" he demanded.

She could hardly tell him she was trying to figure out if some of them really were werewolves. "I'm curious about the Balmoral people. That is all."

"You spent a great deal of time in the bailey today."

She was not surprised he knew how she'd spent her day. He was the kind of man who would keep a close watch over all things to do with his holding, but especially an English captive. "It was a pleasure meeting so many of the clan. You were right. No one but Ulf treats me like the enemy."

"He is fiercely protective of the clan."

"And I insulted you."

"Yes."

"Oh." She couldn't apologize when she still thought it was wrong for them to have sought their revenge in kidnapping an innocent woman. She and Ulf were simply not destined to be friends, but at least the rest of the clan was nice to her.

"Angus does not hold my words against me."

Lachlan frowned. "You have a high opinion of my soldier."

She shrugged. "He has been kind."

"As you feel Ulf and I have not been."

"I did not mean that. Indeed, your desire to teach me to swim is kindness itself."

"I am not a kind man, English."

She did not agree, but she saw that if she argued, he would be insulted. Contrary man. First he was insulted because she thought Angus was kind and not him, and then it annoyed him that she believed he was compassionate. "I appreciate your generosity all the same."

"You were not afraid when you went to the loch with Cait?"

That was not a part of her day she wanted to discuss. "No, but being near the water is not what scares me. I just never go in very deep . . . or I didn't before this morning."

"Why did you go? I did not give permission for you two to venture outside the castle walls."

"You gave us permission to explore the holding . . . it stretches beyond the walls. And Cait wanted to see the lake."

He gave her an odd look. "It is not safe for you to go to the loch unaccompanied."

"Cait and I were together."

"With no warrior to guard you."

"But we did not need one. The lake is close to many of the cottages."

"Just as you did not need a guard when you ventured outside the Sinclair castle walls?"

"We had a guard, but your warriors overpowered him."

"I would not be so easy to overpower."

She did not doubt it. "But since we've already been kidnapped, what else could happen to us?" she asked logically.

"There are wild animals and, pregnant, Cait has no defense against them."

"W-wild animals?" she asked, thinking of Talorc and hoping it did not show on her face.

"Wild boar . . . and wolves." Was he looking at her more keenly when he said that word? Or was that her imagination?

"Oh."

"I do not want you going to the loch without me again."

"All right."

His brows came together in obvious puzzlement. "I expected an argument."

"Did you?"

"Yes."

"Perhaps I am not as difficult as you believe."

"Mayhap you have another reason for being so acquiescent. You have already decided I am right."

Or she did not want to argue and betray what she had seen.

"Did you see any wild animals while you were at the loch today?" he asked, his dark gaze probing.

"Only if you consider a laird a wild animal," she sidestepped, not wanting to lie and hoping he would assume she was talking about him.

"Sometimes that is exactly what a laird is."

After Cait's revelations, Lachlan's words hit Emily with the force of a blow. She would drive herself daft trying to determine if everything he said had more than one meaning, but she could not dismiss his intensity when he uttered those words.

Ulf claimed Lachlan's attention again and soon Emily excused herself to go back to the tower. She had had an exhausting day and she intended to go to sleep early, but found herself strangely alert after brushing her hair and taking care of her other nightly ablutions. It was as if the air crackled with magical energy and she could not settle down to rest.

Donning her clothes again, she decided to go back to the great hall. The night had grown cold and maybe a fire had been built. She'd always found staring into the fire made her sleepy. At the very least, climbing the long spiraling staircase down and up again should tire her out sufficiently to rest.

When she reached the great hall, it was empty but for Ulf and Lachlan. They were arguing and did not notice her. She did not want to interrupt them, but she also didn't want to go back up the stairs so soon.

Perhaps if she waited in the shadows, they would leave and she could sit beside the fire that had indeed been built in the huge fireplace on the other side of the hall. She looked at it longingly as the cold from the stone wall she leaned against seeped into her bones.

Shivering, she sidled sideways, hoping to make it to the fireplace without being noticed. She stayed in the shadows and was as quiet as possible. Not that the two angry men were likely to notice her regardless.

"You do not believe the Sinclair means to do nothing in retaliation?" Ulf demanded sneeringly.

If she were Lachlan, she'd get plenty annoyed with the way his brother always questioned him and did it so provokingly.

"You do not think he believes I was right in gaining restitution through his sister?" Lachlan asked mildly.

"No. He plans war. I am sure of it."

"But our spies have seen no evidence of this."

"He is cunning."

"And you do not think I am equally cunning?" Lachlan asked.

"Not if you are so easily deceived."

"And if I have not been deceived?"

Ulf made that annoying snorting noise of his and Emily stopped her approach to the fire to glare at him. He, of course, did not notice. He didn't even know she was there.

"I say attack before we are attacked."

The words appalled Emily and it was all she could do not to shout a denial. Did the man truly not care how many Balmorals or Sinclairs died over this business?

Lachlan looked past Ulf, and Emily felt as if he were looking directly at her. But that could not be possible. She was in a very dark corner behind one of the stone arches supporting the ceiling of the room.

He said, "I chose a different form of retribution than war."

"It is not enough. We should take Susannah back and kill the blacksmith."

Emily's hand flew to her mouth.

Lachlan frowned. "You are bloodthirsty, Ulf."

"I am my father's son . . . can the same be said of you?"

Instead of being furious, as Emily would have expected, Lachlan looked exasperated. "What would you have me do? Siege the castle?"

"Lead a raiding party over the walls. Effect your vengeance and leave."

"I rejected that suggestion the first time you made it."

"Because you prefer to avoid bloodshed?" Ulf spat.

"Because it is a stupid form of revenge and I liked my plan better." This time his voice was chilling and Emily thought Lachlan's patience had finally been exhausted.

She continued on her journey toward the fireplace, but realized she could not get as close to it as she wanted without revealing herself. Still, some of its heat reached her where she hung back in the shadows.

"You dare to call me stupid?"

"It was your plan I said was stupid, but I ask you now . . . do you dare to challenge me?"

Ulf 's jaw clenched, but he did not answer.

The air inside the great hall crackled and seethed with potential violence.

Emily crowded back into her hidden nook, hoping Ulf would not be *that* stupid. She agreed with Lachlan; his brother's suggestion for revenge was both stupid and horrible. It gained nothing but pain for either clan. Hearing the other option made Emily glad Lachlan had chosen the path he had taken.

Realizing the alternative, she could finally see that his choice to use Cait to effect the redress was not a matter of taking his anger out on an innocent woman. It was, in fact, his solution to a problem that would otherwise have resulted in bloodshed and much grief.

Cait and she were both better off among the Balmoral. Emily could admit that. Cait was either very close to being, or was already in love with her husband, and Emily grew nauseated at the thought of allowing Talorc to touch her the way Lachlan had done. From what Cait said, Susannah was very happy with Magnus. She would be devastated if he were killed by her former clan.

Lachlan had made a choice that embraced life rather than undervalued it. She did not know if her own father would have been as wise. Ulf certainly was not.

Neither he nor Lachlan had moved for the past several seconds. Emily held her breath in anticipation of what would come next.

Lachlan's hands settled on his hips and he seemed to

tower over his brother even though they were close in height. "Show throat or fetch your sword."

"Wolves show throat; I am human."

Emily bit her lip.

"You are Chrechte. You are my brother."

Ulf gave a single jerk of his head and then tilted it sideways, exposing his throat.

Lachlan said something Emily did not understand. It did not sound Gaelic to her. Ulf replied, his words just as incomprehensible, spun on his heel and left the great hall.

Emily silently let out the breath she'd been holding and realized she was shaking violently.

Lachlan looked toward where she hid. "Come here, English."

And in that moment she knew Cait had told the truth, about everything. Ulf had not known she was there, she was sure of it, but Lachlan had known even though he had pretended not to notice. When she had thought he was looking at her, he had been. But most convincing of all was his demand that Ulf show throat. It was not a human tradition and yet it had placated him in the face of terrible fury.

Her father would have demanded a soldier kneel at his feet. Even then, he might have beaten him for his insubordination.

Knowing that she had no hope of hiding, she stepped into the glow cast by the candles lighting the hall. "Why didn't you say something?"

"The situation was volatile enough. You bring out the worst in my brother. I did not want him challenging me out of pricked pride."

"I do not mean to bring out the worst."

"I do not blame you."

"You don't? Even though I have a sharp tongue?"

"I like your sharp tongue, but Ulf is not so tolerant."

"Oh." She licked her lips. "So, I can be plainspoken with you and you will not be offended?"

"If you offend me, I will seek retribution, but not of the kind my brother would like to mete out."

For some reason, that promise made her want to offend him rather than fear doing so.

He smiled as if he knew.

She swallowed. "You do not want to kill your brother."

"Is that such a surprise to you, or do the English not balk at killing their family?" He crossed his arms over his chest, his expression relaxed, but there was a tension about him that the calm stance and expression could not hide.

"I thought you did not care who you hurt as long as you got your own way."

"Did you?"

She licked her lips. "I was wrong."

He gave her a questioning look.

"About the revenge . . . you could have done far worse than to take Cait and see her mated to your first-in-command."

"Do you think?"

Irresistibly drawn by the intensity emanating off of him, she stepped closer until they were almost touching. "Yes, I do think. I also think that if you had wanted to hurt Talorc's pride and were as uncaring of the feelings of others as I accused you of being, you would have used me and then discarded me. But you did not."

In truth, he had not harmed her in any way.

"Only a weak man has to resort to using a woman."

"I don't think Ulf would agree, but that is why you were so sure Drustan would not hurt Cait, isn't it?"

"He is not weak."

"And neither are you."

"Ulf thinks I am."

"Ulf is hotheaded and bloodthirsty. He truly does not seem to care who gets hurt or ends up dead if his pride is satisfied. I don't think he would make a good leader. Your clan would constantly be at war."

"I agree."

"It is a blessing you were born first then." The urge to touch him grew with every passing breath.

"I wasn't. He was born two years before me."

"But you are laird."

"He did not challenge me when I stepped into my father's place upon his death."

"Because he knew he could not win against you."

"Yes. If he were truly stupid, that would not have mattered. He would have challenged me anyway."

"You admire him."

"In many ways."

"It hurts you that he criticizes your choices."

"A warrior is not so easily affected."

Unable to stifle the desire any longer, she reached out and laid her hand against his chest, right over his heart. "I think a warrior is affected, but he does not show it."

Her body jolted in recognition of that slight connection, and that secret place between her legs that only he seemed to affect ached for something she could not name. It also grew moist and she pressed her legs together in private embarrassment and tried to assuage the ache.

Lachlan's nostrils flared and she could swear he knew her body's reaction to being so near him. "I am not so weak."

"Neither was my father, but when he lost my mother, he lost part of himself. Warriors feel, even when they don't want to."

"Your father was a bastard to you."

"He never hurt me again after that time at the pond."

"Physically maybe, but he hurt your tender heart."

"How can you know?" she asked in a whisper.

"He sent you to marry a Highland laird he knew nothing of. He was willing to let you go to pay for his own mistake. He did not value you as a father should value his daughter."

"I told you, I asked to be sent."

"Because you were terrified they would send your deaf sister."

"Yes."

"He forced your hand."

"Sybil did."

"You were wrong about more than my character, you know."

"What else was I wrong about?" she asked with a smile. His arrogance was starting to charm her.

"Abigail would not have been miserable here."

"I think you are right. Given time, I think even Talorc would have warmed to her. She is very sweet."

"Then you two must have a great deal in common."

Emily did not know what to say to that and stared into Lachlan's dark eyes with their intriguing golden rims for several silent moments.

He ran his fingertip over her lips, making her shiver. "You are a good friend to Cait."

"I care for her."

"She cares for you, too."

"Yes."

"Very much. She offended Drustan by insisting she be allowed to check on you."

"He thought she should have trusted him that I was unharmed?" she guessed. She was beginning to understand these Highland warriors.

"Yes."

"You are both so arrogant."

"But not cruel?"

"No. I do not think you are cruel."

"And Angus?"

Confused, she asked, "What about Angus? I never thought he was cruel, except maybe by association."

Lachlan didn't look pleased by that bit of news. "You show a preference for his company."

"Not over yours. I couldn't have."

"Couldn't?"

"No. It would be impossible for me to show a preference for his company because I prefer your company above all others." Perhaps she should not have told him, but part of her needed to let him know how important to her he had become.

Something shifted in his gaze. If she didn't know better, she would think it was relief. "That is good to know."

"Is it?"

"It shouldn't be."

She didn't ask why. She could guess and she didn't want to think about how impossible a future between them would be. "I may be wanton with you, but I am not a wanton. I do not feel for any other man what I feel for you."

"And Talorc?"

"I will ask him not to send me home, but I cannot marry him now. I do not think he will mind." As a werewolf, he would have even less desire to marry Emily than Lachlan did, for no fire of desire burned between the two of them.

"Because I have touched you?"

"Yes," she whispered, not adding that she wanted no other man's caresses. She had revealed enough.

"You are worried he will consider you soiled by my touch?"

"No."

"You do not want him to touch you the same way."

He saw too much, but she refused to answer.

"I have barely begun to touch you, Emily. There is so much more pleasure to be had between us without the breaking of your maidenhead. More intimacy than you can imagine."

Sometimes he was so crude and yet it did not offend her, merely embarrassed her because she could not hope to match his honesty in this matter. Not yet anyway. "I was naked with you," she reminded him. How much more intimate could it get?

"Learning to swim." Without warning he swept her up into his arms. "And now it is time I taught you something else."

He carried her to a chair beside the fire and sat down.

"Here?" she asked, shocked he had not taken her someplace more private.

The great hall was empty, but it might not stay that way.

"If I take you back to your room, I will bury myself inside you and damn the consequences," he admitted in a guttural voice that revealed a depth of feeling his stance and conversation had not hinted at.

"And you cannot do that."

"No."

She knew it to be the case. She even understood why, but it hurt. Terribly. Because werewolf or not, she loved the proud and strong but compassionate laird. It did not matter if the feeling made sense; it was there and she knew to the depths of her soul that from this point forward, it always would be. He possessed her heart, but all he wanted was her body.

She would give that to him, freely and without condition, for the sake of the long, lonely years ahead. She would at least have this.

She put her hands on either side of his face and kissed him, then spoke against his lips. "Make me forget."

"Forget what?"

"Everything."

And he did.

From the moment his mouth touched hers, Emily ceased to think of anything but Lachlan. She sat on his lap, but they did not actively touch anywhere else except their lips. His moved against hers with sensual expertise, but he could have sat there completely still, only pressing his mouth to hers, and she would still be drowning in the need he evoked in her.

Just to touch him was to crave everything he would give her.

Chapter 16

Molding her lips to his, she imitated his movements and inhaled the scent of his utter masculinity. This man might be part wolf, but he was all male, everything she could ever imagine wanting. Her recently discovered love blossomed and consumed her heart until it was a burning but beautiful ache in her chest.

She opened her mouth for his tongue, but he pulled his head back with a curse. "We have to stop."

"Why?" she asked in a dazed voice she barely recognized as her own. She did not want to stop. They had barely begun.

"I thought I could touch you . . . pleasure you, but my control is too shaky right now."

"I don't understand."

"The confrontation with my brother left emotion I need to burn away, but if I burn it the way I want to, I will break the promise I made to you."

"I don't care if you do," she admitted, her voice almost pleading.

He shuddered. "I would care," he said harshly.

She sat up, as far away from him as she could get while still sitting on his hard thighs. There was another hardness there, too, one that moved under his plaid, and she knew he was not stretching the truth when he said his control was precarious. But that did not make her feel better about his rejection.

"Because you would feel committed to me and you don't want to?" she asked painfully.

"Yes. You are a virgin."

"And if I *offer* you my virginity?"

"You offer it because I have enticed you to feel things you are not used to, because it is a full moon, because I am close to my . . . too close to you. I should not have started this tonight, but you make me lose my head."

"So you think we are both out of control?"

"Yes."

"But I do not have excess emotion I need to rid my body of." Unless they were talking about love and they weren't. "If I offer myself, I know what I am doing."

"You don't. There are things about tonight you do not understand. Things you don't know."

"And these things mean I do not know my own mind?"

"Yes."

"Why does it matter so much?"

"I will not break my word to you. I will not take advantage of my beast."

Now that she knew what she did, she understood he wasn't using beast as a euphemism for lust. He meant the wolf inside of him, she was sure of it, but she did not comprehend how his being a werewolf had anything to do with her offering herself. It did not matter though. Not really.

She wouldn't beg. She didn't need to understand his reasoning to realize that if he wanted her anything like she desired him, he would have accepted her offer. With alacrity. It might hurt to admit the truth, but it was obvious that while the feeling might be mutual, it wasn't mutually intense. But then how much of her desire was bound up in the love she felt for him? He liked touching her, but he did not love her.

There would be no comparison between the need generated by the two.

Blinking back tears and swallowing her hurt, she traced the blue pattern that circled his bicep. This was his Chrechte marking, or at least one of them. The other was on his back. She realized now the simplistic beast on his back was probably supposed to represent a wolf, but the tattoo band on his arm was different. None of the other warriors had it.

"Is this to mark you as clan chief?" she asked, wanting to distract herself from thoughts of love.

He gave a strange kind of shiver and gently pushed her hand away. "Yes."

"It's beautiful," she said as the blue markings blurred before her dampening eyes. He would not even allow her to touch him in this innocent way.

"God willing, my son will have the same marking one day."

She blinked furiously. "Your son?"

"I must have sons."

"And daughters?"

"I would welcome daughters, too."

Just not by her . . . because even if it were possible, however unlikely, there was still the risk their children would be born human rather than shape-changers. "Why haven't you married?"

"I was barely past my voice change when I took over leading the clan. Many pressed me to marry then, but I did not want to. I was too wild and there was too much to do to learn how to be a good clan chief. Now, it is a matter of taking the time to select a wife. My position consumes every waking hour."

"Not right now. Not this morning when you were teaching me to swim."

"You make me forget my duties."

Having gained control of her tears, she could meet his dark gaze without flinching. "Is that a good or a bad thing?"

He looked down at her for a long time, the golden circles around his dark irises almost swallowing the brown. They had never looked more like wolf 's eyes to her.

He brushed a kiss across her still lips before pulling back again. "It is a precious thing."

Was she wrong? Did she mean something to him, even if they couldn't have a future? "What I feel with you is precious to me, too."

He stood up, dumping her off his lap. "It is only lust."

She swayed as if struck. "For you, maybe."

"Do not love me, English."

That was beyond anything. Bad enough that he thought he could dictate everything else. He could not dictate her feelings. "I will love you if I want to. If my heart ends up broken because of it, that is my own affair."

She wanted to rush off in anger, but at the last second she remembered her promise to Cait. Though she had almost no hope of her seduction plan being a success, she asked, "You will come for me tomorrow, to my room, before the swimming lesson?"

"Mayhap you should have Cait teach you to swim. You are right. I have neglected my duties too much already in favor of spending time with you."

She had not said that, but it was obviously what he believed. *Precious?* Not likely. She almost gave a snort worthy of Ulf, but stopped herself. The important thing was to keep him from the lake, she had to remember. Not for her to overcome her fear of the water.

"As you wish." She turned and started walking away.

"Damn it, Emily."

She ignored him and kept walking.

His hand heavy on her shoulder, he stopped her in the

shadows between an archway and the wall. Neither said anything for several heartbeats.

Finally she asked, "Was there something you wanted?"

He turned her to face him, his expression an inscrutable mask in the darkness beyond the candlelight. "You did not request permission to leave me."

"I do not believe this." She fisted her hands and settled them on her hips in a way that Sybil deplored. "I am not one of your clan members. I am only a captive. I do not owe you that courtesy, or any other for that matter."

"First you speak of loving me and then declare I am not worthy of your respect. Which is it, English?" he asked in a mocking voice that infuriated her.

"I did not say I loved you, merely that I would if I wanted to. You cannot dictate everything, laird. It would take a very stupid woman to fall in love with a man who sees every moment spent in her company as a waste of his time."

"I did not say that."

"You did."

He sighed, conceding defeat in the only way he knew how maybe . . . silence. After a protracted pause, he said, "I did not mean to hurt you."

"I did not say you hurt me and it is horribly conceited of you to assume you did."

"It is not conceit to note the way your lip quivers when you are trying not to cry or the fact that you cannot wait to be quit of my company because I have told you some unpalatable truths."

"Your truth, as you call it, is not anything I did not know before. You need not concern yourself and if my lip quivered, it is probably because I wanted to kiss you again. More the fool me. Apparently *lust* has no limits, even for an intelligent woman."

"Or an intelligent man," he muttered. "Since it is what we both crave, mayhap I *should* kiss you again."

"Do you think you can spare the time?"

His answer was a kiss so carnal that her body locked in shock. He forced his tongue past her only partially parted lips and took control of the interior of her mouth like the marauder he was. Where before it had all been about lazy pleasure, now he held nothing back. His hands were everywhere, touching her body in impossible intimacy through her clothes and she did not protest, but begged for more with little mewling noises, arching toward his roaming fingers.

This was what she wanted. This was what she craved.

She felt herself lifted and pressed against the cold stone wall, but she was not cold. She was so hot her skin burned with it. He pressed his big, hard body to hers, the bulge she had felt earlier rubbing against the apex of her thighs through her dress. She shuddered in pleasure and pushed back, seeking a relief from the agony of pleasure spearing through her.

He yanked her skirts up, baring her legs, and she wrapped them around his hips with an instinctual sensuality that she did not question. This time when she rubbed against his hardened flesh under his plaid, arrows of sweet pleasure pierced her with each tiny movement. He surged against her, increasing her enjoyment beyond what she thought her body could bear.

Then as suddenly as he had started, he stopped and yanked his mouth from hers.

"Lachlan?" she asked, her tone pleading and she did not care.

"We are no longer alone," he whispered right next to her ear before slowly unwinding her legs from his body and lowering her to the floor.

She stood, swaying before him. And it was several seconds before his words made sense to her. Eventually, the other noises in the hall besides her own labored breathing and fast heartbeat penetrated her consciousness. Though she could not see them, she could hear a group of soldiers that had gathered by the fireplace. From their comments, it was obvious they were waiting for Lachlan to join them.

Tears of frustration welled and spilled over.

Lachlan said something she did not understand, grabbed her and kissed her again. His hand went down her body and rucked up her skirt and then he touched her sweet spot, once . . . twice and everything inside her exploded. Her body bowed against his and he kept his hand where it was, increasing the pleasure until she collapsed against him, her legs too weak to hold her.

He finally broke the kiss and then lifted her into his arms as if she were indeed a precious treasure. He said nothing as he carried her all the way up the spiral steps and to her room. He stopped outside the door and lowered her, helping her to lean against the wall for much-needed support.

"I do not want you to leave this chamber for the rest of the night."

"Are you going to lock me in?" she asked in a voice that sounded slurred as if by too much wine.

"Do I need to?"

"No."

"Promise me, no leaving for any reason."

"I promise." She turned and stumbled into the room, closing the door behind her.

She barely divested herself of her tunic and shift before climbing beneath the covers and sprawling in a boneless heap. The light of the full moon coming in through the windows high in the wall lit her chamber almost as brightly as daylight. Didn't werewolves change at the full moon?

Her thoughts were muzzy from the incredible experience Lachlan had given her, but questions peppered her mind until she was more awake than she wanted to be.

Was that why he had said his control was not as strong as he wanted? Did his animal instincts make it harder for him to control things like lust close to a full moon? She supposed they must. Was her werewolf even now in changed form and hunting, as Cait called it, under the full moon? Would he go to the lake?

Surely Talorc would have been smart enough to leave the island in that case. Or could werewolves tell if another wolf was a werewolf and not just a wild beast? She certainly hadn't been able to tell the difference between werewolves and humans in their human form.

She turned to her side and her body throbbed with remembered pleasure. What had Lachlan done to her? He had touched her and now that she was not drunken with the pleasure that he gave her, the memory of the way she'd responded shamed her. She had made noise. Even with his lips pressed firmly to hers, her moans had been audible.

Especially to werewolf ears, and she somehow thought those soldiers that had been in the great hall were probably exactly that. Had they come to join Lachlan for the hunt? There were so many things she wanted to know, so many questions she had for Cait. But regardless of why the men had been in the hall, they *had* been there and even knowing it, she had done nothing to stop Lachlan touching her so intimately. She had needed his caresses too badly.

But he had not found the same pleasure in her arms. Had he? In truth, she had no way of knowing, but he certainly hadn't gone limp like her. And that hardness that made his plaid protrude had still been there when he carried her up the stairs.

She chewed endlessly on her thoughts until finally, she was so tired, she could not keep her eyes open any longer. As she finally slipped into sleep, she heard the lonely howl of a wolf and something deep inside her insisted it *was* Lachlan in beast form under the cold light of the moon.

Lachlan could see the castle tower from his position near the loch. She was in the tower. His mate.

He shook his big wolf's head . . . the human inside him

denying she could be any such thing, but his wolf cried out to her. He wanted to go to her, he wanted to see her through wolf 's eyes, not just those of a human. He wanted to smell her, to rub his fur against her and mark her with his scent.

Never in his life had his willpower been more sorely challenged than tonight. Leaving Emily outside her chamber had taken all of his strength. If he had gone in with her . . . he would have made love to her. Over and over again. His need for the change would have been supplanted by sexual fulfillment.

But he had not allowed himself that release.

He and the rest of his pack had hunted tonight and he had eaten the kill, sharing with the other wolves in traditions as old as marriage vows and other human bondings. But the pack had long since dispersed. A couple of the bitches had tried to entice him into running with them, but he had snarled and snapped until they had all retreated with their tails between their legs. He was alone now.

He would have run with Drustan if the other werewolf were not back in his quarters . . . with his mate. He had come out for the hunt only. He would take part of the kill back to Cait for her to cook and eat as well. She would not be able to shift until the babe was born, but Drustan had not seemed to mind returning to the castle early. He knew his mate would welcome him home. Bloody hell, why had Lachlan waited so long to mate?

If he were married he would not have this unholy struggle between what he desired and what he knew to be best for the pack.

An image of Emily's beautiful pink and white body rose in his mind to taunt him. She would be the perfect mate if she were a femwolf. She was courageous and compassionate and fiercely loyal. But she was also human and he would not risk a human-wolf mating. He owed more than that to his pack.

Of its own volition, his head raised toward the moon

and he let out a mournful howl that did not dispel the sense of desolation he felt at knowing he had no choice but to let Emily go. Just once he would look on her in wolf form.

He could not mark her with his scent as he longed to do, but he could look.

He loped back toward the castle, changing into human form just before he reached the drawbridge. When he reached Emily's room, the door swung silently open under his careful push.

She was curled on her side facing him. Her long gold and brown curls shimmered around her and the Balmoral plaid covered her. It was right.

Without thought, he changed and looked at her through the eyes of his wolf. She looked the same, but different. His vision was better in wolf form and he could see each individual lash sweeping her cheeks below closed eyelids. Her scent was different, too, both more feminine and more real. He could smell lilacs and remembered she had visited the women hanging the washing. She had endeared herself to them by helping them to gather in the clothes that had dried on the bushes.

He could also smell the scent that was hers alone. It was not a femwolf scent. It was softer, less spicy, less pungent but no less alluring to his wolf 's senses. No female, human or wolf, had ever smelled so right to him. He padded closer as another scent made itself known to his senses. She had gone to sleep still aroused.

He had given her a climax, but it had not been enough. She needed the completion of intercourse as badly as he did, but he doubted she understood that. She was too innocent. Even after tonight . . . she was barely touched. His beast growled for the need to mark her as his, to declare that innocence his and his alone.

He could not resist the urge to kiss her cheek with a delicate lick. She wrinkled her nose and he bared his teeth in a wolf 's grin that faded as quickly as it had come. Soon, things would have to be settled with the Sinclair. Emily would go back to the other holding.

Lachlan did not want to let her leave, but every day she stayed with him put his duty at risk. He had offered sanctuary, but he was glad she had turned him down. If she stayed, he would keep her. It was inevitable. And that would not be fair to his pack or to his clan. The need to join their bodies in total oneness, to plant his seed in her body (even if it would not grow) increased every moment he was in her company.

Right now he wanted to tug the blanket away with his teeth and cover her body with his beast, warm her and scent her and when she woke, change right on top of her so that he could mate her. He would share all his secrets with her and teach her the ways of the Chrechte. The desire was so strong, his wolf 's body shook with the effort it took not to follow through on his thoughts.

Steeling himself to go, he licked her hand and she moaned in her sleep, then whispered his name.

Her dreams were about him. Were they sensual, or did she dream of their time in the lake, or perhaps of things that could never be?

He must leave now, or he would be here when she woke in the morning. He turned and padded toward the door.

"Lachlan?" she said sleepily as he reached it.

He stopped and turned back to face her.

She did not look afraid to find a giant wolf in her room. Her eyes blinked sleepily, but there was no terror in their violet depths. Perhaps she thought she was dreaming.

She sat up, the blankets falling to her waist and revealing the dusky rose of her nipples and perfect curve of her breasts. Physical desire swamped him until he felt like he was drowning.

Her eyes lit with wonder and a joy he did not understand. "It is you, isn't it? I'm not dreaming. You are a wolf and you are here."

He did not move. He barely breathed.

"Can I touch you?"

The words registered in his brain, but he could not make sense of them at first. She wanted to touch him? In his wolf form? She was human, not femwolf. He remembered the way his mother hid from his father's beast nature. She would not touch or talk to him when he was a wolf, pretending that he was no more than a man.

She had been relieved when Ulf did not go through the change. She had died of a fever the following year, after expressing the hope that neither of her sons would have a wolf's nature. Lachlan's change had come early . . . the first full moon after her death. Nothing had been the same since.

But his memories told him that human women did not embrace the beast in their werewolf mates.

"Please," Emily said softly, her hand outstretched.

He craved the feel of her fingers in his fur and he could not stop himself from going back to her, his beast letting out a low whine of need that he doubted she would understand. Had his father felt like this? How hard had it been for him to keep his two natures so separate?

Emily reached out and touched Lachlan's head. "You are beautiful." She trailed her fingers through the fur of his neck and down his back. "And your fur, it is soft. Oh, Lachlan . . . this is such a wondrous thing that you are."

A rumbling sound came from his chest. It was not a sound he'd ever made before. But then he had never known this pleasure. It was beyond physical mating . . . it was a happiness deep inside that his mate accepted and approved of all that he was. *But she was not his mate.* He had to remember.

The rumbling stopped, but the sense of pleasure did not.

He licked her, right between her breasts. He wanted to lick her all over, to taste her with his heightened wolf's senses and imprint all that she was on his memory forever.

She gasped, her hands stilling.

He buried his head in her lap lest he do it again and disgust her. Her feminine scent reached him through the blankets and tormented him with the desire to change and claim her for his own.

"Is it supposed to feel like that?" she asked in a quiet, shaken voice.

He raised his head to look into her eyes, willing her to explain because he could not speak and he could not risk making the change to ask what she meant.

"It felt like magic . . . I don't know how to explain it. Like heat, but it wasn't hot . . . like something fizzled along my skin. You know how the bubbly water from some springs shimmers in your mouth like moving droplets from a waterfall? Oh, I'm making a hash of this. But when you licked me, I felt something more than your tongue on my skin."

He did not know what she was talking about, but he understood one thing. She was not repelled by his action.

He nuzzled her with his head in gratitude.

"Is it all right that I liked it?"

He lifted his head and nodded, then did it again, to make sure she understood his approval.

This time she moaned and it was even harder to force his head into her lap a second time, but he could not allow himself to do what he so desperately wanted to. Besides, she might tolerate one lick, but could she accept more? She was human and he could not forget that important fact.

She scratched behind his ears, her silent approval an incredible gift. What human woman would not scream in fright from a wolf so close? But not Emily. She liked Lachlan's wolf. Had Talorc told her the secrets of the Chrechte? More likely it had been Cait. He would ask Drustan, but Emily was far too accepting for a human who knew nothing of their people. She was too accepting for a human woman at all. It made no sense, especially to his wolf's brain.

"If I lie down . . ." She stopped, her hesitation palpable.

What was she going to say? Did she want him to leave?

"Will you lie beside me and share your magic for just this night? Please, Lachlan. Just this once?"

His head jerked up. He could not believe what she had asked. It was what his wolf craved, he realized, even more than mating . . . the closeness of sharing. If only for just one night.

Her smile was bittersweet. "You are amazing. I will never again experience anything like what I feel with you now. I know that my time with your clan is limited and I will probably never see you in this form again after tonight. Will you stay with me until I sleep, so that in the morning I will believe it was a dream and not yearn for what I can never have?"

Even if he had been in human form, he would not have been able to speak. She said he was amazing, but it was she who was incredible.

He nodded slowly.

She smiled, her eyes shimmering with emotion. "Thank you."

Lying down, she pulled the plaid up to once again cover her modestly. Then, she scooted back toward the wall, making as much room on the small bed for his big wolf's body as she could. He jumped onto the bed and then lay down beside her, his muzzle resting on his forepaws.

She curled an arm over his neck and nuzzled into it with her face. He had never known such contentment, even with the unsatisfied lust making his blood run hotter than lava.

"You do not smell like a dog. I would have thought a wolf would smell like a canine," she said drowsily some minutes later. "But you smell like yourself. It is a fragrance I will never forget."

She fell asleep moments later.

Making no effort to sleep, Lachlan lay listening to her breathe and inhaling her sweet fragrance. Her arm stayed wrapped around him as if she wanted to hold her to him, even in her sleep. The temptation to stay was so strong, he almost gave in to it, but as the sun rose, he crept from the bed. He was careful not to wake her, knowing that if she asked for anything in that sweetly husky voice, he was likely to give it to her.

A few minutes later he had changed to his human form on the landing and then run to his room at full speed so as not to be seen. The bed that had been his own for more than ten years felt lonely for the first time as he fell on top of the furs that covered it.

But as tired as he was, he did not fall asleep immediately. The rocklike hardness of his erection would not allow it. Thinking of Emily's innocent face in repose did not help and when he finally did sleep, he dreamed of her . . . large with his child, smiling and laughing as she swam in the loch, no fear anywhere on her face.

He woke from the dream, an ache in the vicinity of his heart, a few hours later.

He dismissed that ache right along with the desire to see her. He had work to do, reports to hear, soldier training to oversee, and he needed to talk to Drustan. Prior to the evening meal the night before, one of the femwolves had reported that she had spotted a strange gray werewolf near the loch the day before. Lachlan was sure it was Talorc, or one of his well-trained elite guard.

Lachlan had smelled nothing when he had gone to the loch with Emily. Either the wolf had not been there, or he was very good at masking his scent. If it was Talorc, he was spying . . . but to what purpose? To check on the welfare of his sister, or to try to take her back? If he'd wanted to speak to Cait, he would have made himself known when she and Emily went to the loch. Unless he did not trust Emily with the knowledge of his presence.

Or had he? The night before, when Lachlan had asked Emily if she had seen a wild animal, she had said only if he counted a laird such a thing. Talorc was also a laird and

Emily knew of their wolf nature. Had she been trying to avoid answering his question with a clever ploy, or had she not seen anything, as he had assumed?

Lachlan needed to speak to Drustan and then he would seek Emily out and discover the truth of the matter for himself.

Chapter 17

Emily kneaded the big ball of dough while she listened to the kitchen helpers' gossip. She'd woken early, alone in her bed, but the scent of Lachlan had clung to the plaid. Even without that, she would not have been able to convince herself he had been a dream. As unreal as the events of the night should have been, her memory of it was as solid as those she had of her family.

And she had the inescapable feeling that he was now as much a part of her as they were.

She could leave the Balmoral clan, but she would never leave him behind completely. He would live in her heart through eternity. How much less complicated her life would have been if she had felt this way about Talorc on first sight, instead of the deep certainty that she did not belong with him.

What a muddle.

Why had Lachlan come to her, as a wolf no less? She'd been asking herself that question over and over again all morning and she still could not come up with a single reasonable answer. Except that maybe his wolf 's instincts had led him there because of what had happened between them just before she went to bed. Even if that was the case, such an action exhibited a level of trust she knew the man could not have for her.

Yet, he *had* come to her as a wolf. He'd let her touch him, pet him, and he had kissed her like a wolf kisses. Then he had lain beside her until she slept. Probably longer.

She still did not understand what she had felt when his tongue caressed her skin, but it had been extraordinary. As singular an experience as the explosion of pleasure he had brought about in her body earlier, but quite different from it as well. It had not been sexual . . . or at least not entirely so. It had felt good, but it had also felt . . . bizarre.

As if part of his life force was mingling with her own.

And yet, just as he'd said he would not . . . he had not come to collect her for a swimming lesson. It was as if the night before had not mattered to him at all. Perhaps he had not felt the connection she had felt.

"I think that dough is done, lass," one of the older women said to Emily.

She started and looked down. The white mass did indeed look sufficiently kneaded. She patted it into shape and set it aside before taking another ball of dough and placing it on the work space in front of her. She punched it down from its first rising with more than necessary force.

She did not understand him, not one little bit. First he said she meant nothing to him and implied she was a nuisance, then he touched her like a lover. He'd been so careful with her when he carried her up the stairs after giving her the ultimate in pleasure. Like she mattered . . . only he said she didn't.

Then . . . *then* . . . he had come to her as a wolf. That was the most inexplicable thing of all. She hit the ball of dough again with her curled fist even though all it needed now was to be folded in on itself a few times.

"I told Marta not to assign you household chores."

Emily made a face at the ball of dough and muttered about high-handed lairds before looking up. Lachlan was watching her, his expression less than pleased, his big warrior's body making the kitchens feel like a small area in a way that several helpers and she did not.

"She didn't."

His dark brow rose hawklike in a silent demand for clarification.

"Cait has been put in charge of household matters in the keep. She instructed me to help with the bread-making."

"She instructed you?" he asked in a deadly soft voice she did not understand.

"It is only fair. I instructed her to take a nap after we finished assessing the contents of the food storeroom."

"Why were you doing her chores with her?"

"*She* enjoys my company. She does not think I am a nuisance."

"Until you told her to take a nap," he said, his face solemn.

"She didn't consider me a nuisance then, just annoying, and she did not tell me to help with the bread-making in retaliation. She knows I like to keep busy."

"As does she, I'm sure."

"She needed the nap."

His brows rose at her snapping tone. "Did I imply she did not?"

"No," she said grudgingly. "A pregnant woman needs more rest anyway, but she was yawning every other breath. I don't think she got much sleep last night."

In fact, she was sure of it.

Emily had flooded Cait with questions until she understood the full moon hunting ritual and all that it entailed.

She'd learned that although Cait had not hunted with the other wolves, she had stayed up late to share a meal with Drustan. She'd blushed in the telling and Emily assumed that a meal wasn't all she had shared with her husband.

Emily hadn't told Cait about Lachlan coming to her chamber. It had seemed too private a thing to share, even with a friend as close as a sister.

"She is lucky you care for her like you do."

"I am blessed by her friendship as well."

From the sidelong glances she and Lachlan kept getting from the other women in the kitchen area, she guessed her conversation with their laird was highly intriguing to them.

Lachlan looked at the other women and then back to Emily. "I want to speak with you."

She folded the dough over itself and then pressed it firmly together. "I'm almost finished kneading this."

"It can wait."

"No, it can't."

Two of the women at the table gasped and one stared at Emily bug-eyed, no longer making any pretense of not listening. Emily pretended not to notice and continued with what she was doing.

"Dare you refuse me?" he asked, sounding mean.

She grimaced. "You said you liked my plain-speaking."

"I did not say I liked disobedience."

She was not a child to obey without question, though she knew many men saw women that way. As arrogant as he was, she did not believe Lachlan was so shortsighted, but she would take that up with him later. "I did not disobey. I merely told you the truth. If I don't finish kneading the dough now, it will not rise properly. The other women are all busy with their own chores. Would you have me leave mine undone because you have not the patience to wait a minute longer?"

"You have the makings of a termagant, do you know that, English? You remind me of my grandmother."

"Your father or your mother's mother?" she asked as she continued to knead.

"My father's."

She reminded him of a femwolf then. That was interesting, wasn't it? "Did you call her a termagant?"

"Think you I am a fool?"

She shook her head. "Far from a fool."

"Good. Our discussion will be easier if you do not make the mistake of believing me stupid."

"That sounds ominous."

"I wonder why, unless you have secrets you seek to hide?"

Did he know about Talorc? Had Cait told Drustan after all? She had said nothing, but Emily had hardly given her the chance, she'd been so busy asking questions about the Chrechte. Then they had been around others and forced to discuss less sensitive topics.

"Everyone has secrets, laird."

"Mayhap. I will know yours, English."

"And will you tell me yours?" she asked, meeting his gaze directly for the first time since he arrived in the kitchens.

"I already have," he said softly.

A strange sensation settled low in her belly at his look and she swallowed. He was not going to pretend that the night before had been a dream. He would not deny coming to her. Perhaps he would even explain why he had. The day was suddenly much brighter.

She patted the dough into a ball and covered it with a light cloth. "There, that is done. The wait was not so bad, was it, laird?"

"Nay."

Encouraged by his less surly manner, she hurriedly washed and dried her hands before turning to face him once again. "Shall we go?"

He did not respond, but merely turned to leave. She

followed. He led her back to the keep and into the great hall, but he did not stop there as she expected. He continued up a set of wooden stairs to a landing much like the one in her father's keep. Beyond it was the solar, but he did not stop there either. He led her into a bedchamber dominated by a giant bed covered with furs and a plaid.

"Why are we here?" she asked in a squeak.

He closed the door with a resounding thud that seemed to echo through the chamber even though her ears told her it really had not. "Privacy."

"Werewolves can hear what humans cannot."

"Yes, but I'm wondering how you know this."

She stared at him, mute. She could not betray Cait's confidence.

"Actually, I'm not. You could know only one of two ways. Either Talorc told you, or Cait. I'm guessing it wasn't the laird. It had to be his sister. She put a great deal of trust in you."

"We are like sisters," Emily whispered, praying he would not punish Cait for telling her. "Talorc should have told me."

"He refused to marry you. There was no need."

"But Cait was within her rights to tell me."

"Because you are like sisters?"

"Yes."

"She put her life, the lives of her pack in your hands."

"I won't betray her, or you."

"I know, but it amazes me she does. I would not tell another warrior, even one I called friend."

"But you would tell your brother."

"Yes."

"There, you see."

"I see that you and Cait are very lucky in your friendship."

"I agree." But she liked hearing he thought so much of her heart-sister. She licked her lips. "I thought you would try to pretend you had not come to me last night."

"I thought *you* planned to tell yourself it was a dream."

"It didn't work. You left your scent behind and . . . you don't leave me in my dreams." She hadn't meant to admit that, but she did not regret doing so. Her feelings were paltry things if she was ashamed to admit to their existence.

He sighed, his eyes filled with emotions she could not decipher. "I cannot keep you, Emily."

"Because I am human."

"I have a duty to my clan and to my pack."

"Your father married a human."

"And had a human child."

"Ulf."

"Yes."

"We know our own kind."

She wrinkled her nose in consternation. "I can't tell the difference."

"Because you are not one of us."

The words had a chilling impact on her senses. "No, I am not one of you."

"Bloody hell, Emily. I do not want to hurt you, but it is the way it is." He looked angry, but she could not understand why.

She had asked for nothing.

"I know. Truly, I do, Lachlan." Refusing to give into cowardice, she said, "I still want you."

An expression that was almost frightening in its intensity came over his face. "I want you, too, but I cannot take you."

"Why? Cait said you don't practice the same mating laws her clan does."

"Her clan is now the Balmoral."

"You know what I mean. If you take me, we are not wed like the Sinclairs."

"Nor would the Sinclair laird ever wed you then."

"Do you want him to?" she asked, not sure what she would do if he replied in the affirmative.

"No!" He growled and it was no human sound his throat made.

She shivered, but did not mind his ferocious reaction. That was something at least. "I already told you I cannot give myself to him. And he doesn't want me anyway."

Besides, the other laird probably already thought she'd given herself completely to Lachlan. She'd been naked with him and she was now convinced Talorc was aware of it.

"You are a virgin, Emily."

"And you aren't." Was he thinking she did not have the experience to give him pleasure like he'd given it to her?

She could not argue that point, but she was certainly willing to try. Eager even. But she was not so desperate she would say so. She had to maintain some semblance of pride here.

He laughed. "No. I am no virgin. It takes the physical act of mating to give a member of our pack control over the change. As you said, our ways are not the ways of the Sinclairs. We allow noncommitted mating to further the interests of the pack."

"Then why won't you make love to me?"

"You are not a femwolf."

"Are you saying Balmoral werewolves never have sex with human women without the benefit of marriage?"

"No, but there is the risk we will true-bond."

"And you don't want to be bonded with me."

He sighed, but then his expression turned hopelessly grim. "No."

She turned away, the pain of that single word as bad as when her father had shoved her away and called her a useless female child who had caused the death of her mother. Father had wanted a son and she had been a disappointment to him by right of her birth. She was not good enough for Lachlan either.

She had not been born a femwolf and therefore she had no lasting value to him.

"All of our children could be human, not just one. Don't you understand? Every time a Chrechte and a human mate, they risk not passing the wolf nature on."

"And that is so important?" she asked, but she knew it was.

Just as she'd known that being herself had never been enough for her father, Sybil or even her other siblings. Abigail was the only one who had loved Emily for who she was.

"How can you doubt it?" Lachlan demanded in a fierce tone. "We are a special race and to lose that race because we do not care enough to pass our full natures on would be wrong."

She wanted to cry, but she wouldn't. Tears did nothing but relieve some of the ache, and right now, she knew they would not even do that. He was not telling her anything surprising, only hurtful, and that pain would not leave her for a long time, if ever. Wasn't there still a corner of her heart that craved her father's love?

She could never have it either, but that did not mean she had to give up on everything. Was not a small taste of joy better than nothing at all? "You said there was pleasure you could show me without breaching my maidenhead."

"Yes." His voice sounded strangled.

She turned to face him, but did not meet his eyes. "I want that. And I want you to show me how to give you the same kind of pleasure you gave me last night."

He made a feral sound. "Emily . . ."

"What?" She met his eyes then, searching for she knew not what. Certainly she would not find love there, or even unconditional acceptance, but perhaps passion. "Do you not want even that much with me?"

Heat flared in his dark gaze. "Yes. Damn it. I do."

So, at least there was the passion. She was glad because she intended to use it to hide from the pain tearing apart her insides. She had never allowed herself to hide from truth, but right now she planned to do just that. She planned to pretend, for just a little while, that his passion was love.

He would never know and it could not hurt him, but she needed to feel loved just this once. She would live the rest of her life on these memories as she had clung to memories of her father's kindness before her mother's death all through her growing-up years.

Every touch would be motivated by love and a desire that matched her own, every sound would be one of acceptance for her as his *lover*, every response he evoked that of the beloved. She chanted the litany over and over in her head while she waited for him to kiss her.

But he did not.

He reached out and ran his fingers through her hair, his touch so gentle she could barely feel it. "It's so soft, so beautiful. My wolf wanted to bury his muzzle in it last night."

She swallowed, storing the *loving* words in her heart as a treasure no one else could tear from her, not even Lachlan. "He can do it now if he likes."

"You don't mind?"

She shook her head, then watched in fascination as he slowly divested himself of his plaid, revealing himself to her with breathtaking sensuality. He stood before her in all his naked glory. His manhood was engorged and she felt a sense of relief that they were not going to make love completely.

No matter what he thought, they would never fit together, she was sure of it.

"Do you like what you see?" he asked.

She nodded, mute.

"But you still want to see my wolf?" Inexplicable vulnerability to her rejection shimmered in his gold-rimmed eyes.

"Yes."

Then, so fast, she had no idea how it happened, Lachlan the man became Lachlan the wolf.

She'd never seen anything so wondrous, even in her imagination. Not to pass such an ability on to his children would be a tragedy. She remembered her wonder the first time she had seen a shooting star, but this was even more glorious. How incredible that God had made a people capable of such a feat.

She felt privileged to have witnessed the secret miracle. Lachlan had given her another unique gift and she would remember it forever.

As a man, he was everything any woman could desire. As a wolf, he was utterly beautiful. His pelt was glossy black. She'd thought so last night, but moonlight wasn't reliable for revealing color. He was also huge, standing almost as tall as her, but on all fours. His eyes were the same brown with gold around the irises, but they looked sharper.

His head was big, like the rest of him, and he held himself with a regal bearing that reminded her of Lachlan the man. Just as he always had seemed more than a man, he now seemed more than a beast. Human intelligence glowed in his wolf 's eyes.

He watched her intently with those eyes, as if waiting for something.

She could not think what at first, but then it occurred to her that he might be waiting for her to show she was not afraid. Was he waiting for her invitation to touch? Deciding that must be it, she dropped to her knees and put her hand out, welcoming him to come to her.

He padded across the floor, the strange noise he'd made the night before rumbling in his chest. He stopped mere inches away. She tilted her head back and he lowered his so their eyes met.

His spoke secret messages to her heart that she labeled love and a tiny curl of joy pushed some of the pain out of her heart. He licked her cheek delicately and only then did she realize she had allowed a stray tear to escape.

The same sense of connection as the night before shimmered between them and she labeled it love, pushing another chunk of pain deep into the recesses of her heart.

He butted her shoulder gently as if asking for something. She smoothed her hand over his muzzle and the top of his head. He stood still, letting her pet him until, with a small smile, she rested her hand against the side of his neck.

"You like to be touched."

He nodded his big wolf's head and then sat back on his haunches in a single graceful movement.

"I do, too," she admitted. "When you are the one doing the touching."

Did wolves smile? She thought he did because when he bared his teeth, she felt no menace from him. Then he did what he said he'd wanted to, burying his snout in her hair and inhaling deeply. The rumbling in his chest grew louder. She dug her fingers into his fur and massaged down his back. He gave a short bark of approval that made her smile.

They stayed like that a long time, him nuzzling her hair and neck and she petting him and reveling in the incredible miracle of his wolf 's body. She told him how beautiful she thought he was and how amazing. The rumbling in his chest got louder until it vibrated through her body as if he was sharing his pleasure with her.

She was not a wolf, but she felt as if she were inside him and he were inside her.

Without warning, he changed again and he was on his knees facing her, his arms around her and his lips trailing a path of burning kisses from her temple to her mouth.

When he reached it, he kissed her with such sweetness, tears pricked her eyes. "Thank you for accepting my beast, Emily."

"How could I not?" she asked in genuine bewilderment. "He's a special and very wonderful part of you."

He kissed her again, his mouth harder and more insistent until she was melting against him. He pulled his mouth away from hers, but she could still feel his breath on her lips. "I think you are the wonderful one."

"But not special enough to bear your children."

They both went still. She hadn't meant to say that. It was a reality that threatened to crack the fragile shell of fantasy she had surrounded herself with. She could not allow that. She didn't want to give up this taste of joy and pleasure for a reality that could not be changed . . . for a reality she had known only too well for far too long.

"Please forget I said that."

"I'm sorry."

She knew he meant it; she also knew he hadn't changed his mind. "It's all right. Kiss me again. I want to feel your lips on mine." She wanted to forget the truth of their relationship and she knew, as she had the night before, that he could give her that forgetfulness.

"Gladly." And he did, the kiss going from tender to carnal in the space of heartbeats.

Whatever he did not feel for her, he wanted her as much as she wanted him and she reveled in that knowledge, feeding it to her heart in the game she played with herself until the pain was almost completely eclipsed by the pleasure.

He pulled back, breathing hard. "I want you naked, Emily."

She had no thought of demurring. They stood together in one accord and then stepped back from each other. She wasted no time taking off her tunic and then her shift, exposing her body to his scorching gaze.

In one of those lightning quick movements that still startled her, he crossed the distance between them, picked her up and carried her to the bed. He pulled the plaid away and laid her back on the furs. The softness felt incredibly good against her skin and she moaned.

He smiled wickedly and started kissing her again. He used his tongue this time and she loved it. His big body rubbed against her, increasing her ardor to a fever pitch and he had not even touched her as he had on the previous occasions.

When she was moaning over and over again and thrashing below him, he began to kiss his way down her face, stopping at the pulse beating frantically in her neck and sucking there.

Liquid heat pooled between her legs. *"Lachlan."*

"I am marking you," he said in guttural voice. "When others see this love bite, they will know you are mine."

She was so far into her game of make-believe that she was not sure if he actually said those words or if she had made them up in her mind, but she didn't care. He *had* marked her and he was rubbing his body all over hers in a way that seemed strange, but excited her, too.

His mouth traveled to her chest and he licked her where his wolf had kissed her the night before. The feelings his touch elicited were not the same though. This time all she felt was pure sexual pleasure and she whimpered with need.

He kneaded her breasts with knowing movements until her nipples were turgid and aching. His hot mouth closed over one and he began sucking, flicking the tip with his tongue. She cried out and arched toward him. He pinched her other nipple and then began rolling it between his thumb and forefinger with torturous slowness. It felt so good that tears of joy seeped out of her tightly closed eyelids.

Her legs spread of their own volition and she tilted her pelvis up to rub herself against him, but she could not find the relief she sought. She needed his touch *there*, like the night before. Mindless with her pleasure, she demanded it in a voice raw with desire.

He pulled his mouth from her nipple with a pop and laughed, the sound diabolical. But she felt no frisson of fear at the implied threat, only anticipation of what he would do next.

His hand slid down her body until his fingertip was right

above where she most needed it to be. "I will touch you *down there*, my sweet mate, but not like I did last night."

His mouth forged a scorching trail down her body until his face was between her thighs. She was beyond embarrassment and could do no more than express her need with guttural cries. He gently separated her tender, swollen flesh with his fingers and then pressed his mouth against her sweetest spot in a kiss of homage before licking her with one long swipe.

She lost all sense of who she was or what he was doing at that moment. It all became sensation upon sensation. The feelings inside her spiraled tighter and tighter as he did things with his lips, teeth and tongue that made her body jerk and shudder. She cried out her love for him as the storm of passion howled inside her, lifting her body into a bow.

All at once, everything inside her clenched in a crystalline moment of excruciating pleasure. Then her body clenched again and again in a series of increasingly strong convulsions until she could not bear it. Yet she could not stop moving against his mouth either.

It was too much. Too wonderful. Too amazing. Too intense. As the indescribable pleasure spiraled to a peak of sheer perfection, she lost the final thread connecting her to this new reality of being a Chrechte warrior's lover.

Chapter 18

When the waves of pleasure receded and she became aware of her surroundings once more, Lachlan was leaning over her, his eyes glowing almost pure gold. He looked very satisfied with himself. "Good?"

"Unbelievable," she croaked and realized her throat was raw from screaming.

"Sleep and then I will show you how to pleasure me."

"I don't want to sleep. I want to pleasure you now." She needed to see him go wild for her in order for her fantasy to be complete.

"I need time to regain my control."

"I don't want you in control."

"Do you hope to tease me into taking you, Emily?" he asked quietly. "It would probably work. I have never been as out of control with a woman as I am with you."

The admission touched her deep inside, but the accusation stung, threatening to bring back the pain. "I don't want to trick you into anything. I want to pleasure you. Please believe me, Lachlan."

He sighed. "I know."

"If you say we must wait, then we will wait."

He closed his glowing eyes, his face twisting in a kind of agony she now understood. Sexual need had his body in its grip. "Put your hand on me."

"Are you sure?"

"Yes. You pleasuring me will be enough." He said it like he was telling himself as well as her.

She was determined to make the words true. She would satisfy him, for nothing else would satisfy her. "Lie on your back first."

His eyes snapped open. "Why?"

She wasn't sure. It just seemed right. "I want you at my mercy like I was at yours," she said and realized that sounded right, too.

"Unless you tie me to the bed, I will never be at your mercy."

"I'll consider that for sometime in the future." Though how much of a future they had she refused to speculate on at the moment.

He laughed out loud and then rolled onto his back. His erection strained upward, almost parallel to his muscular stomach. She curled her fingers around it. They did not quite touch, but he didn't seem to mind. He sighed in bliss, laid his hand over hers and proceeded to show her how to pleasure him.

He was thrusting up into the tunnel created by both of her hands when she had the idea of kissing him the way he had kissed her. Bending over, she brushed her hair against his thighs. This drove him crazy and he started thrusting against her hand so fast she could barely see the movement.

"Stop," she commanded.

He ignored her.

She released him and demanded again, "Stop, Lachlan."

He glared at her, his body rigid with tension.

She curled one hand around him again and caressed him from tip to root. "I want to kiss you."

She'd succeeded in shocking him. "You don't have to," he strangled out.

"I want to. Is there anything special I should do?"

He shook his head. "Whatever you want."

"And will you like it as much as I did?"

"More."

She liked hearing that and smiled. Then she leaned down and kissed the slit at the tip of his shaft. He growled. She licked him, a single swipe that caught his taste . . . a salty sweetness that gave her tremendous pleasure. She took the broad tip into her mouth and swirled her tongue around. His hips moved in short, jerky movements, but he did not start thrusting again and she explored him with her tongue and lips as thoroughly as he had explored her.

He shuddered. "Suck it, please Emily, suck me."

She sucked as much of him as she could into her mouth and wrapped both hands around his hardness below her lips. He pulsed against her fingers, his skin so hot it almost burned her.

Suddenly he grabbed her hair and yanked her head back from him. "Enough."

Her grip on him tightened convulsively and he thrust upward with an earsplitting shout, then thick white fluid erupted from his male member as it jerked in her hands. She didn't know what to do to prolong the pleasure like he had done with her, so she just held him as his hips thrust up and down and he spurted several more times, but none of them lasting as long as the first one.

Finally, he fell back against the bed, his eyes closed, his face for once devoid of any harsh lines and his body completely slack. She forced herself to climb from the bed on unsteady legs.

"Where are you going?" he asked with his eyes shut.

"My hands are messy . . . I want to wash them."

He said nothing to that and she did as she'd said she wanted to, then searched through a trunk against the wall for a cloth and thankfully found one. She stumbled back to the bed and he allowed her to clean away the evidence of his pleasure without so much as a murmur. Something about his passive acceptance touched her deeply. Perhaps because her ministrations now felt every bit as intimate as what they had just done.

When she was finished, she dropped the cloth on the floor, grabbed the plaid and pulled it over them both as she settled against his side, her head on his chest. "I liked that."

"I did, too, sweeting." His words slurred together and were barely discernible. He said something else, but she didn't understand and finally she wondered if that language was Chrechte.

She asked and he said yes, but didn't volunteer a translation. He sounded far too tired to give one and she did not mind. She'd satisfied him to the point of exhaustion and she was very, very proud of that. Realizing she was a bit tired herself, she let her eyes close.

Lachlan smiled as Emily's body relaxed into sleep. She felt so right next to him with her small hand over his heart. He had never known such a sense of peace as he did in that moment.

He trailed the silken strands of her hair back from her face. She was so lovely, so perfect for him in every way but one. She was not Chrechte, but she was as courageous as a femwolf and she accepted his beast completely. He had never changed in front of a human woman, not even his own mother, but he had felt no inhibition about changing in front of Emily.

She'd touched his wolf's body with obvious delight and affection. Even his prolonged werewolf orgasm had not disgusted her as he had heard it did some human women. In fact, her passion was as uninhibited as any femwolf's.

Their fit had been so perfect that he had even called her his mate in the heat of the moment. She had not seemed to notice, or mayhap she was unaware of the significance of such a claim. But just as he had not been able to hold back from marking her body with his scent and her throat with his love bite, he had made the verbal claiming as well.

If she had been a femwolf, she would expect marriage. By rights, since he had made the claim, he should offer anyway.

Which duty dictated his honor more strongly? That to his clan to wed within the Chrechte or that to his integrity to follow through on the verbal promise he had made? Telling himself that since she did not know it had been a declaration of intention, he was not held to it, did not diminish his sense of obligation. *He* had known what it would mean and he had said the words anyway.

She had not trapped him with her body; he had trapped himself with a need he had been unable to suppress.

Was that how his father had come to be married to a human woman? It was something Lachlan had only asked his father about once and the tough warrior had said that when destiny slapped you upside the head, you listened, or you paid the price for your arrogance. Lachlan had not understood his father's words at the time, but later he thought his father meant that he'd had sex with a woman and found himself true-mated. Lachlan had been determined never to make that mistake.

But he wondered if he had merely been running from his destiny.

He was past the age when he should have taken a wife, and Emily was the first woman he had even considered spending the rest of his life with. He had made excuses for that reality, but the truth was . . . he knew the femwolves of his clan and although he liked and admired many of them, none of them appealed to him as a future mate.

He had considered Susannah, but merely because she

was sister to his first-in-command and Lachlan liked her. He had never felt the consuming passion in her presence he did when he was with Emily. He had known Susannah was in heat at the last full moon and had assumed they would end up mated when she ran with the pack. His wolf's nature would dictate that he fight for her and no other wolf could hope to beat him.

However, one of the reasons Ulf's suggestions for vengeance had been so repugnant to him was that Lachlan had been *relieved* to discover she had mated another. He could hardly go to war over a situation from which he benefited, even if he did not want to admit such a thing to his pack, or even to himself.

He could go to another clan and look for a wife. He had considered that plan many times, but he had never followed through on the intention. Now, he could not imagine finding a woman as perfect for him as the one sleeping so securely in his arms. Even if she had no beast inside to match his own.

And she loved him.

Perhaps it was time he stopped running from his destiny and accepted that God alone could determine the future of the Chrechte. Making love to Emily completely would determine if she was his true mate. If she was, who was he, a mere mortal, to thwart providence?

Emily woke to the sensation of her naked body being caressed by the sun.

Her eyes fluttered open.

Lachlan was watching her with his wolf's eyes, his hands the sun against her sensitive skin. "Good afternoon, sweeting."

She yawned delicately, arching into the delicious sensations he evoked. "I fell asleep."

"I did, too." He sounded bemused by that fact.

She felt his hardness surge against her thigh. "You're not asleep now."

"Far from it."

She smiled, his obvious desire for her and the beautiful dreams she'd woken from putting her in a very good mood.

She'd dreamt of being in the water, of all things, but there had been no terror. Lachlan had finished teaching her to swim and then they had made love. Parts of the dream were vague and unfocused as if even her sleeping mind could not conjure up how to accomplish such a feat in the water, but the remembered pleasure of his caresses still pulsed through her body.

It was easy to slip back into the fantasy that his touch and affection were born of deeper feelings than lust. She had no regrets for allowing him such liberties with her body or taking equally ardent ones with his. If that made her more wanton than a lady, so be it. She was at least happy for this brief moment in time.

She smoothed her hand down his naked flank, loving the feel of hair-roughened skin over muscles as ungiving as a rock. "You are so hard."

"Aye." He thrust against her hip. "Very hard."

Giggling, she pinched his backside, which was as solid as the rest of him. "I meant your body, you wicked man."

"I did, too, but mayhap we each meant a different part of my body."

"You know we did." She moved her hand to his manhood, caressing its length. "Though this is probably the hardest bit of all and that is saying something."

"At the moment it is."

She laughed and he kissed her, his mouth swallowing her expression of joy.

Unlike before her nap when everything had been overwhelming passion and harsh carnal delight, they caressed each other languidly, learning the secrets of one another's bodies while the tension between them built. He touched her everywhere and in doing so gave her permission to do likewise. Her own arousal at a fever pitch, she made him roll onto his stomach, so she could explore his back.

Pushing his long black hair away from his neck and shoulders with one hand, she brushed her fingertips down his nape with the other. He shivered beneath her.

"You like that?" she asked, her voice impossibly husky.

"Yes."

She did it again, but she wanted to touch all of him. She started kneading the bulging muscles of his back. It was a good thing she was used to working bread and had strong fingers because he was so hard everywhere. When she got to his backside, she pushed his thighs apart so she could trail her fingertip down the center of his cheeks to the soft spot just before his scrotum.

He made a harsh sound and then that pleasure growl that made his chest rumble. She bit her lip wondering how she could increase the sensation. She pressed lightly against the tender skin, reaching under him with her other hand to gently cup his stones.

"Yes!" he shouted into the furs on the bed.

She pressed deeper into that small area of flesh between his bottom and his scrotum and he bucked, his entire body jerking. She bent down and kissed him there, reaching with her tongue to tickle his stones.

He erupted from the bed, yanking her onto her back and under his heaving body. He stared down at her, his eyes almost wholly gold and so serious she caught her breath.

He reached down between her legs and caressed her wet heat, gliding his thumb along her sweetest spot. "You offered me your virginity. I ask formal permission to enter your body now."

She moaned and his words took several seconds to penetrate the haze of passion surrounding her. When they did, the sweet fantasy she had created shattered around her. She could not breathe. He did not love her and the last thing he really wanted was to make love to her completely. She did not understand how this time he had lost control so much when their touching had been so much more tender and slow, but he must be nearly out of his head to suggest such a thing.

She should not have touched him like she had, but she had not foreseen the consequences.

She shook her head wildly.

He stared down at her, his brows drawn together in a scowl. "You're denying me?"

She forced words from her suddenly tight throat. "I'm denying you. You don't really want it."

One blunt, man-sized fingertip penetrated her opening. "But I do, Emily. I want to bury myself in your body very much."

It felt so good, but she could not hide behind the physical ecstasy when he threatened his own future. With strength born of desperation and gut-wrenching pain, she shoved him off of her and rolled from the bed, landing on the hard floor with a bruising thump.

She scrambled to her feet. "I won't trap you that way, Lachlan. I won't! Was it sleeping together that broke your control? We can't do that again. I think it would be best if I left. If we share our bodies again, I will be careful not to touch you the way I did just now."

Tears burning her eyes, she searched for her clothes. She spied her shift on the floor and grabbed it. She had started yanking it over her head when it was torn from her grasp.

With a hard hand on her shoulder, Lachlan spun her to face him. "What is the matter with you?"

Wild with grief for the taste of happiness she had lost, she gave a convulsive sob. "I promised I wouldn't trap you with your own lust. Please, I'm sorry, but I must leave."

If she didn't, she was going to give in, and once his lust

had subsided, he would never forgive her. Especially if they turned out to be true mates.

He grabbed her upper arms with both hands, his grip strangely gentle, and pulled her close. His eyes were filled with warmth. "Your conviction to adhere to your promise does you credit, sweet Emily, but I do not require that promise of you any longer. I would much rather you followed through on your promise to give me your body."

"I did not promise that!"

"You offered me your virginity. Do you deny it?"

"No," she choked out, "but that was before I realized how against any sort of lasting attachment between us you are."

"I may have changed my mind about that." He sounded rational, but his member protruded hard and throbbing between them and his body vibrated with tension that belied his calm tone.

"That's lust talking, not you." And she almost hated him for giving in to it. Didn't he know how hard it was for her to tell him no? To refuse her deepest desire? "You don't want a human wife. If we make love and find we are true-mated, you won't have a choice. You'll end up hating me."

"If we find we are sacred mates, that tells us that God created us one for the other."

"You don't believe that. I know you don't. I've got to leave. Please, let me go," she pleaded brokenly.

He shook his head, his expression no longer warm, but implacable. "I want you, Emily. I don't want another woman or a femwolf. Only you."

"That will change after I leave."

"I'd sooner kill Talorc then let him take you back."

"Don't say that! He is Cait's brother, remember."

"But not your mate."

"No. I already told you I won't marry him."

"It does not matter. Marriage or no, you do not belong to the Sinclairs. You belong to the Balmoral clan now and evermore." He picked up her English dress and ripped it into shreds, the violence of his actions further proof that, his words to the contrary, he was out of control. "You will wear our plaid from this day forward."

She stared at the pile of torn strips on the floor that used to be her dress. "I can't."

"You have no choice."

She shook her head, pain twisting her insides. "You can't mean to marry me."

Before he could answer, someone pounded on the door to his chamber. Ulf's voice shouted from the other side, his words indistinct to Emily, but his urgency unmistakable. Lachlan scowled and crossed the room to swing open the door without bothering to dress.

Emily dove for the bed, yanking the plaid over her nakedness as Ulf came into view.

"What is it?" Lachlan demanded.

Ulf glared at Emily. "Not in front of her."

Lachlan sighed with impatience and stepped into the solar, still naked, closing the door behind him.

A moment later, he returned, his expression grim. "Our mating will have to wait, but mark this, English . . . you offered me your body and I will have it . . . along with the rest of you."

The rest? Was he talking about her heart? No. Impossible. And he'd change his mind about her body soon enough, too. Wouldn't he?

He dressed quickly. "I will have Marta bring you a woman's plaid." And then he left without so much as a kiss or explanation of what had required his immediate attention.

But she feared she knew already. Talorc.

She'd finished washing with another cloth from the trunk and the cold water remaining in the pitcher and had donned her shift when Marta arrived with the woman's plaid. The housekeeper helped Emily figure out how to put it on over her shift, her expression worried.

"Do you know what has happened?" Emily asked.

"A young soldier was found dead near the loch. It looked as if a wild animal had gotten him."

Or Talorc. Worried for what this might mean to Cait, Emily thanked Marta, picked up her skirt and ran to the great hall. She skidded to a halt ten feet from a knot of soldiers. She could hear Lachlan's voice, but could not see him.

He was demanding details from someone . . . Ulf . . . who had apparently found the body.

"He was dead when I found him, I told you. But if you think wild animals did this to a Balmoral soldier . . ." His voice trailed off, allowing his listeners to conjecture what he thought of such an assumption.

"There is no scent of an animal on him," Lachlan said with a deadly quiet voice.

"There is no scent at all," Angus, she thought it was, said.

"Talorc." Drustan's voice was filled with fury.

"No." That was Cait's voice and it was laced with torment.

Emily rushed around the soldiers, looking for her friend. She found Cait standing beside her husband, but they were not touching and he was glaring down at her.

Cait's brown eyes were shiny with appeal. "Talorc would no more kill a boy barely out of childhood than I would."

"Didn't you?" Drustan asked.

"What do you mean?" Cait's voice was faint.

"If you had told me the truth, this boy would not be dead."

"That is what you get for trying to make your enemy a member of your clan," Ulf said with disgust. He condemned Lachlan with a look. "Your plan for reparation did nothing but bring grief and loss to our clan. Is she"—he nodded toward Cait with a sneer—"worth this boy's life?"

Emily couldn't believe they were all trying to blame Cait. Even if Talorc had done this dreadful thing, she wasn't responsible. Apprising the Balmoral of his presence at the lake would not have made any difference. If the man didn't want to be found, he wouldn't be.

Which made it difficult for her to believe Talorc was responsible for the young soldier's death. Were they all so steeped in prejudice that they didn't see that?

"Wait," Cait whispered. "You've got to listen to me."

"Anything you had to say worth hearing should have been said yesterday," Drustan replied with disgust.

"You're making a terrible mistake," Cait insisted stubbornly, though she looked as if her heart were breaking.

If she'd had a bucket of cold water handy, Emily would have thrown it over Drustan and Ulf. Both to cool their tempers and just because she wanted to. They were being idiots, and while she was used to that with Ulf, she'd come to expect more from Drustan. She would have said so, but even she could tell right now was not the time for plain-speaking.

"The only mistake I made was believing your marriage vows meant something to you."

"They did!" Cait cried. "They do. If you would only listen."

"Do you know where Talorc is now?"

"No, but—"

"Then you have nothing to add to this situation. Go to our chambers. This is Balmoral clan business."

"I am a member of this clan."

"Are you?"

Cait's eyes filled with tears.

Drustan looked totally unmoved by her obvious hurt. "My clan comes first with me. If you were a member of this clan, it would come first in loyalty with you, too. *I would come first* . . . before your precious brother. You and Emily knew that Talorc was spying, that he was on the island, and yet you said nothing. Emily, I can understand—"

"I can't," Lachlan interrupted in a chilling voice.

Emily's gaze snapped from Cait to him.

His eyes so recently filled with passion now looked on her with dark contempt. "You lied to me."

"I didn't."

"Clever misdirection is still a lie. You knew what I was asking and you deliberately withheld the truth from me."

"I don't want war between the Sinclairs and the Balmorals any more than Cait does."

"What difference does it make to you?"

She wasn't going to use Cait as her excuse. The poor woman had enough blame heaped on her. "I didn't want anyone killed."

"Like this boy?" he asked.

And she looked down at the body at their feet. Bile rose in her stomach. Blood was everywhere and his face was as pale and lifeless as stone.

"I'm not convinced Talorc did this."

"Why?"

"Because he wouldn't need to. He's too good a warrior to be caught out by such a new soldier." The boy could not have been more than thirteen summers.

"Maybe he just wanted to."

Cait gasped out a protest.

Revolted he could even suggest such a thing, Emily said, "That is a horrible accusation to make. Talorc may have the manners of a pig, but he doesn't kill for pleasure."

"How would you know? Or did you know him much better than you told me you did?"

She could see Ulf gloating out of the corner of her eye and she wanted to kick him. Did the man even have a good side?

"What do you mean?" she demanded of Lachlan.

"Did you hope to seduce me into forgetting my duty while your betrothed . . . or is he your *husband* . . . spied on my people and decided best how to attack us?"

Drustan jerked back as if shocked by Lachlan's words, and his expression went from angry to enlightened to remorseful in rapid succession.

"No, it wasn't like that." Emily couldn't believe Lachlan was talking of their time together as if it were something foul. "I am not his wife. I am not his betrothed even. I told you I'm not going to marry him."

"And your word is worth less than your promise."

"My promise is worth everything. You should know."

"You mean because you refused to let me enter your body? I might have found out you were not a virgin. I thought your passion uninhibited, but the way you used your hands and your mouth was a little too knowing."

Emily couldn't speak. She felt like someone had driven a stake through her chest.

Ulf sniggered.

Drustan said, "Lachlan . . ."

"Why so silent, Emily? You are never at a loss for words. Where is your denial? Your so-called desire was nothing more than experience masquerading as innocence, wasn't it?" He shook her by the shoulders. "Answer me, you bloody-minded woman. Where is your sharp tongue now?"

Emily shook her head, the pain inside her too big for any words, and then she shoved against his chest. It was a feeble attempt at best, but he let her go. His expression was one she couldn't decipher, his face almost as pale as the dead soldier at his feet.

And then Cait was there, her hands on her hips, her face inches from Lachlan's. "Don't you speak like that to her, you bastard!"

Drustan pulled Cait around to face him. "Do not dare show such disrespect to your laird." The words were harsh, but the tone he said them in was almost gentle. "You will apologize, my own."

Cait shook off his hold and stepped back, away from all of them. "I don't belong to you and he's not my laird. Our marriage vows meant nothing. You said so."

"I also told you to go to our chambers, but I see that you are still here. Not all words spoken in anger have meaning."

Apparently while Lachlan had been venting his anger, Drustan's had been waning, but Emily didn't think Cait noticed. Or if she did, that she cared.

She glared at her husband, her eyes glistening with moisture. "How remiss of me, to stay where I'm not wanted."

She spun on her heel and ran from the great hall, becoming nothing but a blur of color even as Drustan shouted her name.

"For *that*, we lost a promising soldier," Ulf said.

Drustan punched him straight in the face, and Ulf went flying backward to land with a thud a good dozen feet away. "Do not ever speak of my mate in that tone again or I will kill you."

Ulf sat up, shaking his head, his eyes dazed.

And in that moment, several things became clear to Emily. All of them painful. Most disturbing was a suspicion she had no doubt that if she voiced would go unheeded. After all, in Lachlan's eyes, she was the betrayer.

But looking at his brother, so filled with vindictiveness, spite and a thirst for blood, she could not help wondering if he would kill one of his own soldiers to try to push Lachlan into the one thing his brother had refused to do.

Declare war.

Chapter 19

Knowing that to voice her suspicions would be useless, Emily did not wait around to see Lachlan's reaction to his first-in-command threatening his brother.

She ran after Cait, getting away from the men in the hall as fast as she could. She could not believe Lachlan had said the things he had to her. She might one day forgive him, though that was not a certainty. But she would never forget he'd humiliated her like that in front of his soldiers.

And he had said he wanted to claim her. Hah!

When she reached the door to Drustan's quarters, it was closed, but she was sure Cait was inside. She pushed, but the door would not open. She knocked, or rather pounded on the thick door.

"Cait, it's me," she called, trying to penetrate the wood with her calls.

The door swung open and Cait drew Emily inside, shutting it again with a slam behind her and pushing the bar back into place. Her eyes were red, but she was not crying.

She looked too mad to cry. "How dare he say that to me? He accused me of murdering that boy, did you hear him?"

"Yes, but I don't think he meant it."

"But he said it." The pained guilt in Cait's gaze tore at Emily's heart. "Maybe he was right."

"No, he wasn't! Even if Talorc did kill the soldier, and I suspect strongly he didn't, you would not be responsible just because you did not alert Drustan to the danger. Any fool would have assumed your brother would come himself or send spies to see the lay of the land. And if they were capable of going undetected on Sinclair land, they should have realized the Sinclairs had the same ability here."

Cait hugged herself around her pregnant belly. "Drustan is no fool and neither is the Balmoral."

"So I thought," Emily said with venom, remembering the idiotic things Lachlan had accused her of.

"I don't know if they guessed Talorc was on the island, but Lachlan knew as of last night. A femwolf spotted my brother and reported it. The laird told Drustan this morning."

"So, why are they so angry we didn't tell them yesterday? It would have made no difference to what happened to that boy if we had . . . since they already knew when he was killed."

"That is a logical conclusion, Emily, but I'm not convinced men are always so clearheaded in their thinking."

"No, I think you're right." Lachlan's painful accusations definitely fell in the irrational-thinking camp. "Drustan hit Ulf, by the way, for sneering at you. He threatened to kill him if Ulf insulted you again and I'm sure he meant it, even though his own words to you were much worse."

Cait looked briefly gratified by that news, but was soon frowning again. "Yes, what you heard in the hall was even worse than what he said to me earlier in private."

"After Lachlan told him about Talorc being spotted?"

"Yes. He waited until I'd woken from my nap to ask me

about it. You would think he was being courteous, wouldn't you?" she asked, making it clear with her tone what she thought of her husband's level of courtesy.

"What did he say?"

"He wanted to know if I'd seen my brother. I couldn't lie flat out, so I told him. Emily, I wanted to tell him so much, especially after we discovered we are true mates, but I was so scared and he didn't understand that at all."

"He thought you should not have cared if your brother was killed by the Balmoral?"

"I don't know. He just kept saying I should have trusted him, but how could I? He doesn't love Talorc. He doesn't even like him."

That made Emily smile.

Without any warning at all, Cait burst into tears. "Maybe I should have trusted Drustan. He seemed hurt by my lack of belief in him. He hates me now, you heard him."

Emily put her arm around Cait's shoulder. "But men see things so differently than we do. I remember one time my father had a boy flogged for stealing an apple from our orchard. He did not understand when the boy's mother, who worked in our kitchens, glared at him every time she saw him after that. To his mind stealing was wrong. It shocked him that she would risk his ire over such a trifle."

"But he'd hurt her son," Cait said, making an obvious attempt to stem the flow of her tears.

"Yes, emotions cannot be dictated by the petty rules and wars of men."

Cait laughed, the sound harsh. "Emotions can't be dictated by anything, even sound reasoning. I love Drustan, but I shouldn't. And now he hates me," she repeated.

"I don't believe that. He wouldn't have hit Ulf and threatened him if he hated you."

"His pride would be pricked by an insult to me."

"I think you were right a moment ago when you said that Drustan was hurt by your lack of belief in him. As your husband, he expects to come first with you, but if you are sacred mates, I think that it's more than an issue of pride for him."

"True-mating is not a result of love."

"No, but I'm sure it leads to it."

"I hope so because I don't want to be miserable alone."

Emily laughed at that. "I'm sure he's every bit as miserable. He looked good and upset when you ran from the hall, now that I think about it."

"Did he? Are you sure?"

"Yes."

"He was just worried for the babe."

"It's not even his child; if he worries for it, he does so because he cares for you."

"Do you think so?"

"I am certain of it."

"But earlier he said I might as well wear the Sinclair plaid and be done with it. And in the hall, he said our marriage vows didn't mean anything."

"He said he believed they did not mean anything *to you*. Those are the words of a hurting man, not merely an angry one." She hoped she was right, but even if men were terribly different from women, they couldn't be so nonsensical that no amount of logic could be applied to them.

"I wish I had trusted him, but even now I can't convince myself that to have told him would have been the right course to take."

"It's a matter I think you two should discuss further."

"Are you going to discuss Lachlan's accusations with him?" Cait asked.

"That's different. He is not my husband." But even though she did not think he would give her words any credence, she would have to tell him her suspicions about Ulf.

Cait sniffed the air near Emily delicately. "He marked you with his scent."

"I washed," Emily mumbled.

"But a werewolf 's scent does not wash away that easily. He claimed you."

"No, he didn't . . . he only touched me. We didn't even . . ." She let her voice trail off, but she knew Cait would understand what she was alluding to.

"You came close."

"He wanted to, at the end. I think that was why he was so angry in the great hall. He thought I'd almost tricked him into mating with me, but I wasn't going to allow it. I know he doesn't want a human woman for a wife."

"He wants you, Emily."

"Lust . . . it's not the same," Emily said, her throat constricting with tears she would not shed.

Cait sighed. "No, it isn't." She broke away from Emily's hug and started pacing. "But we cannot afford to be preoccupied with that right now. Both Drustan and Lachlan are so busy being angry with us for deceiving them that they are not looking at things logically."

"Which means we will have to do so for them."

"Precisely."

"Lachlan said there was no scent of an animal on the soldier. Is it possible for an animal to have killed him and not left a scent behind?"

Cait stopped pacing and frowned. "No, but then there should be the scent of a man or a werewolf on him and there isn't. Except Ulf's and that's because he found him and carried him back to the keep. There was no scent in the area where the boy was wounded."

"You said your brother could mask his scent."

"It wasn't Talorc. I'm sure of it."

"I believe you, but he's not the only werewolf with that ability."

"No, it's something you are trained to do from the time of your first change . . . though I never got that good at it. But it doesn't matter. A werewolf can mask his own scent, but not the scent he leaves on others."

"Then how was the boy killed?"

"Without being touched . . . perhaps with a knife that had been cleaned in sand and dirt from the bottom of the loch."

"To remove any scent from his handling of the blade?"

"Yes."

"But that would mean the killer did not touch the young soldier at all . . . not even to subdue him, right?"

Cait looked sick. "Yes. The soldier had to know him and worse, the boy was Chrechte. He probably did not have control of his change yet, but it would take another werewolf or a very strong human warrior to kill him."

"It would have to be a Balmoral and an experienced one at that." Emily's suspicion of Ulf grew. "Lachlan is not going to suspect one of his own people of such an atrocity."

"I agree. We need to talk to Talorc. He may have seen something."

"But how? I doubt we will be allowed out of the keep, much less beyond the castle walls. Lachlan was angry we'd gone out without escort before. He said he was worried for our safety, but he probably did not trust us," she said angrily.

She would wait to tell Cait her suspicions until they heard what Talorc had to say. If she was wrong, she would prefer no one knew what she had thought. She had enough problems with Lachlan's brother without accusing him of a crime she was not absolutely sure he committed.

"Either way, he would have instructed the guards at the gate to prevent our departure."

"What do we do?"

Cait didn't answer, but rushed into the bedchamber. She came back seconds later carrying her Sinclair plaid.

"You're going to change your plaid?" Emily asked in confusion. She knew her friend was irritated with her husband, but to take his words to heart right now seemed a waste of time and effort.

"No. I plan to use this to gain our freedom." With her femwolf strength, she started ripping the plaid into long thin strips.

When she was done, she tied the strips together until she had a thin plaid that was nearly one hundred feet long.

Without waiting to be asked, Emily took one end and, bending her arms, separated her hands so Cait could wind the cloth around them like a thick skein of wool. "What are we going to do with the rope?"

"There is a room at the top of this tower. It can be used to hold prisoners, like your chamber, but it has a window large enough for us to climb through on the side that connects to the outer wall."

"Why on earth would it?"

"I believe it's intended for use in case of a siege, for escape or to get more food supplies. It is too high to be reached by anything but a siege tower, and a tall one at that. But there is only a narrow strip of land between the wall and the cliff. No siege tower could possibly approach the castle from that direction and archers can't get good aim at it either."

"I see . . . but if we're going to escape through it, then couldn't a prisoner?"

"A warrior's plaid wouldn't make a long enough rope and women are rarely captives. Besides, it would only be used if your chamber was already occupied. Do we really need to discuss this now, Emily?"

"I'm sorry. My curiosity gets the better of me sometimes."

Cait smiled. "I like that about you."

Emily grimaced. "Just not right now. I understand. We will have to hope the guards on the wall walk do not see us."

"It's a risk we will have to take. But unless the guard on the tower hangs down to look over the side, he will not. There is no other way out of the keep or the castle walls that I can think of."

Emily bit her lip. "I can't either, but if the room is above this one, the drop to the ground is very long. That is too dangerous for a woman in your condition. I will go to the lake and search for Talorc. I can tell him the situation and ask if he has seen anything."

"No. You'd never find him before the others, but I will. Do not worry, Emily. I am a femwolf, I will not fall." Cait put the plaid rope over her shoulder. "I would do nothing to put my bairn at risk, but we cannot allow war between the clans either. And I will not have my brother killed for another man's crimes."

"Not to mention that if there is a murderer among the Balmoral, he needs to be stopped."

"Exactly."

Cait opened the door and stuck her head out, listening intently. Then she turned to Emily and motioned for her to go ahead. Emily was as silent as she could be climbing the tower steps. Cait was beside her a second later and they made their way to the top room of the tower.

Once there, they maintained their silence even after shutting the door quietly. Cait climbed onto the table, the only piece of furniture in the room. There wasn't even a bed. She tied the makeshift rope to an iron loop in the wall, testament that the window was intended for the purpose she had suggested.

Then she stripped out of her clothing, tied it into a tight bundle with her belt and waited with obvious expectation for Emily to do the same. Apparently, swimming wasn't the only thing she could not do with a dress on. Climbing down a tower wall was another. She wasn't sure that was true, but she wasn't going to waste time arguing.

She didn't know how long she and Cait had before Lachlan began the search for Talorc . . . if he hadn't already. She didn't think their conversation had lasted very long, but she could not be sure.

After only a brief hesitation, Emily quickly stripped off

her plaid and shift. Cait tied both bundles to the free end of the rope before lowering it out the window. Once that was done, she disappeared out the window herself. Emily climbed on the table and then leaned out to watch her friend's progress down the dangerous climb.

The fact that Cait was naked wasn't nearly as disconcerting as how far she would have to fall if her hand slipped on the rope. But Cait reached the ground faster than Emily would have thought possible and then it was her turn.

She climbed out the window, focused on the task at hand and not how far down the ground was. Without her dress on, she could wrap the rope around one leg, giving herself a sense of security, even if it was false. She also wasn't as heavy without her plaid and thought Cait must have considered that.

She used the knots in the rope as natural resting places and took a lot longer to reach the ground than Cait had. A cold wind buffeted her nakedness, but the exertion from the climb kept her from getting chilled. By the time she reached the ground though, her arms were shaking from the strain and she was grateful for her friend's help untangling from the rope. She dressed quickly, noting Cait had already done so.

They left the rope dangling. Although Emily knew they wouldn't use it to reenter the castle, there was no way to hide it. If Drustan or Lachlan found it, they would most likely assume the worst and believe she and Cait had left it there to help Talorc inside the keep. She doubted they would suspect the women had used it for escape instead.

The skies were gray with clouds that threatened rain, and she and Cait hurried as they avoided the path and the Balmoral cottages on the way to the loch. They stayed in the shelter of the trees as they circled to the other side of it.

Suddenly the big gray wolf from the day before was

there, right in front of them. Emily gasped, but Cait ran forward to hug her brother's neck.

"We've got to talk to you," she said to the wolf.

He looked over at Emily and then back at Cait. She sighed and stood. "I think he wants us to turn our backs before he will change. It is considered a very private matter for our kind."

Emily turned away, thinking Cait had been softening the truth. No doubt Talorc did not care if he changed in front of his sister, but an Englishwoman he'd already rejected as a possible wife was another matter.

"What is she doing with you?" he demanded and both women turned to face him.

He was naked. She should have guessed he would be, but she felt herself blushing and averting her gaze. The Chrechte were a lot less concerned about nudity than the English.

"Trying to prevent war between my new clan and my old one," Cait said with some asperity.

"She has mated with the Balmoral."

"No, I haven't," Emily said, "but that's not important right now. Your sister *is* a Balmoral and she doesn't want war. She is my friend and for her sake I want to see it averted as well."

"I will never take you for a mate now."

She rolled her eyes and then met his gaze. "That is hardly news. We established that before your sister and I were ever kidnapped."

He grunted. "True."

"We need to know if you saw who killed the Balmoral soldier," Cait quickly slotted in.

Talorc frowned. "I did, though I was too far away to prevent it. The killer approached me afterward."

"He approached you? Why?" Cait demanded, sounding as shocked as Emily felt.

"He wants me to kill the Balmoral . . . he wants control of the Balmoral clan."

Cait's face flamed with fury. "Drustan would never do that!"

"I did not say it was your new mate."

"But who else would believe they could take over the clan?"

"Ulf," Emily guessed.

Cait just stared at her and Talorc nodded.

"We humans don't think we are nearly as incompetent and useless as the Chrechte do."

Cait looked affronted. "I didn't say you were useless."

"No, but you never guessed a human would believe he could take over a clan with a pack in it and yet isn't that exactly what MacAlpin did when he betrayed the Chrechte? Only he took over all of Scotland."

"You are smart . . . for an Englishwoman," Talorc said. He turned to Cait. "She's right. Our stepmother was another prime example. Look at the damage she did and she wasn't even of Chrechte descent."

"But Drustan would kill Ulf."

"Not if he blamed your brother for Lachlan's death," Emily said.

Cait's face drained of color as she met Talorc's serious gaze. "He would support the murdering pig out of loyalty and try to avenge Lachlan's death by killing you."

"Yes. Ulf *is* a murderer, too. The young soldier did not even have a chance." Talorc's distaste was obvious. "He suspected nothing before the first knife thrust straight to his heart."

"The rest of the cuts were to make it look like an animal had done it. You as a wolf."

"Yes, but if it worked, I'm wondering what kind of fool your new laird is."

"So does Ulf, all the time," Emily said.

"But why do you?" Cait asked.

"Why were you so sure I had not done it?" he asked her in place of an answer.

Cait stared. "You're my brother. You would not murder an untried soldier."

"If he had surprised me, I would have killed in self-defense."

"But he could not have surprised you."

"This is true," Talorc said arrogantly. "But there is another reason I believe you were so sure it was not me or one of my soldiers. Perhaps you did not realize it at the time, but if you saw the body, it played into your certainty."

"You have more Sinclairs here?" Emily asked.

Talorc shrugged. Thunder cracked ominously in the sky.

"I did see the body." Cait looked like she'd just grasped something. "If a werewolf had done it in wolf form, he would have torn out the soldier's throat and he would have left a scent."

"Yes. Now, why hasn't your new laird realized that, I'm wondering?"

"Maybe because I suspected you'd done the killing and wanted it to look like a human had done it instead," Lachlan said as he stepped from the bushes. He was glaring at Talorc with fury-filled eyes.

"How long have you been there?" Emily asked, wondering if he had heard the name of the murderer.

Lachlan ignored her, his gaze never leaving Talorc.

"How did I get close enough to use a knife?" Talorc asked. Before Lachlan could answer, he went on, "Your soldier would never have let me get that close. I could have thrown the knife, but even a young werewolf would have heard it whistling in the air and ducked. Then he would have yelled, or run . . . but regardless, I could not have gotten close enough to kill him without leaving a scent. No, he was killed while I watched, helpless to prevent it, from the other side of the loch."

"And you would have me believe you would have stopped it?"

"The boy was Balmoral, but he was also Chrechte. Yes, I would have stopped his death if I could. For the same reason you chose to kidnap my sister and wed her to Susannah's brother rather than declare war between our clans."

"It was a more fitting form of reparation."

"And an effective one. I'll miss seeing my sister daily and watching her child grow up."

Cait made a soft sound at that. "You will not demand custody of my babe?"

He shook his head. "Do you not know me better than that? You're my sister. I would not hurt you by taking your child. He will be raised to know our ways among the Balmoral just as he would among the Sinclair pack."

"Yes, he will," Cait promised, her relief palpable.

"Your father would have gone to war over the perceived insult," Talorc said to Lachlan.

"I am not my father."

"Nor am I mine. I recognize treachery when I see it. I would have prevented the lad's death if I could."

Lachlan said nothing.

Talorc sighed. "Your brother promised me the return of my sister or delivery of her bairn after its birth, whichever I wanted, if I killed you. He said he would lead you into a trap. If you are alone, he has successfully done so."

No expression showed on Lachlan's face, but Emily knew he was hurting. How she knew she couldn't have said, but she could feel his pain as if it were her own and it was horrible.

"Ulf did suggest I hunt you alone, that I prove my right to lead by challenging you personally," Lachlan said in a flat voice. "I assume you have a guard with you and that Ulf was aware of it, though he told me he saw only one wolf . . . across the loch."

"Dare I assume you ignored your brother's suggestion?"

"If I did?"

"Then you have a full contingent of well-trained Chrechte close enough to give aid and you've earned a measure of my respect."

"Perhaps I should kill you and earn all your respect."

"Or, I could do as your brother desires and kill you."

Chapter 20

"No!" Emily shouted.

"Stay out of it, Emily," Lachlan said.

"I won't. Don't you see how ridiculous this is?" They were like two cocks trying to establish dominance over the roost, but there was no need. They each had their own roost, darn it. "It's clear that Ulf has been manipulating everyone. Trying to kill each other is not going to undo the damage he has done."

Lachlan did not remove his gaze from Talorc, but a muscle in his jaw twitched. "Take Emily back to the castle, Cait. We will discuss how you got out later."

Emily crossed her arms over her chest and looked down her nose at both men. It was quite a feat because she was shorter than them, but she'd learned a few useful tricks under Sybil's tutelage. "I'm not going anywhere."

Cait imitated her actions. "Me, either."

"Drustan," Lachlan said.

The first-in-command came out of the trees on silent feet. It should not have surprised Emily to see him, but it did. Of course, she'd had no idea Lachlan was there until he showed himself either. These Highland men were sneaky as thieves in their movements.

"Escort our women back to the keep."

Drustan nodded and went to grab Cait's arm, but she evaded his touch. "I'm returning to the Sinclair hold," she said, her voice filled with pain. "I do not belong with the Balmorals."

Drustan flinched as if struck.

Emily opened her mouth to deny her friend's words but then snapped it shut again. First, because she thought that was something Drustan should do, and second, because she thought he might already be doing it. He and Cait were looking at each other as if communicating without words.

Were they mindspeaking? What was that like? Did it sound just like a voice, or were there simply thoughts . . . images like a dream? But a dream wasn't necessarily speaking, was it? And Cait had said it was talking in another person's head. How very curious.

Talorc swore, his startling blue eyes lit with amusement if Emily could allow herself to believe it. "He's bloody well true-mated my sister, hasn't he?"

"Yes," Emily answered because it looked like no one else was going to.

Cait was crying now and shaking her head at Drustan. "You don't love me. You called me a murderer."

"I was wrong," he said out loud. "Please don't leave me."

Cait gasped. "You would plead with me?"

"I will do whatever it takes to keep you. You're my sacred mate, you're my wife . . . you're everything to me."

Emily smiled mistily, but both Lachlan and Talorc appeared pained. Cait, however, was looking at Drustan as if he were the sun, the moon and the stars all rolled into one magnificent male.

She gave him a blinding smile through her tears. "I do love you."

"I love you as well. Never doubt it again," he said, sounding quite harsh, but Cait didn't seem to mind.

Whatever she said in his head made him smile, and his reply had her looking all dreamy-eyed. Emily sighed contentedly. She was very glad to see her friend so happy and things finally settled between the married couple. It was as plain as the nose on her face that those two belonged together, no matter how providence had chosen to make that happen.

Drustan nodded as if accepting something Cait had said, though of course . . . she hadn't said anything. "Now, we return to the keep."

"Not yet," Talorc said. "There are things that need to be discussed. As my sister's mate and Susannah's brother, you need to hear them as well."

Drustan looked to Lachlan for permission to stay and it was granted with a slight nod.

That gesture seemed to signal something between all three men because the tension surrounding them all decreased considerably. Lachlan even looked bored, though Emily could not believe it of him. He was being tricky again, she would swear it, but she was equally certain the threat of imminent violence had passed.

His feet planted firmly apart, Talorc crossed his arms over his chest, which was not exactly a conciliatory stance, but it was not a fighting one either. "In my desire to discover my sister's circumstances, I have trespassed on your island without permission, but my soldier did not. Magnus did not kidnap Susannah from Balmoral land."

The fact that he wore no plaid did not minimize his commanding presence one tiny bit. Perhaps because the man showed absolutely no concern that he was naked. Despite the seriousness of the matter at hand, Emily found such a lack of self-consciousness fascinating.

"Magnus?" Lachlan clarified, clearly as unbothered by the other laird's lack of clothes as he was.

She wished she could be so unaffected, but she had only ever seen one other nude man before. Lachlan. Emily chewed her lip, trying to look at Talorc unobtrusively, but she was too curious to ignore his lack of clothing altogether.

"The laird's brother, Ulf, told Susannah that she had permission to hunt on the mainland at the last full moon," he was saying, "but he did not bother to tell her that it was hunting ground for another pack."

"*Ulf* told her this?" Drustan asked, his arm dropping around Cait's shoulder since she had sidled close to him. "But he had no such authority."

"Susannah was not aware of that. She believed he spoke for your laird."

"When did she tell you this?" Drustan demanded.

"She did not. Magnus reported the details of what led to her hunting on our lands when he informed me he had taken a mate in the fur. Susannah was in heat. Ulf had to know she would end up mated to a Sinclair. He withheld the truth that he was the one who had sent her to our lands, did he not?"

"Yes."

"I think he wanted your laird to believe we had insulted the Balmorals so he would try to exact a personal revenge. I have experience with the cunning betrayal of power-hungry humans. I suspect he planned to betray the Balmoral to me so that he would be killed."

"As he believes he betrayed our laird now?" Drustan asked.

"Yes. He told me to wait here and that he would see to it that the Balmoral came after me alone."

"Emily," Lachlan barked.

She jerked and blushed as everyone's attention first went to him and then to her. She met Lachlan's gaze. "Yes?"

He was not smiling. "Come here."

His tone did not suggest she argue and, for once, she didn't. When she was less than a foot from him, he tilted her chin up with his hand. "You belong to me."

"Is this a discussion we need to have now?" she asked.

Rather than answer, he asked, "Do you want me to challenge Talorc?"

They had just gotten past that, hadn't they? "*No*."

"Then look only at me."

He knew she'd been peeking.

Her blush heated and went to the roots of her hair. "I was merely curious."

"I will satisfy your curiosity another time." He pushed her behind him and then looked at Talorc. "I have only your word that my brother is a betrayer."

"And the evidence of your own logic. If I wanted to kill you, I would have done it when I saw you in the water with the Englishwoman. You had no other guards with you. I did. She would have been easy enough to dispose of."

The coldness of those words made Emily shiver. She moved closer to Lachlan until she was almost touching him, and the heat of his body reached out to wrap around her comfortingly.

"You would have had to kill me first."

For no reason she could discern, her throat tightened with tears. She knew he meant it. No matter what he had accused her of earlier, Lachlan would not have let Talorc harm her that day at the lake. He would have protected her with his life. What did that mean? Perhaps it was part of his warrior's honor.

"The point is," Talorc drawled out, "I did not try."

Lachlan shrugged.

"As I said, I came to your island to discover my sister's circumstances."

"The Sinclair guard we left behind when we took the women would have told you she was to wed Drustan," Lachlan said.

"He told me, and I know enough of you to know that if you said that was your plan, it would come to pass, but I had to make sure Cait was not mistreated, that she was not a prisoner."

"And she told you she was content with her marriage," Drustan said, revealing that he must have allowed Cait to tell him at least that much of her exchange with his brother during their initial confrontation.

"Yes," Talorc said. "Just as your sister is."

Drustan nodded and Cait smiled up at him.

"But Ulf told me she was not. He said that Cait had been forced to mate with Drustan against her will." Talorc's voice vibrated with the rage such a thought evoked in him, even knowing it was not true. "He said that she wanted to return to our clan, but that she was being kept here as a prisoner."

"But I'm not!" Cait exclaimed.

"Aren't you?" Talorc asked. "Did you come to this island of your own free will as Susannah came to our hunting lands?"

Drustan stepped in front of Cait. "I acknowledge that she was brought against her will, but she has not been mistreated and she is now my wife and content to be so."

"I don't want to leave," she added from behind him. "I am a Balmoral now."

"So you said." Talorc's voice gave no hint as to how he felt about that. "I will not apologize for not observing ancient pack law. Susannah acted on your brother's word, Balmoral, and you retaliated without all the facts. You should have realized he was a threat to the pack. You are at fault."

Cait gasped, her face going pale. Drustan looked ready to go for Talorc's throat.

But Lachlan merely sighed. It was a sad, rather weary sound, and Emily laid her hand on his back in comfort.

He looked over his shoulder at her, his dark eyes searching for something, but she had no idea what. Then he turned back to face Talorc and the others. "I should have seen his discontent, his greed for power. He hid it well, but there were clues if I had been willing to see them."

Emily was proud of Lachlan's ability to admit he was in the wrong. It showed a strength of character few men in his position possessed. Nevertheless, the reason he had been wrong was of grave concern to her. For if he did not acknowledge it and change his thinking, Ulf 's threat could be renewed from a different source. Perhaps the next time it would go unnoticed until it was too late to change the outcome . . . like it had been with MacAlpin.

"You dismissed the threat Ulf represented because he is fully human. You did not think he was as powerful as a Chrechte, or capable of deceiving you, but you were wrong."

"Thank you for pointing that out, Emily," Lachlan said dryly.

"In believing so fully in your superiority, you put yourself and your clan at risk," she pressed.

Talorc laughed. "She's sharp-tongued, isn't she?"

"Plain-spoken, but she is right." Lachlan sighed. "She often is."

Emily was gratified that he had corrected Talorc's description of her. She was also warm with pleasure at the fact that Lachlan thought she was often right, but that did not make up for the fact that he had accused her of being unchaste because of the passion he had quite deliberately provoked in her. The two lairds might accept a cessation of hostilities without an apology, but she wasn't going to. Lachlan was going to tell her he was sorry, and that was that.

"She said she'd rather be married to a goat than me. Are you the goat?" Talorc asked, his voice still laced heavily with amusement.

"I will be."

"No!"

"I am glad to hear you say so," Talorc said, ignoring Emily's denial. "Since she was sent to Scotland to wed me, she is my responsibility. I had no desire to marry her, but I could not allow her to be compromised without demanding suitable reparation either."

Unbelievably, Lachlan nodded his understanding, just as if Talorc wasn't talking drivel.

"I'm wanting to witness the marriage before returning to my holding." This time there was no humor in the daft man's voice and she wished there had been.

Emily rushed around Lachlan so she could look Talorc in the face when she shouted at him. "I will not marry him and that's that!"

"You want to marry me then?"

"You know I don't, and neither will you marry me."

"You would rather I declared war on the Balmorals?"

"Don't be ridiculous. You aren't going to war over me. I'm English, remember?"

"You are under my protection while you are in the Highlands. My honor is worth going to war over."

"No, Talorc," Cait said, sounding desperate. "They haven't mated."

"I saw him naked with her in the water."

"But that doesn't mean anything," Emily assured him. "You're naked now, but I'm not mating you."

Lachlan growled, the sound inhuman and frightening.

Talorc ignored it as he had ignored her protest a moment before. "I do not believe your father would feel the same."

"You aren't going to tell him?" Emily asked, horrified.

"I'm going to see you wed, or I'm going to war."

Emily looked wildly around her, but no one appeared ready to step in and aid her in dismissing Talorc's daft notion. Cait's worried and faintly sick expression said she knew he meant it and she was worried that Lachlan was going to refuse. Emily was more afraid he wouldn't.

"You don't want to marry me," she cried, facing him.

"Would you rather see our clans go to war?" he asked with interest.

"Of course not."

"Then you will marry me, English."

"No."

Emily was standing in front of a priest an hour later. She was still reeling from Lachlan's confrontation with Ulf upon their return to the keep, which was her excuse for getting this far in a wedding ceremony she was sure should not take place.

Talorc and his soldiers (there were four) had accompanied them back to the castle because he insisted on seeing Emily wed, and Lachlan, for reasons she could not fathom, had agreed to accommodate him. Her continued vehement denials and arguments about why the wedding should not take place were ignored by the two lairds walking side by side.

If she were Chrechte, she would turn into a wolf and bite someone. It was a lucky thing for them all she was ladylike enough not to do it anyway.

Thankfully, Talorc had plaids hidden on the island for him and his soldiers and they were now decently covered. Though Emily had to wonder if the Highland women would have been nearly as shocked by their nakedness as she had been.

Ulf's roar of fury from high on the wall walk splintered her thoughts in that moment and sent a chill skittering down Emily's spine. But when she looked up, she did not see him. She peeked sideways at Lachlan. He acted as if he hadn't even heard the war cry.

But she knew he had and her heart went out to him even though she doubted he would thank her for the concern. Learning his brother was a traitor and a murderer could not have been easy, but he had revealed no emotion at Talorc's revelations. And he didn't expose any now either.

Ulf was not so circumspect. His face twisted with rage,

he was waiting for them in the lower bailey with several other soldiers when their party crossed the bridge. "What the hell is this? You have brought our enemy inside our very gates!"

Lachlan motioned for the rest of them to halt and approached his brother alone. He glared at the other soldiers until the men stepped back from Ulf.

"The only enemy to the Balmoral clan stands before me," Lachlan said when he stood less than two feet from his brother. "In your lust for power, you killed one of our soldiers in hopes of luring me into a trap. You do not even have the courage to fight your own battles."

"I have the courage," Ulf snarled, "but I promised our father I would not challenge you for the position of laird. He did not think I could lead the clan because I have no beast inside me to cloud my thinking. He believed you were his true son, but I am more like him than you ever will be!"

"You have his temper, but you lack his strength and his intelligence."

"That's a lie! I'm everything he could have wanted in a son, but he judged me on the way my body reacts to a full moon."

"Go to the great hall," Lachlan commanded. "You will explain your treachery to me there."

Ulf just sneered.

Moving so quickly, she almost missed it, Lachlan hit his brother straight on the chin, knocking him backward into the dirt and into an unnatural sleep in the process.

"Carry him to the great hall," he instructed two of the warriors that had been hidden in the trees with Drustan when Lachlan confronted Talorc by the lake.

When they moved to obey, he asked the other soldiers if they stood with Ulf or with him. The men went to their knees and knelt before him, one going so far as to explain they had just been called from their duties by Ulf to help protect their laird. As a strong, chilling wind, portent of things to come, whipped around them, the soldier's story was confirmed by others and they were dismissed.

Lachlan went to the great hall and then made sure that no one but Chrechte and Emily and Ulf were in the keep before instructing that the door be shut and guarded by a Chrechte soldier on the other side. And she understood why he had insisted on having the confrontation at the keep. He was protecting the pack's secrets as Chrechte leaders had been doing within the clans since joining them the century before.

Ulf was awake and fuming by the fireplace when Lachlan allowed the rest of them into the great hall a few minutes later.

She and Cait stood between Drustan and Angus, with the Sinclair Chrechte behind them. There were two other Balmoral Chrechte on either side of Ulf. He glared at her and Cait, and then at Lachlan, "What are the women doing here?"

"Your treachery affected their lives. They will hear what you have to say for yourself."

"I need not explain myself to you."

"Like it or not, I am your laird. You will explain."

"Only because our father protected you by demanding that promise."

Lachlan shook his head. "Our father was protecting you from death when he made you promise not to challenge me. But you did not care. You chose to try to take control of the clan through devious means anyway. What honor is there in trying to negate your father's will, or in trying to get the Sinclair to kill me for you?"

"More honor than there is in a younger brother taking my rightful place of laird."

"Our father dictated I be his successor. It was his right."

"He made the wrong choice. It was *my right* to lead!"

"To what end? What could you have done for the clan I have not done?"

Ulf just glared.

"You are guilty of murder."

"You believe the word of your enemy over your brother?"

"You did not deny your treachery."

"I knew it was useless when I saw the two of you from the wall walk. I knew you would stand together as werewolf brothers even though you and I are blood brothers."

A spasm crossed Lachlan's face. "Are you saying now that you deny you plotted to get me killed? That you did not kill that young soldier?"

"Would you believe me if I did?"

"No." The absolute finality of that word could not be lost on anyone in the hall. "I know too much to believe your denial."

"Then why should I attempt one?" Ulf stood proud and erect, his expression filled with contempt and hatred. "You deserved to die . . . just like that soldier. He would have had a position of leadership one day, just as Drustan does, but what of me . . . your brother?"

"You turned down the position of first-in-command."

"It should have been you as my first, not the other way around. Why should I agree to serve you?"

"So, you believe you . . . a murderer and a liar . . . should be laird?"

Ulf was unfazed by the accusations, as if he truly saw nothing wrong with his actions. "I am a Balmoral, son of our father, just as you are."

"If I challenge you, does that negate the promise you made to our father?"

"On what grounds would you challenge me?" Ulf asked sneeringly.

"You murdered one of my soldiers."

"Prove it."

"I don't have to."

"You do if you want the clan to stand behind you."

"You are a fool to believe that."

"Am I?" Ulf asked, his expression taunting. "There is

also your own honor, which would not be satisfied unless you can be absolutely sure I had done the deed."

"But I am."

Ulf just shrugged.

"There are also the many insults, heard by witnesses, you have subjected my mate to."

"You are not mated."

"I soon will be. Emily is my betrothed."

Ulf staggered as if Lachlan had landed him another blow. "You are going to marry a human?"

"Yes."

"I thought you were afraid of having human children like our father."

"If they are as fierce and loyal as their mother, it won't matter if they are werewolves."

Warmth suffused Emily despite the tension of the situation.

"She has tricked you with your lust."

"I'm not so easily deceived. I have told you this. You should have listened."

"Aren't you? You believed me about Susannah."

"I believed the evidence of my own eyes. Susannah was married to Magnus and I knew I had not given her permission to leave the island. Therefore I believed she had been taken without the permission of her clan."

"Now you know I sent her to Sinclair land."

"Why?"

"I wanted you to declare war on the Sinclairs. I could have led you into a trap. It's what our father would have done, but you are not enough like him. You're too soft."

"You're a fool if you believe that. You are the weak one and Father saw the lack in you. He knew you craved power but did not have the character to lead. He should have banished you, or sent you to serve under another laird, but *he* was too soft-hearted toward you. He loved you too much to let you go. You are my brother, but I am strong enough to see you get the punishment your crimes deserve. You were a fool to believe you could manipulate me."

"I wasn't. I had it all under control. If those two whores had not gotten out of the keep, you would not be playing ally with the Sinclair now."

Lachlan backhanded Ulf and the other man slammed against the wall beside the fireplace.

Chapter 21

"Speak respectfully of my intended, or die where you stand."

Ulf wiped at a trickle of blood from his mouth. "I pity her, but most of all I pity the children you might have . . . children that could be like me."

"We will have children if God wills it. If some, or all, are fully human, I will love them."

"Our father loved me until I didn't make the change, but not after. I was his favorite; he trained me to be his next in command, but he dismissed me from the moment it became obvious I was not a wolf. Stupid bloody *animal*."

"It is not your lack of an inner wolf that makes you unsuitable to lead, but your lack of honor. I believe our father saw that."

Ulf attacked Lachlan, but within seconds he was insensate once again. "Lock him in the west tower," Lachlan ordered, his voice harsh.

Cait took Drustan aside for something. The warrior

looked furious for a moment before giving instructions to another soldier. Emily couldn't dwell too long on what had been said by her friend to make her new husband look so angry because Lachlan had just called for the priest.

Which was how Emily had ended up where she was now, facing a priest and hearing the wedding mass spoken for the second time since coming to the Highlands. She'd seen the defeat and pain in Lachlan's eyes. He had lost a brother in the last hour and her heart had gone out to him.

She had been incapable of adding to his torment by opposing him, but how could she allow Lachlan to make this sacrifice? How could she make it herself? He did not want to wed a human and she did not want to wed a man who saw her as less than she was because she was not half-wolf.

Yet, he had agreed to the marriage, had not argued at all in fact. She didn't believe for one minute that was because Talorc had threatened war. Lachlan was too strong to be so easily cowed. No, he had his own reasons for marrying her, but she could not understand what they might be. She loved him so much, but she knew her feelings could never be returned, not while he thought her so inferior.

Only when they had touched it had not felt like he thought of her as inferior. It had not felt merely like an expression of lust either, and she did not think that was entirely the work of her fantasy. He had never treated her like she was "only a human" in his eyes, no matter what he said with his mouth.

When he was talking with Talorc, Lachlan had spoken of her as if he truly admired her. She could do worse than to marry a man who thought that highly of her. Couldn't she?

But when the time came for her to repeat her vows, she opened her mouth and nothing came out.

Lachlan looked down at her. "Is it so hard, lass?"

Mute, she nodded. Too many thoughts vied for supremacy in her mind; she could not give vent to a single one.

"I do not see why. You love me. You told me so. I will make you say the words again later, when I am satisfying your curiosity." He winked at her.

She almost swooned right then and there from shock and embarrassment. It would serve him right if she married him and made his life a misery, the fiend!

"Hush," she hissed.

"It is not a thing to be ashamed of."

"Says you," Talorc said from the other side of Lachlan.

"You don't want this," she whispered, finally getting her throat to work.

"If I did not, the priest would not be standing in front of us."

"But you wanted to marry Chrechte."

"I want to marry you."

"I could not stand for you to reject our children like your father rejected Ulf . . . that is assuming we can even have children."

"I told Ulf it was God's choice whether or not we have children. Do you believe that?"

"Yes."

"If we have children, I will love them no matter what. I promise you this."

"But—"

"Do you trust me, English?"

Tears wet her eyes. "Yes." He was not a man given to breaking his promises.

"Then speak your vows."

"But . . ." she said again, only she didn't know what she wanted to say after.

She would love Lachlan all the days of her life. She had come to the Highlands prepared to do whatever was required to save her sister a dismal fate. She was now being offered a marriage much more hopeful than the one she had contracted to make. Why was she balking?

She could have a measure of happiness while keeping her sister safe. According to the Highlanders, they only obeyed their king when they wanted to. As long as she wasn't returned to England in disgrace, Abigail should be safe. Her father had paid the price his king demanded of him, and by all accounts, it was unlikely the Scottish king would check to make sure his laird had.

But surely, even if he did, he would be as content to have the wild Lachlan "tamed" by marriage to an Englishwoman as Talorc of the Sinclairs.

Still, she wondered if this was the right thing to do. She cast a sidelong glance at Lachlan. He looked so sure. And suddenly she knew it was going to be all right. For him to have had the change of heart he did about marrying a Chrechte, he had to love her. He might not realize it. He might not ever be willing to acknowledge it, but she was confident the feelings were inside him.

He would never, ever consent to marrying a human woman, much less argue for the marriage otherwise. He'd told her he planned to claim her before, but she'd thought he was under the influence of lust alone. After what had just transpired, even he could not be under such an influence at the moment. He must truly want this.

And he'd said he would love their children no matter what. Perhaps one day, he would even acknowledge loving her.

As her thoughts and heart finally settled, Talorc sighed, long and drawn out it was, too.

He asked, "You would rather marry me? With the priest here, that could be arranged."

She practically shouted her vows to the background of his uproarious laughter.

When it was done, Lachlan kissed her with such a wealth of passion she couldn't help wrapping her arms around his neck and kissing him back. He lifted her and cradled her against his chest, then carried her up the stairs and to his chamber. The sound of loud shouting followed them from the great hall.

When they reached his room, he did not give her a chance to stop and think.

They were both naked and in the bed before she became aware enough to warn him, "Once we make love there is no going back."

Despite her certainty that he loved her, she felt the need to give him one last chance to turn back. Marriage to a human woman was so far from what he had planned for his life.

"There was no going back from the moment I met you, but I was too stubborn to see it at first." He sounded too flippant to her.

"I mean it, Lachlan. As long as I am still a virgin, you can obtain an annulment, but once the marriage is consummated, I won't let you kick me out of your life, even if I'm not your true mate."

"I would never let you go." It was a vow and she took it as such, knowing it came from deep inside him. Then he kissed her again.

He touched her in ways he had not done before, bringing her excitement to a fever pitch of need. She widened her thighs, wanting him to join their bodies, to assuage the ache he'd created deep inside her woman's place.

He paused with his shaft pressed against her opening. "I offer you my body and all that I am, Emily of the Balmoral. Do you accept all that I am?"

There was only one answer she could give. "Yes."

"Do you welcome me into your body?"

"Yes. I want you to be part of me, Lachlan."

"I already am, lass, now and forever." He pressed inside then, his hardness stretching her to the point of pain.

She whimpered.

He brushed her face with an incredibly gentle hand that shook. "You must relax your body, love. It is not enough that I take you, but you must will your flesh to accept me."

"I don't know how." Though it was what she wanted. So much.

Reaching down, he touched her sweetest spot with his thumb. The light circular caress sent pleasure shooting through her and she arched up for more. He gave it to her, touching her again and again with the gentlest of strokes.

"That feels so good," she moaned.

"Aye. Think only of the pleasure, love." His voice sounded strained.

She tried, and found herself relaxing around his manhood. He rocked his pelvis, pushing himself inside farther and farther until he hit a barrier that made her cry out and try to scoot back from him in pain.

He held her in place with his heavy body. "This will hurt. I do not know of a way to prevent it." But he wished he could. She could see it in his glowing eyes.

That comforted her as no words could have. "A short, sharp pain is better than a long, drawn-out one," she whispered.

He nodded and thrust, breaking through the barrier and embedding himself to the hilt.

She cried out in pain, tears leaking out of her eyes, but she did not fight his possession. There would be pleasure beyond the pain. There had to be, or all women would join nunneries.

He held his body still and kissed her. "It will get better."

"You promise?"

"I promise."

"But it hurts so much."

"I'm sorry, love." He kissed her again, renewing his ministrations with his thumb. The pain began to get lost in the pleasure.

It was not gone completely, but the pleasure grew until it was more consuming than the pain. She made a small move with her hips and he matched it, increasing the depths of his strokes until he was withdrawing almost completely before pushing back into her, every thrust bringing an intensity of pleasure that astonished her.

She could not help moving beneath him and he urged her on with words of praise and pleas for more. He was as much at her mercy as she was at his. That knowledge sent her pleasure spiraling out of control until their bodies locked together and he yelled something in Chrechte as they both shuddered their completion.

She told him she loved him again.

He collapsed on top of her and then rolled to his side, curving her into his body as if he could not bear to be apart even a few inches.

She did not know how much time had passed before he started speaking. "My father was a wise man, if hotheaded. He must have seen something in Ulf I did not early on. We all assumed it was Ulf's lack of a wolf nature that made our father change toward him, but I remember how Ulf reacted to the fact that he did not go through the change. Each month that went by during that year, he grew more and more sullen. He got into fights with other boys and used his position as laird's son to try to manipulate others. My father saw these things. He and my mother argued about them because she thought Ulf was just showing the tendency to lead."

"But Ulf said your father changed after he showed his lack of a wolf nature."

"Father and Ulf's relationship changed before that, but until I looked back at the past with the eyes of a man, I did not see it. I do think the fact that he was not a werewolf influenced how my father felt. My mother never accepted my father's beast completely and he never accepted the lack of a beast completely in his son. He was still hoping Ulf would go into the change late when he died."

"But he had already named you his heir."

"Because he did not see Ulf as fit to lead. Emily, I meant what I told my brother. If our children have your fierceness and your loyalty, I do not care if they have my wolf nature. You were right to accuse me of being blind."

"I wasn't that plain-spoken."

"Mayhap not, but it is what you meant. I blinded myself to my brother's true nature and the threat he represented, but I will not be blinded to your value, or that of our children if they are as fully human as you are."

"If we have children . . ." she said sadly.

He smiled at her. "Oh, we'll have them."

It was only then that she realized his mouth had not moved once the whole time he'd been talking.

"You mindspoke to me!"

"Yes."

"I want to try."

"Go ahead."

You owe me an apology, she said with her thoughts.

He grimaced. "I do not like saying I'm sorry."

"I don't imagine you do. You're awfully arrogant."

He rolled his eyes. "I'm sorry, truly sorry for the accusations I made earlier today and for not recognizing how important you were to me to begin with."

Her eyes misted. "All right then. I'll forgive you this once, but if you ever do such a thing again, I'll put nettles on your side of the bed."

"We'll share the middle, but I have no doubt you'll find some way to make your displeasure felt."

"I'm glad you realize that."

"Now you will apologize to me."

"For insulting you when you first took us?"

"For looking at Talorc's cock with such interest."

"It wasn't interest, it was curiosity. Surely you can see the difference."

"From this point forward you will reserve such curiosity for me. Promise me this."

"I promise."

He waited.

"And I'm sorry, but I'm a very curious sort of person."

"I know, love, I know."

It was the second time he'd called her that. Perhaps it would not take until they were old and gray before he admitted his feelings. Being who she was, Emily simply asked outright, "Do you love me?"

His smile was warmer than the summer sun. "Can't you tell? I've told you twice now in Chrechte."

"Oh." But the daft man had not realized hearing the words in a language she understood would have made her choice to marry him so much easier. "Say it in Gaelic," she demanded.

He did. Then in English and Latin after that.

She was crying by the time he was done. He kissed her all over her face, sipping at her tears and then gently claiming her mouth in a tender connection that filled her with absolute certainty of his sincerity. Afterward, he kissed her once more on her temple. "I will love you to my dying breath."

"And I will love you just as long."

"You had better."

"Arrogant Chrechte."

"Precious mate."

She smiled, blinking away more tears of joy. He returned her smile and cuddled her into his side. Finally, they slept.

The next morning they heard the news that Ulf had discovered the escape route she and Cait had used to get out of the keep. The walls had been slick with rain and the wind had been blowing fiercely the night before. And as Cait had predicted, *his* plaid had not been adequate to make a sufficiently long rope. He was found at the base of the castle wall with his neck broken.

While it was a terrible tragedy, Emily was relieved for Lachlan's sake. Justice had been met for the murderer, but the man she loved had not been forced to mete it out on his own brother.

Lachlan was furious at the discovery. Not because Ulf was dead, but because the women had risked their own lives climbing out.

Emily tried to explain that it hadn't been raining when they did it, that their rope had been much longer and that she and Cait were never in any danger of falling. But it did no good. Lachlan only yelled louder and Drustan glowered more fiercely until both women ended up promising never, ever to try such a thing again. (Though apparently Cait had *already* promised this once, having told Drustan of their rope the night before. Emily had been too addled by the prospect of marriage to remember.)

"And did you ever consider the security of the keep while you were leaving ropes dangling from windows?" Lachlan demanded. " 'Tis a good thing Cait thought to tell Drustan."

Emily did not take umbrage at the question, for it came after twenty minutes spent harping on her personal safety. She came first, but now he felt the need to slip back into his role as laird. However, she believed her reasons for being forgetful were more than adequate.

"Had you not overwhelmed my attention with a wedding and what came after, I would surely have remembered to tell you about the rope before it could be of danger."

"Are you trying to imply our marriage inconvenienced you, English?"

"Sent the rest of my thoughts flitting from my head more like," she said with a smile.

That pleased him and he smiled as well.

"You can't keep calling me that, you know."

"What?"

"English."

"And why is that?"

"Because I'm Balmoral now. I have it on good authority we're a clan of Highlanders."

"Would you prefer I call you sweeting?"

"I do like that."

He laughed and pulled her into his arms. "You're going to lead me on a merry chase."

"I should not want you to grow bored with me, laird."

"I love you too much to ever do that, but I have a feeling my hair will be silver before the birth of our first child."

"Will your wolf's fur go gray if the hair on your head does?" she asked, her curiosity immediately aroused.

His eyes narrowed warily. "No."

She peppered him with questions after that and he only got her to cease by taking her to bed. Afterward, he taught her how to declare her love in Chrechte.

The next day she asked him if they could send for her sister Abigail and he agreed. "What about your Scottish king? I don't want him making trouble for my sister."

"Talorc has already agreed to go speak with him."

"He's not as bad as I thought he was."

"Our king?"

"Talorc."

"But I'm still the only Chrechte you love."

"You are the only man, Chrechte or human, that I could ever love," she vowed firmly.

"That is as it should be."

She hit his arm and then winced. The man had muscles like boulders. "You are supposed to say I am the only woman you could ever love."

"Do you not know this already?" he asked quite seriously.

She made no effort to stifle her happy grin. "Yes, in fact, I believe I do. But I still want you to say it."

He lifted her and held her close to his chest, his eyes filled with devouring hunger and the love she now recognized had been there as long as her own. "There is no other female, wolf or human, that I could ever love as I do you, sweeting."

"I think I'd like another swimming lesson."

"I believe I might enjoy that myself, but this time I will do what I longed to the first time we were in the loch."

"Drown me?"

He laughed out loud, the sound warming her clear through. "Make love to you."

"It will not take too much time from your important duties?" she teased.

"Nothing is more important to me than you."

And she knew it was true.

She had come to the Highlands to save her sister, but had ended up finding her own happiness. A wound that had opened on her mother's death and been torn wide by her father's rejection, finally closed. She had not thought it humanly possible, but then her husband, the love of her life, was more than human, and she would not have him any other way.